CW00408828

BOW STREET SOCIETY:
The Case of The Lonesome Lushington
By
T.G. Campbell

All characters in this novel are fictional. Any resemblance to persons living or dead is purely coincidental.

Front cover illustration by Peter Spells
Bow Street Society Logo by Heather Curtis
Edited by Susan Soares
Copyright © 2017 Tahnee Georgina Campbell
All Rights Reserved

Printed by KDP

TABLE OF CONTENTS

ACKNOWLEDGEMENTS

Thank you to Karen McDonald for her proofing skills and unending levels of patience during many a late-night Skype rant. Thank you also to my sister, Bronia, for her proofreading skills and support. Also, to Pashen and Thayne for their continued support in this endeavour.

While researching the historical context for this novel, I had assistance from certain individuals and organisations. The assistance they gave me, and the information they provided me with, was both invaluable and appreciated beyond measure. Those individuals who assisted me included: Paul Robert of The Virtual Typewriter Museum who, for a second time, was generous enough to answer my question. Thanks to him, I could describe the brand, and history, of the typewriter used by Dr Weeks. Also, Julie Mathias, head of learning at the Old Operating Theatre & Herb Garret Museum in London. The advice and information she graciously granted to me, in answer to my question, enabled me to form a more historically accurate description of the dissection tables used by Dr Weeks. Furthermore, she supplied me with the name of an additional source of reference which shall undoubtedly prove invaluable as I write more *Bow Street Society* books.

I'd also like to thank artists Heather Curtis and Peter Spells. Heather designed the Bow Street Society logo on the front of this book (which also appears on my website and social media). Peter created the amazing central illustration on the cover. Peter also designed the central illustration of my first book *The Case of The Curious Client*.

Finally, I'd like to thank all my family and friends for their patience and support while I've been writing this book.

PROLOGUE

BLAGGARD OF BOW STREET HANGED, read the headline of the *Gaslight Gazette*'s evening edition. It had come as a relief to everyone involved in the case. The unexpected 'not guilty' plea at the trial's start had caused a ruckus both inside the courtroom and out. Whilst looking upon the newspaper, Inspector John Conway recalled the harsh questioning the defence had given Thaddeus Dorsey. Testimony from an independent doctor, submitted by the Crown, had then successfully argued that Dorsey saw things which weren't there because of his bad eyes, something a bloke called Charles Bonnet had found out about years back. In the end, the jury wasn't convinced by the prisoner's lies, and the judge had put on the black cap before sentencing. Now, a month of appeals later, the rope had sent the blaggard to meet their maker. Yet even as night fell to end this cold February day, the grizzled policeman knew London's darkest corners would be bearing the next sensation to hit the press.

"This so-called 'Bow Street Society,' what do you make of them?" Inspector Calcb Woolfe's deep baritone voice enquired from behind the newspaper as his small eyes peered over its top.

"They're a group that wanna do good," Inspector Conway's rough voice replied. His accent had continued to reflect his upbringing in the East End district of Stepney despite his exalted position at Scotland Yard. His well-maintained, dark-red beard and moustache were in stark contrast to his weathered features which had aged him beyond his years. Nevertheless, his attire of a dark-grey waist coat with matching trousers, a crisp, white shirt, and dark-blue tie was testament to the pride he took in his appearance.

"Humpf. A group of *amateurs* who aren't even retired coppers but members of the public. Reading this though, you'd think the sun shone from their backsides," Woolfe said as his large hand reached around the newspaper to bring the pint of ale to his lips. At forty-nine, he was six years older than Conway and considerably taller, too. Six feet four inches to Conway's five feet nine, to be precise. Both men were broad shouldered, but Woolfe's build was solid. This, along with his height, leather-like skin, red nose, and unkempt black hair and brows, had earnt him the nickname 'Big Bad Woolfe' from coppers and criminals alike. His swift pace, provided by his long stride, further strengthened his reputation as a relentless hunter. With his thirst sated, he read aloud, "The hanging was welcomed by the clerk of the Bow Street Society, Miss Rebecca Trent, who is quoted as saying it was the members' hard work which exposed Mr Arthur Perkins' murderer."

"She would though," Conway pointed out, drinking some of his own pint.

Woolfe lowered the newspaper and glared at him. "*You* were the investigating officer; *you* brought the blighter in, not her and not *them.*"

"Yeah," Conway drained his glass, "but they got the rope, and now it's done."

The tension in Woolfe's frame eased as he mumbled his agreement and put the newspaper down. "Another?" he enquired as he cast his shadow over Conway upon standing.

"Nah. Thanks."

"Suit yourself," Woolfe replied and left the table to approach the bar.

Given its name and location upon the promenade of the River Thames' Victoria Embankment, one could be forgiven for expecting to find washed-up old fishermen and sailors in the Ship & Anchor pub. In reality, its

8

clientele comprised almost entirely of Metropolitan Police officers. All of whom were enjoying a smoke and a drink. The plain-clothed officers turned a blind eye to the handful of uniformed ones on the grounds they weren't drinking on active duty. Regardless of their status, though, the officers' preference for the establishment was due to Scotland Yard being a mere mile south down the river. Geographically, the pub was closer to Blackfriars' Bridge than Westminster Bridge but remained within walking distance of the Metropolitan Police's headquarters.

The Victoria Embankment was one of three divisions which made up the Thames Embankment. The second was the Albert Embankment running from the south end of Westminster Bridge to Vauxhall, and the third ran from Millbank to Battersea Bridge. Costing over £1.5 million, the three divisions were constructed between 1864 and 1870 and were the work of Sir J. W. Bazalgette. Although not certain, it was presumed by Ship & Anchor proprietors that the pub had been built around the same time as the Embankment upon which it stood.

Set back from the bank of the River Thames by the hundred-foot-wide promenade, the pub was entered by a set of double doors which led into the specious, open-plan bar area. To their right were two immense windows with framed navy-blue and frosted glass checked panels on their lower halves. Low-backed benches formed a line beneath them, whilst low stools provided the remainder of the seating. Although the former were considered more comfortable, both options were well-maintained and upholstered in navy-blue fabric. Low tables with wooden, round tops, and black, curved, cast-iron legs littered the room. All were covered with glasses, used ashtrays, pipes, and hats. A uniformed sergeant sat at a piano set against the far wall to one's right upon entering the pub. Despite the din of conversation, he played an upbeat tune to no one in particular. To the left of him was an immense hearth with a cast-iron surround and a large fire burning within. The half-hexagonal-shaped bar occupied the room's back-left corner. Behind it was a door leading to the cellar and the landlord's private rooms upstairs. The landlord Mr Arnold Fairchild and his barmaid Pearl moved along the bar to greet Woolfe as he'd approached. Despite the limited amount of room at the bar, the crowd of officers had also parted like the Red Sea with Woolfe easily being head-and-shoulders taller than them all.

Conway lit a cigarette and tossed the spent match into the ashtray. Exhaling the smoke from his lungs a moment later, his dark-blue eyes then watched his friend through the dissipating cloud as he ordered ahead of the others and strummed his fingers upon the bar. No one complained; no one even spoke to Woolfe. Instead, they gave him a wide berth and only returned to their jostling and chattering when he was on his way back to his table with a pint in hand.

"You put the fear of God into them lads," Conway remarked with a smirk as Woolfe plonked down onto his stool.

"It doesn't take much, unfortunately."

"Takes more than you think, mate," Conway retorted.

Woolfe gave a soft grunt of acknowledgement, taking a large mouthful from his pint, and resumed his reading of the newspaper.

ONE

"It's a disaster, the absolute *worst* that could've happened. All you had to do was move five pieces of furniture from Endell Street to here. *Five*! From *one* street away, and *you* have somehow managed to perform a trick even the Great Locke would be envious of! You have achieved the impossible and *lost* my typewriter between *there* and *here*. Do you have *any* notion of its cost?" Miss Rebecca Trent admonished the two removal men standing before her as they twisted the caps in their hands.

"No, miss," the first replied.

"We'll find it, miss," the second added.

"Then please *do* so," Miss Trent replied.

Both men hurried out the front door like rabbits fleeing a warren, and Miss Trent released a deep sigh. At twenty-eight years of age, she would've been considered 'old' by late nineteenth century standards, but she placed little worth in such shallow-minded opinions. In anticipation of moving furniture, she'd pinned up her chestnut-brown hair and left a fair number of its shorter strands hanging loose about her face. The mauve skirts she wore were plain but practical, whilst her corset was foregone in favour of greater movement. Thus, her slender silhouette beneath the closely fitted, long-sleeved light-cream blouse was wholly natural.

"It'll prob'ly be back in the old place," Mr Samuel Snyder's rough East End voice remarked from the other side of the hallway. His broad shoulders almost touched the frame of the open doorway where he stood, whilst his hands dwarfed the cloth he used to wipe away the dust. Needless to say, he could deliver a devastating punch despite his five feet six inches height. A full twenty years older than Miss Trent, his bushy side-burned face was weathered, and his hands calloused from years spent driving a two-wheeler hansom cab. More accustomed to wearing a heavy, black cape as a result, he savoured the opportunity to set it aside and wear only his indoor clothes. These consisted of a cheaply made, brown-tweed jacket that had been ripped and sewn here and there with a shirt, greyer than white, beneath. The tip of his long, black tie rested on his rotund belly, whilst the cuffs of his black trousers were tucked into the tops of his heavy, scuffed, well-worn, black-leather boots. His deep-set, brown, beady eyes regarded the Bow Street Society clerk with genuine warmth as he invited, "Come on, let's ge' a cuppa."

Although now the legal property and new headquarters of the Bow Street Society, the house's previous life as Mr Thaddeus Dorsey's home could still be seen in the hallway's burgundy-embossed, flock-patterned wallpaper, and black-and-white-check tiled floor. The grand staircase, with its smooth, oak handrails, rounded balusters, and burgundy carpet, had also remained unchanged. It led to a narrow landing that encircled the hallway to form a first-floor balcony. From there, numerous oak doors led into empty rooms. Meanwhile, back on the ground floor, the hallway continued past the left and right sides of the staircase to meet the doors leading into the kitchen. It was the door on the left that Mr Snyder now held open.

"If they don't find my typewriter, I swear there shall be another murder here," Miss Trent remarked as she walked past him.

"You don't mean that, lass," Mr Snyder replied with a chuckle and followed her inside.

"The garden still needs a lot of work," Miss Trent observed upon looking through the windows. She then slid back the three bolts and turned the key in the recently installed lock to open the back door. A wave of cold air hit her in an instant.

"It's only been a month," Mr Snyder pointed out as he hung a cast-iron kettle over the stove to boil some water.

"A month without any new cases," Miss Trent replied, closing and securing the back door once more. Crossing the kitchen to hold open one of its doors, she then watched as Mr Snyder brought in the first of several second-hand chairs from the hallway and set it down beside the battered, wooden table. "We're relying wholly on member contributions to keep the Society afloat."

"Sumin'll turn up, lass," Mr Snyder reassured as he brought in the next chair and propped the door open with a discarded piece of wood.

"Probably our eviction notice," Miss Trent retorted and checked the stove's coal levels.

"Hello?" a woman's voice called from the hallway. "Is anyone here?"

Mr Snyder shot Miss Trent a questioning look.

"I've already deposited this month's mortgage repayment," Miss Trent responded.

Mr Snyder glanced at the door and suggested, "Best go see who it is."

"*Hello*?" the woman repeated in distress.

"Wait here," Miss Trent instructed and, after receiving Mr Snyder's agreement, removed the piece of wood propping the door open and entered the hallway.

Standing at the foot of the grand staircase was a petite woman of perfect proportions. Around thirty-five years old, she had pale, almost translucent, virgin skin that embraced the soft contours of her face. Her chestnut-brown eyes were shaded by the wide brim of a pale-yellow straw hat. Nonetheless, Miss Trent was struck by the intense desperation they held. Studying her attire next, Miss Trent saw hints of restricted wealth in the fit of her dark-brown tweed, long-sleeved jacket, and the marginally higher calibre of material of her ankle-length, light-brown bustle skirts. Catching movement around her visitor's waist, Miss Trent lifted her gaze and saw she was toying with the fingertip of her leather glove despite it being on her hand, still.

"Good morning, madam," Miss Trent greeted as she rounded the staircase. "May I help you at all?"

"Is this the Bow Street Society?" the visitor enquired.

"It is. I'm Miss Rebecca Trent, the Society's clerk—" She paused as her visitor gave a curt nod, downcast her eyes, and intensified her glove tugging. "I'm also responsible for deciding whether or not our Society accepts a commission set before it—"

"But you are a woman," the visitor interrupted, astounded, with a sharp lift of her head.

"And perfectly capable of making such a decision, I can assure you. Mrs—?"

"Suggitt, Mrs Diana Suggitt." Mrs Suggitt pursed her lips momentarily. "The Society *must* accept this commission, Miss Trent, without question. The most dreadful thing has happened and only the Society can see to its resolution." Although her lips trembled, and her voice was strained by emotion, her eyes remained dry. With a swift sudden ceasing of her glove-tugging she looked squarely at Miss Trent and went on, "I immediately thought of the Bow Street Society upon hearing the news…" She pursed her lips once more and finished, "…They shan't investigate her death properly, Miss Trent."

"Who shan't? And who has died?"

Mrs Suggitt took a moment to compose herself before she answered. "The police… And my sister. Maryanna Roberts. She…" The glove tugging resumed, and Mrs Suggitt closed her eyes. "Murdered… She has been murdered… *Brutally* so." She opened her eyes as some stray tears slid down her cheeks. "Yet she was a fallen woman, Miss Trent. If they wouldn't find the monster of Whitechapel, why should they find the fiend who slayed my sister?"

"When was she murdered?" Miss Trent enquired.

"I'm afraid I don't know. I spoke to my husband, Clement—on the telephone—but fifteen minutes ago and came straight here."

"Where is your husband?"

"I assume he is with the police. He told me he would find out what was happening, but I mustn't, under any circumstances, go to my sister." Mrs Suggitt swallowed. "Yet how can I not? At this moment, as we speak, my sister is lying in Oxford Street for all of London to gape at."

"Mrs Suggitt, if your husband *is* with the police, they will already be—"

"*Please,* Miss Trent! I ask not for myself, or my husband, but for my sister." Mrs Suggitt turned away, and her voice trembled as she continued, "What you see before you is not what I have always been. I am that rarity of a poor woman who has married well but my sister—my whole family in fact—has remained where I started." She faced Miss Trent, again. "Yet *I* have money and can pay whatever fee you deem appropriate so, please, I ask you to heed my sister's call as you have heeded others."

"Mrs Suggitt—" Miss Trent began but was interrupted by Mrs Suggitt gripping her hand. The desperate look in her eyes was enough to quash the clerk's concerns about taking the case. Yet, even if it hadn't, Mrs Suggitt's words would've succeeded just as easily.

"I ask only for justice," she said.

Miss Trent smiled and, giving Mrs Suggitt's hand a firm squeeze, replied, "Then both you and she shall have it."

"Thank you," Mrs Suggitt whispered and withdrew her hand.

"You said your sister lies on Oxford Street; where, exactly?" Miss Trent enquired.

"The London Crystal Palace Bazaar."

"I shall allocate some members to your case and send them to Oxford Street. If you do wish to join your husband, I can arrange for our cabman, Mr Samuel Snyder, to take you free of charge."

"Yes, please. *Thank you*, Miss Trent."

"If you'd like to wait here, I shall ask him to prepare the cab."

"Of course," Mrs Suggitt replied, moving away to compose herself whilst Miss Trent returned to the kitchen for a few moments.

When the clerk returned, though, she was struck by how adrift Mrs Suggitt's solitary figure seemed in the hallway's vast emptiness. Feeling her heart ache for her even more, she approached and said, "Mr Snyder will be with you shortly, if you could wait here still?"

Mrs Suggitt gave another curt nod as a fresh wave of sorrow passed over her, compelling her to turn away once more. Knowing she could do little to ease her grief, Miss Trent took comfort in knowing she could at least do something about its cause. She therefore excused herself again and entered the room which had formerly served as Mr Thaddeus Dorsey's bedroom. Her desk was stood in the middle, facing the door, with a chair in front. Behind the desk was another chair and then the window. Her filing cabinet was stood against the back corner to the right of the window whilst the hall telephone was now mounted to the wall to the window's left. Taking several index cards from the filing cabinet, she copied their addresses onto some small envelopes and sat down at her desk. Lifting her hands to begin typing the letters, she gave an angry sigh at the offensive space and muttered, "By hand it is."

* * *

Mr Joseph Maxwell scratched his head, hummed, and rubbed his pale chin with long, ink-stained fingers as he regarded the clump of four typewriter arms jammed together against the paper with a pencil wedged beneath. Aged twenty-one years, he possessed an average stature, slender form, and broad shoulders. His high cheekbones and freckles invariably drew the eye to his sunken cheeks before his distinctive red hair distracted one's gaze. It was kept neatly combed into a left-hand side parting and complemented the dark green of his waistcoat. The remainder of his attire consisted of black trousers, a black frock coat, high-collared white shirt, and black, silk cravat with a tiny bow over his Adam's apple.

"Where's your article, Maxwell?!" Mr Morse's voice bellowed through the open doorway of the editor's office.

"C-coming, sir!" Joseph Maxwell cried as he stood and wiped his hands upon his frock coat.

"Hurry up! We've not got all day!"

"Yes, sir!" Panic-stricken, Joseph Maxwell simultaneously yanked at the paper and jammed typewriter arms. The former tore with a loud rip whilst the latter relented long enough to allow the pencil to drop and his fingers to become trapped instead. Yelping and pulling his arm back in response to the pain shooting through his digits, Joseph Maxwell then released a sharp cry as the typewriter remained attached to his limb and slid across his desk. Notebooks, papers, pencils, a half-eaten sandwich, and even a cold cup of tea toppled from the desk whilst he tugged at the tortuous typewriter arms. Another lightning bolt of pain struck his poor fingers as they were freed from the wretched device, and he released a second anguished cry.

"Still a clumsy fool, I see," a man's nasally voice remarked with disdain.

Joseph Maxwell looked up and stared at the older gentleman in astonishment. "F—Father, I—I wasn't—"

"Get the words out, man!" Oliver Maxwell interrupted, and his thin lips contorted into a scowl. "Only idiots stutter."

"Sorry, Father…"

"I still live in hope you'll one day show me you're *not* an idiot, Joseph, but my hope fades each time we meet." Oliver Maxwell was in his mid-fifties and like his son, was of average height with defined cheekbones. Patches of salt and pepper hair disrupted the natural black colouring of his slanted eyebrows, and the hair above his ears and around his off-centre parting. His high forehead was exaggerated further by his receding hairline. This, like the rest of his hair, was also plagued by the salt and pepper signs of ageing. "*Sit* down."

Joseph Maxwell sat without taking his eyes off his father.

"You are to come to dinner with your brothers tomorrow night. Your mother wants to see you."

"Yes, Father. But—"

"This is *not* up for debate."

"Murder on Oxford Street!" a messenger boy yelled across the office.

Joseph Maxwell looked past his father and knew it was just a matter of time before one of his fellow journalists took the assignment. Prior to the boy's proclamation, Joseph had intended to ask his father why he hadn't sent a written invitation to dinner. Yet, this sudden—and rare—opportunity to claim an exciting story before his editor could assign a dull one had distracted him. He therefore swallowed hard under his father's scowl, rose from his chair, and began, "Please excuse me but I must—"

"And what exactly is it you *do* here?" Oliver Maxwell enquired. "Other than peddle lies and cause scandals. This newspaper has ruined many a man." His eyes narrowed when he caught his son reaching for his overcoat. "*Where* are you going? *Sit* down!"

Joseph Maxwell clutched his overcoat but remained standing.

"You always were an insolent little wretch," Oliver Maxwell sneered. "Why couldn't you have been more like your brothers? Both successful, and both married well."

"I want someone on Oxford Street, *now*!" Mr Morse bellowed as he stood in his office doorway.

"When are you going to find some stupid, wealthy woman to marry you?" Oliver Maxwell enquired. "Dowry, Joseph. That's what you need, a decent dowry."

"Maxwell, *where's* your article?!" Mr Morse interjected.

"C-coming!" Joseph Maxwell called back, attempting to step around his father who easily blocked his retreat.

"You've never shown any inclination toward women or mentioned any women on the rare occasion you deign to grace your mother and I with your presence," Oliver Maxwell said. "Do something about it."

"Yes, Father," Joseph Maxwell replied through a sigh as he saw his colleague, Mr Baldwin, grabbing his coat and hurrying from the office.

"*Don't* you sigh at me, boy," Oliver Maxwell growled. "Arrive promptly at eight."

"Yes, Father," Joseph Maxwell repeated and dropped down into his chair. Watching his father leave, and feeling the tension brought on by his presence going with him, Joseph Maxwell then realised he could still reach Oxford Street before his rival if he ran. He therefore leapt to his feet, pulled on his overcoat, and walked straight into the corner of his desk with a grunt. Hissing as he rubbed his sore thigh, he then plucked the torn article from the floor, deposited it upon Mr Morse's desk, and hurried from the office before his editor could bite.

TWO

Ranked amongst London's most famous thoroughfares, Oxford Street was over a mile and a half long and acted as one of the main arteries between the fashionable residential quarter and the capital's counting house. As a result, near constant streams of traffic ran from the east to the west, and vice-versa. Included within Oxford Street was New Oxford Street whilst Oxford Circus—known as Regent Circus on account of its location at the top of Regent Street—formed Oxford Street's central point. Regent Circus was also where the communication lines of the four compass points crossed, and where the first ladies' public lavatory was erected in 1884. The latter convenience being an undoubtedly welcomed addition when one realised that Oxford Street was brimming with shops dear to the heart of country and city lady alike. One such establishment was the London Crystal Palace Bazaar. Found on Oxford Street's east side, just past the circus, it sat opposite Argyll Street with entrances on both Oxford Street and Great Portland Street. Constructed from glass and iron to the designs of Mr Owen Jones, its most striking feature was its roof of coloured glass. Amongst the commodities on sale at the Bazaar were toys and the "cheaper kind of fancy goods."

At eight thirty on a typical morning, the bazaar's sellers would be preparing to admit the first customers of the day. Yet as the clocks chimed the half hour on that morning, they were instead embroiled in hushed conversations around the Oxford Street entrance. A uniformed constable from the Metropolitan Police stood guard on the inside of the doors, whilst his colleagues had formed a human barricade against the immense crowd of gawkers gathered outside. Identical methods had also been employed at the Portland Street entrance. As a result, the sellers were denied access not only to the outside world but also to the truth of what had caused their predicament in the first place.

Amid the Oxford Street crowd was Mr Joseph Maxwell who, with pencil and notebook in hand, was jostled in all directions before breaking free. When he did, he found himself beside a constable. Leaping at the chance of an interview then, he kept his elbows pinned against his sides whilst putting pencil to paper and enquiring over the din, "P-Pardon me, Constable, but what's happened here?!"

"A murder," the constable replied before addressing the crowd at large. "Stay back! There's nowt to see!"

Mr Maxwell doubted that. His view was shared by the crowd, too, as no one heeded the request.

"Is it true the body's been mutilated?!" Mr Baldwin yelled.

Mr Maxwell cast a swift glance around him but couldn't see his rival anywhere. Perturbed by Baldwin's threat to *his* story, but bolstered by the constable's silent response to the question, he enquired, "Wh-who was murdered, Constable?" Realising he hadn't been heard over the din, he cleared his throat and repeated in a louder voice, "Who was-oof!"

A shove from behind cut off his words and propelled him to the ground. Although he'd thrown his hands down to break his fall, he'd done so too late and hit the wet, horse filth-covered cobbles face-first. He'd also lost his grip on his pencil and notebook upon impact. Both were tossed onto the ground in front of him; the former to be snapped under foot and the latter to be kicked away. Releasing a soft sigh, he pushed himself up onto all fours and peered through the fleeting gaps in the crowd's legs for his notebook. When they parted to show him the bazaar's doorway, though, he saw a man crouching there and recognised him at once.

"Dr Weeks!" Mr Maxwell yelled, using his shoulders to push the crowd aside as he crawled to the front. Emerging into the bright light, he looked ahead to the doorway and yelled, "Dr Weeks, sir! Doctor!"

"'Ere, what's your game?" a constable demanded whilst taking Mr Maxwell by the scruff of his overcoat and dragging him off his feet.

Startled by the sudden disappearance of the ground beneath him, Mr Maxwell scrambled to get to his feet with the constable's 'assistance.' Fighting to calm his pounding heart when he was once again standing upright, he replied in a higher-than-normal pitch, "No game, Constable." Clearing his throat to reset his voice, he added, "I'm a journalist." The constable furrowed his brow but rewarded Mr Maxwell's honesty with a shove so hard it sent him off balance. Yet, even as he stumbled, Mr Maxwell cried, "And a friend of Dr Weeks!"

Hearing his name, the Canadian turned hazel-brown eyes toward the hapless journalist and muttered a curse under his breath. Taking the lit cigarette from the corner of his mouth, Dr Weeks then rose to his feet, rested the heel of that hand against the top edge of a book, and wrote some notes with his other. Dark circles were visible under his eyes, his jet-black hair was unkempt, and his small, black moustache was devoid of wax. In fact, the only neat parts of him were his short-haired, black sideburns. Even the grey, woollen, fingerless gloves, black overcoat, and grey, woollen scarf were a far cry from the smart suit Mr Maxwell had seen him wear previously.

Having caught Dr Weeks looking his way, Mr Maxwell attempted to wave him over. Within moments, though, he was surprised into abandoning this course of action by a broad chest moving into his line of sight and blocking his view. Swallowing hard, he looked up at the newcomer's neck before tilting his head further back to see their face. Squinting against the low sun, he shielded his eyes with his hand and met the hard gaze of a man with black, bushy eyebrows.

"What's your name?" The man demanded—or perhaps it was the deepness of his voice that made it sound that way? Mr Maxwell was certain it could make even the most ridiculous of requests sound like a serious demand.

"Mr Joseph M-Maxwell, sir," he replied. "Journalist with the *Gaslight Gazette.*"

"You're not a friend of Dr Weeks' then."

"W-well, y—yes, I am. That is to say, we, um, we have worked together—" Mr Maxwell cut himself short as he realised it may not be wise to reveal such information. Giving a weak smile instead, he therefore corrected, "Not *worked* together, but we have a mutual friend…" He swallowed hard. "M-May I speak with him, Mr…?"

"*Inspector* Woolfe, E Division, and, no, you can't."

Mr Maxwell looked down and searched his mind for a more persuasive argument. Yet no sooner had he thought of one did he realise Inspector Woolfe was walking toward the bazaar's doorway. Frustrated by his own ineptitude, Mr Maxwell scanned the scene for someone else to interview and noticed another plain-clothed man he didn't recognise. Presuming him to be a sergeant, he watched him make notes whilst speaking to a gentleman in a tan, knee-length coat. The quality of its material, and the pristine appearance of his fingernails, suggested he was a man who enjoyed a comfortable financial existence. This observation did little to ease Mr Maxwell's disappointment, though, since he couldn't hear what was being said.

"Better luck next time," Mr Baldwin taunted from behind.

Mr Maxwell looked over his shoulder at his rival's

smirking face and retorted, "At least I spoke to a senior officer."

"And what good did it do you?" Mr Baldwin sneered and gave Mr Maxwell's shoulder a firm shove. "*None!*"

"What do you *mean* I cannot visit Messrs Drysdon and Drysdon, Constable? I have an order to be collected for my dear nephew's birthday; it must be collected today, or his special day shall be ruined, *ruined*! And after the tragic loss of his parents in the bicycle accident, I shall hold the Metropolitan Police *personally* responsible if I do not collect my order today!" An offended, high-pitched voice demanded, thereby drawing Mr Maxwell and Mr Baldwin's gazes to a woman several metres away.

She was in her late-forties with a fair complexion and warm, chestnut-brown hair styled in tight curls beneath a fantastic headdress of small, black ostrich feathers. The latter, in addition to her court (or 'Louis') shoes, made her appear taller than her natural five feet. Her slender, but wide-shouldered, form, complemented the contours of her face and was wrapped in a black, fur coat that hung about an inch off the ground.

Standing behind her was another woman of around twenty years old. While her companion was adorned in expensive fur, she'd opted for an open, cropped, black jacket. Its sleeves were of the fashionable "leg-of-mutton" shape (tight on the lower arms, puffed on the upper) and its back flared out into two, small points. Underneath the jacket was a loosely fitted, burgundy, cotton blouse (or 'waist'). It was tucked into a dark-brown, brass-buckled belt below her bust to accentuate her naturally slender waist. Her skirts had plain, burgundy panels on their front and a minimal bustle at their rear. The latter shifted into dark-brown pleats of accumulative sizes which cascaded toward the ground. Yet, despite the apparent thought given to her attire, her chocolate-coloured hair was wrapped into a plain bun at the base of her skull. This, coupled with the narrow hat pinned to the front right-side of her head at an unfashionable angle, meant the young woman's overall appearance was underwhelming. Her hands, covered by brown cotton gloves, held the curved handle of an immense, black umbrella as it rested vertically against her skirts. Although she could never be considered 'beautiful' in a traditional sense, the way she kept her broad shoulders squared and back erect whilst scrutinising the scene gave her an irrefutable—and attractive—air of strength. As if feeling Mr Maxwell's eyes upon her, the young woman cast a glance in his direction and stepped closer to her companion.

In doing so, she revealed a third member of their group. As soon as he saw them, Mr Maxwell's eyes widened, and he muttered, "Georgina…" At only five feet tall, Miss Georgina Dexter had been completely hidden by the second lady. Perfectly proportioned for her height, Miss Dexter was also fair complexioned with red hair kept tightly pinned and half-hidden beneath a dark-turquoise bonnet. Its colour matched that of her dress, whilst the black panels on the latter's straight-lined skirts matched the bonnet's black, ruffled edging. Her modesty was preserved by the dress's high neckline, whilst a cropped black jacket guarded against the cold. A brown leather strap ran diagonally across her torso and was attached to a satchel sitting against her hip. In her hand was a peculiar looking box. At eighteen years old, she was the youngest of the group.

She was several metres away, with many people in between, but Mr Maxwell was determined to reach her. Forcing his way through the crowd therefore, he soon came within mere feet of her. The final barrier of people proved resistant to his efforts to break through, however. Feeling his fear of losing Miss Dexter overcome his fear of a confrontation, though, he slipped his fingers between the shoulders of those in front and attempted to push them apart. Yet, just as he was about to straighten his arms, one of them moved, and Mr Maxwell stumbled forward, narrowly missing his fiancée in the process.

"Mr Maxwell!" Miss Dexter exclaimed in startled amazement and gripped his arm to steady him. "Are you hurt?"

"No, I'm fine," he replied, brushing the dirt from his frock coat with her assistance. "It was a tight squeeze—through the crowd."

Miss Dexter glanced behind him. "You need to be more careful; you'll hurt yourself." Noticing his sore fingertips, then, she took his hand in hers and said, "Your *poor* fingers."

"Typewriter," Mr Maxwell replied and felt his cheeks burn at her confused expression. Deciding to change the subject, he smiled and said, "I had to see you. It's been a long time since we last spoke." Mr Maxwell's smile died as he saw the sadness blot out the confusion on her face. Moving closer to her, he continued, "I want to make amends, Georgina, for the night at your parents' house when I—"

"I'm glad you're unhurt, Mr Maxwell," she interrupted and turned toward the bazaar's doorway. Although Mr Maxwell couldn't see them, her lips trembled under the strain of containing her emotions. Her voice was therefore subdued as she said, "I... I really must take these photographs for Lady Owston."

Mr Maxwell watched her lift the peculiar looking, rectangular-shaped wooden box to her chest and press a button on its top. A click sounded, followed by a second and third as she pressed the button twice more. Looking ahead of them, he saw the ghastly mutilated body of a naked woman slouched in the doorway of the bazaar. Realising Miss Dexter was photographing the crime scene, Mr Maxwell tugged upon his cravat to loosen it but felt unable to draw his eyes away from the macabre sight. Due to the shadows cast by the walls of the doorway's porch, Mr Maxwell found it difficult to see exactly *how* the poor woman had been mutilated. There was certainly a great deal of blood on her chest, stomach, and shoulders. Her chin rested on her chest and… was that a cap on her head? Mr Maxwell squinted against the bright sunlight but soon wished he hadn't. *Not a cap,* he thought as his stomach lurched. *It's her skull!*

He turned his back upon the scene, but the damage had already been done. A violent retch overcame him, forcing him to clap both hands over his mouth. All thoughts of documenting the scene were forgotten—he'd lost his notebook anyway—as he gave another retch and added to the small amount of vomit already in his mouth. Unable to hold it in any longer, he bent over and emptied the contents of his stomach into the gutter beside the curb. Several in the crowd's front row moved back to avoid getting their shoes soiled.

"Mr Maxwell!" Miss Dexter cried as she came to his aid once again. Frowning upon seeing the vomit, she then rubbed his back and enquired, "Are you feeling better?"

"Yes…" Mr Maxwell replied, spitting out the remnants.

"Good," Miss Dexter said with obvious relief.

Mr Maxwell straightened and, wrapping his arm about his stomach, nodded to her to continue with her work. It surprised him she could bear to look at such things. Then again, the more he watched her, the more he noticed how she repeatedly swallowed back her own disgust.

He didn't dare look back at the bazaar. Instead, he shifted his weight from one foot to the other and began, "Georgina…" His last shred of courage deserted him, though, and he cast his eyes downward. Unable to find the strength or answers needed to remedy the rift between them, he took a deep breath and remarked, "I tried calling to Dr Weeks, but he couldn't hear me." He paused as something occurred to him. "Is the Bow Street Society investigating this murder?"

"Haven't you received a letter from Miss Trent?" Miss Dexter enquired. Holding the camera closer to the scene, she pressed its button again before pulling it back to rest against her stomach. Recalling how Mr Maxwell hadn't been given such a correspondence at the start of the Dorsey case, though, she explained. "Miss Trent sends letters to everyone she wants to give a case to."

"Oh." Mr Maxwell frowned. "In that case, no, I haven't."

"I can't talk to you about it, then," Miss Dexter replied. "I'm sorry." Yet the sadness with which she spoke those two simple words suggested far more than was immediately apparent. "Speak with Miss Trent. I'm certain it's just a mistake?"

"I will make it right," Mr Maxwell promised.

Miss Dexter's lips trembled at the thought of the words' true meaning, and she turned her back before her tears could fall. Wiping her eye with her finger, she took a soft, shuddering breath and resumed her work.

"Do you have *any* idea who I *am*, Constable?" challenged the woman in the black fur coat. "I am Lady Katheryne Owston and this," she indicated her companion holding the umbrella, "is my secretary, Miss Agnes Webster. Where is the investigating officer? I *demand* to speak with him."

"I'm he, what's going on?" Inspector Woolfe enquired as he approached.

Lady Owston cast a disapproving glance over the odd-looking man and announced, "I wish to collect a most important gift for my nephew from Messrs Drysdon and Drysdon."

"You can't," Inspector Woolfe replied.

"I know *that*, Inspector—I assume you *are* an inspector?" Lady Owston enquired. "Otherwise I *demand* one be brought to me."

"I am Inspector Caleb Woolfe from E Division."

"How unfortunate for you," Lady Owston remarked upon the first name with distaste. "I want to know *why* I can't collect my order."

"There's been a murder," Inspector Woolfe informed her. "The poor girl's body's in the doorway of the bazaar so we can't let anyone in or out until we've done what we need to do and moved her."

Lady Owston stifled a gasp with her hand and cried, "Oh, how *very* awful! The *poor* girl! Agnes, my smelling salts." She held out her hand as she enquired from Inspector Woolfe, "Did she have a name? Any family? I would like to send them a monetary gesture of support." Feeling the weight of a bottle upon her palm as Miss Webster handed her the smelling salts, Lady Owston then removed its cork and took a swift sniff of the strong scent emanating from its contents.

"Why would you want to do that?" Inspector Woolfe enquired with a mixture of confusion and suspicion.

"Why would I *not*, Inspector?" Lady Owston retorted with a stern tone and sombre expression. "We are all Christians here; charity is the responsibility of us *all* who can afford to give it. Will you deny me such a Godly deed?"

"Fine," Inspector Woolfe replied through a soft sigh. "Her name's Mrs Maryanna Roberts. She's got a husband, Abraham, and a daughter."

"How did she die, Inspector?" Mr Maxwell interjected as he stepped forward.

Lady Owston and Miss Webster simultaneously turned toward him. The former was aghast with her lips parted and clear irritation in her eyes, whilst the latter cast a subtle glance of mild curiosity over the newcomer. Miss Dexter, meanwhile, took the opportunity to slip her camera into a fur hand muff without Inspector Woolfe noticing.

"We don't know yet," Inspector Woolfe replied, annoyed by the intrusion.

"Will the family know she is dead?" Lady Owston enquired in a sympathetic tone for all she threw Mr Maxwell a warning glance to mind his own affairs. "If she's only just been found, I don't wish the news of her demise to be in the form of my gesture."

"They do," Inspector Woolfe confirmed. "She was found at six o'clock this morning by Constable Fraser when he was on patrol. Now, if you'll excuse me, Lady Owston, I've got a job to do."

As he watched Inspector Woolfe return to the crime scene and speak with Dr Weeks, Mr Maxwell felt the ladies' eyes boring into him.

"Exactly who *are* you?" Lady Owston demanded but lifted her hand to prevent his reply. "*Never mind*! I do not have time for this. Agnes, Miss Dexter, this way." She stepped around him and, after passing a small, leather-bound notebook and pencil to Miss Webster, headed for Mr Snyder's horse-drawn, two-wheeler hansom cab parked some distance away. Miss Webster followed with the umbrella's handle hooked into the crook of her arm whilst she set about making some short-hand notes on what had occurred.

"Please don't follow us," Miss Dexter warned Mr Maxwell and moved to follow the others.

"When will I see you again?" Mr Maxwell enquired.

Miss Dexter halted at the question but kept her back to him. After a moment's consideration, though, she bowed her head and replied, "I don't know…" Looking at him across her shoulder, she added, "Goodbye, Joseph," before hurrying to catch up with her fellow Bow Streeters.

The further away she got, the more adrift and helpless Mr Maxwell felt. Compliments, reassures, and promises swarmed around his mind but he doubted any were adequate to mend his fiancé's hurt. When he saw her reach the cab and climb inside, he noticed it was facing away from him. An idea struck him at once and, swallowing hard, he made his way from the crowd and toward the vehicle.

Mr Snyder glanced around as Mr Maxwell neared, though, thereby forcing the latter to duck beneath the elevated driver's seat where the former was sitting. Keeping low, Mr Maxwell placed his hands upon the cab's slanted back wall, pressed his ear to its smooth surface, and listened.

"Mrs Suggitt, I'm Lady Katheryne Owston, an independent journalist for the Women's Signal and Truth publications," introduced the first voice. It was markedly quieter, and lower in pitch, than when she'd addressed the constable. "Miss Agnes Webster is my secretary, and Miss Georgina Dexter is a most talented artist. Miss Webster shall be taking some short-hand notes during our discussion but, rest assured, these shall remain confidential."

"And you are all members of the Bow Street Society?" Another female voice enquired. Mr Maxwell didn't recognise it, but logic dictated it belonged to 'Mrs Suggitt.'

"Yes," Lady Owston replied. "Miss Trent's correspondence gave us the facts you've already disclosed, Mrs Suggitt, but we must know absolutely everything if we are to discover the identity of your sister's murderer."

"I understand," Mrs Suggitt said.

"When was the last time you saw your sister?" Lady Owston enquired.

"About a week ago but I…" Mrs Suggitt's voice faltered. "I almost saw her yesterday."

"Almost?" Miss Dexter's voice interjected, and Mr Maxwell's heart ached at the sound. It grieved him to know she was so close with not just the cab wall keeping them apart.

"Yes," Mrs Suggitt replied. "She visited the *Queshire Department Store* in search of me, but I wasn't there."

"I know the *Queshire Department Store* well," Lady Owston remarked. "But why would she think to search for you there? Had you arranged to meet her?"

There was a long pause, during which Mr Maxwell felt the first drops of cold rain against his hands.

"No, I hadn't," Mrs Suggitt replied. "My husband is the store's assistant manager."

"Ah yes, of course. Mr Clement Suggitt," Lady Owston recalled. "I assume your sister also knew of his employment there?"

"Yes. And how I often meet my husband for lunch," Mrs Suggitt replied. "Yesterday though I was late—I can't remember why—and, when I arrived, I was informed by Mr Queshire himself that my sister had caused a most despicable scene with the husband of one of his wealthier customers. She'd *propositioned* him with his wife standing there! I was mortified and, naturally, understood utterly when Mr Queshire informed me he'd had to escort her from the premises. Yet, when I enquired if he knew where she'd gone, he replied he didn't know, but it was more than likely the nearest pub."

"A surprisingly flippant remark from Mr Queshire," a fourth voice observed. Although it had spoken in a monotone, Mr Maxwell assumed it belonged to Miss Webster.

"Hmm. He's usually a most accommodating man—to women of all social classes," Lady Owston said.

"Oh, he is," Mrs Suggitt agreed. "But even Clement was surprised by how angry he was."

"I'm quite certain he was," Lady Owston replied. "I have met your husband on several occasions, Mrs Suggitt, while conducting research for my Women's Signal articles. In fact, I saw him only minutes ago speaking to the police outside of the bazaar."

"Clement knows I'm here?" Mrs Suggitt enquired.

"Not presently, but if you wish him to, Miss Dexter may accompany you to him?" Lady Owston offered.

"Yes, I…" Mrs Suggitt's voice broke a little. "…I would like to see him."

"Did Mr Queshire give any reason as to why he thought your sister would go to a public house?" Lady Owston enquired after allowing Mrs Suggitt a moment's grace to compose herself.

"No, he walked away after stating such to me," Mrs Suggitt replied.

A creak sounded above Mr Maxwell's head as Mr Snyder shifted within his seat. Glancing up at him, Mr Maxwell was relieved to see his gaze remained fixed upon the cab's horse. A deep sigh from Mrs Suggitt then drew Mr Maxwell's attention back to the conversation.

"Drink was my sister's demon, Lady Owston; it took her under its spell several years ago following the deaths of her other children in infancy," Mrs Suggitt said. "She couldn't come to terms with them. She blamed herself even though we all reassured her there was nothing else she could've done."

"We?" Miss Webster enquired.

"Clement, Abraham—Maryanna's husband, her only surviving child, Regina, and I," Mrs Suggitt replied. "All the children died of disease: polio, cholera. We were all as heartbroken as she, but she took it the worst. Neglecting her duties as a wife and mother and finding

34

solace in the arms of a gin bottle. Her husband stood by her until he could no longer keep her in the house. He said she needed to sober up before coming back. Regina and I have tried to give Maryanna the help she so desperately needs—" Mrs Suggitt's voice faltered as she corrected, "Needed. But my sister continued to drown in the liquor."

"She remained close to her daughter, though?" Miss Dexter enquired.

"As much as her husband would allow, yes," Mrs Suggitt replied.

"I'm sure you can appreciate, Mrs Suggitt, why we will need to speak to Mr Roberts," Lady Owston said.

"Yes," Mrs Suggitt replied in a soft voice. "I shall give you his address."

"Can you think of anyone who would want to see harm come to your sister?" Miss Dexter enquired.

Mrs Suggitt took in a deep, shuddering breath and answered, "When she wasn't under the influence of drink, my sister was the kindest, most considerate woman you could ever hope to meet. Under it, she could be vile, vulgar, and erratic but not to the degree anyone would want to see her *dead*. Not even Abraham, and he had been shamed by her the most."

"Forgive me, Mrs Suggitt," Lady Owston began, "but I *must* ask this: where were you last evening and the early hours of this morning?"

"At home," Mrs Suggitt replied.

"Thank you. You will need to speak to Inspector Woolfe about what you have told us," Lady Owston said. "Feel free to inform him you have hired the Bow Street Society if you so wish. If you don't, we shan't reveal the fact either. We do recommend you be as honest and open with the police as you can though; none of us wish to be arrested for perverting the course of justice. Do you have an address where we may reach you?"

"Yes… here," Mrs Suggitt replied, her voice strained with emotion. Since no address was uttered, Mr Maxwell presumed she'd given it to Lady Owston in note form. This was confirmed when Mrs Suggitt enquired, "Would you like me to write Mr Roberts' address on the back?"

"If you could, please," Lady Owston replied.

A long pause followed, during which Mr Maxwell assumed Mrs Suggitt wrote down the address.

"Thank you," Lady Owston said afterwards. "Miss Dexter shall take good care of you, Mrs Suggitt. Agnes, I believe a visit to the *Queshire Department Store* is in order."

The softly spoken words of gratitude from Mrs Suggitt in response were Mr Maxwell's cue to depart. Remaining bent over, he crept away from the cab toward the crowd. Yet no sooner had he emerged from beneath the driver's seat did he hear Mr Snyder state, "Be seein' you, Mr Maxwell." Mr Maxwell straightened at once and, turning upon his heel, discovered Mr Snyder looking over his shoulder at him. Feeling his cheeks warm at the embarrassment of being caught, Mr Maxwell gave the cabman a curt nod, tugged on his frock coat, and hurried away.

"There he is again," Lady Owston observed upon alighting the cab.

"Who?" Miss Webster enquired as she joined her.

"The pale fellow who kept asking questions," Lady Owston replied.

Miss Dexter poked her head out of the cab and became perturbed at the sight of Mr Maxwell disappearing into the crowd. *Miss Trent shan't be pleased by his eavesdropping*, she thought.

"Mr Joseph Maxwell," Mr Snyder explained to the others. "Journalist with the *Gaslight Gazette.*"

36

Although she was surprised Mr Snyder hadn't alluded to Mr Maxwell's membership of the Bow Street Society, Miss Dexter nevertheless felt grateful for the cabman's discretion. News of her engagement to Mr Maxwell would've only caused Lady Owston and Miss Webster to congratulate her and, given the circumstances of his proposal, Miss Dexter would've felt uncomfortable accepting such sentiments.

"A fine thing he had the sense to depart. Come, Agnes!" Lady Owston said and took off down Oxford Street. Miss Webster followed with long, swift strides and soon fell into step beside her. The moment they were beyond Mrs Suggitt's earshot, Lady Owston stated, "Let us test our client's account."

"Do you think she's lying?" Miss Webster enquired in surprise.

"No, but we mustn't accept all she tells us as Gospel either."

Miss Webster agreed, not having thought to take such precautions.

Meanwhile, Miss Dexter had mouthed a 'thank you' to Mr Snyder upon giving him her camera for safe keeping. After all, there was little point in making further attempts to photograph the crime scene whilst the line of police constables remained in place. Accompanying Mrs Suggitt as she made her way to the bazaar, Miss Dexter felt her heart pounding in her chest at the thought of encountering Inspector Woolfe again. She could well imagine him confiscating her camera if she tried photographing Mr and Mrs Suggitt in front of him. Such was in the best-case scenario. *A night in a police cell*, she thought. *Newgate Jail!* She shuddered. *Yes, best to leave my camera with Mr Snyder*.

THREE

Magnificent buildings of awesome size lined Oxford Street as testaments to the religion of capitalism and consumerism. Like preachers in a pulpit, the store owners called forth their flock through strategically placed signs and alluring window displays. All implicitly promising an unobtainable state of utter completion and happiness if one purchased their goods. Many a female worshipper, cocooned from the offensiveness of city life by her private carriage, could be seen waiting outside her chosen temple. Time and again, store employees would bring forth offerings for silent approval or loud rejection. Only once she felt happy and complete would she make a glittering 'donation' and claim her prize. Such women had been discouraged from visiting the bazaar and its surrounding stores for obvious reasons. Yet Lady Owston and Miss Webster saw an increasing number as they walked further along Oxford Street.

Paying them little heed, they instead focused on scanning the plethora of signs above their heads for the familiar dark-red and gold one of the *Queshire Department Store.* Lady Owston, a veteran "wor-shopper" of that temple, caught sight of it first. Without breaking her stride, she proclaimed, "There it is!"

"Where?" Miss Webster enquired as she slowed her pace to examine the signs more closely. The wind had also picked up, obliging her to hold her hat against her head. In doing these things, though, she fell behind Lady Owston and soon lost her amidst the swelling numbers of pedestrians. Thinking she'd seen a glimpse of her ostrich feathers a few metres away, she stretched her arm as high as it would go, waved, and shouted, "Lady Owston!" All the while side-stepping those rapidly approaching from the opposite direction.

A gentleman neared with his hand cupped around a cigarette perched between his lips. As he lit its end with a match, Miss Webster's breath caught in her throat at the sight of the flame. Although both it and the gentleman had disappeared in a matter of seconds, Miss Webster immediately felt lightheaded. The deafening noise of Oxford Street also became muffled by the sound of her racing heart as her chest tightened, and she fought to fill her lungs. "I cannot breathe…" she gasped, her voice drowned out by those around her. Darting her gaze between their faces in a desperate search for her employer, she soon realised Lady Owston was nowhere to be seen. Too disordered in her thoughts to use her umbrella, despite the torrential rain, she instead kept its handle hooked over her arm and tightened her grip upon it. Her fellow pedestrians swarmed along the pavement but all she could see were dark, indistinguishable shapes flying past her, worsening her dizziness and disorientating her as a result. Fearing she might faint, as she had in the past, Miss Webster rushed to the nearest wall and leant against it. She took in several gulps of air, but they did little to alleviate her panicked state. Her heart continued to pound, her lungs refused to expand, and her mind whirled with fast-moving black shapes and blinding, golden flames. Noticing the rain, she opened her umbrella and felt short-lived relief at seeing her fellow pedestrians divert their route to avoid colliding with its spokes. Being permitted room to breathe as a result, she gripped the wall, leant forward, and felt a hand gently rub between her shoulders.

"Deep breaths," Lady Owston reassured.

A sob escaped Miss Webster, and she gripped her employer's arm to confirm it was really her. They stood beneath the umbrella for several minutes whilst Miss Webster's fear dissipated. When her lungs felt able to expand once more, she took several deep breaths and met Lady Owston's gaze.

"How did you find me?" Miss Webster enquired, still a little dazed.

"You found me, child," Lady Owston replied and turned Miss Webster by the arm. To the latter's amazement they were standing beside the *Queshire Department Store*'s impressive façade. Lifting her head, she saw the dark-red and gold sign swinging from a pole. In its centre was an oil painting of a beautiful woman sitting sideways on, looking outward over her shoulder. The wavy, brown mound of hair atop her head was wrapped in a veil of fine, almost translucent, cotton that flowed down her back. Her flawless face, head, and shoulders were bathed in heavenly light while her red, sleeveless dress was touched by shadows. The gold of the bands adorning her head and upper arms echoed that of the store's name and thick line painted along the sign's inside edge.

"So I did," Miss Webster remarked, allowing the corner of her mouth to lift into a fleeting smile before her natural stoicism fell back into place. Resting her hand upon Lady Owston's, she added, "And I'm now ready to continue."

"*Excellent*," Lady Owston replied in delight.

The *Queshire Department Store* stood back from the pavement by several feet. This, coupled with the fact it was two storeys shorter than its neighbours, could've spelt disaster for its visibility. Yet the light being emitted by the gas lamps both above the main sign and within the store meant its dark-brown brickwork was lifted from the shadows. Elaborate displays housed within the immense, curved windows either side of the door provided additional enticement to investigate further. Leather-bound books, decorative perfume bottles, and the program of a popular play being performed at the Theatre Royal, Drury Lane formed the backdrop to several tailors' dummies adorned in the latest trend of shirts, blouses, ties, and costume jewellery. The door was painted in the same burgundy as the sign, whilst a stained-glass window depicting a repetitive pattern of red and gold diamonds filled its central pane. Its colours glistened in the candlelight of a cast-iron lantern suspended above the doorway. Unable to see inside, Lady Owston and Miss Webster obeyed the instinct of many curious shoppers before them and entered the store.

The interior was larger than expected compared to the dwarfed façade. Three glass display counters, formed into an inward-looking horse shoe, filled the immediate space upon entering. The Millinery Department's counter on the left was covered by wooden stands displaying a vast array of ladies' hats, from the broad-brimmed Olympia, with its chipped edging and upturned back edge pinned into a flourish, to the popular staple of a Murray Hill Ladies' Leghora. Most were reinforced with wire to maintain their characteristic shape, and all were available to purchase either in plain or readily decorated forms. Examples of the latter option showcased elaborate arrangements of pleated chiffon, silk ribbons, steel buckles, velvet, silk or lace nets, and even wildflowers. Each element was displayed at varying heights to increase the visual drama of the headpiece. Free-standing mirrors, tilted upward, stood on the counter's two front corners, whilst trays of hat and hair pins were laid out on its interior shelves. The former were made from steel, brass, gold, and silver with styles varying from the plain and cheap to the intricate and expensive. Likewise, the hair pins were constructed from brass, steel, and rubber with the most popular design being that of a plain, brass pin with its end bent into the shape of a daisy.

The Haberdashery Department's counter on the right, meanwhile, had folded samples of fine silks and lace laid out on its top. Mounted upon the wall behind were five columns of horizontal brass poles in rows of ten.

Threaded upon these poles were paper tubes holding rolls of plain and patterned materials waiting to be measured and cut to order. A trio of tailors' dummies stood to the right of the counter. The first wore a pale-pink, cotton blouse with puffed out shoulders and a cream-and-pale pink polka dot cravat. It's lower half was covered by a dark-brown, straight-lined skirt as a leather, small buckled belt sat around its waist. The second dummy wore a traditional mourning ensemble consisting of a black-cotton bustle dress and black, lace veil. Finally, the third dummy was dressed in a lightweight, pale-yellow, cotton bustle dress with cut-out floral detail on its skirts to complement the yellow daisies of the forest-green, crocheted shawl draped around the dummy's shoulders. The third counter appeared to be an extension of the Haberdashery Department due to the neatly stacked pyramids of boxed leather and cotton gloves in each of its corners.

While Lady Owston headed for the Haberdashery Department's main counter on the right, Miss Webster approached the one in the middle and requested to see inside one of the boxes. The moment the shop assistant had lifted the lid Miss Webster smelt the unmistakeable aroma of new leather. Admiring the craftsmanship of their stitching, Miss Webster reached to try them on but was prevented from doing so by Lady Owston calling her over. "I'll return," Miss Webster promised, and the shop assistant returned the box to the pile.

Beyond the Haberdashery Department was a set of stairs leading to the first floor. Running from the back of the shop to the front, the stairs' summit could only be seen from their base. Thus, when Miss Webster joined her employer, she was at the wrong angle to discreetly see what was there. Opposite the stairs, against the back wall, was the Perfumery and Hosiery Departments. From her vantage point, Miss Webster saw boxes of stockings, various styles of corsets (from plain to nursing), and undergarments tastefully displayed on both the interior shelves of the Hosiery Department's counter and those on the wall behind it. Meanwhile, the Perfumery Department displayed pyramids of soap wrapped in brown paper bearing the store's stamp on its countertop, and intricate, hand-blown glass perfume bottles on its interior shelves. Between the Perfumery and Hosiery Departments was a plain, wooden door. Gas-lit chandeliers were suspended from the ceiling throughout the store to illuminate each department, whilst each counter had its own cash register for convenience.

"Mr *Queshire*," Lady Owston said as the store's proprietor approached.

Miss Webster, having been in the midst of retrieving her notebook and pencil, paused when she caught sight of him. *Surely this couldn't be the Mr Queshire we are seeking,* she thought. His physique and boyish facial features placed him no older than eighteen and yet, when he spoke, his voice came from someone beyond those years. Scrutinising his face further, she saw he was fair complexioned and clean shaven with mildly defined cheekbones and a soft jawline. His olive-green eyes were warm as he regarded them both, and his short, fine, chocolate-brown hair was combed into a side-parting.

"Lady Owston, good day to you," Mr Queshire greeted, smiling at both women but nonetheless waiting for Lady Owston to make the formal introductions.

"This is my secretary, Miss Agnes Webster," Lady Owston said. "Agnes, this is Mr Edmund Queshire."

"Good day to you, too, Miss Webster. And welcome to the *Queshire Department Store.*" From both he enquired, "Are you looking for something in particular today or merely browsing?" He indicated the Perfumery Department. "I perfected a new soap only this morning. I think you would approve of it, Lady Owston. Rich, creamy, and excellent for the skin."

Miss Webster knew her employer would relish the opportunity to hold a prolonged conversation with Mr Queshire so took the opportunity to scrutinise him further. Frockcoats had become associated with the older, or more conservative, gentleman which is why, she supposed, he had chosen not to wear one. Instead, his attire consisted of a fashionable dark forest-green cotton suit with matching waistcoat and tie, and a white shirt with turned down, starched collar.

"The Bow Street Society, of which we are members, has been commissioned to investigate a most hideous crime," Lady Owston said.

Having missed the statement preceding it, Miss Webster decided she'd better listen more closely from then on. She therefore opened her notebook and began to take notes.

"A *murder*, Mr Queshire," Lady Owston added.

Mr Queshire's cheerful expression contracted into sombreness. After a significant pause, he said in a heavier tone of voice, "Of course… I trust you refer to the slaying of Mrs Maryanna Roberts." Lady Owston nodded, prompting him to release a thick, sad sigh. "Naturally news reached us here soon after the poor woman was found. The constable who made the discovery recognised her as a customer of ours and, of course, sister-in-law to my assistant manager, Mr Suggitt. Mr Suggitt went immediately to the police upon being told the news when he came to work this morning." He paused, again, as a thought occurred to him. "Why are you here, then? I assume it was he who commissioned the Society?"

"I'm afraid we can't divulge such sensitive information," Lady Owston explained. "But it is actually you to whom we wish to speak. I understand Maryanna Roberts was here yesterday and caused an incident of a *most* regrettable nature."

Mr Queshire lifted his brows and replied, "She

did, but how did you know of it?"

"Our client said you'd witnessed it and told them of it afterward," Lady Owston replied whilst being careful to sound non-judgemental. "Is that correct?"

"I can't confirm the last part without knowing who your client is, but I did see the end of the incident, yes—" Mr Queshire said, cutting himself short when he saw some customers approaching the Haberdashery Department. Glancing at Lady Owston and Miss Webster, he then made a sweeping motion with his hand to indicate he wanted them to follow before leading them to a corner. Once there, he lowered his voice and continued, "One of our shop assistants, Miss Rose Galway, saw the beginning."

"May we speak to her? I promise it shan't take long," Lady Owston said. "If it's more convenient, we could even talk to her together?"

"Of course," Mr Queshire replied with his usual, charming smile. Noticing a group of women hurrying into the store to shelter from the rain, he indicated the plain, wooden door and added, "Let's retire to the storeroom, however, where it's quieter and more discreet. I'll invite Miss Galway to join us along the way."

* * *

"Your husband's identified the body, Mrs Suggitt," Inspector Woolfe informed her. Rain had soaked his coat, unkempt hair, and face since Miss Dexter had seen him last, but he showed no sign of being troubled by it. He was standing with his back to the crowd, facing the *London Crystal Palace Bazaar's* doorway, as Mrs Suggitt huddled beneath an umbrella with her husband at her side and Miss Dexter behind. Due to Mr Clement Suggitt being marginally taller than his wife, he was able to keep all three reasonably dry whilst holding the umbrella aloft. Nevertheless, his tan coat was damp from rain whipped up by the wind and his polished, brown-leather shoes were semi-submerged in a dirty puddle. Beneath the coat, he wore a double-breasted, dark-brown suit, a light-mustard cravat, and a white, starched-collar shirt. In the coat's outer pocket was a dark-brown, cotton handkerchief. His bushy, brown moustache and hair were neatly combed, the latter into a central parting between his small, hazel eyes. His most striking of features were his large ears and nose. As Inspector Woolfe delivered the news, Mr Suggitt felt his wife tighten her grip upon his arm.

"Thank you," Mrs Suggitt whispered to her husband, a hint of appreciation gracing her otherwise melancholy eyes.

The news had also prompted Miss Dexter to look toward the bazaar. Fortunately, a camera mounted upon a wooden tripod blocked her view of the ghastly scene. She noticed a man emerge from beneath the black cloak attached to the camera's rear and converse with Dr Weeks. The surgeon pointed at the doorway and gave instructions as to which part he wanted photographed. Miss Dexter shivered at the memory of the poor woman.

Prior to the discussion, Inspector Woolfe and Mr Suggitt had settled the contentious issue of Mrs Suggitt's unexpected presence at the crime scene. The revelation the Bow Street Society had not only been hired but brought along by the victim's grieving sister hadn't been warmly received by Inspector Woolfe either. The glare he'd cast Miss Dexter's way when Mrs Suggitt had introduced her was proof enough that he didn't care for meddlers. He'd then gone on to deliver a speech about the shortcomings of members of the public investigating murders, followed by a recommendation he and his officers be permitted to do their duty. Mr Suggitt had agreed but, so far, Mrs Suggitt had held her tongue on the matter. This had irritated Inspector Woolfe further because it insinuated that she lacked faith in his ability. Unable to prove his suspicions, though, he had instead resolved to keep a close eye on the Bow Street meddler and continue with his interview.

"Do you know why your sister would've been at the bazaar this morning?" Inspector Woolfe enquired. Rather than comfort the woman—her husband's job, in his mind—he scrutinised her reactions. Thus far, she'd been the typical mourning relative, but her request for guidance from her husband in the form of a glance had piqued his interest. Whilst this wasn't unusual, Mr Suggitt replying with a shake of his head was.

"No, I'm afraid not," Mrs Suggitt said, addressing the policeman.

Inspector Woolfe knew Constable Fraser had recognised the victim for *two* reasons and, going by the Suggitts' reluctance to speak, they did too. It was true she'd been a regular customer of the *Queshire Department Store* on account of her familial connection to its assistant manager. He wanted to test his theory regarding the extent of the Suggitts' knowledge, though, and so enquired, "Was she living with Mr Roberts?"

"No," Mr Suggitt replied.

"Mr Roberts is a good man," Mrs Suggitt added.

Having had his suspicions strengthened by Mr Suggitt's lack of elaboration, Inspector Woolfe decided to reserve his judgement of Mr Roberts' character for when they met. "Where does he live?"

Unlike his wife, Mr Suggitt kept his gaze on the policeman as he gave him the address.

Miss Dexter looked to Mrs Suggitt in the hope she wouldn't reveal the Bow Street Society had also been given the address. From the little she'd seen and heard of Inspector Woolfe, she doubted she could dissuade him should he demand the truth from her. His countenance alone was sufficient to send a feeling of dread through her. Fortunately, Mrs Suggitt remained silent, and Miss Dexter moved closer to her to hide.

"They've got a child between them, a daughter—" Inspector Woolfe began.

"*Regina*!" Mrs Suggitt cried. Pressing her hand to her mouth to stifle a sob, she half-whispered, "She'll be so upset."

"Was she close to her mother?" Inspector Woolfe enquired.

The Suggitts exchanged glances for a second time but neither looked certain of the answer.

"There were tensions within the family, Inspector," Mr Suggitt replied.

"What about?" Inspector Woolfe probed.

"Maryanna's drinking," Mr Suggitt retorted. Releasing a soft sigh at his loss of control, he went on, "I've already gone over this with your sergeant, Inspector. What more—"

"Did you ever give Maryanna Roberts money, sir?" Inspector Woolfe interrupted.

Mr Suggitt stared at him a moment and demanded, "I *beg* your pardon?"

"Maryanna was a fallen woman, wasn't she, sir?" Inspector Woolfe enquired with a glance to Mrs Suggitt. "Addicted to the gin and giving out 'favours' to pay for it. Constable Fraser, who found the body, knew her not just because she was your sister-in-law but because he'd arrested her numerous times for prostitution. Now, it's obvious you both knew this, so it makes sense you would have—maybe in the past—given or offered her money. You'd not disowned the family, after all."

"*My* financial affairs are my *own* business, *Inspector,*" Mr Suggitt said, attempting to steer his wife away from the policeman. "Diana, we're leaving."

"You told my sergeant you were at home all evening," Inspector Woolfe said, halting the pair in their tracks. "Am I correct, sir?"

"You are," Mr Suggitt replied.

Mrs Suggitt turned her head sharply toward him with wide eyes.

"And were you with your husband?" Inspector Woolfe enquired.

"Yes," Mrs Suggitt snapped despite looking like a startled rabbit when she did so.

"She was, Inspector," Mr Suggitt interjected as he put his arm around her. "We have no reason to want Maryanna dead."

"Just routine, sir," Inspector Woolfe remarked. "When was the last time you saw your sister alive, Mrs Suggitt?"

"About a week ago," Mrs Suggitt replied. "But you saw her yesterday, didn't you, Clement?"

"*Did* you?" Inspector Woolfe enquired. Recalling Mr Suggitt's statement, recounted to him by his sergeant, Inspector Woolfe couldn't remember any mention of such an incident. He therefore hardened his tone as he enquired, "Did you neglect to tell my sergeant that, sir?"

"He never asked, and I didn't think it relevant since it was at the *Queshire Department Store* and *not* here," Mr Suggitt replied. "I'm sorry, Inspector, but my wife and I are very distressed by this whole business. As unwell as she was, Maryanna was still part of our family. I'm also finding your line of questioning *very* offensive, not to mention intrusive. So, if you'd excuse us, we would like to visit our niece."

"I will," Inspector Woolfe replied and watched the Suggitts visibly relax. "When I've finished asking my questions." Mr Suggitt's face contorted with anger but Inspector Woolfe didn't provide him with an opportunity to protest as he continued, "As you saw Maryanna yesterday, sir, you can tell me what she was wearing."

The colour drained from Mr Suggitt's face as the tension in his brow and jaw eased. "Yes…" He glanced at the bazaar and felt his stomach lurch at the recollection of what he'd been obliged to witness when he'd identified the body. "Of course... Erm, I believe it was... a green dress—"

"Long or short, sir?" Inspector Woolfe enquired.

"Long, past her knees, boots, and a shawl," Mr Suggitt replied. "I *think* it was the shawl Diana gifted to her."

"It's crocheted," Mrs Suggitt said. "Dark green with yellow flowers on it. If she was wearing it."

"Thank you," Inspector Woolfe said and, closing his notebook, looked between them. "That's all for now, but I'd like to continue this discussion tomorrow, sir." He eyed Mr Suggitt with suspicion; he was *certain* he would've been asked about the last time he'd seen the victim. Alas, it would be his sergeant's word against Mr Suggitt's, so there was little to gain from pressing the point.

"Whatever for?" Mr Suggitt challenged.

"New information comes our way all the time in these sorts of cases, sir," Inspector Woolfe replied. "There might be something I need to ask you about."

"Very well," Mr Suggitt reluctantly agreed.

"I'll come by tomorrow morning around ten o'clock, if it suits?" Inspector Woolfe enquired.

"It does," Mr Suggitt replied despite his concerned expression. Steering his wife away from the policeman, relieved at being permitted to depart this time, he then led her toward Mr Snyder's cab.

"Mr Suggitt, would you be so good as to visit the Bow Street Society's headquarters later today?" Miss Dexter enquired as she went after them. Once she'd acquired Mr Suggitt's full attention, she further explained, "I'm an artist by profession; if you, again, describe Maryanna's missing clothing to me, I can draw it. I may then make minor adjustments, under your guidance, so we may distribute the sketch to locate her clothes."

"Very well," Mr Suggitt replied, and the two of them agreed upon an appropriate time. After assisting Mrs Suggitt into the cab, he gave Mr Snyder the address of Mr Roberts's home and climbed inside. The cabman tipped his hat to Miss Dexter, geed his horse forward and, within moments, had driven the vehicle out of sight.

Returning to the bazaar, Miss Dexter was reassured to find Inspector Woolfe distracted by the crime scene and not preparing for her arrest. Concluding there was nothing more to be done, she decided to meet Lady Owston and Miss Webster at the *Queshire Department Store*. Yet, as even as she turned her feet in that direction, she heard Inspector Woolfe yell, "Get the photographs taken and the body away from here! I'm going to the *Queshire Department Store*!" Miss Dexter stopped abruptly and looked over her shoulder. Seeing Inspector Woolfe approach, she then hurried toward the store as swiftly as she could. Finding no sign of either Lady Owston or Miss Webster along the way, she contemplated running to reach the store ahead of the inspector. Just as she thought this, though, Inspector Woolfe passed and put several metres between them in a matter of seconds.

"Inspector!" Miss Dexter shouted but he didn't stop. "Um, *Inspector Woolfe*!" Hitching up her skirts to her ankles, she ran after him. Fortunately, he heard her swift footfalls and stopped to see what was going on. "Inspector…" Miss Dexter said, quite out of breath, when she'd finally reached him.

"Yeah?" Inspector Woolfe enquired with a glare— at least it looked like a glare. She couldn't be sure since he towered so highly over her.

"Miss… Miss Georgina Dexter." She took a few deep breaths and, straightening, added, "Mrs Suggitt's friend?" Inspector Woolfe narrowed his eyes but, to her amazement, Miss Dexter found the courage to continue,

"Please, sir, may I ask… do you have any idea where Maryanna Roberts' clothes could've disappeared to?"

A deep, guttural growl sounded from the policeman as he pointed at her. "Look, Miss Decker—or whatever your name is—I *don't* help amateurs who think they're better than us coppers—"

"But will you help her poor sister—Mrs Suggitt? She will naturally want to know," Miss Dexter said, fearing Inspector Woolfe might gobble her up like the wolf in the fairy tale.

"No," Inspector Woolfe replied, much to Miss Dexter's disappointment. His next words took her quite aback, however, for not only were they calmly spoken but there was genuine regret in his voice. "I don't know where they've gone. Was that all you wanted?"

Miss Dexter was quite surprised; she hadn't expected him to agree for Mrs Suggitt's sake—she thought she'd been clutching at straws. Now at a loss as to what else she could do to stall him, she realised she felt rather lightheaded after her run. Placing her hand upon her head, therefore, she said, "I think I feel faint…"

FOUR

The storeroom to which Mr Queshire took Lady Owston, Miss Webster, and Miss Galway was dimly lit. Though small, there was sufficient space for a table and chairs beneath its window, a pot-bellied stove in its corner, and at least four piles of boxed stock. The window overlooked a bland yard surrounded by a high, brick wall. Beyond it was the service alleyway running adjacent to the row of buildings. Brown, striped wallpaper added optical warmth to the space whilst the stove's orange, glowing coals heated the air. A pot of French Breakfast coffee and the *Gaslight Gazette*'s morning edition were laid out upon the table.

Prepared twice weekly, the coffee was left to cool and only heated on the stove when required—usually midmorning or lunch time, as per the habits of the English middle classes. Under normal circumstances, only Mr Queshire and Mr Suggitt were permitted to enjoy the beverage due to the high expense of its pre-roasted, pre-ground kernels. An exception was made on this occasion, however, as Mr Queshire served Miss Galway a cup and offered the same again to his guests. Lady Owston and Miss Webster politely declined with the former adding, "I'm more of a tea drinker myself."

"I'm sorry, sur," Miss Rose Galway mumbled with her head bowed as she accepted the drink.

"Whatever for?" Mr Queshire enquired.

"Whatever it is I've done, sur," Miss Galway replied, her natural, East End of London accent breaking through on the last word. It was the only hint of her background since the store's uniform of a cream-coloured blouse, brown belt, and ankle-length skirt hit her poverty well. An attempt had also been made to tame her wiry, dirty-blond hair, but the result was an unkempt, loosely pinned bun at the back of her head. Perched upon the chair as she was, her petite build would've made her appear childlike if it hadn't been for the crow's feet in the corners of her eyes.

"*Have* you done something wrong?" Lady Owston enquired.

"I dunno, Milady," Miss Galway mumbled.

"Then what reason have you to apologise?" Lady Owston enquired.

"None, Milady," Miss Galway replied. Looking at Mr Queshire, she added, "I just thought I had because you asked me in here, sur."

"No, Rose," Mr Queshire replied.

"Sorry, sur," Miss Galway mumbled and bowed her head once more.

"*Stop* apologising, Rose—" Mr Queshire cut himself short and, offering a contrived smile, said in a softer tone, "You have nothing to worry about." Shifting his smile into a more sincere one, he indicated his guests. "Lady Katheryne Owston and her secretary, Miss Agnes Webster, here wish to know what happened yesterday between Maryanna Roberts and the customer."

"She didn't do her in," Miss Galway responded in disbelief.

Mr Queshire's smile faltered, and he replied, "No one is saying she did; Lady Owston and Miss Webster just want to know because they've been commissioned to investigate the poor woman's murder."

Miss Galway's head shot up, and she looked between the two Bow Streeters in amazement. "What, you're police? Didn't know they let women in."

"They don't," Miss Webster replied in her usual monotone. "Lady Owston and I are part of the Bow Street Society."

"*Really?*" Miss Galway enquired with wide eyes.

"Yes," Miss Webster replied.

Miss Galway's face lit up with delight as she cried, "I read all about your last case! With the old blind boy? Hung onto every word the newspapers printed, I did. You couldn't have gotten better people to go after Mrs Roberts' killer, sur."

"*I* didn't enlist their services," Mr Queshire replied.

"And the Thaddeus Dorsey case was investigated by my fellow members," Lady Owston interjected. "Not Miss Webster and I."

Miss Galway's shoulders slouched at the news. She enquired, "You're still gonna get them, though, yeah?"

"We shall do our best," Lady Owston reassured.

"Mrs Holden didn't do her in though; she's too much of a lady for that," Miss Galway said.

"*Rose!*" Mr Queshire cried, causing Miss Galway to flinch.

"*What'd* I do, sur?!" Miss Galway cried in return.

"I wasn't intending on giving the Bow Street Society our customer's name," Mr Queshire explained, and Lady Owston cast a knowing smile at Miss Webster. She'd assumed such would be the case given Mr Queshire's apparent unwillingness to elaborate upon the incident when they'd been on the shop floor.

"I—I didn't know, sur!" Miss Galway insisted as she sat bolt upright.

"It's fine, Rose," Mr Queshire replied.

"But I swear, sur," Miss Galway began. "If I'd have known you wasn't gonna tell them Mrs Holden's name I wouldn't of—"

"*Rose*," Mr Queshire interrupted with a hard voice and harsh look. Seeing the fear in her countenance, though, he added, "It's fine. No harm has been done."

"We shall treat the information with the utmost confidence, Miss Galway," Lady Owston reassured.

The tension visibly eased in Miss Galway's face and shoulders, and she took a large mouthful of coffee to calm her emotions further. Taking another sip from the cup, she reflected on the monetary value of the beverage as its strong, bitter flavour lingered in her mouth.

"Tell Lady Owston and Miss Webster what happened with Mrs Holden," Mr Queshire prompted.

"Well…" Miss Galway put the cup down on the table. "I was serving Mrs Holden in the haberdashery department when Mrs Roberts got in the middle of us and asked where her sister was. I told her she wasn't there. Mrs Roberts walked a little way and I got on with serving Mrs Holden. The next thing I hear is Mr Holden saying, 'I beg your pardon?' His wife and me look over and see Mrs Roberts trying to hold the poor man's hand. She was telling him she could keep him warm at night, too. Mrs Holden was mad when she heard this and told me as much. She announced she was leaving, got alongside her husband, and started walking out."

"This is where I come in," Mr Queshire interjected. "I was in the millinery department when I overheard Mrs Holden announce she was leaving. Naturally, I was dismayed by what I heard so I intersected Mrs Holden at the door. I enquired if all were well, and she informed me she'd expected more from my establishment and intended never to set foot here again. I apologised, profusely, and enquired what had happened. She pointed directly at Mrs Roberts, still standing at Miss Galway's counter, and exclaimed 'her!' Still somewhat dumbfounded by the whole matter, I at once went to the haberdashery department only to see Mrs Roberts swaying quite markedly. I don't like to speak ill of the dead, but Mrs Roberts had a very particular scent about her person."

"Hence your explanation to Mrs Suggitt when she enquired after her sister's whereabouts," Miss Webster observed as she wrote down the key points in her notebook.

Mr Queshire nodded and, releasing a heavy sigh, replied, "An uncharacteristically callous remark on my part. I was, I'm ashamed to say, angry and embarrassed by Mrs Robert's conduct—both toward Mr Holden and myself. When I'd approached, she'd made lewd, and *very* false, suggestions about our acquaintanceship. She forced me to take action." He frowned. "I'm not proud of myself."

"What did you do?" Miss Webster challenged, meeting his gaze.

"Whatever it was I'm *certain* you were justified, Mr Queshire," Lady Owston interjected. "Especially given the *outrageous* behaviour of Mrs Roberts."

"Thank you," Mr Queshire replied with an appreciative smile. Yet his smile vanished as he turned cold eyes to Miss Webster and said, "She was removed from the store. We don't have any security officers here, so I had to remove her myself. I tried to do it discreetly, but her drunkenness kept her tongue sharp. My strength was greater than hers, so she was outside within moments but, in between, she drew the full attention of the other customers with her foul language. Furthermore, the Holdens decided against remaining and left the store."

"Was a constable not summoned?" Miss Webster challenged further.

"The woman was already miserable," Mr Queshire countered but, taking a moment of consideration, added in a subdued voice, "I didn't want to make matters worse."

"Couldn't Mr Suggitt have intervened on your behalf?" Lady Owston enquired.

"Rose, could you fetch me a bar of the new soap, please?" Mr Queshire requested.

"Yes, sur," Miss Galway replied and hurried from the room.

"As you've witnessed, Miss Galway has trouble holding her tongue," Mr Queshire explained once the door had closed behind her. "I didn't want her to hear this for that reason."

"You may speak freely with us," Lady Owston said. Though both her curiosity and excitement were piqued at the prospect of the impending revelations, she nevertheless kept them well hidden.

"Mr Suggitt didn't intervene, but... nor did I ask him to," Mr Queshire said with a deep frown. Sitting on Miss Galway's chair, he rested his hand upon the table and went on, "You see..." He knitted his brow and turned his face away. After a few moments of reflection, he relaxed his features and said, "He would always distance himself from Mrs Roberts whenever she came to the store."

"Did Mrs Roberts realise he was doing so?" Lady Owston enquired.

"No," Mr Queshire replied. "But it was never him she wanted to see."

"Who, then?" Lady Owston enquired.

"Her sister, Mrs Diana Suggitt," Mr Queshire replied. "Mrs Suggitt comes here every day, without fail, to escort her husband to lunch. When the store is—very often—busy and I require all assistants to forego their break to meet demand, Mr Suggitt usually does the same even though, for him, it's not mandatory. Mrs Suggitt still comes, even then, and asks after her husband. He'll eventually be brought to her, but in the meantime, she'll browse the departments and discuss the store's apparent level of busyness with the assistants. And, when Mr Suggitt does join his wife, she'll speak with him for half an hour while customers fill the space around them." He momentarily pursed his lips into another frown. "It can be rather irritating."

"Presumably, Mrs Roberts has come seeking her sister prior to yesterday's incident?" Lady Owston enquired.

"Yes, many times, and I'm sorry to say, many times inebriated," Mr Queshire replied. "As I said, Mr Suggitt would distance himself from Mrs Roberts, though he has never denied his familial connection to her when directly asked. His wife, on the other hand, would speak openly with her in the store. Admittedly, Mrs Roberts had never behaved so incorrigibly before yesterday. The particular scent I spoke of always lingered around her, however." Mr Queshire knitted his brow once more. "He's never spoken to me of this. I'm afraid I therefore don't know the reason why he'd distance himself. After having observed how much of a concerted effort he'd made to do so in the past, I felt reluctant to ask him to break the habit during the incident yesterday."

"And yet you say Mrs Suggitt spoke openly with her sister *in* the store?" Lady Owston enquired. "Despite her husband avoiding her?"

"I know how my words may make things appear, Milady," Mr Queshire replied. "But Mr Suggitt is a good man; he would never deny his wife the reassurance of speaking to her sister."

"Of course," Lady Owston said with a soft smile. "Was Mrs Suggitt very worried about her sister's welfare?"

"Yes, and with very good reason," Mr Queshire replied.

"Did Mrs Roberts acknowledge her sister's concern at all?" Miss Webster interjected.

"It's not my place to say," Mr Queshire replied. "But she did always become calmer whenever Mrs Suggitt spoke to her."

"Did Mrs Suggitt ever give her sister money?" Miss Webster enquired.

Mr Queshire closed his hand into a fist upon the table and replied, "I don't know. *Mr* Suggitt is the one you should ask, not I."

"Mr Queshire," Lady Owston intervened to distract him from Miss Webster's poor choice of question. Her ploy seemed to work, too, for his annoyance dissipated as he shifted his gaze back to her. Upon seeing this, Lady Owston offered a charming smile of her own and enquired, "Was Mrs Suggitt there when you removed her sister from the store yesterday?"

"No, she arrived about half an hour later," Mr Queshire replied. "Which was unusually late."

"Did she say why?" Lady Owston enquired.

"She spoke to her husband, who told her of the incident with her sister," Mr Queshire replied. "She then enquired if I knew where Mrs Roberts had gone. That's when I made the awful, awful remark. I was still angry about the whole thing." He released a soft sigh. "I'm sorry, I don't know if she gave a reason for her lateness or not. I wish I could be more helpful."

"I'm *sure* the Suggitts would be *most* appreciative of the help you've already given us, Mr Queshire," Lady Owston said as she gave his hand a gentle pat. "After you had removed her from the store, did Mrs Roberts return at all? Perhaps still seeking her sister? Presuming you were at home all evening, of course."

"I was, and no, she didn't," Mr Queshire replied. "After shouting obscenities at my store, she walked away. I wasn't paying attention to the direction she went; I was happy to be rid of her." He rested his forehead in his hand and released a deep breath. "If she had returned... even after the store had closed... I could've kept her safe and sent for her sister. She wouldn't be..." He shook his head but kept his eyes covered as he added with deep regret, "Her poor family."

The door opened, and Miss Galway entered with the soap in her hand. "I got it, sur," she said, offering the bar to Mr Queshire.

"Thank you, Rose," Mr Queshire replied. Taking the soap, he then offered it to Lady Owston and said, "A gift from the *Queshire Department Store*."

"*Oh!* I couldn't *possibly*—!" Lady Owston exclaimed with her hand upon her chest.

"I *insist*," Mr Queshire urged, holding the soap closer to her as his usual relaxed demeanour and charming smile returned. "I'll be *very* offended if you don't."

"Very *well*!" Lady Owston replied with a coy chuckle. "If you *insist*." Taking the soap, she held it under her nose and inhaled its sweet scent. "*Oh,* Mr *Queshire*! It's *divine*! Agnes, smell this." She stuck it under Miss Webster's nose, prompting her fellow Bow Streeter to jerk her head back in surprise.

When she realised what it was, Miss Webster took a reluctant sniff of the bar and remarked, "Mhm, very nice."

"*Agnes,* you didn't even smell it properly," Lady Owston said. "*Here—*" Yet, both her words and movement of the soap stopped when she caught sight of the stairs through the open doorway. "How very peculiar…" she mused aloud.

"Is there something wrong with the scent?" Mr Queshire enquired.

"No," Lady Owston replied, pulling her gaze back to him. "The soap is *lovely,* but I'm certain I just saw one of your customers entering the room at the top of the stairs."

"She'll be going to the hairdressing salon, Milady," Miss Galway said, pointing to an open doorway on the right of the small landing at the stairs' summit.

"No, you misunderstand," Lady Owston replied as she lifted her gloved hand and gave a brief shake of her head with her eyes closed. "I saw her go through the door marked *Staff only.*" Miss Galway paled and darted her eyes to Mr Queshire. Concerned by this reaction, Lady Owston enquired, "Is everything well?"

"Absolutely," Mr Queshire interjected. "I'll go up and make sure no one is lost. Excuse me, ladies." Rising to his feet, he then closed the door behind him as he left.

Yet, despite his confidence, Lady Owston remained dissatisfied with his answer. She therefore placed a gentle hand upon Miss Galway's arm and enquired, "Are you ill?"

"No, Milady," Miss Galway replied.

"It's just you seemed—" Lady Owston began.

"How does somebody become a member, then?" Miss Galway interrupted.

"A member…?" Lady Owston enquired, taken aback by the shop assistant's sudden change in demeanour. Exchanging glances with Miss Webster, she decided to humour Miss Galway in the hopes of gaining her trust. "You have to be interviewed by the Society's clerk, Miss Rebecca Trent. I could put you in touch with her and… put in a good word for you, if you'd like?"

"You'd do that for me?" Miss Galway enquired.

"Of *course*," Lady Owston replied with a broad smile. "The Society would be enriched to have someone with your talents as a member. Being a member does mean you have to share information with one another, however. Sometimes *very* confidential information."

"But I don't know anything," Miss Galway replied.

"Why were you so alarmed when I spoke of the customer entering the *Staff only* room at the top of the stairs?" Lady Owston enquired.

Miss Galway paled for a second time and replied, "I can't say, Milady. I was being foolish, that's all." Turning sharply toward the door, she added, "I must be getting back to work or Mr Queshire *will* be angry at me."

"Thank you, Miss Galway, you've been most helpful," Lady Owston said, delaying the young woman's retreat long enough to add, "And my offer still stands if you wish to take advantage of it."

"Thank you, Milady. I will, Milady," Miss Galway replied, hurrying from the storeroom and leaving the door ajar behind her.

Allowing her a few moments' grace to return to her department, Lady Owston opened the door wide and scanned the area. Finding no sign of Mr Queshire, she mused, "How *very* curious…" Glancing behind her, she added, "Come, Agnes," before leaving the storeroom and heading for the stairs. Miss Webster, having finished her writing, put away her notebook, and duly followed.

Yet no sooner had they climbed halfway up the stairs did the door marked *Staff only* open, and Mr Queshire stepped out. He paused upon seeing them but then gifted his charming smile and greeted, "Lady Owston." Descending the stairs, he went on, "It was a misunderstanding; the poor lady thought she was going into the salon. May I assist you with anything else?"

"No, thank you," Lady Owston replied. "You've been *most* helpful. Let us go, Agnes!"

"Yes, Milady," Miss Webster agreed and, descending the stairs ahead of her, waited at their base until Lady Owston had made her goodbyes to Mr Queshire and joined her. Allowing Lady Owston to lead the way out of the store, Miss Webster tried to keep as close to her as the densely populated floor space permitted. When they neared the haberdashery department, though, a blond-haired lady blocked their path. She placed a shawl upon the counter and, pointing to its material, told the shop assistant, "Mark the loosening of the weave, miss."

"I can assure madam none of the items in the store are second-hand," the shop assistant replied.

"Excuse me," Lady Owston said, and the blond-haired lady stepped aside to allow them to pass. "Thank you." Once they were outside, Lady Owston remarked, "Something isn't quite right, Agnes." Yet before Miss Webster could respond, Lady Owston strode down the street and exclaimed, "*Inspector* Woolfe! What *are* you doing to Miss Dexter?"

The large man twisted his torso upon hearing his name, thereby revealing his grip upon Miss Dexter's shoulders.

Lady Owston quickened her pace at the sight and, with Miss Webster hurrying along behind, cried, "I've heard of police intimidation, but *really*!" Putting herself between Inspector Woolfe and Miss Dexter, she then took a gentle hold of Miss Dexter's arm once he'd released her and enquired, "Are you hurt?"

"N—No, Lady Owston," Miss Dexter replied. "I—I was feeling faint and Inspector Woolfe assisted me." She offered him a nervous smile. "Thank you, Inspector, I feel much better now."

Lady Owston clasped her hand over her mouth and said, "Oh, I *do* apologise, Inspector! I quite misunderstood the situation."

"Forget it," Inspector Woolfe replied and, stepping around them, entered the *Queshire Department Store*.

"I believe it's time to leave, ladies," Lady Owston said as she linked her arms with Misses Dexter's and Webster's.

"I have Mr Roberts' address, but Mr Suggitt took Mr Snyder's cab," Miss Dexter explained when some distance had been put between them and the store. "I think he may have taken his wife to Mr Roberts' home to see their niece."

"Then we wouldn't want to impose," Lady Owston said.

"Unless they are coordinating their stories," Miss Webster remarked.

"Even if they are, it shall do them no good," Lady Owston replied. "We shall *still* find the truth of it."

"Inspector Woolfe was also given Mr Roberts' address," Miss Dexter said. "He's arranged to speak to Mr and Mrs Suggitt again tomorrow morning."

"*That* is when we shall speak to Mr Roberts and his daughter," Lady Owston said. "We also have the Holdens to speak to."

"Do you think we should find out if Mrs Roberts knew anyone at the bazaar before leaving?" Miss Dexter enquired.

"We shan't get near it with all the police around, my dear," Lady Owston replied. "Alas, I suspect poor Mrs Roberts wasn't there to see *anyone* at the bazaar when one considers she was found so early in the morning. Though I have known women who loved shopping so much, they have had their servants sleep in the doorways overnight so as to be the first to make a particular purchase, I think it *highly* unlikely this was the reason for Mrs Roberts' presence. No, *first* we shall return to Miss Trent and divulge our findings thus far. *Onwaaard*!"

FIVE

Miss Trent's footsteps echoed around the room as she crossed the bare floorboards to the window. Torrential rain pummelled the glass whilst dark-grey clouds smothered the sky and thunder rumbled in the distance. Although gas lighting was fitted throughout the house, lack of use meant the rooms above ground floor level were seldom illuminated. Thus, she stood in practical darkness as she observed a private carriage travelling down Bow Street on its way to the Opera House. Noticing a separate vehicle slow to a halt outside her own front door, she put down her cup, and hurried downstairs. Keen to avoid losing *any* potential client, she rushed across the hallway, slid back the door's bolts, and turned its key in a matter of moments. As she opened it, though, she was immediately driven backward by Lady Owston charging toward her.

"*Well!*" Lady Owston exclaimed as she passed the clerk, turned upon her heel, and slapped her gloved hands together. "What a *most* intriguing morning *we* have had, Miss Trent!"

"Where shall I place this?" Miss Webster enquired, holding up her soaked umbrella.

"What was so intriguing about it?" Miss Trent enquired as she took the umbrella and rested it against the staircase. Meanwhile, Miss Dexter, having followed the others inside, closed the door and gave it a gentle tug.

"Was this where the poor man was murdered?" Lady Owston enquired and, ascending to the third step, twisted her torso to address the others. "*Never mind*! It's *irrelevant*!"

"*What* was so intriguing?" Miss Trent repeated with one hand upon her waist.

"A man who not only distanced himself from his sister-in-law in spite of her closeness with his wife, but

66

also became irate when it was suggested he may have given his sister-in-law some money," Lady Owston replied in a sing-song voice whilst climbing to the top of the stairs. "Also, information being held back from the police, and shop assistants becoming alarmed over allegedly trivial matters such as customers entering storerooms." She moved her hand in a circular motion. "The usual detective fare." Strolling along the landing a short distance, she then descended the stairs to join the others. "It is *rather* spacious here. You *must* give Agnes and me a tour sometime."

"Was Maryanna Roberts where Mrs Suggitt claimed she'd be?" Miss Trent enquired, moving to meet her.

Lady Owston passed her, however, and, removing her gloves, replied, "She was."

"I was able to take some photographs of the body," Miss Dexter interjected. "But my camera is with Mr Snyder, and he has taken the Suggitts to Mr Roberts' home to see Maryanna's daughter Regina."

Several firm knocks sounded from the door, and the four women looked at each other.

"Are you expecting anyone?" Lady Owston enquired.

"I never *expect* anyone," Miss Trent replied as she went to the door. "Only clients." In opening the door, she both inadvertently hid Miss Dexter behind it and revealed Mr Snyder standing on the porch. Water dripped from the broad brim of his hat and onto his sodden cloak as he stepped inside with a squelching of his boots. Draping his cloak over the stairs' handrail and resting his hat on top, he then retrieved Miss Dexter's camera from a satchel slung over his shoulder. It, like the rest of his clothes, had remained dry despite the onslaught of rain. Passing the camera to Miss Dexter, he said, "Kept it as dry as I could."

"It's perfect, Sam," Miss Dexter replied once

she'd turned it over several times and inspected it. "Thank you." Slipping it into her own satchel, she informed Miss Trent, "I'll develop the photographs this afternoon."

"Did the Suggitts go to Mr Roberts' residence?" Lady Owston enquired from Mr Snyder.

"They did, Milady," Mr Snyder replied. "Woz the same address Mrs Suggitt gave."

"Ah, so you *were* paying attention?" Lady Owston remarked, impressed.

Mr Snyder gave a soft chuckle and replied, "A cabman sees and hears more than you'd think."

"May I see your copy of the *Post Office Directory*, Miss Trent?" Miss Webster enquired. "Mrs Roberts offended a Mr and Mrs Holden at the *Queshire Department Store* yesterday; I would like to check if they're listed."

"Do you have Christian names?" Miss Trent enquired in return as she went into her office.

"I'm afraid not," Miss Webster replied, moving to the open doorway and watching Miss Trent retrieve the required tome from beneath the wall-mounted boxed telephone. Accepting it from her with a quietly uttered "thank you," Miss Webster laid it on Miss Trent's desk and searched its pages as swiftly as if it were her own diary. "Here they are," she announced a few minutes later. Making a note of the address, she then carried the directory into the hallway and placed it upon the stairs for the others to see.

"How can you be sure they are the Holdens from the store?" Miss Dexter enquired.

"Mrs Holden was described as being too much of a lady to commit murder by the store's shop assistant, Miss Rose Galway," Miss Webster began. "Ergo Mrs Holden is wealthy—either upper middle class or upper class. We know her husband was with her as it was he who Mrs Roberts propositioned. We can therefore assume they reside together. Due to my accompanying Her Ladyship to various balls, dinner parties, and afternoon teas at wealthy ladies' homes to discuss the latest fashion trends, I have come to know which addresses are the more affluent. The Holdens residing in these areas are the ones we should be searching for in the directory. Fortuitously, there is only one: Mr and Mrs Bartholomew Holden who reside at 200 Hill Street in Mayfair."

"Agnes is *very* clever," Lady Owston remarked.

Miss Dexter was certain Miss Trent could've come to the same conclusion, with Mr Snyder's assistance. *At least Miss Webster and Lady Owston have personal experience of these places, though,* she thought.

Miss Webster closed the directory and gave Lady Owston the piece of paper with the address. Upon reading it, the latter smiled and said, "Not too far from the *lovely* Mrs Braithwaite in Berkeley Square, either!" Pausing as a thought occurred to her, she mused aloud, "I wonder if she knows the Holdens?" She dismissed the idea with a wave of her hand. "Ah well, *never mind*!"

"You'll be going to question them now?" Miss Trent enquired as she picked up the directory from the stairs and held it close.

"There's no time like the present," Lady Owston replied.

"And what of Mr Roberts?" Miss Trent enquired. "Have you spoken to him?"

"Inspector Woolfe intends to speak with Mr Roberts this afternoon," Miss Dexter replied. "And the Suggitts again tomorrow morning."

"I thought it best we not risk the inspector's wrath by attempting to speak to Mr Roberts today," Lady Owston interjected and ushered Miss Webster toward her umbrella. "Would you be so kind as to take us to the Holdens residence, Mr Snyder?"

"Yeah, I'll jus' ge' the cab," Mr Snyder replied.

Upon heading for the door, though, Lady Owston stayed him with a lifting of her hand.

"As wealthy as I am, I am still a woman," Lady Owston said, addressing Miss Trent. "We are not weak but—some, not all—men still believe us thus. Therefore, I request a gentleman to speak to Mr Holden whilst Agnes and I speak to his wife."

"Will you be accompanying them?" Miss Trent enquired from Miss Dexter.

"N—No, I don't believe so…" Miss Dexter replied with a nervous glance cast toward Lady Owston. "I've arranged for Mr Suggitt to pay a visit here later today to describe Mrs Roberts' missing clothes to me so I may draw them."

"Very well," Miss Trent said. "Lady Owston, I'll arrange for another of our members to meet you at the Holdens' residence." She held out her hand for the piece of paper.

"May we have his name?" Lady Owston enquired as she gave it to her.

"He'll make himself known to you if you wait inside Mr Snyder's cab," Miss Trent replied after reading the address and making a mental note of it. Passing it back to Lady Owston, she then went to the door for a third time after yet another knock sounded. Releasing a deep sigh upon seeing her latest visitor, she kept one hand on the door whilst her other went to her hip. "Yes, Mr Maxwell?"

"S-Sorry for bothering you, but—" Mr Maxwell began but cut himself short upon catching sight of Miss Dexter over Miss Trent's shoulder. "Georgina…?" Miss Trent half-turned toward Miss Dexter, thereby giving Mr Maxwell an unadulterated view of her. Rather than be reassured by this fact though, he felt his heart rate increase, his face flush, and the back of his neck warm. "I—I didn't know y—you were here. I came to speak to Miss Trent. About the murder of Mrs Roberts and why I wasn't assigned to investigate it. I—I didn't follow you here, I swear."

"I didn't think you had," Miss Trent replied in a dry tone.

"Had you not heard enough whilst you were eavesdropping?" Lady Owston demanded.

"No. Yes, I mean-no," Mr Maxwell replied. "Which is to say I—"

"*Save* your excuses, *sir*!" Lady Owston interrupted. Passing both Miss Trent and Mr Maxwell, she descended the external steps to the street and called, "Good day to you, Miss Trent, Miss Dexter. Agnes!"

"Goodbye," Miss Webster said to the others as she collected her umbrella. The rain had stopped so she hooked it over her arm and followed Lady Owston to the street. Mr Snyder, having put his hat and cloak back on, bid farewell to Miss Trent and Miss Dexter and departed for his cab. Opening it up, he held each lady's hand in turn as she climbed inside, before carefully closing the doors over their knees. After paying a street urchin for watching the vehicle, he climbed up to his seat at the back of the cab and settled into it. His hands once again found the reins and geed the horse into motion, sending both the cab and the Bow Streeters on their way.

"I was in the *Gazette's* office when the story came in," Mr Maxwell explained, resting his hand upon his cravat. "And I decided to cover it but when I arrived, I saw Georgina—" He flinched. "Miss Dexter… and so I went over to her and naturally, I was surprised to find she had been assigned, by you, to investigate the case for the Society when *I* had received no such note. I thought, perhaps, it was a mistake, so I came here."

"Not every member is assigned to every case," Miss Trent replied. "This was explained to you at your initial interview."

"Yes, I remember," Mr Maxwell said. "But I'd

thought—I'd *hoped*—after the success of the Dorsey Case, that…" He gave a weak smile. "you would've thought to assign me to *this* case. I—" He cut himself short as Miss Dexter passed him. "You're not leaving already, are you?"

Miss Dexter stopped at the porch's edge and, looking over her shoulder at him, replied with a frown, "I must return home and develop my photographs."

"Then allow me to accompany you to the omnibus stop," Mr Maxwell suggested, stepping out onto the porch as he did so. "Obviously, I misunderstood, Miss Trent," he informed her. "Please, forgive me."

"Of course," Miss Trent replied.

"Shall we?" Mr Maxwell enquired with a broad smile as he offered Miss Dexter his arm.

Looking from it, to Miss Trent, to Mr Maxwell's face, and back to Miss Trent, Miss Dexter said, "I will return in time for Mr Suggitt's arrival, if that's acceptable?"

"It is," Miss Trent replied with a smile. "Good day, Miss Dexter, Mr Maxwell."

"Good day," Miss Dexter replied and hurried down the steps without taking Mr Maxwell's arm.

Perturbed by her silent refusal, his smile shifted into a frown as he lowered his arm.

"I'd follow her if I were you," Miss Trent suggested and closed the door.

Realising he hadn't done so, Mr Maxwell dashed down the stairs and ran down the street to catch her up. Fortunately, Miss Dexter's pace wasn't a fast one, so she'd hadn't gone far by the time he fell into step beside her. He said, "Father has invited me to dinner tomorrow evening."

Miss Dexter fought the urge to return to the Bow Street Society's house. She didn't feel unsafe in Mr Maxwell's presence—far from it—she just wasn't sure she wanted to act as if nothing had happened as he was doing. Something *had* happened; something truly terrible, in her mind, and it couldn't be swept away by a nice walk and idle chatter.

"…Will you meet my parents?" Mr Maxwell enquired.

Miss Dexter halted and stared up at him, stunned. "I *beg* your pardon? Did you… *truly* ask what I thought you did?"

"Erm, I'm not sure," Mr Maxwell replied. "What did you think I asked?"

"To meet your parents."

"Oh," Mr Maxwell smiled in relief. "Yes, you did." Miss Dexter's lack of enthusiasm caused his smile to disappear and her utter bewilderment brought a deep concern to his heart. "I've met yours," he pointed out, feebly. "We *are* engaged, Georgina."

"Without the proposal," Miss Dexter's voice broke on the last word despite the angry bewilderment it held. Unable to even *look* at him, she turned her back and attempted to compose herself.

Mr Maxwell moved closer and lifted his hand as if it reach for her. Changing his mind at the last moment, though, he instead closed his fingers and lowered his arm once more. "I'm trying to make amends…"

Miss Dexter took out her handkerchief and pressed it to her lips.

"I'm sorry for the way I did it," Mr Maxwell continued, moving closer still. "But I'm not sorry for being engaged to you."

Miss Dexter bowed her head, compelling Mr Maxwell to do the same.

"I… I love you," he confessed.

For several long, excruciating moments she remained silent. When she did finally speak, her soft voice was filled with regret. "I'm very fond of you, too, Joseph, but what you did… you trapped me in an engagement I neither wanted nor asked for. And in so doing, you have planned a future I never wanted for myself, the future of a housewife and mother when all I've ever wanted is to be an artist. To be independent, doing what I love."

"You can still be an artist, Georgina. I'll do whatever it takes to make you happy."

Miss Dexter immediately lifted her head and turned toward him with lips parted and eyes widened in astonishment. Furthermore, she discovered a part of her was hopeful that he was sincere. Not for his sake but her own. She scrutinised him for the slightest hint of deceit but could find none. "You do not know the brevity of what you say. Of what you *offer* me, Joseph—"

"I do—!"

"Then *promise* me," Miss Dexter replied as she closed the gap between them and looked straight into his eyes. "Give me your word what you say shall come to pass with both your support and blessing."

"I promise," he took her hand in his and placed it upon his chest. "With all my heart and word as a gentleman, I'll do whatever it takes to make you happy, to make you the successful—independent—artist you want to be."

Her heart rate quickened as she again found sincerity in his eyes. Feeling her bosom swell with a deluge of relief and happiness, she placed her other hand upon his and said, "I believe you."

Mr Maxwell held her hands between his and kissed them.

"So, yes, I shall meet your parents," Miss Dexter said.

Having forgotten about his earlier request, Mr Maxwell was at first taken aback and then delighted by her answer. Slipping his arms around her petite form and holding her close, he said, "Thank you." Their eyes met, making them both blush, before they broke their embrace, and Mr Maxwell offered her his arm. "I think you'll really like my mother," he said once she'd slipped her small hand into the crook of his arm and they were walking toward the omnibus stop.

"If she's anything like you, Joseph, I'm certain I shall."

* * *

The cold water's surface tension was broken with the thorough rinsing of a flannel covered in the residue of lavender-scented carbolic soap. Water then poured into the hand-painted, Chinese-inspired bowl as the flannel was withdrawn and placed upon bare skin. Its circular motions followed the well-defined contours of a male abdomen before brushing against the waistband of his trousers. Feeling another's hand upon his own, the flannel's owner lifted his emerald-green eyes to regard their reflections in the mirror opposite. Although shirtless, his unchecked, small, golden-blond curls atop his head, closely cut hair beneath, and sideburns running to the corners of his jaw remained dry. His slender face, high—yet delicate— cheekbones, and pristine nose gifted him with a handsomeness adored by many who attended his performances at the Paddington Palladium.

Standing behind him with her free hand upon his shoulder was a dark-blond haired lady with dark blue-green eyes and a fair complexion. At six feet, she was an inch taller than him. The high mound of wavy hair pinned to her crown made the deficit even more pronounced, however. Her white, long-sleeved blouse with pale-blue floral print was tucked into the high waistband of her plain pale-blue, straight-lined skirts. As a result, her narrow waist was accentuated despite the blouse's loose fit. Both her blouse and the dark-blue, thigh-length cotton jacket she wore over it had "leg-of-mutton" shaped sleeves. A gold brooch, inlaid with a single blue sapphire at its top, was pinned to the jacket's lapel.

A warm feeling flooded him as he both watched and felt her hand exploring his abdomen. Lowering his voice, he said, "I thought the door was locked."

"It was," she replied, kissing his neck whilst moving her hand lower.

His hand remained upon hers until he felt her fingers toy with his waistband. Allowing her hand to rest upon it, he then held her gaze as her breath trembled in his ear and her cheeks became tinged with pink. "I see," he replied and, in a heartbeat, had gripped her wrist, pulled her hand free, and turned her around in front of him.

The sudden movement had brought a sharp gasp from her and her chest rose and fell quickly as he pinned her against the desk's edge with his body. Gripping the furniture with both hands, she thrust out her chest and enquired, "I suppose you are amused?"

"But of course, darling," he replied, reaching around her with a muscular arm to drop the flannel into the bowl. In doing so, his lips came tantalisingly close to hers. Knowing it would be improper to succumb to her desire, though, she instead licked her lips whilst maintaining close eye contact with him. He, on the other hand, had no such qualms. He therefore slipped his arm around her waist and held her against him as she instinctively parted her lips and felt the delicate caress of his tongue against her own. Feeling her knees weaken as a result, she placed her hands upon his back and relaxed against his body. Yet, the longer the kiss lasted, the lower her hands went until they rested upon his firm behind.

"You are a dangerously attractive man, Mr Locke," she said, softly, when he'd broken the kiss. Resigned to the fact their liaison would go no further, despite their blatant desire, she moved her hands to the crooks of his arms and smiled.

"A fact I cannot deny, Mrs Locke," he replied, mirroring her smile.

"Is that so?" She enquired in mock surprise as she moved back her head and shoulders.

"It is," he replied and captured her lips in another, gentler kiss.

Sliding her hands down his forearms as she savoured his taste, she began, "Let no woman say modesty is one of your virtues, darling—" She stopped as her fingers felt something unexpected. Glancing down at his arm, her lips flattened, and her eyes cooled as she demanded, "*What,* pray tell, is *this*?"

"I believe it is called a needle mark, darling."

"A *fresh* one," she retorted, pushing his arms away. "I thought we had come to an agreement over this, Percy."

Mr Locke flicked up his gaze and pulled away. Moving behind an oak folding screen with Chinese dragons, lotus flowers, and bamboo carved into it, he retrieved his shirt and said, "I do not wish to hear a lecture, Lynette."

"And *I* do not wish to have a dead husband!" She cried and followed him to the screen. Behind it was an immense trunk with a curved lid and a dark-blue chaise lounge set further back against the wall. Standing between the chaise and the screen to prevent her husband from retreating anywhere else, she demanded, "When did you poison yourself with it?"

"Excuse me," Mr Locke replied as he attempted to move past her, nonetheless.

"Answer me!" Lynette insisted, stepping-aside but then following close behind when he returned to the desk. It took up the wall's entire length and had three deep drawers at either end. Its surface was highly polished whilst its edges and drawer fronts were adorned by hand-carved stars, moons, and signs of the zodiac.

Tubes of grease paint, boxes of talc, and bottles of black hair dye lined the desk's rear edge, whilst combs, hair scissors, nail files, and nail scissors were arranged in a line to the left of the bowl. To the bowl's right were a bar of lavender-scented carbolic soap, a box of powdered talc, a round, ceramic pot of chalk dentifrice and a horsehair toothbrush. A jug, matching the bowl in decoration, stood at the back of the desk beside the mirror. When her husband ran the comb through his curls, Lynette marched up to the desk, turned her back toward the mirror to face him, and said, "You cannot rehearse with such *filth* in your body, Percy."

"Is that a challenge?" he enquired in a sardonic tone.

"It is my advice as your doctor *and* your wife."

A gentle tapping sounded from the door, and Mr Locke reached for the key.

"Will you not even *listen* to me?" Dr Locke pleaded.

Mr Locke looked back over his shoulder, and their eyes met. Yet the moment was brief for he looked away almost immediately and turned the key in the lock with a click. "Come in," he instructed and retreated behind the screen once more. Dr Locke's hard eyes followed him, though, as she pursed her lips and gripped the desk behind her. She heard James, her husband's personal valet, enter the room and caught a glimpse of him as he joined his employer behind the screen to assist him with dressing. Folding her arms across her chest, she waited a little longer before clenching her jaw, shaking her head, and heading for the door, saying, "Good day to you, *Husband*." The door slammed a moment later, signalling her departure.

"Two notes have arrived for you, sir," James said while smoothing down the back of Mr Locke's shirt and assisting him into his black waistcoat.

"I will read them presently," Mr Locke replied, grateful for the distraction.

James retrieved two envelopes from his own pocket, formed them into a fan, and offered them to his employer. The first emitted a strong scent of rose perfume, and the second had a familiar red 'B' stamped into its corner. Taking both at once, Mr Locke read the first letter whilst James tied a white-cotton cravat around the former's neck. Giving a wry smile upon reading the words written in a feminine hand, he then cleared his throat and slipped the letter into the inside pocket of the black frock coat hanging on the wall. Turning his attention to the second letter, he read the instructions contained therein and tossed the piece of paper onto the chaise lounge. "It would appear my services are required by the Bow Street Society once again. Is my carriage ready?"

"Yes, sir," James replied, taking the frock coat from the wall and holding it up.

"Excellent," Mr Locke said, slipping his arms into the garment's. Allowing his valet to lift it onto his shoulders, he added, "If my wife returns, inform her I have departed on Bow Street Society business."

"Yes, sir," James replied, smoothing down the last of the frock coat's creases and stepping back to admire his work. Mr Locke turned around on the spot and, after getting a nod of approval from his valet, checked himself in the mirror and left.

SIX

Running southwest from Berkeley Square toward Park
Lane, Hill Street gained its name from a slight rise in the
ground when it was farmland. Developed in the first half
of the eighteenth century, Hill Street joined its Mayfair
counterparts in becoming the fashionable residence of
choice for lords and admirals. Arguably Hill Street's most
notable resident was Mrs Elizabeth Montagu who, with
Elizabeth Vesey and Frances Boscawen, hosted the Blue
Stocking Circle in her home. A group of artists, writers,
and thinkers, its name derived from a decision made by
scholar Benjamin Stillingfleet to obey Vesey's call to
"come in your blue stockings," thus abandoning formal
evening wear. Although Mrs Montagu had died in August
1800, she and the Blue Stocking Circle had often been
discussed by the ladies of the *Writer's Club*, of which
Lady Owston and Miss Webster were members.

"Perhaps *I* should host such salons?" Lady Owston
mused aloud as Mr Snyder held her hand and assisted her
in alighting from his cab. "Thank you."

"You practically do already," Miss Webster
replied, accepting identical assistance from the cab man.
Once stood on the pavement, she held out her hand to
check for rain. Feeling none, she put her umbrella onto her
seat whilst Mr Snyder climbed back into his own.

"Possibly, but giving our gatherings a *name* would
give them further credibility, don't you think?" Lady
Owston enquired. Holding her ostrich-feathered headdress,
she peered up at the building and added, "Are we here?"

Constructed from red bricks on its upper levels
and immense, smooth, white stone on its lower-ground
floor, the building's stately façade was muted by years of
blackening by soot-laden air. A stone portico, crowned by
a triangular-shaped pediment, provided shelter for the

solid, dark-green front door. Above it was a plain-glass window with an iron ring. Sharp spikes pointed inwards from the ring's edge to discourage attempts to gain entry by pint-sized house breakers. A single, stone step led from the portico to the pavement. Wrought-iron, spear-headed railings ran either side of the portico. On their far right was a gated entrance to a set of steep, stone steps leading to the lower-ground floor. Sash windows with white wooden frames, wide stone sills, and fan formations in the brick-work above, lined the building's main storeys, whilst dormer windows lined the roof. Yet, despite the apparent abundance of rooms, only those either side of the portico were illuminated by the bright glow of electrical lighting.

"Yes, we are here," Miss Webster replied.

"*Good*!" Lady Owston said, clasping her hands together. "All we need now is Miss Trent's gentleman." Looking up, down, and then back up the street, she turned toward the cab and enquired, "Mr Snyder, are you able to see any vehicles approaching?"

"Nah, Milady," Mr Snyder replied with a sniff.

"Where *is* he?" Lady Owston complained.

"Perhaps if we had been told the gentleman's name…" Miss Webster remarked.

"You'll know him when you see him, miss," Mr Snyder interjected, and the heads of both ladies' jerked upward. A tentative smile formed upon Lady Owston's lips as she realised her foolishness and, the more she thought about neglecting to question Mr Snyder, the larger her smile grew. Miss Webster, meanwhile, pursed her lips at the idea that Mr Snyder could've been taken into Miss Trent's confidence instead of them. If he had, then Miss Webster saw no rhyme or reason to it. Unless he, too, was assigned to the case, of course.

The sounds of hooves and carriage wheels clip-clopping and crunching against cobblestones reached their ears, prompting the ladies to step away from the cab to gain a better view.

"'Ere 'e is," Mr Snyder announced.

The four-wheeled carriage was pulled by two chestnut-brown mares and driven by a middle-aged man wearing a black, leather cloak and top hat with cream band. Painted in black lacquer with gold leaf on its handles and the door's central panel, the carriage also had the letters 'P' and 'L' intertwined beneath its window. As it slowed to a stop behind Mr Snyder's cab, a slender, black-leather clad hand slipped out from behind a red-velvet curtain and opened the door using its external handle. This was immediately followed by a polished shoe stepping down onto the carriage's metal step as a top hat wearing gentleman emerged and alighted onto the pavement.

The moment she saw his face Lady Owston clasped her hands over her mouth to stifle a gasp. Holding out her arms as she then approached with a broad smile upon her face, she cried, "Mr *Locke*! What an *absolute* pleasure it is to make your acquaintance! Miss Webster and I are *tremendous* admirers of yours, aren't we Agnes?"

"Yes, Milady," Miss Webster replied, a smile tugging at the corners of her mouth despite her best efforts to remain stoic.

"I am pleased to hear it, ladies," Mr Locke replied. "Mr Snyder."

"Mr Locke," Mr Snyder greeted with a touch of his hat.

"Miss Trent's letter briefly outlined the ghastly goings on at Oxford Street but, without having witnessed them myself, I must place myself into your hands," Mr Locke began. "You are Lady Katheryne Owston, I presume?"

"*Oh*! How *remiss* of me!" Lady Owston cried. "*Yes*; I'm she and this is my secretary, Miss Agnes Webster." Lady Owston held her clasped hands in front of her bosom as she tilted her head and continued to smile, unable to keep her eyes off him. Miss Webster, meanwhile, bowed her head by way of formal greeting at the introduction.

"And this is the Holden residence?" Mr Locke enquired as he looked to the building.

"It is, sir," Lady Owston replied. "Miss Webster discovered it in the *Post Office Directory*. We were awaiting your arrival before we made our presence known. Are you familiar with the Holdens?"

"Only by name," Mr Locke replied and lifted his hand toward the door. "Ladies first."

Lady Owston's smile broadened in an instant, and she strode into the porch with Miss Webster following closely behind. Joining them, Mr Locke took his position in the middle and used the silver handle of his ebony cane to knock on the door.

A middle-aged butler with neatly trimmed tan sideburns, perfect posture, and green eyes flecked with brown answered the door. He wore his morning uniform of dark-grey trousers with a black tie, dress coat, and high, double-breasted waistcoat. He regarded each of them in turn and, with faultless enunciation, said, "Good morning. May I help you?"

"Indeed, you may," Mr Locke replied, offering him his calling card. "I am Mr Percival Locke, and these are my associates: Lady Katheryne Owston, an independent journalist, and her secretary, Miss Agnes Webster. We three are also members of the Bow Street Society and would like to request an audience with Mr and Mrs Holden—if it is not too inconvenient? Please pass on our apologies for the unscheduled visitation but circumstances have forced us to forego the etiquette of polite society in this instance. We have been commissioned to investigate a murder, you see."

The butler's stoic expression faltered at the news, but he nevertheless maintained his decorum long enough to respond, "I shall make enquiries."

"Thank you," Mr Locke said. "Perhaps it would be appropriate for us to await our answer inside?"

The butler pushed back his shoulders and parted his lips to refuse but hesitated when he recalled how overlooked the property was by the neighbours. He therefore stepped aside and indicating the first door on the left with his hand, said, "If you would be so kind as to wait in the library."

"Of course," Mr Locke replied and entered the hallway. Removing his top hat and gloves, he placed the latter into the former and put both into the butler's waiting hands. Lady Owston, having joined them, relinquished her hat and coat to the servant, whilst Miss Webster surrendered her coat but chose to keep her hat upon her head. Satisfied his fellow Bow Streeters were taken care of, Mr Locke led them through the indicated door.

Although it had been introduced as a library, the room's furnishings suggested it was also used as a study; a flat-top desk stood before the window and two bookcases stood against the wall to one's right upon entering. Identical in design, each bookcase was made from oak and filled with innumerable volumes of expensive, leather-bound books. A gigantic, iron hearth, housed within an oak surround, occupied the wall opposite the door. Beside it was an oak fireguard with a thick, hand-stitched tapestry in its centre. Lady Owston crossed the room at once upon entering and moved the fireguard in front of the fireplace. Going to Miss Webster at the bookcases afterwards, she placed a hand upon her arm and said in a whisper, "The fire guard's in place, dear."

"Thank you," Miss Webster replied. "I'll be fine now."

Lady Owston gave her arm a gentle squeeze and returned to the fireplace to warm her hands.

Meanwhile, Mr Locke had approached the desk the moment the butler had closed the door. Made of oak, the desk was approximately two feet wide by five feet long. Its top had also been polished to such a high shine the window was reflected in it. Stepping back from it, Mr Locke then bent forward to gain a closer look at it. The superior carpentry skills which had gone into its construction could be seen in its joins but Mr Locke's interest laid in its drawers. Running a finger over one of their locks, he thought, *automatically locking drawers: weak enough to pick within seconds rather than minutes.* Concluding his idle curiosity was insufficient reason to break into their host's property, though, he instead straightened and pushed aside the window's lace curtain. Seeing a rather mundane view of Mr Snyder's cab, his own carriage, and the houses opposite, he let the curtain fall back into place.

"We should have sent word ahead of ourselves," Lady Owston remarked. "Wouldn't you agree, Mr Locke? After all, they only have our word we are who we claim to be."

Miss Webster glanced at her employer whilst keeping to the outskirts of the room. She was impressed by the amount of light being emitted from the electrical lamps and wondered if Lady Owston would consider having something similar installed at their home.

"Provided we do not give them reason to doubt our honour, Lady Owston, I suspect we shall be well-received," Mr Locke replied.

Lady Owston and Miss Webster exchanged unconvinced looks.

A few minutes passed before the butler returned. When he did, he stepped into the room and announced, "Mrs Holden shall see you now."

"And Mr Holden?" Mr Locke enquired.

"Away from home, sir," The butler replied. Waiting a few seconds to allow the news to sink in, he then continued, "However… I have Mrs Holden's authority to inform you he is to be found at *The Royal Coachman Public House* located on the far end of Hill Street. Now, if you would like to follow me, the mistress is awaiting your introductions in the lounge."

"She shall have to be introduced to Lady Owston and Miss Webster alone," Mr Locke replied and, slipping past the butler, retrieved his hat and gloves from the hall table. "Ladies, we shall reconvene at Bow Street in…" He checked his pocket watch. "An hour. Good day to you all." Without waiting for an answer, he strode back down the hallway and left.

Having turned upon his heel when Mr Locke had gone past him, the butler now stared at the front door in disbelief.

"To the lounge…?" Lady Owston encouraged.

The butler looked at her and, realising he'd been addressed, pushed back his shoulders, and pressed his heels together. "Yes," he replied. "My apologies, ma'am. This way."

"Thank you," Lady Owston said. With Miss Webster by her side, she followed him across the hallway to another door that he opened and placed his back against.

"Lady Katheryne Owston and Miss Agnes Webster of the Bow Street Society, ma'am," he announced.

Entering the room first, Lady Owston greeted the woman therein with a warm smile and said, "Thank you for agreeing to speak with us."

"Only my curiosity permits your presence here," Mrs Ruth Holden replied. Although she couldn't have been a day younger than sixty, her voice was strong and assertive. Her skin, once firm and fair, hung from her chin and neck to rest in loose, paper-thin grey folds upon the neckline of her dress. Made from plain, dark-grey material, her dress covered her form and bagged around her arms and hips. A white blouse peeked out from beneath it at her neckline and cuffs. Her long, wiry, grey hair was scraped back and largely concealed by a white, cotton bonnet whose ribbon was tied into a large, white bow beneath her chin. As Lady Owston and Miss Webster came further into the room, her faded-blue eyes followed them as if they were mice invading her territory. Nonetheless, she said, "That will be all, Wolston."

"Yes, ma'am." The butler gave a slight bow and departed.

"I was told there would be three of you," Mrs Holden remarked. "Mr Locke has departed in search of my husband, I presume?"

"He has," Lady Owston replied. Having only met the gentleman a few minutes ago, she thought it inappropriate to offer apologies on his behalf. She therefore refrained from doing so, choosing to glance at the vacant chairs instead.

"He shan't have far to look," Mrs Holden commented.

"I believe he was travelling to *The Royal Coachman Public House*…?" Lady Owston enquired from Miss Webster.

Mrs Holden tightened her features and, in a cool tone, replied, "My husband's favourite pastime; he has not permitted a drop of liquor to pass his lips these twenty years, but he enjoys the 'atmosphere' of the place." She turned her head away and, with a sweeping motion of her hand, added, "Please, sit down."

There were two low-backed, leather sofas stood facing one another on either side of a fireplace identical to the one in the library. Relieved to see a fireguard already in place, Miss Webster distanced herself from the fire's cracking, snapping, and popping by sitting on the sofa's far end. Lady Owston then sat beside her, with Mrs Holden occupying the sofa opposite. Confident the task of recording the conversation would also distract her from her fears, Miss Webster took out her notebook and pencil and began writing some shorthand notes.

"What is she doing?" Mrs Holden enquired.

"If you consent, we would like to record our conversation so we may refer back to it if necessary," Lady Owston explained.

"Whatever for?" Mrs Holden demanded.

"Scotland Yard, specifically an Inspector Woolfe, is investigating the matter about which we have come to speak with you today," Lady Owston answered. "And you know how *intrusive* the police can be, not to mention *incompetent* and *corrupt.* They will come here—"

"Let them come!" Mrs Holden interrupted. "They shall speak to the door."

"Consider the scandal the mere presence of a policeman could cause, though, should your neighbours catch sight of him," Lady Owston pointed out, and Mrs Holden's features tightened once more. "It is a scandal our client wishes to avoid also, which is why she has commissioned the Bow Street Society to investigate," Lady Owston continued. "To achieve this, though, we need a record of the conversations we have with *all* witnesses—so we may read, and reread, what was said in case an important clue has been missed. A clue you yourself could be in possession of but not realise it. I think it unlikely though since you strike me as a highly intelligent and shrewd woman."

The tension in Mrs Holden's features eased as, in a warmer tone, she thanked her and said, "I must confess I have heard your name spoken among my acquaintances; they speak highly of you and now I see why." She lifted her chin and, addressing Miss Webster, said, "Very well, young lady, you may take your record."

"I can assure you it shan't be passed on to anyone beyond the Bow Street Society without your explicit consent, Mrs Holden," Lady Owston reassured.

"Which I shall never give," Mrs Holden retorted. Resting her hands within her lap, she kept her tone formal as she enquired, "What is the matter you wish to speak to me about? Wolston spoke to me of a murder."

"Yes; Mrs Maryanna Roberts," Lady Owston replied, watching Mrs Holden's face. It betrayed no hint of recognition, however. In fact, it betrayed no emotion at all. "You met her, I believe, at the *Queshire Department Store* yesterday…?" Lady Owston probed further.

Again, Mrs Holden's stoicism remained firmly in place.

"There was an incident," Lady Owston continued, "between Mrs Roberts and your husband—?"

"Oh *her*!" Mrs Holden interrupted with a swift twisting of her features. "An *awful, awful* creature! Straight from the slum and the gin house, there can be no doubt about it! Absolutely no idea how to behave, though one should not expect manners from those of *that* class; the *criminal* class is what they call them, do they not?"

"I have heard the terminology used before, yes," Lady Owston replied with reluctance. "Mrs Roberts was, unfortunately, found murdered this morning—"

"Nothing unfortunate about it!" Mrs Holden interrupted with venom. "The *creature* propositioned my husband, in *public*, and became violent and abusive when Mr Queshire escorted her from the premises." Placing her hand upon her bosom, she looked up and said, "We are told we must be Godly and sympathetic toward the plight of the poor," dropping her hand, she met Lady Owston's gaze with hard eyes and added, "but I couldn't be either when she did *that*."

Lady Owston's back stiffened as she pursed her lips to prevent her desired retort from escaping her lips. Recalling past failed attempts to convince women of Mrs Holden's kind that the poor were often obliged to resort to immoral or criminal measures to survive, Lady Owston decided it would be just as futile to pose the argument now. She therefore diverted her line of questioning elsewhere as she said, "There is some belief Mrs Roberts was murdered last night. Her body being found on Oxford Street this morning. Naturally, you were not on Oxford Street last night, were you?"

"I was not," Mrs Holden replied. "Mr Holden and I were at the *Theatre Royal*, Drury Lane until nine thirty. We arrived home at ten o'clock. Mr Holden wished to read in the library, so I retired to bed without him."

"Could you recall what time he eventually retired to bed?" Lady Owston enquired.

"No; Mr Holden knows not to disturb me when I am sleeping," Mrs Holden stated matter-of-factly.

"And this morning, did either of you have need to visit Oxford Street?" Lady Owston enquired. "To collect an order from the *Queshire Department Store*, perhaps?"

"We both rose at seven thirty," Mrs Holden replied. "My maid dressed me, and my husband's valet dressed him. We breakfasted together in the morning room before he retired to the library and I sat at the bureau in here to write some letters. It was only a half hour ago he departed for his favourite pastime."

"Thank you," Lady Owston said with a contrived smile.

Mrs Holden's features tightened as she asserted, "Neither Mr Holden nor I would have ended the wretched creature's existence." She lowered her chin to peer down upon the Bow Streeters and continued, "Aside from it being utterly against *God's* Commandments, neither of us would waste our time or strength on such a foul human being."

"I believe you," Lady Owston replied with conviction. In her opinion, Mrs Holden was herself a "wretched creature" but, ironically, it was this very wretchedness which had convinced her of Mrs Holden's innocence. The question of Mr Holden's guilt would have to be settled once she'd heard Mr Locke's account back at Bow Street, however. Rising to her feet, she said, "There are no further questions we'd like to ask. Come, Agnes. We'll see ourselves out, Mrs Holden."

* * *

Miss Trent left behind the ice-cold air of the *Royal Botanic Gardens* to enter the warmth of the *Water Lily House*. One of the most attractive greenhouses at Kew, the *Water Lily House* stood adjacent to the instantly recognisable *Palm House*. Whilst the latter boasted an impressive 362-foot length, hundred-foot breadth, and sixty-six-foot height, the former was a much shorter, domed structure. Found within the *Palm House* was a veritable tropical forest of full-sized tree ferns, date palms, betel nuts, coconut trees, upas trees, bamboo, cotton plants, coffee shrubs, tamarinds, and even the clove. By contrast, the *Water Lily* House, with its tank of rare water lily varieties, the Sacred Bean of Egypt, the Telegraph Plant of India, and the Sensitive Plant, was a hidden oasis of serenity to both horticulturalists and ignoramuses alike. The tank, located in the centre of the *Water Lily House*, was thirty-six feet in diameter. Chest-high iron railings lined its circumference to prevent anyone from reaching into its waters, and a fine papyrus plant grew from its middle.

Having glimpsed the hordes of visitors inside the *Palm House*, Miss Trent was pleased to find the *Water Lily House* deserted. A further advantage was the abundance of foliage confined to a smaller space. Not only did it block the view of passers-by, but the mammoth leaves also served to obstruct one's view of the path encircling the tank. Releasing a soft hum of approval, therefore, she pushed aside a vine dangling from the white, wrought-iron beam above her and approached the tank. She rested her hands on its railing and, inhaling the earthly scented, damp air, admired the lilies with a gentle exhale. Keeping her attention upon the water, she strolled along the path until she heard the door open.

At which point she opened the penny guidebook she'd purchased upon entering the Gardens and listened. Footsteps came toward her but ceased soon after. Unable to see their owner's face without lifting her own, Miss Trent turned the page of her guidebook and waited for them to come closer. Alas, the next sound she heard was the footsteps walking back toward the door. *Bother*, she thought and stole a glance at her fellow visitor. Seeing a woman leaving the green house, Miss Trent lowered her guidebook with a frown. A moment later, though, a man emerged from the foliage holding the door, and closed it. Recognising him at once, Miss Trent ran her hand along the railing and continued her stroll with a subtle smile.

The newcomer wore a brown-tweed suit, white shirt, and dark-brown tie beneath a shin-length, black overcoat. A hand-knitted, burgundy scarf was wrapped around his neck whilst matching, fingerless gloves covered his hands. Short, dark-brown hair was concealed by a brown bowler hat except for neat sideburns framing his slender face. The remainder of his most noteworthy features were hazel-brown eyes which exuded warmth despite being partially obscured by his hat's brim, a combed moustache that dominated his upper lip, and a set of clearly defined, high cheekbones. Miss Trent knew he was thirty-three years old; an uncommon age for someone of his high rank.

"A nice-looking fern," Chief Inspector Richard Jones remarked as he came up alongside her.

"I believe it's a papyrus," Miss Trent replied, turning toward the tank.

"Ah. So it is." He cleared his throat while Miss Trent bowed her head.

"There is much more to see than this," Miss Trent remarked as she offered the guide to him. "I think you'll find it an interesting read."

Taking the book, he opened it a fraction to see the typed report concealed within before slipping it into his overcoat's interior pocket. "Indeed," he replied. Looking out across the pond, he then enquired in a softer voice, "Who have you chosen for this case?"

"Lady Katheryne Owston, an independent journalist with the *Women's Signal* and *Truth* publications, her secretary, Miss Agnes Webster, and artist, Miss Georgina Dexter," Miss Trent replied in a tone matching his.

"Not Mr Maxwell?"

Miss Trent continued her stroll around the tank and, when she heard his footsteps a short distance behind her, replied, "His clumsiness and ineptness make him a liability."

"And it has nothing to do with the fact he and Miss Dexter are in the midst of a disagreement?"

Miss Trent turned upon her heel to find him smirking. "Personal feelings have no place in an investigation," she replied with as much formality as her amusement at his behaviour would allow. "You taught me that."

"I did?" He enquired with a raised brow. Recalling the incident she referred to, whilst she walked on ahead, he then followed at a respectable distance and enquired in the same low voice as before, "What did they find when they went to Oxford Street?"

"Mrs Maryanna Roberts' mutilated body and the usual circus of gawkers being held back by police," Miss Trent replied with a glance over her shoulder. "Mr Clement Suggitt, Maryanna's brother-in-law, was already there when Mr Snyder drove Mrs Diana Suggitt to Oxford Street." Pausing to admire the Sacred Bean of Egypt, she continued, "Mrs Suggitt told Lady Owston, Miss Webster, and Miss Dexter that Maryanna had been seen alive by Mr Suggitt at the *Queshire Department Store.* After speaking with Mrs Suggitt, Lady Owston and Miss Webster interviewed Mr Edmund Queshire, the owner of the store, about an incident which had taken place between Maryanna and one of the store's wealthier customers, the Holdens. Lady Owston, Miss Webster, and Mr Locke are questioning the Holdens as we speak, while Miss Dexter is developing her photographs of the scene to bring to tonight's meeting. Finally, it's been arranged for Mr Suggitt to describe Maryanna's missing clothing to Miss Dexter so she may draw them."

The door opened behind them and a young man carrying a large sketchbook entered. His glasses steamed within seconds, obliging him to rest the sketchbook upon a large, ceramic pot and fumble around in his pockets for a handkerchief. Chief Inspector Jones, meanwhile, walked ahead of Miss Trent, retrieved the guidebook from his pocket, and pretended to look up a plant. In his natural tone of voice, he said, "Almost at the week's end. Soon we shall be meeting another week, shan't we?"

"We shall, sir," Miss Trent replied as Dr Weeks' face appeared in her mind's eye.

"At such close quarters, the Weeks don't know the impact they have on our lives, do they?" Chief Inspector Jones enquired.

"They don't, sir," Miss Trent replied. "But nonetheless we must appreciate what the Weeks bring us."

"And be cautious of their gifts at the same time,"

Chief Inspector Jones warned, glancing at the bespectacled young man now sketching the papyrus. When he looked back to Miss Trent though, he saw her retracing her steps to the door. He therefore took his pipe box from his pocket to give her more time to widen the distance between them before following. By the time he caught up to her, she was standing on the steps outside.

"Dr Weeks still needs to be careful, as do you and the other Bow Streeters," he warned, lighting his pipe. Seeing a couple approaching, he mimicked Miss Trent in stepping aside to allow them to enter the *Water Lily House*. "It's cold outside, isn't it, miss?"

"It is, sir," Miss Trent replied, "but I am well versed in guarding against turbulent weather."

Chief Inspector Jones moved in closer and, tilting his head forward with his eyes locked upon hers, warned in a low voice, "Inspector Caleb Woolfe is a determined police officer and a cynical man. He doesn't let anything lie, no matter what the consequence."

"We will be cautious," Miss Trent whispered.

"Yes, *we* will," Chief Inspector Jones replied and, maintaining the intense eye contact for a moment longer, then lifted his head and stepped back. "We must." He tapped his breast pocket. "Thank you for the guide, miss. I shall enjoy reading it."

"You're most welcome, sir." Miss Trent took a moment to gather her thoughts and added, "I'm sure we'll be fine provided we *all* guard against the turbulent weather."

The briefest of smiles swept across Chief Inspector Jones's lips before he descended the steps and strolled deeper into the gardens. Deciding it was better not to linger, Miss Trent made her way back to the gardens' main entrance whilst repeatedly turning over the warning in her mind. *Why can't every case be investigated by Inspector Conway?* She mused despite knowing the answer. Folding her arms across her chest, she felt the muscles in her jaw tighten against both the cold and the prospect of an unfamiliar inspector asking awkward questions. When she considered where such questions could lead, her chest and stomach simultaneously tightened. She therefore pushed the thoughts from her mind and tried to concentrate on the agenda of that night's meeting instead.

SEVEN

With a history dating back almost two hundred years, *The Royal Coachman Public House* had once served as a coaching inn where weary travellers could lay their heads and fill their stomachs. By 1896, its days of renting rooms were over, and its main function was to quench its patrons' thirst. Located on the corner where Hill Street met Hays Mews, it was constructed from brown brick with tall windows on its ground floor and smaller on its first. The cellar was accessed via a hatch at the building's rear while its main door led into the small bar room. Its interior had white-washed plaster on its walls, exposed, oak support beams on its ceiling, and a sprinkling of fresh sawdust across its wooden floor to absorb dirt and spills. The oak bar and round, squat tables which littered the room were polished, clean, and unmarked.

Mr Bartholomew Holden lowered his pipe and rested his withered hand upon his knee as white smoke poured from his pale lips. His pale-green eyes, nestled beneath a stern brow, surveyed the calm activity happening around him. He'd always enjoyed watching others going about their daily business; it was why he'd taken to sitting in *this* chair, in *this* corner. A lead-latticed window on his right overlooked Hays Mews, whilst a large hearth was positioned diagonally from him on the other side of the small room. The latter combated any chill the sixty-three-year old man may have felt from the former. From this, his little patch of England, he could observe the subtle shifts in his habitual environment without feeling obliged to be a part of them. That particularly irritating responsibility was the foundation of his dreary working life. Repetitive questions, repetitive meetings, and repetitive correspondences all demanded his undivided attention on an hourly basis—despite his tireless input never having any tangible impact on the workings of the wider business. Nevertheless, it kept him in bread and water. He smiled as he remembered there was 'none of that here.' The additional recollection that today was his day off then broadened his smile further.

He had spent the entirety of his adult years working in the City of London's financial district. Luxuriant, russet locks, which had once covered his head, were now limp, white/grey strands hanging from a receding hairline. Many of his peers had retained full beards and moustaches, but he had done away with both on the grounds they added too many years to one's appearance. Instead, he'd kept his thinning sideburns to frame the jawline that bore a closer resemblance to a lacklustre oil-painting than a chiselled sculpture. The remainder of his face hadn't fared any better; cheeks which drooped past his chin and swollen bags under his eyes were just two of his least favourable features. The third being his nose as, with its broad bridge and pointed snout, it seemed to exaggerate the harsh line of his brow. This physical peculiarity was in stark contrast to his personality as he wasn't an angry man by any stretch of the imagination. Even his clothes, consisting of a black waistcoat and cravat, and dark-grey frock coat and trousers, hung upon his frame without formality. From the outside, he was a man who seemed comfortable in his own skin.

He hooked his pipe onto his bottom lip and took several puffs from it. Around the corner from where he sat, the front door opened and a stranger crossed Mr Holden's line of sight a short time later. It was rare for him not to recognise a patron but, when it happened, he always found it unnerving. Familiarity was security and peaceful familiarity was bliss. The young gentleman who'd approached the bar and spoken to the landlord had shattered it all. *Was my name uttered?* He thought with a frown, thereby causing his cheeks to droop further. Leaning forward, the only words he caught were muffled.

Damn my ears! He inwardly cursed, poking one with his finger. In doing so though, he was too distracted to notice the landlord pointing at him or the young gentleman approaching his table.

"Mr Bartholomew Holden?" The young gentleman's voice enquired from above.

Mr Holden lifted his head sharply and jolted when he saw who it was. Gritting his teeth against his pipe, he scowled at the newcomer and considered ignoring his blatant rudeness under the pretence of not hearing him. The realisation that a stranger had sought him out, though, soon overpowered his initial irritation, and he found himself replying, "I am he; to whom am *I* speaking?"

"Mr Percival Locke. I am a magician who—"

"*Not* interested, young man," Mr Holden interrupted with bitter disappointment. "Take your parlour tricks elsewhere."

"Pardon me, but you misunderstand, sir. I *am* a magician, but I am here in my capacity as a member of the Bow Street Society. Perhaps you have heard of them?"

Mr Holden reflected on the name. Somewhere, from the depths of his mind, he pulled forth a memory of a newspaper article. Knitting his brow as he looked sideways at Mr Locke, he then enquired, "Dorsey Trial?"

"Yes. I was one of the Society members who investigated the case. May I join you?"

Mr Holden appraised the gentleman before him; blonde curls which would've looked adorable on a child but which were utterly amiss on a grown man, and an air of arrogance born from youth. *A dandy,* Mr Holden concluded with distaste. Nevertheless, he was curious. This man, a stranger, wished to converse with him—why? He glanced out of the window but dismissed the unpalatable notion of returning home. Deciding he wanted to hear the reason for the visit, whilst also knowing he wasn't obliged to tell the gentleman anything in return, he said, "If you so wish."

"Thank you," Mr Locke replied. Removing his top hat and gloves, he put the latter into the former and placed it onto the vacant chair beside him as he sat. "Your wife informed me of your whereabouts," he went on. "My associates—Lady Katheryne Owston and her secretary, Miss Agnes Webster—are currently visiting upon her. I therefore wish to beg both of your pardons for the unscheduled, and uninvited, intrusions upon your time and home."

"It is given," Mr Holden replied with a curt nod. The smile of appreciation Mr Locke offered him in return was received with contempt, however. *Charmers, the lot of them,* Mr Holden thought. *Insincere charmers. It's a good thing he's speaking to me and not my wife. Though, on second thoughts, attempting to charm a statue in Trafalgar Square would yield better results.* He took another puff from his pipe as Mr Locke's voice cut through his ponderings.

"As you are no doubt already aware, the Bow Street Society is a group of lawfully minded individuals who work to solve cases on behalf of their clients. Its current client is Mrs Diana Suggitt, sister of Mrs Maryanna Roberts—a lady who, we have been led to believe, made your acquaintance under less-than-respectable circumstances at the *Queshire Department Store* yesterday."

"If I did, it's no business of yours," Mr Holden snapped.

"Even if I were to tell you Mrs Maryanna Roberts was murdered last night?"

"*Are* you telling me?" Mr Holden enquired in an accusatory tone as he leant toward him.

"I am," Mr Locke replied.

Mr Holden broke eye contact at once and stiffened in his chair. Tapping the side of his pipe's bowl as his complexion paled and his face became drawn, he enquired in a soft voice, "When did it occur?"

"Last night," Mr Locke replied.

Mr Holden stood and shuffled across to the hearth where he deposited the remnants of his spent tobacco. Although Mr Locke wasn't sitting beside the hearth, the room's small dimensions meant he could still see Mr Holden running his finger around the inside of his pipe's bowl and flicking out the stubborn fibres. Seemingly unable to achieve his goal, Mr Holden threw the pipe against the cast-iron grate with a loud clang and placed his hand upon the brickwork above. With a bowed head and slouched shoulders, he muttered, "Dear God... What is the world coming to?" He closed his hand and dug his nails into the brick. "Poor woman..." Lowering his hand to wipe it over his mouth, he took a deep breath and gently shook his head. "Dear God," he repeated. He glanced over his shoulder at Mr Locke and, retrieving his pipe, returned to the table. His face appeared haggard and red from the hearth's heat. Mr Locke therefore remained silent whilst Mr Holden put down his pipe and wiped the sweat from his brow with a handkerchief. When he was once again settled, Mr Holden said, "Mrs Suggitt has my condolences."

"I am certain she shall appreciate them," Mr Locke replied. "Would you like a brandy, sir?"

"No," Mr Holden said with curt shake of his head. "You mentioned the Bow Street Society; the group is looking into this matter on behalf of Mrs Diana Suggitt, then?"

"We are."

"What is it you wish to know?" Mr Holden enquired as he prepared his pipe with fresh tobacco and lit it with a match.

"About the incident at the department store yesterday, and after," Mr Locke replied.

Mr Holden's gaze was on the table as he took a couple of puffs from his pipe and replied, "An unfortunate one, but resolved nonetheless."

"Resolved how?"

"My wife and I left the store. There's no need to rake it up again."

"Mrs Roberts has been murdered; you do not think the incident in the department store could bear some relevance?"

"Absolutely not," Mr Holden snapped with a scowl.

"Even if someone, who had witnessed the altercation, had possibly taken it upon themselves to confront her about her behaviour?" Mr Locke ventured in a lower tone.

"I do not see *who*," Mr Holden retorted for all he'd glanced away as he'd said it. "As I told you, the matter was resolved."

"And you did not see Mrs Roberts again?"

"Absolutely not," Mr Holden repeated. Knitting his brow, he leaned forward and enquired, "Should I have done?"

"I do not know; should you?" Mr Locke countered.

Mr Holden's eyes widened as he straightened in his chair. Staring at Mr Locke for a moment, he then hooked his pipe back onto his lower lip and looked out of the window. Allowing several white clouds of smoke to escape his lips as he puffed upon the pipe with glazed eyes, he remained like that for several moments more. Eventually, after much contemplation, he rested the pipe-holding hand upon his knee, turned toward Mr Locke, and enquired in a soft voice, "May I rely upon your discretion?"

"You may," Mr Locke replied, keeping his voice quiet, also.

"Thank you," Mr Holden said with a glance to the landlord and other patrons. They were all engrossed in their own mundane lives, however. "Would you agree a gentleman has certain needs, Mr Locke?"

"I would."

"Needs a wife cannot satisfy for the sake of propriety."

Mr Locke leaned forward, prompting Mr Holden to do the same.

"I know to what you refer," Mr Locke began in a softer tone. "May I assume Mrs Roberts… dealt with these needs?"

"You may," Mr Holden whispered. "Naturally, she was paid for services rendered."

"Naturally," Mr Locke repeated.

Mr Holden scowled as he challenged, "Do you mock me, sir?"

"I do not. I myself do not limit myself to my wife alone." Mr Locke smiled. "Though for reasons perhaps different to your own."

"Indeed," Mr Holden agreed. Although he was certain they were in no way alike—despite what the *dandy* said—he conceded Mr Locke was at least able to appreciate the matter's sensitivity. An ally was still an ally, after all. "Our marriage was one of convenience," he continued. "When our son was born, we at least had his welfare in common but, now he has a family of his own…" Mr Holden trailed off as he realised he'd revealed more than was proper. Clearing his throat, he muttered, "The least said of that the better." Taking another puff from his pipe to underline the sentiment, he then went on, "Maryanna was one of my regulars. Yesterday wasn't the first time I had met her, but it was the first time she'd met my wife." He sighed deeply. "Ruth of course knows I am not always here when I go out on an evening, but it isn't for her to say where I take my pleasure, is it?"

"Indeed, it is not," Mr Locke agreed and not entirely without sincerity. "It is a gentleman's prerogative to do as he wishes."

"*Precisely.*"

"You left Oxford Street, returned home, and departed company from your wife to seek out Mrs Roberts, then?" Mr Locke enquired as he attempted to form a clear picture of Mr Holden's movements in his mind.

Mr Holden shook his head and replied, "My wife and I visited the theatre after dinner and returned home at around ten o'clock. Once she had retired to bed, I slipped from the house and sought out Maryanna—not to harm her, you understand, but to remind her of her place." He took another puff from his pipe. "Naturally, I took advantage of the service she offered following our discussion. Afterward, I gave her only half of what I do usually, partly because she was inebriated at the time and partly because I wanted her to understand she couldn't approach me in such a manner in public again. I warned her she would get no more coin from me in future if she did."

"At what time did you locate Mrs Roberts?"

"It was around ten forty-five, I believe."

"And when did you part company?"

"Only a short time later," Mr Holden replied. Lowering his voice further, he added, "Services were rendered orally, you understand."

"Yes…" Mr Locke replied, attempting to push the unwanted image from his mind. Recalling a point mentioned in Miss Trent's note to him, then, he enquired, "Can you recall what Mrs Roberts was wearing?"

"A dress—hanging a long way past her knees, some heavy boots, and a scarf; all dirty and tattered."

"When you parted ways, did she tell you where she was going?"

"No. We merely bid good night. I returned home and retired to bed."

"May your wife corroborate your account?" Mr Locke enquired despite being uncertain of its importance. After all, as a married woman, Mrs Holden was forbidden from giving evidence against her husband in open court. On consideration, though, Mr Locke concluded it would at least allow the Bow Street Society to verify Mr Holden's story.

"I very much doubt it," Mr Holden replied. "It was quarter to midnight by the time I crept under the blankets, and she was asleep. I am always careful not to wake her."

"Then you could have murdered Mrs Roberts," Mr Locke stated.

Mr Holden's complexion paled as his jaw and pipe lowered in unison. "I couldn't…" He said in a soft voice. Leaning closer to Mr Locke, he insisted, "I *couldn't*. Despite what I am, and what I did with Mrs Roberts, I'm not a heartless or unfeeling man. Murder isn't a vice I indulge in."

Mr Locke scrutinised Mr Holden's eyes and face. Whilst maintaining a stoic expression, he picked up his top hat and stood.

"I'm aware you only have my word to support my claim of innocence," Mr Holden continued. "But I shall tell you again, Mr Locke. I couldn't have murdered Maryanna Roberts. Fumbled pleasures in darkened streets? Yes. Deceiving my wife for the sake of propriety? Indeed. But *never* murder."

Mr Locke put on his gloves and hat as he resumed his scrutiny. Forming his conclusions, he said, "I am inclined to believe you, Mr Holden."

Mr Holden sat back in his chair, and the tension vanished from his form in an instant.

Taking a calling card from his pocket, Mr Locke placed it on the table in front of him and said, "Should you recall anything further. Good day to you, Mr Holden."

"Yes, of course…" Mr Holden slid the card toward him with a stubby finger. "Thank you, Mr Locke—and good day."

* * *

"A darker shade of green, I believe… Although, perhaps, it was lighter but made darker by the dirt?" Mr Clement Suggitt mused aloud as he studied the drawing in Miss Dexter's sketchbook. Propped up on the easel usually reserved for her oil paintings, the sketchbook was positioned between them. They were sitting on chairs borrowed from the kitchen in the otherwise barren parlour of the Bow Street Society's house. Although the chairs were angled toward the easel, sufficient space had been left between them to ensure a respectable distance was kept between Mr Suggitt and Miss Dexter.

"I can sketch it again for you, but with a dirty dress so you may compare the colouring?" Miss Dexter suggested, the echo of her voice making it sound louder than it was. With gentle encouragement when Mr Suggitt had expressed frustration, and patient silence when he'd procrastinated, she'd spent almost an hour drawing Maryanna's lost clothing.

"No… I don't think it will be necessary," Mr Suggitt replied. Leaning back in his chair, he clasped his knees and admitted, "Without seeing the items in the flesh, so to speak, I think your depiction is as close as we shall get to what I remember."

Miss Dexter picked up the sketchbook and, offering it to him, enquired, "Would you like to take a closer look?"

Taking the sketchbook, he ran his gaze over the

106

drawing to absorb its detail. At its top was a worn, dirty straw hat adorned with even dirtier, white-cotton posies. The front of its brim had become pointed from innumerate tugging down of its sides to shield the owner's ears. A ragged, forest-green woollen scarf then lay over the top of a dark-brown, tweed jacket. The sleeves ended midway down the forearms whilst the stitching on its left shoulder had been ripped open to reveal the dirty, yellow, cotton lining beneath. The jacket's singular button was fastened in the middle. Beneath the jacket was a forest-green dress that hung loosely around the shins like an apron. Its skirt had also been ripped and tied in many places. A dark-green, almost black, crocheted shawl with yellow flowers lay over the jacket with its ends tucked into the crooks of the arms. Finally, at the bottom of the drawing, was a pair of black-leather ankle boots which were scuffed, faded, and caked in mud.

Miss Dexter felt a weight in the pit of her stomach as she, too, looked at the last thing Maryanna had worn. At what was the *only* thing she'd ever worn, at least according to Mr Suggitt. The thought that she and the Bow Street Society would expose Maryanna's murderer eased the weight in her stomach. It was soon replaced by a feeling of confusion, though, as a question dropped into her mind. She said, "Begging your pardon, sir, but do you know why anyone would want to steal Mrs Roberts' clothes?"

"I'm afraid I don't," Mr Suggitt replied and passed the sketchbook back. "They certainly weren't valuable—at least not in a monetary sense."

"The shawl was a gift from your wife," Miss Dexter recalled in an unobtrusive voice.

"Yes, she crocheted it herself last spring," Mr Suggitt replied with a fleeting smile. "I'd offered to pay for one to be made, and to even purchase something similar from the store, but Diana wouldn't hear of it. She told me she wanted to be sure her sister would be warm enough during the coming winter. She used the thickest wool she could find. It wasn't as expertly finished as it might have been, had a seamstress created it, which was probably for the best in hindsight."

"It sounds beautiful," Miss Dexter said, looking down at the sketchbook in her lap.

"Charming, yes, but not beautiful," Mr Suggitt replied as he stared at the vacant easel. "If it had been, it would've been sold to procure monies for gin."

Miss Dexter felt the weight return but in her chest this time. Running her fingers along the shawl in her drawing, she tried to imagine how desperate for gin one must have to be to part with such a precious item. Abandoning her attempt when she realised her imagination could never come close to the realities of such a situation, she instead enquired, "Do you recall what colour Mrs Roberts' hair was?"

"Yes… a mousey brown, I believe. Long, possibly to her shoulders," Mr Suggitt replied. Checking the time on his pocket watch, he then announced as casually as if he were about to catch a train, "The doctor gave my wife a sedative this afternoon and I want to be there when she wakes."

"I understand," Miss Dexter replied, putting the sketchbook back onto the easel as they stood. "I will inform you at once if the clothes are found, sir."

"Thank you," Mr Suggitt replied and deposited his pocket watch back into his waistcoat. "My wife and I greatly appreciate all you and the Bow Street Society have done for us, and Mrs Roberts, in this matter. However," he straightened his coat and met her gaze, "after some consideration, I feel it best we all take a step back and allow the police to do their work without being hindered by our meddling."

"But—"

"You've done nothing of the kind—far from it,"

Mr Suggitt interrupted. "The truth is my wife shouldn't have hired your group in the first place. I had told her over the telephone I had everything in hand; there was no need for her to come here—" He cut himself short as he realised he was babbling. Taking a moment to gather his thoughts, therefore, he smoothed down his coat and continued, "She was upset and shocked, as we all are, and she wasn't in her right mind. Please, by all means, attempt to locate my sister-in-law's missing clothes—if only to put my wife's mind at ease on the point. As for the murder though, I think it would be better all-round if we forget about trying to solve it ourselves." He crossed the room but stopped when he'd reached the door. Turning toward her, he added, "If you could pass the news of our decision on to Miss Trent and your associates, I'd be most grateful. Good day, Miss Dexter, and thank you."

"Good day, Mr Suggitt," Miss Dexter replied and watched him leave. Waiting until she heard the click of the front door, she then hurried across the hallway to Miss Trent's office.

EIGHT

"Thank you, dear," Lady Owston said with a gentle touch of Miss Webster's wrist. The steaming cup of tea she'd poured for her was most welcome after their cab ride in the wind and rain.

"You're welcome," Miss Webster muttered with a meagre twitch of her mouth in place of a smile.

Although others may have considered such a reaction rude, Lady Owston accepted it as the small quirk it was. Having raised Miss Webster since the tragic loss of her parents all those years ago, Lady Owston was habituated to her ways and felt grateful for every piece of affection she showed her—regardless of the form it took. She therefore left Miss Webster's reaction unchallenged to allow her to pour her own tea.

Yet, as she did so, Miss Webster noticed another cup beside hers. She glanced around the table but saw Miss Trent, Mr Snyder, and Miss Dexter all had full cups. Having had a desire to please Lady Owston by serving her tea, she'd allowed Miss Dexter to serve the others. She'd not seen who'd placed the additional cup, however. Holding the teapot above the table as she scanned the vacant chairs for clues as to the identity of the cup's owner, she then winced as Mr Locke's voice suddenly sounded from behind her.

"If you would be so kind, Miss Webster?" He requested.

Miss Webster turned to face him with hard eyes. In a cool tone, she replied, "I would; if you would be so kind as to apologise. You shouldn't creep up on a woman."

"My sincerest apologies," Mr Locke replied with a brief dip of his head. "I shan't loiter around your person again."

Miss Webster lifted her chin and replied, "Apology accepted." Pouring some tea into his cup and placing it before a vacant chair, she then added sugar and cream to her own.

"Will you not ask me how I was able to enter undetected when the door was so clearly locked?" Mr Locke enquired.

Miss Webster's gaze remained upon her cup as she took a sip from it and replied, "No."

"Most of us are aware of your talents," Miss Trent remarked.

"*Indeed*," Lady Owston agreed, glancing at Miss Webster as she sat beside her. "Agnes and I read of your exploits in the *Gaslight Gazette* during the Dorsey case, Mr Locke, but I'm curious; is the breaking of locks a skill you learnt for your performances?"

"Call it a hobby of mine," Mr Locke replied. On his way to his own seat, he said to Miss Trent, "It was worryingly simple. I had assumed you would have had the lock switched for a far superior one following my recommendation regarding the back-door's security." Adding sugar and cream to his tea, he then lifted its cup to his lips and added, "But clearly not."

"Perhaps you would care to pay for it?" Miss Trent suggested.

"If that is what it shall take to have it replaced—" Mr Locke began.

"It is," Miss Trent interrupted.

"If you would permit me to finish," Mr Locke said with a contrived smile as he replaced his cup upon its saucer. "I was about to say I would be more than happy to put forth the capital."

"I'll expect to receive a cheque tomorrow, then," Miss Trent replied.

"Consider it done," Mr Locke said and placed a fine quality cigarette between his lips. Miss Webster averted her gaze when he then struck a match to light it, but her reaction appeared to go unnoticed.

The group was gathered around the table in the kitchen of the Bow Street Society's house. The combination of gaslight from the wall lamps and warmth from the stove created a cosy atmosphere. Meanwhile, the dark abyss of night filled the windows either side of the solid back-door as rain beat against their glass. As a result, one could only see the group's reflections, distorted by water trails, when one looked outside.

"Thank you all for coming this evening," Miss Trent began. "We—"

A loud bang tore through her words, causing Miss Dexter to jolt in her chair and Lady Owston to choke on her tea. When a second, identical bang sounded, they all turned toward the backdoor and saw a pale face, sodden by rain, pressed against the window to the door's right. Miss Dexter clapped her hand over her mouth to stifle a gasp at the sight, whilst Lady Owston gripped Miss Webster's arm.

"One of ya wanna let me in?!" Dr Weeks yelled over the din of wind and rain.

"Who *is* he?" Lady Owston enquired from Miss Trent in a hushed voice.

"Dr Percy Weeks, a surgeon," Miss Trent replied. "Sam, will you let him in, please?"

Lady Owston's lips parted as she stared at her in disbelief. Hearing movement from the other side of the kitchen, though, she pursed her lips and watched as Mr Snyder unlocked the backdoor. No sooner had he pulled it ajar though did Dr Weeks attempt to get inside by throwing his weight against it. Yet Mr Snyder's solid frame refused to budge, and Dr Weeks cursed as a sharp pain erupted from his shoulder and shot down his arm.

"Should've waited," Mr Snyder said.

"I didn't know ya were behind the door, *did I?*" Dr

Weeks retorted with a glare as he gripped his shoulder and half-stumbled into the kitchen carrying a Gladstone bag.

Locking the door, Mr Snyder retrieved a towel from a nearby counter and offered it to him. He said, "Sit by the stove and ge' a warm."

"I'll give ya somethin' warm alrigh'," Dr Weeks replied with a hard shiver as he snatched the towel from him. "Righ' where the Goddamned sun don't sh—"

"*Sit* down," Miss Trent interrupted, her hard gaze fixed upon the newcomer.

Lady Owston tightened her grip upon Miss Webster's arm as she looked between Miss Trent and Dr Weeks. Miss Webster, on the other hand, ran her eyes over the mess-of-a-man and wondered if anyone had ever seen his alleged qualifications. Meanwhile, Miss Dexter had glanced at the cupboards behind her as she'd considered making Dr Weeks some coffee, whilst Mr Locke was smirking as he continued to smoke.

"If you *want* every constable at Bow Street police station to hear you then please continue as you are," Miss Trent said.

"That's the las' thing I want and ya know it," Dr Weeks replied.

"Then *sit* down and get dried," Miss Trent said and, checking her notes, mumbled, "before you catch your death of cold."

Dr Weeks narrowed his eyes but nonetheless strode over to the vacant chair beside Miss Webster's and tossed his bag onto the table with a thud and rattling of china. Using the towel to dry his face, he dragged the chair across the floor, plonked down onto it, and put his wet feet onto the table. His features contorted into a scowl as he took a packet of cigarettes from his pocket and discovered it had become a crumpled, wet mess of paper and tobacco.

"Please, take one of mine," Mr Locke said, holding out his cigarette case.

"Thanks," Dr Weeks mumbled. He tossed his packet onto the table and, taking one of the slender, white sticks, put it into the corner of his mouth. Once Mr Locke had lit it with a match, Dr Weeks took a deep pull and rested the back of his head against the top of his chair. He exhaled the smoke in a long, upward stream and, giving a guttural groan of satisfaction, took the cigarette from his lips to admire it. "Not as good as sex but sure damn close."

Miss Webster released a soft tsk and rolled her eyes.

"In case you were wondering, Doctor," Miss Trent began in a sardonic tone, "This is Lady Katheryne Owston, an independent journalist for the *Truth* and *Women's Signal* publications, and her secretary, Miss Agnes Webster."

Dr Weeks lifted his head and, looking at each of them in turn, smiled at Miss Webster. "Evenin', ladies." Putting the cigarette back into the corner of his mouth, he returned his gaze to Lady Owston and thought he recognised her from earlier. He couldn't be sure, though, as it had been chaos on Oxford Street. Glancing around the table, then, he enquired, "Where's the fool from the *Gaslight Gazette*?"

"He's not—" Miss Trent began, only to be interrupted by another noise coming from outside. This time, though, it was a series of polite knocks against the window to the left of the backdoor. Seeing Mr Maxwell's pale face looking back at her, she felt her heart sink. "Here," she finished through a sigh.

"Hello?" Mr Maxwell enquired with a few further knocks. "May I come in, please?"

Miss Trent met Mr Snyder's gaze, and the latter rose to unlock the door. Unlike Dr Weeks before him, though, Mr Maxwell waited until the door was opened wide before entering. Drenched from head to foot, his shoes squelched upon the kitchen's hard floor as he walked around the table to Miss Trent. Parting his lips to speak, he then hesitated as he noticed the amount of people gathered. "You're not holding a meeting, are you?"

"Nah, we jus' thought we'd take turns starin' at each other," Dr Weeks quipped.

"Oh…" Mr Maxwell replied. "Why?"

"*Mr* Maxwell," Miss Trent began as she rose to her feet, thereby drawing his attention back to her. "This *is* a meeting and *you* are interrupting. *Why* are you here?"

Mr Maxwell shifted his weight from one foot to the other and toyed with the damp knot of his cravat. Darting his eyes to Miss Dexter and back again, he replied, "to see Miss Dexter; she told you earlier she was coming back in time for an appointment with Mr Suggitt."

Miss Trent's expression hardened, and she put her hands upon her hips.

"B—But I saw Dr Weeks walking down the alleyway and…" Mr Maxwell cleared his throat and, resting his hand upon his chest, continued, "…my curiosity got the better of me."

"Jus' like it got the better of ya on Oxford Street?" Dr Weeks challenged.

"Yes," Mr Maxwell replied but immediately shook his head and corrected, "I mean, no…" Feeling his heart beat faster under Dr Weeks' intense glare, he gripped the lapel of his frock coat and swallowed the lump forming in his throat. "I—I wasn't there as a Bow Street Society member but as a journalist. You see, my editor, Mr Morse, wanted someone to cover the story and—"

"I don't *care* what yer reasons were," Dr Weeks interrupted. "That damned stunt of yours could've cost me my job!"

"This isn't getting us anywhere," Miss Trent interjected.

"Didn't you see Mr Maxwell following you?" Miss Webster enquired.

"He wouldn't of," Mr Maxwell hastily replied. "He walks faster than me. By the time I came to the gate, he was already inside, so I followed."

"*Enough*," Miss Trent ordered.

All eyes turned to her in an instant.

"Mr Maxwell, you have no right to be here because you were not assigned to this case," Miss Trent continued. "However, since you *are* here and I don't want to waste any more time or effort expelling you, *sit* down, *be* quiet, and *listen*." Retaking her seat, she made a note of his presence and added, "Consider yourself assigned."

"*Thank* you, Miss Trent! You won't be disappointed—" Mr Maxwell began with a broad smile.

"*What* did I *just* say?" Miss Trent interrupted, feeling her blood pressure rise.

"Oh… yes… forgive me…" Mr Maxwell replied and hurriedly sat down.

Taking in a slow, deep breath through her mouth, Miss Trent then pursed her lips and exhaled through her nose. "Dr Weeks," she began after a moment to regain her composure. "Please give us your findings."

"Whatever ya say, Miss Trent," Dr Weeks replied and retrieved a folder from his bag. He opened it upon his thighs and flicked the ash from his cigarette onto a spare saucer.

Upon seeing the folder, Lady Owston's stomach tightened at the prospect of what it would contain. She therefore braced herself against the horrors she was about to hear by gripping the arms of her chair. At the same time, Miss Webster had poised her pencil over her notebook despite the intense feeling of anticipation causing her heart to beat faster. Miss Trent, although not entirely unaccustomed to these things, was nonetheless grateful to have her own trepidation momentarily replaced by irritation at the soft sound of Miss Dexter offering to pour Mr Maxwell some tea. She glanced over at the pair

116

but, seeing they were doing their best to be quiet, picked up her pencil and turned her attention back to Dr Weeks.

"The meat were sittin' on the ground in the doorway of the *London Crystal Palace Bazaar*—" Dr Weeks began, having rested the heel of his cigarette-holding hand against the table's edge.

"Pardon me," Lady Owston interrupted in a subdued voice. "But… 'meat?'"

"Yeah, the 'meat.'" Dr Weeks replied and took another deep pull from his cigarette. Seeing Lady Owston give a gentle shake of her head whilst momentarily lifting her shoulders, he flicked the ash onto the saucer and elaborated, "Mrs Maryanna Roberts."

"Good *gracious*!" Lady Owston cried through a gasp.

"He always calls them that," Mr Maxwell explained. Feeling Dr Weeks' eyes boring into him as a result, he bowed his head and sipped his tea to hide his flushing cheeks.

"*Like* I were sayin'; she were sittin' on the ground," Dr Weeks continued, his glare lingering on Mr Maxwell until he was obliged to refer to his report. "She had her back to the door and her head down. She were naked, and her scalp and breasts were missin'."

"Do…" Mr Maxwell began with his head still bowed. Clearing his throat before daring to look up, he then enquired, "Do you think she could be another Jack the Ripper victim?"

"My *goodness*!" Lady Owston exclaimed. "The idea had never even *occurred* to me!"

"It ain't him," Dr Weeks replied, taking a final pull from his cigarette and crushing its end upon the saucer. "I checked the body 'gainst the Ripper files myself; he left the clothes with his victims, killed 'em in Whitechapel, and done his last murder eight years ago. Mrs Roberts ain't one of his."

"Oh, *thank* God," Lady Owston said, slumping back in her chair as Miss Webster rubbed her hand. "Thank you for being so diligent, Dr Weeks."

"Would you like some more tea, Lady Owston?" Miss Dexter offered.

"No. Thank you, child," Lady Owston replied in a subdued voice. "Please continue, Dr Weeks." She squeezed Miss Webster's hand, "You too, Agnes; back to your note-taking."

Miss Webster frowned but obeyed, nonetheless.

"Breasts and scalp were cut from the body with a blade blunter than a surgeon's or butcher's," Dr Weeks resumed as he reached into his bag. Retrieving a silver hip flask, he unscrewed its cap and took a swig of the whisky it held. Giving a soft groan at the burn in his throat, he replaced the cap and put the flask down beside his legs. "The wounds had jagged edges, and there weren't s'much blood 'round 'em as I'd expect to find if the heart had still been beatin' when they were cut. I reckon they were cut off after she died. No blood on the ground under or 'round the meat in the doorway. Also found hessian fibres in her hair." He glanced at the others. "What it gets us is this: she were killed someplace else, put in a sack, and dumped at the bazaar."

"She was put into a *sack* to be moved?" Miss Webster enquired.

"That's what I said, weren't it?" Dr Weeks countered.

"I only ask, *Doctor,* because I'd imagine such a feat would be quite difficult," Miss Webster replied in a cool tone. "I run the household accounts for Lady Owston and therefore arrange the purchase and delivery of sacks of potatoes every month. I couldn't imagine trying to get a body into one of those."

"D'pends on 'ow many bushels' worth you ge'," Mr Snyder interjected. "I've seen several bushels worth being loaded up with coal from ships at the docks. Farmers hire the big sacks from the sack hiring companies, too. They've got depots at places like railway stations and coal merchants."

"Yes, you're right, Mr Snyder," Miss Webster agreed. "We only tend to get the smaller amounts as there are so few of us in the house." She considered the sack's origins for a moment and mused aloud, "the sack could've come from any number of places, then. Including from the kitchen of anyone who knew her."

"We've gotta ask Mr Queshire, the Suggitts, and Mr Roberts, and his daughter if they can ge' those sacks," Mr Snyder said.

"If it *was* one of them who murdered her…" Mr Maxwell interjected.

"Clearly, whoever murdered Mrs Roberts couldn't afford to leave her body where the deed had been done," Miss Webster mused aloud. "Possibly due to the likelihood of it being discovered."

"It was discovered on Oxford Street, however," Mr Locke pointed out. "In plain sight of anyone walking past."

"Preciscly; *anyone* could've walked past *or* placed her there," Miss Webster replied. "*Not* someone who could be linked to the crime by where her poor body was found."

"Maybe the murderer was so sickened by his, or her, act they wanted her to be found to ease their shame?" Lady Owston suggested.

"I would have cause to doubt such a notion," Mr Locke replied. "In addition to leaving the body where it could be found, a feeling of shame could also encourage smaller, more subtle, acts to ease the murderer's sense of guilt. For example, ensuring Mrs Roberts' body was covered to protect her modesty. Yet Mrs Roberts' body was devoid of clothing, correct?"

"Yeah," Dr Weeks replied.

"Which suggests to me not only a measure of arrogance in our murderer but also a desire to humiliate our victim," Mr Locke continued. "He wanted to expose her to the world by presenting her in the most vulnerable state possible."

"Foulness, utter, utter foulness," Lady Owston remarked, twisting her lips in disgust

"D'ya mind if I continue?" Dr Weeks enquired in a sardonic tone.

"Please, do," Miss Trent replied.

"Ain't my fault people keep interruptin'," Dr Weeks retorted, picking up his hip flask and unscrewing its cap once more. "Rigor Mortis starts takin' hold after 'bout thirty minutes or so but can take several hours to finish doin' its work to the point where a body can't be manipulated," he took a mouthful of whisky and rested the open flask upon his thigh. "It had to have been put in the sack before it happened. There were some bruisin' on her face, chest, and arms but not enough to say it were done before she were killed. Small scratches on her skin—forearms and thighs—which ain't what I'd call defensive. I reckon the murderer beat her after she died and tore her clothes off. They're missin'. All of that would've taken a good slice of time. I reckon the bastard that done this didn't know the body would stiffen up like a pisser in a whorehouse so ya'll ain't lookin' for a medical man.

"There were traces of semen in her mouth, on her lips, in her throat, colon, vagina, and stomach. Not to put too fine a point on it, ladies and gentlemen," he scratched his cheek, "but my snake's been stroked by enough ladies' mouths to know what trace it leaves on their lips."

Lady Owston shuddered.

"Our lady were covered in it," Dr Weeks continued. "She'd had sex with a lot of men before she died and didn't give a damn about disease." He took another mouthful of whisky. "When I cut open her belly, her stomach were inflamed, makin' me think of some kinda poison bein' what killed her. There were the smell of gin but, on testin' some of the juices, found only a small amount. There were no food but there were coffee—'bout half a pint's worth." He paused to screw the cap back onto his hip flask and toss it into his bag. "'Cause of the gin, I checked her liver; were showin' disease but not enough to kill her and, 'sides, her skin weren't yellow as yer'd expect to find with liver failure. So, I went back to my theory on the poisonin'. Dunno if yer've seen cases of long term poisonin's in the 'papers but it's hard to prove poison in the hands as a murder weapon. Now, I'm talkin' *arsenic*, ladies and gentlemen. I tested s'much as the coffee in her belly as I could usin' somethin' called the Marsh test. Got some traces of arsenic at the end of it and even the smell of garlic."

"Garlic?" Mr Maxwell enquired.

"S'what arsenic smells like when ya heat it," Dr Weeks replied. "And there were enough to kill her after I weighed it—'bout three teaspoons worth. Ya'll remember I told ya'll 'bout the semen in her throat? There were some vomit, too, there and in her gullet. I tested some of the vomit usin' the Marsh test; were arsenic in it. I tested her stomach tissue, skin tissue, and muscle tissue—no arsenic. What that tells us is she weren't poisoned by someone over a long period. I reckon the arsenic were what the murderer had to hand but it weren't a murder done when havin' the mother of all arguments. Folks have knives and things for those times. Nah, the murderer were actin' on a thought put in his head shortly b'fore he killed her, but he chose to do it with arsenic and watch her die. The vomit were her initial reaction after swallowin' the poison. Arsenic, in a big dose like that, can start workin' in as little as one minute. He could've held her down or locked her in to stop her gettin' help to make sure she died."

"You said proving arsenic as a murder weapon is very difficult, however," Miss Webster reminded him. "Yet it sounds to me as though you have done an excellent job at proving it."

"Thanks for your vote of confidence, but this is jus' a theory of mine based on what I know," Dr Weeks replied. "But even that's been called bull by others in the past."

"How so?" Miss Dexter enquired.

"Arsenic is one of the most commonly used metals," Dr Weeks replied. "It's used in farmin', wallpapers—Hell, it's even used to make the apparatus the Marsh test relies on. That and the sulphuric acid and zinc ya gotta use could have arsenic in 'em if ya don't make sure they're free of impurities first. Then yer've got 'normal arsenic' to think 'bout."

"Does such a thing exist?" Mr Locke enquired.

"Yeah," Dr Weeks replied. Seeing the confusion on the faces of those around him, though, he released a soft sigh and continued, "We've all got arsenic in us; least that's what a fella called Orfila found out— 'im and his associate, Jean-Pierre Couerbe. Orfila were also the one who gave folks suggestions 'bout gettin' rid of impurities in the Zinc and Sulphuric Acid in the Marsh test. Couerbe had been testin' dead folks who they reckoned hadn't been poisoned with arsenic—rotten dead folks. He found arsenic so took it to Orfila. They worked on it together." Dr Weeks gave a deep exhale. "Cuttin' a damned long story short, Orfila's work showed how 'normal arsenic' ain't soluble in boilin' water whereas yer poisoner's arsenic is. So, I done a Reinsch test on the coffee from her stomach; it showed arsenic, too. Only thing with that is ya gotta make sure the copper ya use is pure 'cause that, too, can mess up yer findings. Like I said, damned hard provin' arsenic as a murder weapon in the hands of a poisoner."

"Yet you believe Mrs Roberts *was* killed by arsenic?" Miss Webster probed.

"Yeah; I know I made my tests as near accurate as I could get 'em," Dr Weeks replied. "And I know in my gut that Mrs Roberts were killed by it. Ya'll and Inspector Woolfe are gonna need more than that if this gets to court though."

"Yes, well, we will deal with that when—or if—it arises," Miss Trent interjected as she wrote her own notes on the matter. "Do you know when Mrs Roberts was murdered, Dr Weeks?"

"Wondered when ya'll were gonna bring that up," Dr Weeks replied and glanced over his report. "I reckon it were sometime between midnight and four o'clock this mornin'."

"You can't be any more precise?" Miss Webster enquired.

"Nah, I can't," Dr Weeks replied. "And that's jus' an informed guess as it is. Take it or leave it."

Miss Webster recorded the approximate time of death and enquired, "And she was discovered at six o'clock this morning, correct?"

"Yeah, by Police Constable Fraser," Dr Weeks replied. "How did ya know that?"

"Inspector Woolfe himself told us this morning," Lady Owston interjected.

"If the latest she was murdered was four o'clock, why was she not discovered until two hours later?" Mr Locke enquired with a lofted brow.

"Maybe it was too dark to see?" Mr Maxwell suggested.

"No," Mr Locke replied. "As I have told you previously, patrols are conducted at least ten minutes apart. If Mrs Roberts' body were in the doorway prior to six o'clock, she would have been found. Ergo, her body was not placed until at least ten minutes prior to Constable

Fraser passing. In which case, it would be necessary for our murderer to have had somewhere secure to store the body. Furthermore, a reasonable knowledge of the area."

Mr Maxwell hummed.

"How did you reach the conclusion it was the coffee and not the gin which was poisoned?" Mr Locke enquired.

"Cause the coffee weren't digested and I found it in the vomit in her throat and mouth—along with the arsenic," Dr Weeks replied. "'Sides, a murderer ain't gonna give the lush a poisoned bottle of gin and, as she lay dyin', pour coffee down her throat."

"A 'lush'?" Lady Owston enquired.

"Short for Lushington," Mr Snyder replied with a soft smile. "Someone addicted to the drink."

"It's what's called a 'slang' term," Mr Maxwell interjected.

"Yes, I'm quite familiar with the notion of 'slang,' thank you," Lady Owston replied in a sardonic tone. "It is a vulgar butchering of the English language." Turning her attention to Mr Locke, she went on, "Mrs Suggitt informed us her sister was a fallen woman and her drinking was to blame. I would therefore be inclined to agree with Dr Weeks; coffee isn't the usual beverage of choice for someone who wishes to become inebriated. The fact she drank it at all also leads me to suspect she was offered it by someone she both knew and trusted. I know *I* wouldn't accept a drink from a stranger."

"Took a lot of comparin' but I got it down to the French Breakfast kinda coffee, too," Dr Weeks said.

"We need to find out which of those close to Mrs Roberts had this coffee, as well as access to arsenic and hessian sacks," Lady Owston mused aloud.

"If they're guilty though, they're not going to admit to owning arsenic, are they?" Maxwell enquired with a frown.

"Ya'll gotta check the poison books of pharmaceutical chemists 'round where them folks live to get that kinda information," Dr Weeks replied. "Since the Pharmacy and Sales of Poisons Act of 1869, no one can sell the stuff without bein' one of those. People can't buy it if they ain't known to the chemist either, and they gotta give their name and address. If the chemist knows yer murderer, they'd sell the arsenic to 'em—or if they knew someone who introduced 'em to the chemist. So, yeah, chemists 'round where they all live is a good place to start."

"I can do it," Mr Maxwell said as he lifted his hand. "And maybe Miss Dexter would like to…?"

"Miss Dexter would be better suited to speaking with Mrs Roberts' daughter," Miss Trent replied. "Miss Webster, given your experience with ledgers, you shall accompany Mr Maxwell."

"Very well," Miss Webster replied.

Miss Dexter meanwhile cast an apologetic look in Mr Maxwell's direction.

"Was there anything else, Dr Weeks?" Miss Trent enquired.

"Yeah; this," Dr Weeks replied and tossed a sepia-looking photograph onto the table. It depicted Mrs Maryanna Roberts sitting against a plain background with her hands against her chest. Her fingers were spread wide as they framed a rectangular piece of slate hanging from a piece of string around her neck. Written on the slate, in white chalk, were some numbers and the date. Her hair was intact, but the photograph's various shades of brown made its colour hard to distinguish. It was clearly shoulder length, however. Her glazed eyes, pronounced leaning to the right, and need to be held upright by the hands of unseen guards suggested she was drunk at the time the photograph was taken.

Upon seeing her pose and slate, Mr Locke

remarked, "Her photograph from the Convict Supervision Office at Scotland Yard."

"Yeah," Dr Weeks replied, causing Lady Owston and Miss Webster to regard Mr Locke with curiosity.

"May I capture it with my camera?" Miss Dexter enquired in a meek voice as she retrieved it from under the table.

"Do what ya like," Dr Weeks replied with a shrug of his shoulders. "S'long as I get it back."

"Thank you," Miss Dexter said in a soft voice and, holding her box-like camera above the photograph, pressed its button several times.

"I presume Mr Suggitt's identification of the body was correct?" Lady Owston enquired in a grave tone. "This photograph is of the same woman found in Oxford Street?"

"Yeah; Inspector Woolfe asked me to check," Dr Weeks replied. "He also said she'd been arrested for prostitution when I told 'im about the semen in her different holes." Suddenly taking his feet off the table, he snatched the photograph and stuffed both it and his report back into his bag, saying, "Yer've seen enough." He then tossed the bag under the table and put his feet on it.

"The fact she had a criminal record as a prostitute certainly gives credence to Mr Holden's account," Mr Locke revealed nonchalantly. When everyone looked at him as a result, he felt a burst of adrenalin surge through him.

"You speak of the incident at the department store?" Lady Owston enquired.

"Though it *is* a consequence of her behaviour then, it is not the incident to which I refer," Mr Locke replied before pausing for not only dramatic effect but to savour the almost palatable anticipation exuding from Lady Owston and Miss Webster. "Following a respectable night at the *Theatre Royal,* Drury Lane, the Holdens returned

126

home. After waiting for his wife to retire to bed, however, Mr Bartholomew Holden departed again, this time to seek out Mrs Roberts."

"Did he find her?" Mr Maxwell enquired.

"He did," Mr Locke replied. "He told me his intention was not to harm her but to remind her of her place. He admitted to me he paid for 'services rendered' following their discussion, but he had only given her half of his usual amount. In parts, he said, to her being intoxicated and to his wish for her understanding behaviour, such as she had displayed at the store, could not be repeated should she ever meet him in public again. He said he found her at around ten forty-five, and they parted company a short time after. The way he put it, Dr Weeks, is the 'services' were 'rendered' in an 'oral' manner. It would therefore explain why you found that particular substance not only in her throat and mouth but also in her stomach."

Dr Weeks grunted his agreement.

"Mr Holden could not present his wife as a witness to the time he returned home for she was asleep when he slipped into bed, and he did not dare wake her," Mr Locke continued. "Personally, I have severe doubts of Mr Holden's guilt. If nothing else, he was saddened to hear of her demise; his marriage is, by his own account, one of convenience and loneliness."

"We were given much the same story by Mrs Holden," Lady Owston said. "Aside from the account of her husband visiting Mrs Roberts for…" She lowered her voice, "you-know-what."

"Maybe they concocted the whole story to prevent the truth from being exposed?" Mr Maxwell suggested.

"No; *too* improbable," Lady Owston replied. "Mrs Holden spoke so vilely of Mrs Roberts; I think murdering one so far down the social ladder would be positively beneath her in her mind. She even told us as much." She lifted her hand. "No, I have to concur with you, Mr Locke. Neither Holden were responsible for Mrs Roberts' murder."

"We're ruling them out as suspects, then?" Mr Maxwell enquired.

"Yes," Lady Owston and Mr Locke replied in unison.

"Very well," Miss Trent began. "Unless we come by new evidence which makes us question our stance, we should consider the Holdens as irrelevant. Miss Dexter, will you show everyone the sketch of Mrs Roberts' missing clothes you did under Mr Suggitt's direction?"

"Yes, Miss Trent," Miss Dexter replied and softly cleared her throat, taking the sketchbook from the shelf behind her. "Mr Suggitt had some difficulty resting on a final depiction," she began, opening the sketchbook and placing it in the table's centre. "After almost an hour of trying, and some gentle encouragement, he declared these to be Mrs Roberts' missing clothes. He was also able to tell me her missing hair was mousey brown in colour." Her eyes became downcast as she sat down and clasped her hands tight within her lap. "Mr Suggitt doesn't want us to continue with our investigation. He said... his wife wasn't in her right mind when she hired the Bow Street Society, and he thought it best if we let the police do their duty. Inspector Woolfe told the Suggitts the same when he questioned them outside the bazaar." She lifted her gaze to focus on Miss Trent alone. "There was something else, too. When Mr Suggitt told the inspector they were both at home the night Mrs Robert died, Mrs Suggitt was surprised." She frowned. "Perhaps I am seeing things which weren't there."

"Go on," Mr Maxwell encouraged.

Miss Dexter gave a weak smile and continued, "By his behaviour, and his responses, I couldn't help but feel Mr Suggitt was hiding something; what, I know not."

"Ya didn't ask 'im when ya were doin' the drawin'?" Dr Weeks challenged.

"We spoke only of the clothes," Miss Dexter replied. Having not thought to question Mr Suggitt about her suspicions at the time, she lowered her gaze once more.

"Mr Queshire told Milady and me of Mr Suggitt's habit of distancing himself from Mrs Roberts," Miss Webster said as she consulted her notes from earlier in the day. "Furthermore, this was the reason why he'd not been requested to intervene when she'd behaved so deplorably with the Holdens. Given what we now know about Mrs Roberts' 'other' activity, isn't it possible Mr Suggitt was also paying her for sex?"

"*Agnes*!" Lady Owston scolded. "Such questions are *improper* for a lady to be asking."

Miss Webster rolled her eyes but, choosing to ignore her employer, enquired from Dr Weeks. "Well? Isn't it?"

"Sure, it is, darlin'," Dr Weeks replied with a grin.

"Thank you," Miss Webster said with a curt nod of her head. "I suggest we speak with the Suggitts again tomorrow, milady."

"Once Inspector Woolfe has finished his interrogations in the morning, yes, we shall," Lady Owston replied with a hard edge to her voice. "*And* once Mrs Roberts' daughter and estranged husband have been spoken to." She shifted within her chair as she cast a look of disapproval Miss Webster's way. "Of course, it's *equally* possible Mr Suggitt distanced himself from his sister-in-law due to her drinking so we shouldn't leap to any conclusions."

Miss Webster pursed her lips and returned to her notetaking.

"*Now,* back to your absolutely *fantastic* sketch, Miss Dexter," Lady Owston said.

Miss Dexter's cheeks flushed a bright pink as she replied, "Thank you."

"Credit where credit is due, child," Lady Owston said as she pulled the sketchbook across the table toward her. Upon seeing it in closer detail, she tapped the part depicting the shawl and mused aloud, "I do believe I've seen this garment before. The question is, *where*?" She went over the places she'd recently visited in her mind and suddenly exclaimed, "*Yes, I have*! Agnes, do you recall? In the *Queshire Department Store*, on the dummy in the haberdashery department."

"I do," Miss Webster replied, referring to the notes she'd made at the time. Yet an additional memory caused her to doubt her employer's assertion. "But it can't be the same garment," she said, meeting Lady Owston's gaze. "Don't you recollect, as we were leaving, one of the assistants explained to a customer none of the items in the store were second-hand?"

"*Pish-posh!*" Lady Owston exclaimed with a wave of her hand. "I can assure everyone here the *Queshire Department Store* does sell second-hand goods for *I* have, in the past, purchased garments displaying minute signs of wear. Mr Queshire simply doesn't wish for the fact to be known due to the negative connotations associated with such garments. Now, while it *is* true garments which pass hands in the Rag Fair *are* of a questionable quality, those I've purchased from the *Queshire Department Store* would be acceptable to *anyone* who couldn't recognise the subtle signs of previous ownership."

"What's the Rag Fair?" Mr Maxwell enquired.

"A dark, dirty street that's got more in common with the Thames than a place to do business," Dr Weeks interjected.

"I'm surprised you've heard of it," Lady Owston replied. "Very few have. Even those who have resided in London for years."

"I had the misfortune of havin' to visit the hellhole when someone were murdered there," Dr Weeks replied. "Crouchin', ankle-deep in muddy water, ain't fun."

"Quite," Lady Owston remarked with a sympathetic smile. "Nonetheless you are mistaken." Turning her gaze back to Mr Maxwell, she explained, "The Rag Fair is held in the vicinity of Houndsditch. It begins at the end of Cutler Street, leads out of Houndsditch, and proceeds in an eastward direction. It then embraces a narrow street called White's Alley, and extends towards the north. There it turns eastward and proceeds in a direct line to extend as far as Petticoat Lane, where it turns to the north and south. Probably the entire length of the area wherein the patrons of the Rag Fair may be found is nearly a quarter of a mile of the vicinity; while the width of the space the Fair occupies varies with the breadth of the streets and lanes on which it is held. The lane, of which you spoke, Dr Weeks, is the largest, I believe."

"And people can buy second-hand clothes there?" Mr Maxwell enquired.

"Buy *and* sell," Lady Owston replied. "It is frequently members of the Jewish population who do the buying, usually behind the closed doors of the sellers' residence." She placed her hand upon the sketch. "But Mrs Roberts didn't sell her shawl in the Rag Fair if this is indeed the same item. I'd have to inspect the garment to be certain."

"Mr Suggitt told me she couldn't have sold the shawl as it wasn't nice enough," Miss Dexter interjected.

"A donation, perhaps?" Miss Webster suggested.

"If it was, it would have had to have been made between the time when Mr Suggitt saw her at the store and Mr Holden's rendezvous with her last night," Mr Locke pointed out. "For, when I asked Mr Holden if he could recall what Mrs Roberts had been wearing when he had last seen her, he never mentioned a shawl. Of course, it could be the weakness of memory preventing him from recalling such a garment, yet he was able to tell me she was wearing a scarf, dress, and boots. If Mr Suggitt did indeed distance himself from her at the store, and her sister was nowhere to be seen, Mrs Roberts could have donated the shawl from some sense of spite."

"Or whoever killed her," Dr Weeks interjected as he tilted his chair back and returned his feet to the table.

"But wouldn't Mr Suggitt have recognised it?" Miss Dexter enquired.

"Another question only Mr Suggitt knows the answer to," Mr Maxwell replied with a frown.

"I will pay another visit to the *Queshire Department Store,* take a closer look at the shawl, and speak again with Mr Queshire. He may be able to shed some light on the matter," Lady Owston said. "Such a *charming* man he is—and generous, too." She retrieved her bag from beneath the table and, rifling through it, added, "He gave me a bar of soap he'd made only this morning and didn't charge."

"As charming as he may be, we must not remove him from our list of suspects without just cause," Miss Trent replied. "Aside from her rendezvous with Mr Holden, the last place Mrs Roberts was seen alive was Mr Queshire's store."

"I would beg to differ," Lady Owston said while still searching. "But nevertheless, I shall *bow* to your experience."

"Good," Miss Trent replied. Adding to her notes, she then read them aloud. "Mr Maxwell and Miss Webster are to visit the chemists located in and around Oxford Street, and near to the homes of the Suggitts and the Roberts. Meanwhile, Lady Owston shall speak to Mr Queshire whilst Miss Dexter speaks with Mrs Robert's daughter, Miss Regina Roberts. Sam," she looked to Mr

Snyder, "given your working-class background, I think Mrs Roberts' husband, Abraham, would feel more at ease in your presence than anyone else's. Therefore, could you accompany Miss Dexter?"

"Yeah," Mr Snyder replied.

"In the meantime, I'll contact Mr and Mrs Suggitt and arrange a meeting between them and Lady Owston, Miss Webster, Mr Locke, and Mr Snyder tomorrow evening," Miss Trent continued. "I'll be sure to choose somewhere Inspector Woolfe wouldn't expect to find you."

"If they are indeed hiding something, I think speaking to the Suggitts separately would be an excellent tactic," Mr Locke said. "They may reveal information they are otherwise hiding from one another."

Miss Trent hummed her agreement and added, "Ensure you all return to me in the morning with your findings, though."

"*Here* it is!" Lady Owston exclaimed upon finding the soap in her coat pocket. Holding it in one hand as she rested the other on top, she added, "He makes *all* of his own soap on site; his father would be proud."

"His father?" Mr Maxwell enquired. Thoughts of his own father drifted into his mind at the question. They reminded him to purchase a new shirt to wear to the family dinner tomorrow evening.

"His father owned the store—it was a simple haberdashery back then—prior to Mr Queshire," Lady Owston replied. "When Mr Queshire Senior was tragically killed by a horse and carriage, the business was passed to his son and heir. Mr Queshire Junior's hard work has made the department store into the success it is today."

"You seem to know a lot about it," Mr Locke observed.

"I've covered the *Queshire Department Store* and its many delights in several of my articles for the *Truth* publication—in addition to being a loyal customer of theirs," Lady Owston replied and smiled wistfully at the soap as if it were a precious gem. "It's truly a remarkable story." She put the soap down on the table. "With so much tragedy in his life, one would think Mr Queshire would be bitter, but one couldn't hope to meet a *nicer* man!"

"Who else has died?" Mr Maxwell enquired.

"Well, there was his sister—she was only fifteen when she died," Lady Owston replied. "Then his father, as I've already explained, and many years later, his poor mother. Oh! I *almost* forgot! While we were at the store, there was a *most* peculiar incident concerning the room at the top of the stairs." She pointed upward. "One of the customers entered a room marked *staff only*." She dropped her hand. "I remarked upon it to Mr Queshire and one of his *many* assistants, Miss Rose Galway." Lady Owston took a sharp inhale. "Oh *my,* she turned as *white* as a sheet, didn't she, Agnes?"

"She did," Miss Webster replied.

"Mr Queshire investigated and reported to us a customer had simply become lost," Lady Owston continued. "Yet Miss Galway's reaction was *most* strange, wasn't it?"

Miss Webster nodded.

"Even when Agnes and I tried to encourage the reason for her fear from her she refused to reveal it," Lady Owston said. "She practically fled the room. I think I may speak to Mr Queshire of her odd behaviour tomorrow." She knitted her brow. "Something about the way the customer entered the room, however… I may attempt to see for myself what is in there during my visit."

"Nothing illegal unless you have good reason," Miss Trent reminded her.

"*Perish* the thought!" Lady Owston cried with her hand upon her chest.

"Miss Galway also enquired about becoming a

member," Miss Webster interjected.

"Of *course,* she did," Lady Owston agreed.

"A member of what?" Miss Trent enquired.

"Why the Bow Street Society," Lady Owston replied. Noticing Dr Weeks pick up the soap, she exclaimed, "Yes, take a *sniff*!" Watching as he did so, she then enquired, "Have you *ever* smelt anything *more* divine?"

Yet before Dr Weeks could give his answer, the sound of someone violently braying upon the front door filled the room.

"Are we expecting anyone else?" Mr Maxwell enquired from Miss Trent.

"Open up!" a male voice demanded from beyond the front door. "This is the police!"

NINE

"It's *Woolfe*!" Dr Weeks cried, using his foot to drag his bag toward him. Snatching it from the floor and pushing his chair back with a loud scrape, he tossed the soap onto the table in front of Lady Owston and fled through the backdoor.

"Wh—what's he doing here?" Mr Maxwell enquired, having leapt to his feet the moment the inspector's name had been mentioned. He rested his thumb and forefinger either side of his Adam's apple and considered following Dr Weeks' lead.

"I don't know," Miss Trent replied as she stood.

"*Open this door or I'll kick it down!*" Inspector Woolfe bellowed.

"But I intend to find out," Miss Trent added and went to let the bad-mannered policeman in.

Although the medical report and Mrs Roberts' photograph had left with Dr Weeks, the sketchbook containing the drawing of Mrs Roberts' missing clothes remained open on the table for all to see. Realising Inspector Woolfe would recognise it at once, Miss Dexter hurried to close the sketchbook and put it back onto the shelf.

"We're in the middle of a meeting—" Miss Trent's voice called, only to be cut off by Inspector Woolfe barging into the kitchen. Entering behind him, she stood to one side and continued, "This is Inspector Caleb Woolfe of the Metropolitan Police's E Division. Inspector, may I introduce Lady Katheryne Owston, Miss Agnes Webster, Miss Georgina Dexter, Mr Samuel Snyder, Mr Joseph Maxwell, and Mr Percy Locke." She put her hand upon her hip. "Now that the formalities have been dealt with, what do you want?"

Inspector Woolfe moved around the table with squared shoulders and tense arms. His unkempt brow was also furrowed as his cold eyes moved from face-to-face. When they met Lady Owston's gaze, he said, "You've been questioning *my* witnesses." Shifting his glare to Miss Dexter, he added, "I *told* you to let me do my duty." By this point, he'd reached Mr Maxwell. "And *you*," he snarled, taking a tight grip of Mr Maxwell's shoulder to drag him around to stand in front of him. "First, you tell me you've worked with Dr Weeks," he released Mr Maxwell's shoulder but stepped forward to pin him between the table and him. "And now I find you *here*?"

"*Stop* bullying our members," Miss Trent warned as she strode over. Standing beside Mr Maxwell, she added, "Step away from him."

Inspector Woolfe stepped back to allow Mr Maxwell to slip out, but then moved closer to Miss Trent instead. Despite the marked difference in their stature, Miss Trent lifted her chin and, closing the gap between them, warned, "Don't think you can intimidate me, Inspector."

Inspector Woolfe lowered his chin and straightened his back with a scowl.

"Continue as you are, and you shall get no cooperation from us," Miss Trent warned.

"I'm not getting any as it is," Inspector Woolfe countered.

"That is because you have come charging in here like a bull into the ring," Mr Locke pointed out. "Whatever Mr Maxwell may have said to you has nothing to do with either this Society or its client."

"A client who, until now, has cooperated with the police on account of the advice I gave her," Lady Owston interjected.

"She may have a change of heart, though, upon hearing of your conduct this evening," Mr Locke said.

"Are you threatening me, *magician*?" Inspector Woolfe growled.

"Threats are the reserve of crude criminals; I endorse neither," Mr Locke replied as he stood and held out his open cigarette case to the policeman.

Inspector Woolfe looked from it, to Mr Locke, and then to Miss Trent. Seeing her fold her arms across her chest and lift a brow in stern expectation, he realised he was getting nowhere. Glancing around the room, the only hint of fear he found was on Mr Maxwell's face. Irritated that they'd backed him into a corner, he grasped what little power he had over the situation by ordering him, "Sit down."

Mr Maxwell dropped onto a chair like a sack of potatoes.

Pleased by this minor victory, Inspector Woolfe smirked. Yet, the moment he looked back to Miss Trent, his smile vanished, and he stepped back with a scowl. Noticing Mr Locke was still offering him a cigarette, though, he took one from the case and sniffed it. Persuaded by the strong scent of tobacco to place it between his lips, he then allowed Mr Locke to light it with a match and filled his lungs with the high-quality smoke.

"How did you discover Lady Owston had spoken to a witness?" Mr Locke enquired once he'd re-taken his seat.

"The witness told me," Inspector Woolfe replied.

"Which of the witnesses was it?" Miss Trent enquired as she moved to stand between Mr Maxwell and the policeman.

"I'm not telling you," Inspector Woolfe replied.

"Inspector, *please*," Mr Locke said in a condescending tone. "You cannot play judge, jury, and executioner without permitting us to put forth a case of defence. Furthermore, you have not fully enlightened us as to the charge."

"Attempting to pervert the course of justice for your own gains," Inspector Woolfe replied. Taking a further pull from his cigarette, he then reached across the table to tap its ash onto the saucer. Catching sight of the crumbled, wet mess of Dr Weeks' cigarette packet whilst doing so, he picked it up and turned it over.

"Her Majesty's British Empire does not restrict the exchange of conversation," Mr Locke said, his gaze moving from the cigarette packet to Inspector Woolfe's face. When the latter showed no hint of recognition, Mr Locke enquired, "Shall you pay a visit to all of London's citizens? For the brutal murder of Mrs Roberts will undoubtedly be discussed among them."

"They've not been commissioned by her sister to investigate," Inspector Woolfe countered, tossing the packet onto the table.

"Inspector," Lady Owston began as she stood and approached him. "You were kind—so *very* kind—when you told me of Mrs Roberts' family, and when *dear* Miss Dexter felt faint. I mistook your good deed for a foul one and I, again, apologise for it." She placed one hand over her heart and the other on his arm. "Please, do not make a mockery of my apology by behaving like the beast I know you are not. You are a good man, a *just* man." She offered a sympathetic smile. "Miss Rose Galway is the witness, isn't she?"

Inspector Woolfe felt his anger weaken at her generous words. Irritated by his sentimentality and sense of obligation to repay her kindness, he muttered, "Yeah, she is."

"And did she tell you I had instructed her *not* to speak to you or the police?" Lady Owston enquired.

"She didn't," Inspector Woolfe conceded.

"Then you already have the truth of it," Lady Owston replied with a broad smile.

"We don't want to assist Mrs Roberts' murderer

any more than you do, inspector," Miss Trent began. "The Bow Street Society has been hired to investigate her death and we intend to honour our commitment. However, we aren't against you or the police. If you're willing to permit our pursuing our own lines of enquiries, we'll be sure to let you know what we discover."

"No," Inspector Woolfe said, feeling his anger strengthen at the suggestion. Crushing out his cigarette upon the saucer, he went on, "You've got no jurisdiction over this case, in the eyes of the Metropolitan Police or in the eyes of the law." He opened the door into the hallway. "You say whatever you want to Mrs Suggitt; if she's guilty, I'll see her twitching on the end of a rope regardless. And you'll all find yourselves breaking rocks at Dartmoor if I find out you've been questioning my witnesses again." He left the kitchen and strode back to the front door, yelling, "This is your final warning!"

TEN

The following morning, Mr Maxwell and Miss Webster parted company from Lady Owston outside the *Queshire Department Store*. After the Society's meeting, they had discussed the location of the Suggitts' residence with Mr Snyder. From the address given to them by their client, they knew they lived on Reeves Mews, a small street between South Andle to the east and Park Street to the west. To its north was Upper Grosvenor Street that led to Grosvenor Square, and to its south was Mount Street that eventually led to Berkeley Square. A little further afield was the vast expanse of Hyde Park to the west and Oxford Street to the north. According to Booth's Poverty Map of 1889, Reeves Mews housed people who were "fairly comfortable" with "good, ordinary earnings," whilst the remaining named thoroughfares were the territories of the "upper middle and upper classes wealthy" and the "well-to-do middle class." Mr Snyder was able to confirm the class of Reeves Mews' residents—much to Miss Webster's surprise—based upon his knowledge of the area. Furthermore, he could list the omnibus and tram routes from that location. Although, by his admission, many of the omnibus routes included Oxford Street, the Suggitts would be obliged to walk to their home regardless of where they disembarked. The fact a private carriage hadn't collected Mr Suggitt from Oxford Street or Mrs Suggitt from Bow Street on the previous day also suggested they didn't employ a domestic driver. This, when considered alongside the short distance between Reeves Mews and Oxford Street, the Suggitts' apparent wealth, and the ease in which Mr Suggitt hired Mr Snyder's cab, led them to conclude the Suggitts relied upon hansom cabs.

As far as chemists were concerned, a search of the

Post Office Directory by Miss Webster had revealed those on Oxford Street to be the closest to the Suggitt residence. They'd considered the possibility the Suggitts could've visited a chemist further afield to purchase arsenic. Yet, they'd dismissed the idea on the grounds the Suggitts would've known a visit to a chemist who didn't know them could be construed as suspicious compared to visiting one who did.

Huddled beneath Miss Webster's immense umbrella, she and Mr Maxwell made their way along the crowded pavement toward the first chemist. As they grew near, they discovered it was on the opposite side of the road. Now, if Londoners considered attempting to cross major thoroughfares as foolish, they'd certainly consider attempting to cross Oxford Street during heavy rain as insanity. Standing on the pavement's edge, Miss Webster and Mr Maxwell watched the endless stream of carriages, carts, omnibuses, and cabs.

"We should've asked Mr Snyder to stop on the other side," Mr Maxwell said.

"There must be a way across," Miss Webster replied. Watching the traffic for a little while longer, she then passed her umbrella to Mr Maxwell, hitched up her skirts, and strode into the road the instant she saw a gap between the vehicles.

"Miss Webster!" Mr Maxwell cried as he saw her narrowly avoid an oncoming coach and horses.

"Come on, Mr Maxwell!" Miss Webster yelled back before disappearing behind a passing omnibus.

"I don't think—!" Mr Maxwell began but cut himself short when he couldn't see her anymore. Feeling a knot form in his stomach as he knew he'd have to follow, he looked left, right, and left again. Finding the umbrella obscured his view, he put it down and stepped out into the road.

Suddenly, an omnibus sped past him. The

vehicle's conductor, perched upon a narrow ledge at the rear, shook his fist at Mr Maxwell and shouted, "*Get outta the road*!"

"I'm trying!" Mr Maxwell replied but the omnibus was already out of sight. Whirling around to find Miss Webster, he came face-to-face with a shire horse pulling a brewer's cart. The animal nodded its head several times and gave a loud snort. Startled, Mr Maxwell walked rapidly backwards and into the path of a hansom cab travelling in the opposite direction.

"Behind you!" Miss Webster cried from the pavement.

Mr Maxwell spun around and felt a sharp tightening of his chest at the sight of the vehicle.

"Hurry!" Miss Webster cried.

Glancing in the direction of her voice, he saw she was only a few feet away. Hearing the cab getting closer at the same time, he closed his eyes and lunged for the pavement. A second later, he heard the yell of the cab's driver, followed by the screeching of the horses as their reins were pulled taught and their front legs were lifted off the cobblestones. Fortunately, he'd reached the safety of the pavement so, when he peeked at the horses' kicking legs above him, he was already out of harm's way.

"Are you hurt?" Miss Webster enquired as she helped him to his feet.

"N—No, thank you," Mr Maxwell replied, looking behind him at the thud of the horses' hooves landing upon the cobblestones.

"Do you wanna get yourself killed?! Watch where you're goin'!" the driver shouted.

"Apologies, sir!" Mr Maxwell replied.

"Where is my umbrella?" Miss Webster enquired.

"It's—" Mr Maxwell began, only to cut himself short when he discovered it was no longer under his arm. Although his heart was still racing from the close encounter with the hansom cab, it beat even faster at the loss of his fellow Bow Streeter's property. Turning toward the road, he caught sight of it lying on the cobblestones and said, "There it is." A coach and horses then ran over it; the latter's feet kicking it back and forth across the ground, before the former crushed it beyond all recognition beneath its wheels. He felt the knot return to his stomach and his temperature rise as he looked to Miss Webster.

Having also witnessed the umbrella's destruction, she clenched her jaw, spun around, and marched off down the pavement. Their destination was just a few doors down from where they'd been standing. Therefore, when she'd reached it, she looked over her shoulder at Mr Maxwell and ordered, "come on, we have a task to complete."

"Y—yes, s—sorry," Mr Maxwell replied and hurried to join her.

The façade of *Drummond's Pharmaceutical Chemists* was typical of its kind. Glass carboys, from the Persian word 'Quarabah,' meaning a wine or rose-water holding vessel, lined the shelves behind a single, rolled plate window. Originally created to hold an apothecary's tinctures and extracts, to enable the sun's heat to assist with the process, carboys were now used as display pieces. Meanwhile, the tinctures and extracts had been moved to the shop rounds kept behind the counter. Consisting of the popular 'onion,' 'pear,' and 'swan neck' designs, the carboys were filled with varying levels of coloured water. Whilst some believed the colours represented bodily fluids, others preferred the notion the colours served as a subtle announcement of a chemists' shop due to them vaguely symbolising chemicals. Regardless of their purpose, though, the colours' lovely hues rarely failed to lure customers toward them. Especially when the carboys were illuminated by the shop's interior gaslight during the darker evenings of the winter months. Amongst the carboys was a specie jar which, like its more elegant counterparts, served no practical purpose beyond being a display piece. Large in dimensions, the jar had a white label of MAGNESIA painted on its inside; white being used to also denote its contents. Finally, a white sign in the window's bottom-right corner announced *Medicines Dispensed with PURE DRUGS ONLY* in thick, black print.

Miss Webster entered the shop ahead of Mr Maxwell, but neither could venture further than a couple of feet due to customers crowding the ten-foot squared space. As far as the Bow Streeters could see there were two queues leading to the counter dominating the shop's right side. Serving a stern-faced governess at the head of the queue on the far side was a man no older than thirty. He was attempting to measure a dose of powdered medicine using a set of scales and Troy weights. Despite Avoirdupois weights and measures being favoured in the Medicinal Act of 1858, Troy weights were still preferred for the prescribing and dispensing of medicines. The governess's hand was on the handle of a large pram she'd positioned flush against the counter. As a result, the customer at the head of the queue nearest to the Bow Streeters was obliged to lean over the pram to be heard by the much older gentleman behind the counter.

The wall opposite the counter was adorned by polished-mahogany panelling covered in advertisements. These featured an array of products including cod liver oil emulsion, live pills, pain-relieving embrocation, and food products to supplement the normal meals of invalids and infants. Due to the tumultuous weather, number of people, and meagre gas light, the shop's interior was gripped by gloom. This, added to the customers' combined body heat, the mustiness of their damp clothing, and the malodorous odour of their chest-infection fuelled coughing made the shop a thoroughly unpleasant place to be.

Having no choice but to wait their turn, though, Miss Webster and Mr Maxwell joined the queue for the older gentleman. As they waited, they overheard snippets of conversations from their fellow customers. Whilst some focused on the weather, friends and relatives, most were about Mrs Roberts' body being found on Oxford Street.

"Do they think it's another one of his?" enquired the man standing in front of Mr Maxwell.

"Nothing's been said so far," his companion replied.

"If it is, the Ripper's a long way from Whitechapel," the first man remarked.

The queue moved forward a few paces, and Mr Maxwell could see the older gentleman behind the counter taking monies from customers in both queues whilst operating a large, brass cash register. Cylindrical jars, containing a variety of lozenges and other products, lined the counter's front edge. Behind the counter was a wooden cabinet stood atop a solid, mahogany unit. Within the cabinet were numerous small, square drawers. Each had a brass frame fixed to its front with a card slipped inside. The cards showed the handwritten names of the chemicals the drawers contained. Shelves above the cabinet held a multitude of decorative shop rounds and bottles. The bottles with wide mouths and bulbous stoppers held powders, the bottles with narrow necks and lips suitable for pouring held liquid preparations, and the glass-domed, collared bottles with sharp-pouring, spouted stoppers held oil. The blue bottles with tin-capped necks contained the syrups, whilst the bottles labelled ETHER had heavy, close-fitting domes over their stoppers. All the bottles were labelled with either the full or abbreviated name of the substance it contained. As a result, Miss Webster and Mr Maxwell were able to locate the pair of bottles holding the poison. Positioned on a high shelf, the bottles were green in colour with vertical ridges down their sides and the word ARSENIC written upon their labels. Regardless of what the label said, though, ridges on poison bottles were an obligatory design feature to ensure a chemist could identify its contents though touch alone.

"Good morning and welcome to *Drummond's Pharmaceutical Chemists*. I am Mr Drummond. I sincerely apologise for the wait," the older gentleman greeted when Miss Webster and Mr Maxwell finally reached the front of the queue. He was in his mid-forties with ebony-coloured hair, short sideburns, and moustache. His chin had a pointed appearance due to his lower jaw jutting out from beneath his top, whilst his complexion was pale from many hours spent in the shop. Although his five-foot-eight frame was thin, it nevertheless seemed healthy beneath his white shirt, black waistcoat and cravat, and ankle-length apron. The sleeves of his shirt were rolled up to his elbows, whilst the apron's ties were fastened into a knot over his stomach. He leaned forward, and peering at them with pale-blue eyes, enquired, "How may I be of assistance?"

"Good morning," Miss Webster replied. "We would like to purchase some arsenic, please."

"For some rats," Mr Maxwell added.

"Yes, Cook almost leapt out of her skin when she saw one scurrying across the floor," Miss Webster said.

"Dear, dear me," Mr Drummond muttered, shaking his head. "I would like to assist but neither of you are known to me. As such, I couldn't," he momentarily lifted his heels, "*possibly* sell you arsenic."

"I understand," Miss Webster replied in a flat tone. "Perhaps something else—?"

"We're willing to sign your poison book," Mr Maxwell interrupted.

"I should *think* so, too, sir," Mr Drummond scolded.

Mr Maxwell averted his gaze and, with a soft clearing of his throat, mumbled, "Yes, of course."

"I haze lozenges for coughs—syrups, too, if you

prefer," Mr Drummond said, addressing Miss Webster. Turning toward the shelves, he continued, "We are amid the sneezing season, after all. Perhaps a meal supplement if you are unable to swallow your food?"

"If you'd be so kind as to sign the poison book, sir," the younger gentleman directed his own customer at the other end of the counter. Shorter than Mr Drummond at around five feet, he had scrawny limbs, a dry, pale complexion, neatly combed, pallid-blond hair, and dark rings under his eyes. His apron, although identical to Mr Drummond's in style, was too big for him. As a result, the dark-grey jacket he wore underneath was all but hidden from view. He placed a small, narrow brown paper parcel upon the counter and, after sniffing several times, asked his customer to excuse him whilst he wiped his nose with his handkerchief.

"Dear, dear, me, Mr Collins," Mr Drummond said as he picked up the parcel. "This isn't four grams, this is *eight*." To the customer, he added, "Apologies, sir, but I'm obliged to measure it again before you can sign the book."

"Very well, but be swift about it," the customer replied and stepped away from the counter.

Meanwhile, Mr Drummond closed the poison book and slid it across the counter to the register whilst Mr Collins climbed onto a stepping stool to retrieve a bottle of arsenic from the shelf.

Seeing both chemist and assistant were preoccupied, Mr Maxwell edged his way along the counter to the book. Glancing behind him at the few remaining customers, he saw they were either deep in conversation or reading the advertisements. He therefore rested his hand upon the counter, met Miss Webster's gaze, and looked between her and the book. Releasing a soft cough as he slid the book closer to her, he then stood perpendicular to the counter with his back to the book. Leaning upon his elbow on the counter, to further shield the book from view, he kept a close eye on the chemist and his assistant whilst Miss Webster opened the book. Whilst she read its entries, he lifted the lid of a nearby jar and peered into its contents. Deciding against putting his hand in, though, he replaced the lid and released a loud cough to disguise the sound of Miss Webster turning a page.

"What will you be using the poison for, sir?" Mr Drummond enquired from Mr Collins' customer.

"A mice infestation," the customer replied.

Mr Maxwell turned his head and browsed the shelves. Humming a quiet tune, he strummed his fingers in time with the melody and released another loud cough when Miss Webster turned another page.

"One moment, sir, and I'll dispense some syrup for your cough," Mr Drummond informed him.

"Thank you," Mr Maxwell replied, thumping his chest a little too hard with his balled-up fist. Disguising his subsequent wince with another abrupt cough, though, he rubbed his chest, dipped his chin, and coughed for a fourth time. "Terrible… I've had it for weeks."

The other customers eyed him with suspicion and stepped back.

"Here you are, sir; four grams of arsenic," Mr Drummond said to Mr Collins' customer as he put a second small, brown paper parcel on the counter. "Now, where did I put the poison book…?"

"Done," Miss Webster whispered into Mr Maxwell's ear and slid the poison book back across the counter.

"Is this what you're looking for?" Mr Maxwell enquired, picking up the book for the chemist to see.

"*Yes,* thank you, sir," Mr Drummond replied as he took it from him. "Syrup, wasn't it? However, I would recommend a visit to a physician if you've had the cough for several weeks."

Mr Maxwell released another loud cough, and Mr

Drummond took a swift step back.

"If you think it's for the best," Mr Maxwell said. "That's what I'll do. Thank you, Mr Drummond, and good day."

"Good day, sir, miss," Mr Drummond replied and watched the two leave.

"We must return to the *Queshire Department Store* and speak with Lady Owston at once," Miss Webster said once they were outside.

"Why? What did you find?" Mr Maxwell enquired.

"A name I hadn't expected to see."

ELEVEN

Lady Owston faced a sea of feminine forms upon entering the *Queshire Department Store.* Modest headwear of governesses and maids mingled with the elaborate hats of middle-class ladies as the customers formed human blockades at the counters. Standing near the door, Lady Owston was elbowed and nudged by boxes and umbrellas of those both arriving and departing. Casting her gaze across the room, she was unable to locate the dummy amongst the swathes of dark coats. Becoming increasingly keen to safeguard her personal space at the same time, she ventured further into the store whilst avoiding ladies coming from all directions. Her progress was slow as, whenever a gap appeared in front of her, another body filled it. Yet, when she'd finally reached the haberdashery department's trio of dummies, her heart sank; the shawl wasn't there.

"*Bother,*" she muttered. A brief, visual check of those around her confirmed no one had recently picked it up. Deciding against checking the remaining customers on the grounds of impracticality, she was also obliged to abandon the option of enquiring with the department's assistants since the crowd was more than two-deep in places.

"Good day to you, Milady," a familiar voice greeted from her left.

"*Mr* Queshire," Lady Owston said through a sigh of relief as she turned toward him. "Thank *heavens.*"

"Are you well?" he enquired, concerned.

"Yes," she replied with a broad smile. "You would do well to add telepathy to your many talents, for I was just contemplating how I may seek you out in this commotion."

"You flatter me; I merely caught sight of you as I

was passing," Mr Queshire said with a coy smile. "I hope my soap was satisfactory?"

"Of *course,* it was," Lady Owston replied. "Admittedly, I've not had the opportunity to sample it, but I have *every* confidence it shall be *sublime.*" She gestured toward the dummy. "I saw a shawl I'd hoped to purchase but it's gone…?"

"Remind me of which shawl you are referring to?" Mr Queshire enquired as a gap formed to allow them to approach the counter.

Lady Owston retrieved Miss Dexter's sketch from her coat, and smoothing it out upon the glass, tapped the depiction of the forest-green, hand-crocheted shawl. She said, "*This* one. It was draped over the shoulders of your dummy only yesterday."

"Then I'm afraid it must have been sold," Mr Queshire replied.

Lady Owston frowned. "Would you know to whom?"

"We don't keep a record of who purchases which garments unless they require delivery," Mr Queshire replied. Turning to the assistant, he pushed the sketch toward her and instructed, "Please check the delivery ledger for this shawl, Miss Lemon."

"Yes, Mr Queshire," Miss Lemon replied and retrieved the delivery ledger from a shelf hidden behind some fabric.

"If it's not too inconvenient, Lady Owston, I'd like a private word with you afterward," Mr Queshire said.

"You have again read my mind," Lady Owston replied, her smile growing.

"There's no record of it having been delivered, sir," Miss Lemon said.

"Thank you," Mr Queshire replied with a small bow of his head. "If I'm required, I'll be in the storeroom."

"Yes, sir," Miss Lemon replied and, closing the

ledger, returned it to its hiding place.

"Please, follow me," Mr Queshire invited once Lady Owston had put away her sketch.

Utilising his gentlemanly manners and renowned status amongst his clientele, he forged a path through the crowds surprisingly quickly. Allowing Lady Owston to enter the storeroom ahead of him, he then closed its door upon the chaos and invited her to join him in sitting at the table.

"Inspector Woolfe of the Metropolitan Police came here yesterday," he began. "He enquired about a crocheted shawl also, one worn by Mrs Roberts. I presume your sketch is of the same garment?"

"It is, in addition to the other garments she was last seen wearing by Mr Suggitt here in this very store," Lady Owston replied. "I'm surprised you didn't recognise them immediately."

"Though I'm a connoisseur of clothing, I didn't pay much heed to her apparel. As I explained yesterday, I allowed my emotions to get the better of me." He looked to the table. "I was forced to admit such to Inspector Woolfe, too."

"The inspector is only doing his duty as an officer of the law," Lady Owston reassured. "He was *frightfully* angry at the Bow Street Society being hired to investigate the matter."

"I had no choice but to tell him of your visit here yesterday," Mr Queshire admitted with regret.

Lady Owston momentarily placed her hand upon his arm and replied, "I would've asked you to have done so anyway. We've no interest in keeping information from the police. But I apologise for deceiving you earlier. I wanted to look at the shawl to satisfy myself that it indeed belonged to Mrs Roberts."

Mr Queshire smiled and said, "I can at least ease your mind in that respect. There's no possibility the shawl you saw on the dummy yesterday could've belonged to Mrs Roberts for none of the items we sell are second-hand."

"Come, come, Mr Queshire," Lady Owston teased with a wagging finger.

Mr Queshire's smile vanished as he enquired in a hard tone, "Do you call me a liar?"

Lady Owston blinked and moved her head back at the dramatic change of demeanour. Staring at him in stunned silence for several moments, she then kept her voice soft as she said, "In actuality, Mr Queshire… I do."

Mr Queshire's facial muscles tightened, and a coldness entered his eyes.

"I've purchased goods from your store that have clear signs of previous wear," Lady Owston continued. "Clear to those with an eye for these things anyway."

Mr Queshire thrust back his chair and stood over her.

Lady Owston held her breath.

"You have found me out," he said. "And now have me at a disadvantage." Placing his fists upon the table, he leaned over them and enquired in a low voice, "What do you intend to do with your… newfound information?"

"I shan't be making scandalous revelations in the *Women's Signal*, if that's your concern," she replied with indignation.

"Many would be interested in publishing such a story, however, given my store's reputation," Mr Queshire straightened and, peering down his nose at her, enquired, "Do you mean to say such monetary incentive isn't appealing to you?"

"I have enough money already, thank *you*!"

Mr Queshire furrowed his brow. "The knowledge has no value to you, then?"

"On the contrary; it's *highly* valuable as far as Mrs Roberts' murder is concerned."

The corner of Mr Queshire's mouth twitched, and he folded his arms across his chest. "If I should tell you all I know about the shawl, may I rely upon your utter discretion regarding how I came to own it?"

"You may," Lady Owston replied.

Mr Queshire freed a hand to rub his chin as he turned away and considered his predicament.

"Very well," he said and retook his seat. "I'll place my trust in you."

"Thank you," Lady Owston replied with a contrived smile. Relieved an escalation of their disagreement had been avoided, she enquired, "When did the shawl come into the store's possession?"

"I don't know," Mr Queshire replied. Standing, he pushed aside a stack of boxes to reveal a large, wicker basket secured with a thick, dark-brown, leather strap. He said, "I came across it among the donated garments in here. Two nights ago, I believe."

"The night Mrs Roberts was murdered?" Lady Owston enquired, feeling a chill course through her.

Mr Queshire spun around with wide eyes and replied, "You're right... it was." He dropped back onto his chair and muttered, "Dear God..."

"When did you put it on the dummy?"

"I..." His glazed eyes glanced over the table as if searching for the answer. "Inspected it for faults," he met her gaze, "as I do with all the garments we receive, and mended any flaws. Sometimes I have to make additions to garments to lift their overall quality, but I don't recall... no, I didn't need to with the shawl. I put it on the dummy once I was finished—the same night I found it in the basket." The tension in both his face and form eased and a weak smile slipped onto his face. "It's remarkably easy to sell worn garments as new with a few adjustments. You're the first to notice the deception. New fabric is so expensive..." He released a deep sigh. "I honestly had no idea it was Mrs Roberts' until you pointed out the connection."

"Inspector Woolfe didn't notice the shawl at all?"

"No; he asked me if I could recall what Mrs Roberts had been wearing when I saw her last. I couldn't."

"Do you know who donated it?"

"We don't keep a record. For obvious reasons."

"Who else has access to the basket?"

"Mr Suggitt." Mr Queshire settled into his chair and rested his arm upon the table. "We've kept it a secret from even the assistants for fear of loose lips fuelled by greedy hearts."

"Has Mr Suggitt ever told his wife about its existence? Could she have put something in there without your knowledge?"

"I suppose she could have…" Mr Queshire frowned. "I would be disappointed if Mr Suggitt *had* told her of the basket, though."

"Why?"

"Betrayal of professional trust, naturally." Mr Queshire tilted his head as, in a quiet voice, he enquired, "Do you believe her to be involved in her sister's death, then?"

"I'd prefer not to speculate at this point in our investigations," Lady Owston replied in a subtle tone. "May I ask you to check the basket now? For her other items of clothing."

"Of course," Mr Queshire replied, and the two rose to their feet. With Lady Owston beside him, he opened the basket and peered into the mound of fabric. He shifted several garments aside and delved into the deeper layers. After comparing a couple of items against Lady Owston's sketch, he dropped them into the basket and closed the lid. "Nothing, I'm afraid."

"Bother…" Lady Owston murmured. Clasping her hands together as she returned to her seat, she went on,

"Never mind." She offered him a weak smile. "You were here *all* night, correct?"

"Yes; my rooms are upstairs, as you know," Mr Queshire replied as he sat across from her. "I worked in the store until eleven thirty and retired to bed."

"Did you not eat at all?"

"Only a cold supper which I ate here in the storeroom."

"And *no one* came to the store after it had closed?" Lady Owston probed.

"No one whatsoever," Mr Queshire replied with a shake of his head. In a voice laden with regret, he added, "I wish I could be of more help."

A quiet knock sounded from the door, followed by the swift entrance of Miss Rose Galway.

"How many times must I tell you to *wait* to be invited into a room before doing so?" Mr Queshire scolded.

"I'm sorry, sur," Miss Galway replied, bowing her head. "I forgot, sur."

"It's fine… no harm done," Mr Queshire replied with a soft sigh. "What is it?"

"Miss Webster is here, sur," Miss Galway replied. "She and her friend want to speak to Lady Owston."

"Ah yes—" Lady Owston began but stopped when she thought she'd caught a glimpse of someone she knew exiting the *Staff only* room at the top of the stairs. Realising neither Miss Galway or Mr Queshire had seen the same, though, she decided against airing her suspicions and said, "I asked them to meet me here." She rose to her feet. "Thank you, once again, for sparing your precious time, Mr Queshire."

"You're most welcome," Mr Queshire replied as he stood. "Rose, you can make amends for your behaviour by escorting Lady Owston to her friends."

"Yes, sur," Miss Galway replied.

"Good day to you, Lady Owston," Mr Queshire said, leaving the storeroom to be beckoned over to the perfumery department by a customer. Meanwhile, Miss Galway led Lady Owston back through the crowd to where Miss Webster and Mr Maxwell were waiting at the millinery department.

"If that is all, madam, I must return to my counter," Miss Galway said once they'd greeted one another.

"Actually, Miss Galway, there is something further," Miss Webster said.

"What, miss?" Miss Galway enquired with trepidation.

"May you explain why your name appears in the poison book at *Drummond's Pharmaceutical Chemists* shop?" Miss Webster enquired.

TWELVE

"You'd better have a bloody good reason for waking me," threatened a man's voice as he pulled open the door. His jaw was covered in thick stubble and his gaunt, weathered face aged him beyond his thirty-five years. At only five feet tall, it was clear childhood malnourishment had stunted his growth. Yet his enlarged biceps and broad shoulders suggested a long career in manual labouring. He was attired in a pair of old, brown-cotton trousers, darned socks, and a stained vest. Once his burnt umber-brown eyes had adjusted to the gloom of the corridor, they regarded Mr Snyder and Miss Dexter in turn. He noticed the former's worn complexion and calloused hands first. Marking him as a working man in his mind, therefore, he lowered his guard a little. The higher quality of Miss Dexter's attire marked her out as middle-class, but he thought she looked about as threatening as a damp rag. Retrieving a thin coat from a hook on the back of the door, he put it on and enquired, "Who're you?"

"I'm Mr Snyder and this 'ere's Miss Dexter. Can we talk to Mr Roberts?"

"You don't look like peelers," the man countered.

"That's 'cause we're not," Mr Snyder replied. "I'm a cabman, and Miss Dexter's an artist. We're also Bow Street Society members. Are Mr Abraham Roberts and Miss Regina home?"

"I'm Abraham Roberts. Regina's out working. Maryanna's sister said you'd be coming by." Mr Roberts stepped aside. "Come in."

The home was a single room approximately fifteen feet long by ten feet wide. The wall to one's left upon entering was dominated by a coal-burning stove. A cubby hole opposite held a straw-filled mattress that served as a bed for all. Mr Roberts crossed the room and pulled the hole's faded, ochre-coloured curtain back into place to hide the bed's disturbed blankets. In the centre of the room was a square table and three mismatched chairs. Cupboards with broken doors held clothing of all shapes and sizes, whilst a handful of garments hung above the stove to dry. Mr Roberts invited his guests to sit and went to the stove to prepare some tea. Mr Snyder took the chair facing the stove while Miss Dexter sat to his left.

"Do you live here alone with your daughter?" Miss Dexter enquired.

"Yeah," Mr Roberts replied as he lined up three mugs on the table. "We had another family sharing with us, but they left for America last week."

Shifting her gaze to the drying clothes, Miss Dexter noticed two dresses which were markedly different in both style and size. Glancing around the cramped room, she saw it was tidy and well swept. Although she assumed Miss Regina Roberts must've done the housework, the contrast in dresses made her question whether Mr Roberts was being honest with them. For, unless Miss Roberts had experienced a dramatic change in weight recently, Miss Dexter would swear the dresses belonged to two different women. The kettle's shrill whistle disrupted her ponderings. She watched Mr Roberts pour the hot water into the mugs through a tiny tea strainer containing a meagre clump of leaves. Deciding any insinuation Mr Roberts was lying to them would be ill-received so soon after their meeting, she pushed aside her suspicions and took a sip of the weak tea.

"You drink French Breakfast coffee, Mr Roberts?" Mr Snyder enquired, pointing to a shelf on the stove's right.

Mr Roberts glanced over his shoulder at it and replied, "No, Diana bought Maryanna that last Christmas; forgot we even had it." Even from where they were sitting, the Bow Streeters could see the coffee tin wasn't covered in as much dust as the rest of the shelf's contents. Mr Robert's use of Mrs Suggitt's first name had also piqued their interest.

"Are you close to Mr and Mrs Suggitt?" Miss Dexter enquired.

"They've treated us well," Mr Roberts replied in a quiet voice as he warmed his hands on the mug. "Despite all that Maryanna done."

"They were here yesterday, weren't they?" Miss Dexter enquired. "Mrs Suggitt loved her sister dearly."

"As did I," Mr Roberts snapped. "It was the drink what made Maryanna the way she was. I done my best, we all did, but she wouldn't have any of it. In the end, she was drinking away the housekeeping money." He bowed his head and, rubbing the mug with his thumb, stared into the dark liquid. He muttered, "I couldn't let her do that." He furrowed his brow and hunched his shoulders over the mug. "Regina's the only one I got left now."

"You said she woz workin'?" Mr Snyder enquired.

"Yeah…" Mr Roberts replied in a voice strained by emotion. "She helps sell flowers at Covent Garden Market." He took a mouthful of tea. "Any way she can, really. Anything to make ends meet."

"Was she working the night her mother died?" Miss Dexter enquired with reluctance. She detested the insinuation the question posed, despite knowing the question's importance.

"Only until it got dark," Mr Roberts replied. "Then she came home, and we had supper together."

"Did either of you go out again after that?" Mr Snyder enquired.

"No, Regina and I got knocked up at four o'clock," Mr Roberts replied. "I then left to sleep outside the dock gates, and she went to the Market."

"When will your daughter be home?" Miss Dexter

enquired.

Mr Roberts frowned, prompting Miss Dexter to think he didn't know.

"Depends on the selling, don't it?" Mr Roberts enquired in return. Alas, Miss Dexter couldn't hope to give him the answer. "Regina's the wandering sort, too, if there's no work to be had," Mr Roberts continued. "She picks up railway ticket stubs and brings them home." He took a swig of tea. "When it's dark is when she comes home."

"Do you sleep outside the gates every night?" Mr Snyder enquired.

"You've got to if you're not a Royal; only way you give yourself a good chance of being picked by the ganger is to be at the front," Mr Roberts replied.

Miss Dexter looked to Mr Snyder for clarification.

"Royals are the blokes on the ganger's list," Mr Roberts explained instead. "You get on that and you can be all but sure you'll be picked to unload the goods." He rubbed his neck. "The rest of us've got to take our chances."

Feeling her cheeks warm, Miss Dexter gave a meek smile of thanks and sipped her tea.

"Woz you picked this mornin'?" Mr Snyder enquired.

"Nah," Mr Roberts replied. "All the Royals got picked but the quay-gangers didn't want any others. Sometimes a ship comes in late, so I waited around but nothing."

"What time did you leave?" Mr Snyder enquired.

"Was about two o'clock this afternoon, give or take a few," Mr Roberts replied. "When I got home is when I was told about Maryanna—found an inspector here."

"Where woz your daughter?" Mr Snyder enquired.

"Gone to stay with Diana and Clement, he told

162

me," Mr Roberts replied.

"Mr Roberts," Miss Dexter began in a tentative voice. "I know this may sound a queer question, but do you own any hessian sacks?"

"What?" Mr Roberts enquired, confused. Glancing around afterward, though, he shook his head and replied, "Nah."

"And you haven't had any in the past few days?" Miss Dexter enquired with a discreet, visual sweep of the room to confirm his claim's validity.

"Maybe when Regina got a bushel of potatoes?" Mr Snyder interjected.

"We can't afford them by the bushel," Mr Roberts replied and waited for any further questions from the two Bow Streeters. When none came, he resumed his hunched position, gripped his mug, and enquired in a quiet voice, "Police told me she was found on Oxford Street... cut up. That right?"

"Yes," Miss Dexter replied, softly.

Mr Roberts put his elbows upon the table and bowed his head into his forearms. As he clasped his hands above his head, his shoulders began to shake. This was followed by the quiet sound of sobbing as he lowered his hands to grip the back of his head and dug his nails into his skin. "Get out..." Mr Roberts' muffled voice demanded. "*Please*, just... get out!"

With her heart aching at the sight of the poor man's grief, Miss Dexter stood without hesitation and allowed Mr Snyder to lead her from the room. She remained close to him as they descended the stairs. Feeling her own eyes stinging with unshed tears, she whispered, "His grief was sincere, Sam. Whatever the cause of it... his grief was sincere."

* * *

Miss Rose Galway had the distinct feeling of déjà vu as she once again sat at the storeroom's table. Sitting opposite her was Lady Owston with Miss Webster and Mr Maxwell standing behind her. The din of conversations and movement from the shop floor was muffled by the door. Nevertheless, its sound jolted Miss Galway's mind into action, and she straightened in her chair, saying, "I should fetch Mr Queshire."

"No, Rose," Lady Owston replied. "It's time for you to speak freely, and openly, with us."

"But I've already been doing that," Miss Galway replied, rubbing her hands within her lap.

"You didn't tell Miss Webster or me the truth of the room at the top of the stairs," Lady Owston pointed out.

"But there's nothing to tell—!" Miss Galway began.

"*How* can I trust you?" Lady Owston interrupted. "To risk my own reputation with Miss Trent when you *still* refuse to cooperate with me?"

"Please, Milady," Miss Galway begged. "It's nowt to do with Mrs Roberts' murder." She pressed her blouse's cuff to the underside of her nose and sniffed.

"Could you give her your handkerchief, please, Agnes?" Lady Owston requested.

"Yes, Milady," Miss Webster replied. Retrieving her handkerchief from her pocket, she offered it to Miss Galway and enquired, "Why was your name written in Mr Drummond's poison book the day before her murder?"

"I bought it for Mr Suggitt, didn't I?" Miss Galway snapped as she took the handkerchief and wiped her nose with it. "Who'd said Mr Queshire wanted it for rats in the cellar." She blew her nose. "None of us killed her."

"Where were you the night Mrs Roberts died?" Mr Maxwell enquired as he sat down beside her.

"At the lodgings 'round the corner with all the other assistants," Miss Galway replied as she crushed the handkerchief into a ball and wiped her eyes. "Ask anyone; I've got no reason to murder the bloody woman."

"None of that now—" Lady Owston scolded.

"Why not?" Miss Galway interrupted. "You're all saying I killed her… or suggesting it was someone here. Why don't you ask her mum? She was the one who disowned her."

"Oh?" Miss Webster enquired as she placed a reassuring hand upon Lady Owston's shoulder.

"Yeah," Miss Galway replied. "You heard what Mrs Roberts did here the other day; she was a nasty piece of work. Pulled the wool over her sister's eyes and her daughter's, but not Mr Suggitt's or Mrs Yates'."

"Her mother?" Mr Maxwell enquired.

Miss Galway nodded and continued, "Her mum hated the way she treated her husband and always told her she'd abandoned her daughter when she'd chosen the drink. Maryanna was her dad's daughter, that's what she used to call her. He died from the drink, leaving the family destitute."

"How do you know all this?" Mr Maxwell enquired.

"Hear things, don't I?" Miss Galway replied with a shrug of her shoulder. "Things said by Mr Suggitt and his wife when they think no one's listening. Her mum told Mrs Suggitt that her sister was squeezing her for all she was worth, and she was a fool for letting her. That Mrs Roberts was past all hope, and she should worry about Regina and Mr Roberts more. Mrs Suggitt couldn't take that though, could she? Was always in here, complaining to her husband about how it wasn't fair and how Mrs Roberts just needed help. From what I saw of her, the only help she needed was directions to the nearest pub."

"You liked Mrs Roberts as much as her mother

did, then," Miss Webster coolly remarked.

"Doesn't matter what I thought of her," Miss Galway replied as she put the handkerchief on the table. "I'm just telling you what I've seen and heard."

The three Bow Streeters exchanged glances.

"I didn't kill her!" Miss Galway insisted. "I got the poison for Mr Suggitt like I've done loads of times! Ask him! Ask Mr Drummond! Ask Mr Queshire!"

"Calm yourself," Lady Owston soothed.

Miss Galway folded her arms across her chest and, nibbling on her thumbnail, rapidly tapped her foot.

"Calm yourself," Lady Owston repeated with a soft smile.

Miss Galway lowered her hand and wiped her eyes with her blouse's cuff.

"Who drinks the French Breakfast coffee?" Mr Maxwell enquired, pointing to a shelf behind her.

"Only Mr Queshire and Mr Suggitt are allowed to," Miss Galway replied as she turned in her chair to look at it.

"Who else has access to this room?" Miss Webster enquired.

"Anyone, I suppose," Miss Galway replied. "The door isn't kept locked."

THIRTEEN

The remaining chemist shops within a ten-minute walk of the *Queshire Department Store* failed to yield any further results for their persons of interest. The time it had taken Miss Webster and Mr Maxwell to gain access to each establishment's poison book meant they'd spent two-thirds of the available daylight at Oxford Street. By the time they'd arrived at *Eastleigh's* chemist shop on Queen Street at four thirty, dusk was drawing in. The second address Mrs Suggitt had supplied them—that of Mr Abraham Roberts and his daughter, Regina—was located on the adjacent Moore Street. Whereas Booth's Poverty Maps classified Queen Street's residents as being "fairly comfortable," those on Moore Street were deemed the "lowest class" of the "vicious, semi-criminal." By stark contrast, Edgware Road to the east of Moore Street housed the "well-to-do" middle classes. Finally, the residents of Nutford Place to the south of Moore Street were akin to those of Queen Street.

The façade of *Eastleigh's* chemist shop had paint crumbling from its grubby sign and a window marred by dust on the inside and soot on the outside. Additional signage advertising a photographic service also hinted at the shop being in poor financial health. When Miss Webster and Mr Maxwell entered the shop, a bell shook above their heads but made no sound. The interior's weak gaslight and dark, wooden panelling exaggerated the gloom caused by the fading daylight, whilst the dusty, stained floor and yellowing advertisements echoed the façade's drabness. A closed door stood opposite the main entrance and a large counter ran alongside the shop's right-hand side. To the Bow Streeter's surprise, the proprietor was nowhere to be seen.

Approaching the counter, Mr Maxwell lifted the

hatch and took a bottle of arsenic from the shelf. Realising anyone could do as he had, with the chemist being none-the-wiser if the thief were quick, Mr Maxwell felt nauseous and replaced the bottle. The idea had also occurred to Miss Webster as she joined Mr Maxwell behind the counter, checked the bottle for herself, and then crossed the room to open the other door. Finding a set of steep, narrow stairs spiralling upward to a closed door, she listened a moment but could only hear muffled voices.

"Photographic session in progress. Please ring bell for assistance." Mr Maxwell read aloud from a small card he'd found propped against the cash register. "We shan't be doing *that*, Mr Eastleigh."

"It nonetheless means he is nearby," Miss Webster replied. She left the door ajar and joined Mr Maxwell behind the counter once more. "Upstairs, I believe. It must be where he carries out his photography." Noticing a ledger sitting on a shelf beneath the countertop, she slipped it out and discovered it was the poison book. "Listen for any sound of Mr Eastleigh or his customer approaching the stairs," she instructed as she found the record for the day of Mrs Roberts' death and worked backwards.

"Right…" Mr Maxwell replied, smoothing down his frockcoat and heading over to the door to listen.

Miss Webster ran her finger down the column of names but found none which were familiar either on the day prior to Mrs Roberts' murder or the two days previous. Pursing her lips as she discovered more of the same on the next page, she then paused as she caught sight of a name she knew—*Mrs Sarah Yates.* She mused aloud, "Miss Galway didn't tell us Mrs Yates' first name."

"Pardon?" Mr Maxwell enquired.

The door at the top of the stairs opened and a man's voice said, "Bring your wife and children back tomorrow, Mr Fields, and I'll capture their likenesses as well as I have yours."

Miss Webster looked along the row but garnered little additional information.

Two pairs of feet thudded their way down the stairs, and Mr Maxwell retreated to the counter.

Miss Webster memorised Mrs Sarah Yates' entry in the poison book and slipped it back onto the shelf. She'd just managed to get back onto the other side of the counter when the door swung open and a large-set man stepped down into the shop. Following him was an equally stout man with thick, unkempt, blond hair, a bulbous, red nose, and beady, green eyes.

"Goodbye, Mr Fields," said the blond-haired man.

"Goodbye, Mr Eastleigh," replied the large-set man.

Noticing Miss Webster and Mr Maxwell by the counter once Mr Fields had left, Mr Eastleigh enquired, "Can I help you at all?"

"N—No… thank you," Mr Maxwell replied.

"You don't appear to have the lozenges we need," Miss Webster interjected. "Good day to you."

"Good day…" Mr Eastleigh replied, with a scratch of his head, as the Bow Streeters left.

"What did you say about Miss Galway?" Mr Maxwell enquired as he and Miss Webster walked briskly toward their rendezvous with Mr Snyder and Miss Dexter on Edgware Road.

"She didn't tell us Mrs Yates' first name," Miss Webster replied. "I found a record of Mrs Sarah Yates purchasing arsenic four days prior to Mrs Roberts' murder. The reason given was an infestation of mice. I'd be interested to hear how Mr Snyder and Miss Dexter's visit to the Roberts' residence went, too."

"Why?"

"Because the address belonging to the Mrs Sarah

Yates in the poison book is the same as Mr Abraham Roberts. It may be two families share the same living space but, if this is so, it would be an incredible coincidence."

FOURTEEN

Founded in 1892 by journalist Frances Low, the *Writers'*
Club aimed to assist female authors who, in the main,
devoted themselves to writing pieces for the journalistic
press and magazines. Occupying the ground floor of
Hastings House on Norfolk Street, its proximity to the
Strand and Fleet Street meant those wishing to leave copy
of their work at newspaper and magazine houses could do
so on their way home. Although the club lacked member
accommodation, it nonetheless had other excellent
facilities, such as a dining room, kitchen, cloak room, two
reception rooms, and a writing room with a strict policy of
absolute silence. For the ladies wishing to spend the day at
the club, a plain dinner, tea, and supper could be had at a
moderate cost. Guests of members could also be
entertained with an afternoon tea every Friday; something
Lady Owston had taken advantage of on numerous
occasions.

At present, she was reading the latest membership
applications pinned to the bulletin board above the mantel
shelf in one of the reception rooms. She knew Princess
Christian was the *Writers' Club*'s honorary president,
while Lady Seton, the Duchess of Sutherland, and the
novelist Mrs. G. Linnaeus Banks were among its many
vice presidents. Yet none of those distinguished ladies had
been the customer Lady Owston had seen leaving the
mysterious *Staff only* room at the *Queshire Department*
Store. That had been Mrs Peter Gromwell, a long-time
member and a creature of habit. Every Thursday, Mrs
Gromwell would dine at the *Writers' Club* while her
husband dined at his—and today happened to be Thursday.

Hearing Mrs Gromwell's voice in the main hall,
complaining about the inconsideration of a British winter,
Lady Owston faced the doorway and saw another of the

club's members pass. When Mrs Gromwell then followed, though, she stilled the moment she looked within. She was a woman of average height in her late fifties. Wiry, washed-out, brown hair was pushed beneath a modest, beetroot-purple, square-brimmed bonnet with a loose-cloth back. The bonnet's brim cast the top half of her face in shadow, while its strings were tied behind the flaccid roll hanging from her chin. Her dress followed tradition in its style and fit—wide skirts, narrowed shoulders, and a marked bustle at the rear. Her corset, though shapely, wasn't as tight as it may have been in her youth. Her light-olive eyes widened as she regarded Lady Owston who offered a smile of invitation. Yet, rather than join her, Mrs Gromwell hurried from sight instead.

"Mrs Gromwell?" Lady Owston called as she rushed to catch her up. Finding her in the main hall, still, she approached and repeated, "Mrs Gromwell?"

Mrs Gromwell spun around and, with a contrived smile, said, "Lady Owston, I didn't see you there."

"Well, we are *all* getting *rather* short-sighted in our old age, aren't we?" Lady Owston replied in a sickly-sweet tone. "I thought I saw you at the *Queshire Department Store* earlier."

"You did…?" Mrs Gromwell enquired in a soft, trembling voice.

"Yes," Lady Owston replied, "coming out of the room at the top of the stairs." She looked up. "Now *what* is the name of that department again?"

"The salon?"

"No, no, the *other* door at the top of the stairs."

"I really do not know what you mean…" Mrs Gromwell murmured.

"Surely you know which department you were in?" Lady Owston enquired and gestured toward the second reception room. "Perhaps if we ask one of the other ladies—?"

"*No!*" Mrs Gromwell cried. "I *tell* you I do not *know*. Now, *please*, leave it be." She attempted to exit the hall but halted when Lady Owston stepped into her path.

"I cannot," Lady Owston replied in a quiet, sombre voice. "A woman was murdered on Oxford Street two nights ago. Whether the room at the top of the stairs has some bearing on the matter or not, I *must* know what is in it. Quite honestly, I'm losing my patience with it, for everyone is hiding its contents as if it were the Ark of the Covenant." She put a hand on Mrs Gromwell's arm. "Whatever it is, please know you may rely upon my absolute discretion."

"Peter doesn't even know," Mrs Gromwell confessed in a whisper.

"Know about what?" Lady Owston enquired as she moved in closer.

"My shame," Mrs Gromwell whispered.

Lady Owston's mind was at once filled with all manner of possibilities. Intrigued, and yet fearful of what she may hear, she lowered her voice and enquired, "What have you done…?"

"I've deceived you all…" Mrs Gromwell replied.

The door to the dining room opened behind her and two of their fellow club members entered the hall. Due to the limited space, Lady Owston was obliged to remove her hand from Mrs Gromwell's arm to allow them to pass. Mrs Gromwell slipped away at once and, within seconds, Lady Owston had lost sight of her.

"*Bother,*" Lady Owston muttered under her breath and peeked into the dining room. Seeing no sign of her quarry, she moved onto the cloak room, kitchen, writing room, and both reception rooms. None sheltered Mrs Gromwell, however. Reluctantly conceding Mrs Gromwell must've left the *Writers' Club*, she returned to the dining room where three of her fellow members were deep in conversation.

"Mrs Gromwell didn't stay for her supper," Mrs MacBride remarked.

"How queer," Mrs Vaughn replied.

"Perhaps she was unwell?" Miss Karlson suggested. "She did look *frightfully* pale when she passed me in the hall."

"I do not know how you could tell under that bonnet of hers," Mrs MacBride replied with a smirk. "I've never seen her without it."

"You know... neither have I," Mrs Karlson admitted with astonishment.

Yet Lady Owston was only half-listening to their conversation. Having checked the time, she realised she'd be late for dinner with Miss Webster. Although such a thing wouldn't be important under normal circumstances, she and Miss Webster were due to attend an appointment with the Suggitts that evening. She therefore prepared to leave and, on her way out to hail a hansom cab, cried, "Good evening to you all!"

* * *

"Very handsome, dear," Mrs Maxwell complimented as her arthritic thumbs fumbled to straighten her son's midnight-blue cravat. Next, she smoothed out his white shirt and tugged down his black waistcoat embroidered with midnight-blue flowers. Standing upon her tiptoes, she used her fingers to brush the shoulders of his frock coat before she stepped back to admire him.

She was a petite woman with genial, dark-green eyes and impeccably pinned, auburn hair greying at the edges. In her late forties, she had a face as pale as porcelain with the occasional wrinkle in the corners of her eyes and mouth. She wore long, cream-coloured, silk gloves and an emerald-green, silk bustle gown with simple embellishments.

Mr Joseph Maxwell swallowed the lump forming in his throat and looked to the study door. He enquired, "Will you accompany me, Mother?"

"I will," she replied, "but only for as long as he tolerates my presence." She used her silk handkerchief to wipe the sweat from his palms and said, "Deep breath now," she smiled. "You know how your father detests any form of weakness."

"Yes, Mother."

"Good boy." She placed her hand upon his cheek and gazed lovingly into his eyes. Lowering it again after a few moments, she then took her own advice as she turned to the door and knocked.

"Come!" Mr Oliver Maxwell's voice commanded from the other side.

Mrs Maxwell entered with her son behind her and said, "Forgive me for disturbing you, but Joseph is here; he wishes to speak with you."

"He's early," Oliver Maxwell muttered. Sitting in an immense chair behind his desk, he finished the line of correspondence he'd been writing and held his pen between his hands. Casting a cold glance over his son, he twisted his brow and demanded, "*Well*? Out with it."

"I—I simply wanted to tell you that I've invited a lady to dine with us this evening," Joseph Maxwell replied, moving around his mother to stand in front of his father's desk.

Oliver's brow formed a hard line as he put down his pen and stood. In a cool, low voice he said, "I don't recall authorising such an invitation."

"You didn't, Father, which is why I wanted to speak with you before she arrives—"

"Who is she?" Oliver interrupted.

Joseph flinched and his heart raced. Yet, as he

thought of Miss Dexter, his heart rate slowed, and his body warmed with a flushing of his cheeks. He replied, "My fiancé, Father: Miss Georgina Dexter."

"Isn't that wonderful news?" Mrs Maxwell interjected.

"*Leave* us, woman," Oliver ordered.

Mrs Maxwell bowed her head and hurried from the room. When he heard the door close, Joseph felt like the room had grown larger and his father taller.

"The Dexter's are not a family I'm aware of," Oliver said as he advanced upon his son. "How did they come into their money?"

"Um, they d—didn't. Mr Dexter is a—a clerk, I believe," Joseph replied. The resultant scowl from his father forced his gaze to the floor, however.

"You *snivelling*, foolish *wretch,*" Oliver said through a clenched jaw. "You *dare* come to me and speak of a *wench* you have invited to *my* home and to *my* table?"

"She's not a wench, Father—"

"*Don't* lie to me! *You* are not *valuable* enough, or *charming* enough, to find a fiancé in a *day*!"

"I didn't—"

"You will cancel her dinner invitation and nullify your preposterous engagement." Oliver leaned over his son and, in a low voice, enquired, "Do I make myself clear?"

"I thought you'd be happy—"

"This family will *not* be shamed by your *vile, filthy* habits, Joseph!" Oliver glanced over his son's quaking form. "*Stop* shaking and do as I say!"

"Y—Yes, Fath—"

"*At once!*"

Joseph cowered at the yell before stumbling out the door, saying, "Y—yes, Father. Forgive m—me, Father. G—Goodbye, Father."

FIFTEEN

The *Turk's Head* public house was a dilapidated
establishment whose nightly entertainments included gin-
fuelled knife fights. Located on the corner where Edgware
Road met Queen Street, its interior was filled with round,
wooden tables and stout, unstable stools. Sun-faded church
pews beneath the dirty windows offered an uncomfortable
alternative. The windows were set at right angles to the
main door on the corner and promised 'fine ales' in
chipped, white paint. Meanwhile sparse, alcohol-soaked
sawdust was sprinkled across the floorboards with little
suggestion it had been changed in recent months. Despite
the pub's proximity to the wealthier neighbourhoods, its
regular patrons consisted of the "vicious, semi-criminal"
residents of Moore Street and the lane located to the rear
of Molyneux Street and south of John Street.

"And you are *quite* certain *this* is it?" Lady
Owston enquired as she gazed upon the pub's filthy
façade.

"Yes," Miss Webster replied. "I passed by earlier
today."

"*Please* do check again?"

Miss Webster retrieved Miss Trent's note from her
bag and read aloud, "The *Turk's Head* public house,
corner of Queen Street and Edgware Road."

"Evening, ladies," a deep voice greeted from
behind.

"*Mr* Snyder," Lady Owston said as she saw him
standing beneath the weak gaslight of the streetlamp.
Extending her gloved hands to him, which he took, she
continued, "We appear to have become confused in our
unerring enthusiasm to assist the Suggitts. Agnes is
convinced *this*," she indicated the pub, "is where we shall
be gathering. But *I* have reason to doubt her conviction—

purely based on what is inside, you understand. Agnes isn't *usually* wrong."

"Nah, this 'ere's the place," Mr Snyder replied.

Lady Owston's face crumpled, and Miss Webster smirked in triumph.

"I hope you didn't mind my not bringin' you 'ere," Mr Snyder continued. "But the Missus had my supper on the table and I'd not seen the little ones since this mornin'." He thumbed behind him. "I've got the cab tonight though, so I'll take you back."

"How very kind you are," Lady Owston replied in a flat tone.

"Not me… Miss Trent," Mr Snyder teased.

Lady Owston threw a momentary scowl his way before adjusting her coat and marching into the pub, saying, "Shall we go inside?" Commandeering a vacant pew to the right of the door, she plonked her bag onto her lap and hugged it. Miss Webster, having sat beside her, did the same and tried to ignore the suspicious looks from their fellow patrons.

"What are you ladies drinkin'?" Mr Snyder enquired.

"*Drinking*? In *here*?" Lady Owston scoffed. Surveying their surroundings, she twisted her lips as if she'd tasted something bitter. Realising her temperament wouldn't allow her to stay for long without being bolstered by alcohol, though, she glanced at the drinks on nearby tables and replied, "I'll have a sweet sherry. Agnes?"

"The same, please," Miss Webster replied.

"Wait a moment," Lady Owston instructed as she opened her bag.

"Keep your coin," Mr Snyder said. "I've got money enough."

"Oh… very well," Lady Owston replied and graced him with a warm smile. "Thank you, Mr Snyder."

"Thank you," Miss Webster repeated. Watching

178

him head over to the paltry bar, she then looked around the room for the fireplace. After much searching, she found it on the opposite side of the room. Not only was it small, but the flames it held were blocked from view by the many patrons sitting in between it and her. Relieved, she settled against the pew and looked back to the bar.

A haggard woman in her late fifties was serving behind it. Her dirty-blond hair was loosely pinned with several strands hanging about her face. She had permanent, large, dark rings under her puffy eyes and creased skin riddled with wrinkles. Her sunken cheeks and a narrow, flat nose gave her an almost witch-like appearance. A knitted, light-grey shawl was draped about her shoulders whilst a long, white-cotton apron covered her straight-lined, plain, dark-grey woollen dress.

Movement from the door suddenly diverted Miss Webster's attention, and she saw Mr Clement Suggitt standing there with Mr Edmund Queshire. In Mr Suggitt's hand was an envelope displaying the unmistakeable mark of the Bow Street Society in its top-right corner. Mr Suggitt said, "My wife's note from Miss Trent."

"I'm here at Mr Suggitt's request," Mr Queshire interjected.

"Please, sit, gentlemen," Lady Owston invited as she indicated the vacant stools opposite.

"Thank you," Mr Suggitt murmured and, checking the stool for dampness, sat. "Mrs Suggitt was too distressed by the note's arrival to attend this evening. She, like me, had assumed your enquiries to be over."

"Why? Because you'd asked them to be?" Miss Webster challenged.

Mr Suggitt took a deep breath and released it as a soft sigh. He replied, "I'm quite certain the police are capable of identifying, and arresting, Mrs Roberts' murderer. My wife agrees she should not have hired the Bow Street Society at all."

Lady Owston and Miss Webster exchanged glances.

"Miss Trent shall require Mrs Suggitt's formal withdrawal of her commission in writing," Miss Webster said.

Lady Owston couldn't recall such a clause yet, upon reflection, suspected Miss Webster was calling Mr Suggitt's bluff.

"I'll have her write Miss Trent first thing in the morning," Mr Suggitt replied.

Having taken a seat on the stool beside Mr Suggitt's, Mr Queshire now raised his hand and said with regret, "I may, inadvertently, be responsible for some of this confusion. I told Mr Suggitt of your discovery regarding Mrs Robert's shawl, of it having been unwittingly… 'passed on' by my store."

"My wife takes much comfort from knowing it's found a good home, Edmund," Mr Suggitt replied with a half-hearted smile.

"Thank you," Mr Queshire murmured. In a louder voice, he went on, "After you'd left, Lady Owston, I naturally considered the other clothing depicted in your sketch. I checked our stock again and the remainder of the storeroom, but there was no trace of them anywhere."

Mr Suggitt gave a beleaguered sigh and admitted, "I have no recollection of the mannequin from that morning."

"You were not the one who procured the shawl and placed it into the store's 'possession,' then?" Miss Webster enquired as she prepared to transcribe their conversation.

"Pardon?" Mr Suggitt enquired.

"Perhaps on behalf of Mrs Roberts herself?" Miss Webster probed. "Or your wife?" Pausing to refer back to her previous notes, she continued, "You told Miss Dexter the shawl was of little monetary value. Being her brother-in-law though, you could've gifted a generous sum in exchange for it, correct?"

"Absolutely not," Mr Queshire interjected. "The items are donated, not purchased."

"Perhaps such an arrangement applies to others, Mr Queshire," Miss Webster replied. "But your wife had always held a deep-seated concern for her sister, Mr Suggitt. Furthermore, you knew of the arrangement at the department store. If Mrs Roberts had approached you— possibly the very night she died—and asked to sell the shawl, would you have not granted her request? If only to appease your wife's troubled mind? Or, perhaps, you have broken Mr Queshire's trust and told your wife of the arrangement concerning donated stock? *She,* in that case, could've been the one to place it in the—"

"*Enough!*" Mr Suggitt cried and leapt to his feet.

The corner of Miss Webster's mouth twitched whilst her eyes blinked out of reflex at the sudden movement. Her stoic expression remained firm, however. At the same time, Lady Owston had released a soft gasp and pressed herself against the pew's back.

"Clement," Mr Queshire began as he stood. "Please sit down—"

"*No,*" Mr Suggitt snapped. "I don't have to stay here and be accused of such dastardly things—and by a woman no less!"

"Why is it you become irate whenever the idea of Mrs Roberts receiving money from you is mentioned?" Miss Webster enquired in a cool tone.

"Because my financial affairs are precisely that, *MY* financial affairs!" Mr Suggitt cried.

"Oi!" the haggard-looking barmaid shouted across the room.

Mr Suggitt spun around and straightened the moment he saw her face. The pub's other patrons, having had their peace disturbed by the wealthy man, watched the spectacle.

The barmaid repeatedly thrust her finger in Mr Suggitt's direction as she warned, "You being my daughter's husband, don't stop me from getting the landlord to toss you out on your ear."

Mr Suggitt balled his hands into fists, gritted his teeth, and glowered at the woman with more malice than was necessary to remind someone of their place. Holding his stance for a few, tense moments, he then turned upon his heel and sat. His hard gaze and rigid back remained, however.

"Such *unnecessary* behaviour," Mr Queshire remarked as the other patrons resumed their conversations.

"How did you know my mother-in-law worked here?" Mr Suggitt enquired in a low voice.

"We didn't," Lady Owston replied. "Miss Trent simply chose this location as she thought it was unlikely Inspector Woolfe would find us here. I presume she was already familiar with the establishment. *Personally,* neither I nor Agnes has *ever* set foot within its walls before tonight. Good evening, Mr Locke!"

"Forgive my lateness, Lady Owston, but I was delayed at the Palladium," Mr Locke explained.

Mr Queshire stood and offered his hand to him, saying, "Mr Edmund Queshire, owner of the *Queshire Department Store* on Oxford Street."

Mr Locke removed his glove and, taking the offered hand, replied, "Mr Percival Locke. Illusionist, owner of the *Paddington Palladium*, and member of the Bow Street Society."

"Mr Clement Suggitt, Assistant Manager at the *Queshire Department Store*," Mr Suggitt introduced as he, too, stood and extended his hand to the newcomer.

"My sincere condolences to you and your wife," Mr Locke replied, shaking his hand.

Meanwhile, Mr Snyder watched the haggard-looking barmaid pour his pint from a tap inserted into one of two barrels standing on a counter behind the bar. Lady Owston and Miss Webster's sweet sherries had already been poured from a dusty bottle on the shelf above. Mr Snyder swept his thumb across his nostril and enquired, "You'll be Mrs Sarah Yates, then?"

"How'd you know?" Mrs Yates enquired in return as she put his pint on the bar and wiped her hands upon her apron. "You're not one of the regulars."

"I've been workin' for your daughter, tryin' to find out who done in her sister," Mr Snyder replied. "Me and the other Bow Street Society members."

"Waste of bloody money," Mrs Yates scoffed and wrapped her shawl tight about herself. As she'd moved, Mr Snyder thought he'd caught a glint of gold on her marriage finger. The light behind the bar was too dim to be certain, however. "Was probably one of her customers who did it," Mrs Yates continued. "I told Diana that but, like always, she wouldn't take a blind bit of notice of what I had to say. Was the same when Maryanna was alive, the devious beggar. All she cared about was the drink, sod everything, and everyone, else."

"Is that why you're livin' with your other son-in-law?" Mr Snyder enquired.

Mrs Yates lifted her head sharply and narrowed her eyes. Inclining her head, she enquired in an accusatory tone, "Did Abraham tell you that?"

"Nah," Mr Snyder replied.

Gripping the corners of her shawl, she folded her arms across her chest and challenged, "How'd you know, then?"

"Saw your dresses hangin' 'bove the stove when I woz there talkin' to Mr Roberts today," Mr Snyder replied. Although, truth be told, he'd only been guessing at the dresses belonging to Mrs Yates. "Thought 'e would've told you we'd been."

Mrs Yates unfolded her arms and replied, "I've been here all day, ain't I?" She glanced along the bar to ensure there weren't any customers waiting before adding, "Anyway, someone had to take care of him and her daughter when she walked out on them."

"I thought 'e told her to leave?"

"Only because he caught her stealing the housekeeping money," Mrs Yates retorted. "And that was her choice, weren't it? Take the money to get the drink or keep it to put food in her daughter's belly. She chose the gin. Was her father's daughter all right, bloody drunks. I hate 'em."

"But you work in a pub," Mr Snyder pointed out as he handed over the monies for their drinks.

"Never let 'er come in 'ere, did I? She was barred for running her mouth off—as usual. Anyway, we've all got to do what we can to make ends meet, don't we?"

Mr Snyder hummed in agreement and took a sip from his pint. Feeling her eyes boring into him, though, he said, "Only havin' the one."

"I prefer lemonade myself," Mrs Yates replied as she filled a glass from the jug on the shelf.

"Woz you workin' the night she died?" Mr Snyder enquired.

"Yeah." Mrs Yates took a sip from the glass. "Wouldn't of made a difference to her if I'd not been."

"Why's that?"

"We wasn't talking on account of her drinking, and of her pulling the bloody wool over Diana and Regina's eyes." She made a dismissive sweep of her hand. "I tried telling them she'd only break their 'earts but…" She sighed. "What can you do?"

"What time did you work to?"

184

"Half past ten. If you don't believe me, I can fetch the landlord; he won't talk to the police, but he'll talk to someone from the Bow Street Society. You done right by that blind fella."

"Nah, I don't think we'll need that," Mr Snyder replied with a soft smile.

"Good," Mrs Yates said. Leaning over the bar, she continued in a quieter voice, "I'm s'pposed to work until eleven but I had an old friend come in on one of the ships. Sailed back out this morning, he did."

Mr Snyder didn't need any further explanation; if her words weren't enough, the wistful look in her eyes certainly was. Thumbing over his shoulder toward Mr Suggitt, he enquired, "You don't think much of him? Your other son-in-law?"

Mrs Yates glanced over to Mr Suggitt and replied, "He loves Diana right enough but still likes to lord it over the rest of us." Taking another sip of lemonade, she lowered her voice once more and added, "But he doesn't know that I know he was in here asking after Maryanna the night she died."

"How come?"

"Asked Mr Ratchett if he'd seen her, didn't he?" Mrs Yates replied with a smirk. "And Mr Ratchett told me he'd been in. God knows why he was wanting her at that time of night."

"What time woz it?"

"Dunno, but it was before I left because Mr Ratchett told me about half past nine," Mrs Yates replied. "I was upstairs seeing to Mrs Ratchett then; poor blighter's been sick for days." She drank some more lemonade. "When Mr Ratchett told him she wasn't 'ere, Mr Suggitt asked if she'd been in at all that night. When Mr Ratchett told him she hadn't, Mr Suggitt got all agitated and left again." She finished her drink and put the empty glass under the bar.

"You bought arsenic from *Eastleigh's* chemist shop, yeah?" Mr Snyder enquired.

"Yeah," Mrs Yates replied. "Mr Ratchett wanted it for the mice he got upstairs." She swept her gaze over him and revealed, "I read what they're saying in the 'papers. Killed with arsenic, wasn't she? I'll save you the trouble and tell you now." She chopped the air once with the side of her hand. "I might've wanted to throttle her at times, but I didn't do my own daughter in."

Mr Snyder nodded and, hooking two fingers around the sherry glasses, picked up his pint and said, "Thanks for the drinks." He returned to the table and served the ladies their drinks. Putting his pint down, he retrieved another stool from nearby and placed it between Mr Locke's and the pew's end. Due to the bulk of his frame, though, he was obliged to not only set the stool back from the table but also tuck his arms in as he sat.

"This is Mr Samuel Snyder, the Bow Street Society's cab driver and, I must say, *invaluable* expert on London's transportation networks," Lady Owston introduced to Mr Suggitt and Mr Queshire.

Mr Snyder twisted sideways on his stool to shake their hands. Once the formalities were over, he said, "Had a good little chat with your mother-in-law, Mr Suggitt. How come you and your wife never told us Mrs Yates is livin' with Mr Roberts?"

"I didn't think it was relevant," Mr Suggitt replied. "And I am supposing my wife thought so, too."

"Even though Mrs Yates and Mrs Roberts didn't get along?" Mr Snyder enquired.

"The root of their dispute was Maryanna's drinking," Mr Suggitt replied. "Not Mrs Yates living with Abraham."

Mr Snyder shifted on the stool to get comfortable and, scratching his cheek, mused aloud, "What woz it you told the inspector about where you woz when Mrs Roberts was done in?"

Mr Suggitt averted his gaze and replied, "The truth; that I was at home."

"Why'd your mother-in-law tell me you woz in 'ere askin' after Mrs Roberts, then?" Mr Snyder enquired.

Mr Suggitt met his eyes in an instant. Staring at him a moment, he began, "I…" Yet his voice trailed off as he looked to Mr Queshire and then the others.

Miss Webster referred to her previous notes and said, "If I recall Miss Dexter's account correctly, your wife was surprised when you told the inspector you were home all evening. She naturally confirmed your story but was startled when Inspector Woolfe enquired if she was with you."

Mr Suggitt had watched Miss Webster with intense concentration as she'd spoken. Lost for words, he looked down with a grimace and clasped his hands tight upon his lap.

"Perhaps it's time you told us the truth," Lady Owston encouraged.

SIXTEEN

Mr Suggitt wetted his lips but kept his head bowed as he rubbed his cuticles. "I didn't murder her…" he began in a strained voice. "I *was* looking for her that night, yes," he took in a deep breath, "but I never found her."

"Why were you seeking her out at all?" Mr Locke enquired as he opened his cigarette case and held it before Mr Suggitt's gaze. Mr Suggitt took a cigarette with trembling fingers, and putting it between his lips, lifted his head to allow Mr Locke to light it. When Mr Locke struck the match against the side of its box, though, he caught sight of Miss Webster's flinch from the corner of his eyes. Igniting Mr Suggitt's cigarette, he then glanced at Miss Webster, intrigued, as he extinguished the match with a shake of his hand and discarded it into the ashtray.

Meanwhile, Mr Suggitt took several deep pulls from the cigarette before resting both hands upon his knees. Whilst one held the cigarette, the other rubbed at his leg as he replied, "I'd presented Mrs Roberts— Maryanna—with a proposition only the day before." He took another deep pull from the cigarette. "A rather generous sum of money in exchange for leaving London." He took a final pull from the cigarette and crushed it out in the ashtray. "She was making our lives a misery."

"Whose?" Mr Locke enquired as he tapped another cigarette against the side of his case. Placing it between his lips, he then lit it with another match.

"Her daughter's, her husband's… but mostly my wife's," Mr Suggitt replied. "Diana cared a great deal for her sister, too much, in all honesty. Too many times, she would offer assistance, which Maryanna would take with promises of giving up the gin, and too many times Diana's heart was broken. I couldn't bear to stand idly by and see her in pain any longer. If Maryanna wished to drink herself into the grave, then so be it." His eyes became downcast once more. "But she refused. Two *hundred* pounds I offered her to leave London and that... *Lushington* wouldn't accept it." He drew in a deep breath and pinched at the skin between his thumb and his forefinger. "After her usual vile insults, she threatened to tell my wife everything. I knew she wouldn't understand *why* I had done it; all she'd see was an attempt by her husband to rid himself of a parasitic relative who he despised." He glanced sideways at the Bow Streeters and added, "I'd never made a secret of my dislike of the woman."

"We know," Lady Owston replied with glance to Mr Queshire. "You thought you could persuade her not to tell your wife. You therefore resolved to find her the night she died, having presumed she'd come to the store that day to tell your wife, correct?"

"Correct..." Mr Suggitt replied with another grimace. "I didn't know *how* I would persuade her—more money, probably. I checked the usual doss and public houses my wife had told me she frequented. Even when I came here, I had doubts I'd find her. She and her mother haven't spoken since Maryanna spent her housekeeping money on gin." He looked over at Mrs Yates. Satisfied he'd not been overheard, he continued, "I spoke to Mr Ratchett, the landlord here, but he'd not seen Maryanna all evening. It didn't even occur to me he would tell her mother of my visit."

"Where was she?" Miss Webster enquired.

"Upstairs, he told me," Mr Suggitt replied. "His wife is unwell, and she was tending to her, a sickness of the lungs—or something."

"When did you arrive here?" Mr Locke enquired and took a brief pull from his cigarette.

"It was around quarter past nine, I believe," Mr Suggitt replied as he lifted his head and met his gaze. "I left home at eight thirty—after dinner. My wife *was* at home when I left so, *yes,* she lied for me but, at that time, didn't know where I'd gone or why. I cannot say I'm proud of myself for allowing her to do so." Mr Suggitt took in a deep, shuddering breath. "I stayed here for only a few minutes and continued my search. I gave up around ten thirty and arrived home just after eleven thirty."

"Was your wife still at home when you returned?" Mr Locke enquired.

"Yes; she was sound asleep when I retired to bed at around a quarter to midnight," Mr Suggitt replied. "I... made every effort not to wake her. I didn't want her knowing I'd returned so late."

"Does she now know the reasons for your leaving home?" Mr Locke enquired.

Mr Suggitt nodded and replied, "I told her during the cab ride to Mr Roberts' home. She wasn't best pleased, but she understood why I did what I had."

The Bow Streeters knew it would be pointless to ask if Mrs Suggitt would confirm her husband's story; she'd already lied once for him so, undoubtedly, she'd do the same again.

"Does the police know?" Mr Locke enquired, tapping his cigarette's ash into the ashtray.

"We told Inspector Woolfe this morning," Mr Suggitt replied. "He threatened to arrest me should Mr Ratchett not confirm my whereabouts. I have not had another visit from the inspector since, so I assume he must have."

"Mrs Roberts was murdered using French Breakfast coffee laced with arsenic, a tin of which is in the *Queshire Department Store's* storeroom," Lady Owston began, deciding to approach the conversation from a different angle. "Miss Galway's name was also found in the poison book of *Drummond's Pharmaceutical Chemist's* on Oxford Street. She had purchased arsenic for, she claims, an infestation of rats."

190

"That's correct," Mr Suggitt replied. "I'd sent her to fetch some as I'd forgotten to do so, and the store was particularly busy that day. As for the coffee, it's well known among the assistants it's there as its consumption is restricted to Mr Queshire and me alone. The door is also never locked; the assistants regularly replenish goods from the stock we hold in there."

"Your easy access to the method by which the poison was administered does place you both under suspicion, however," Mr Locke pointed out.

Mr Suggitt and Mr Queshire exchanged incredulous glances before the former said, "But I have a tin of it at home, too. My wife and I developed a taste for it while we were honeymooning in Paris. I wouldn't even *think* to lace it with *arsenic* and I would *certainly* not serve such a deadly drink to *anyone*. Who, on God's green Earth, *could* do such a thing?"

"Most certainly someone known to her," Mr Locke replied. "Whether the coffee used was attained from the storeroom, Mr Roberts' home, your own home, or elsewhere, the fact remains she accepted coffee—far from her usual choice of beverage—from her murderer and, without any hint of hesitation, drank enough of it to be struck down by the poison."

"No… I can't believe it…" Mr Suggitt said as the colour drained from his face. "She was murdered by a madman… a stranger in the street."

"Would you accept coffee from a stranger?" Mr Locke enquired.

Mr Suggitt's eyes darted from face to face as he replied, "No, I would not, but—"

"Why did you think the inspector would wish to arrest you," Mr Locke interrupted, "if he did not think someone she knew had murdered her?"

Mr Suggitt shook his head in disbelief as he replied, "He accused me of the deed but didn't enlighten my wife and I as to the method used to administer the arsenic."

"Do you have any hessian sacks at the store?" Mr Snyder interjected, causing Mr Suggitt and Mr Queshire to shift their gazes to him in an instant.

Parting his lips, Mr Suggitt glanced at Mr Queshire and replied, "I don't recall…"

"Why?" Mr Queshire enquired, keeping his gaze fixed upon Mr Snyder.

"Her body was carried in a hessian sack to where she was discovered outside the bazaar," Mr Locke replied.

Mr Suggitt paled whilst Mr Queshire remained stoic.

"They are not something the store usually utilises," Mr Queshire said. "But I'll check nonetheless."

"And at home? Perhaps a sack of potatoes or coal?" Miss Webster enquired.

"You'd have to ask my wife about that," Mr Suggitt replied.

"I have a small sack of potatoes, but I use a scuttle for my coal," Mr Queshire added.

"Mr Suggitt," Lady Owston began with a smile. "I'm certain Mr Queshire shan't mind my asking this: what is at the room at the top of the stairs in your store?"

"Another storeroom; chairs and stock for the salon," Mr Suggitt replied with another glance to Mr Queshire.

"Lady Owston, I do not know *why* you are fixated upon a mere storeroom," Mr Queshire interjected with a hint of irritation in his voice and a contrived smile.

"I am fixated, Mr Queshire, because I do not believe it to be such," Lady Owston replied with hard eyes. "Why would ladies leave it, on several different occasions, if it was as you say?"

Mr Queshire's smile faltered as he released a soft sigh. His facial muscles then became tense as he forced a larger smile and said, "Because our customers know the salon to be at the top of the stairs, and presume the first door they come to is it. They don't think to look to the open doorway where the salon actually is."

"Oh my God…" Mr Suggitt whispered with wide eyes as he stared past Lady Owston. When the others turned to see what he was looking at, they, too, were taken aback by the sight of Mrs Roberts' crocheted shawl. It was draped around the shoulders of a blond-haired woman carrying a black-leather Gladstone bag.

Mr Locke stood at once and, crushing out his cigarette in the ashtray, approached her. He said, "Darling?"

"Good evening," Dr Locke greeted.

"My wife Dr Lynnette Locke," Mr Locke introduced to the others. "Darling, this is—"

"I thought women were not permitted to become doctors," Mr Queshire interrupted in a cool tone. "Where did you train?"

Mr Locke lofted his brow whilst his wife gave Mr Queshire a condescending smile and replied, "The *London School of Medicine for Women* and, before you ask, that institution is legally approved to train women doctors. Furthermore, my training's respectability is equal to that of my male colleagues." Turning to her husband, she placed her hand upon his chest and said, "Introductions shan't be necessary, darling. Contrary to the whisperings of your ego, I'm not here in pursuit of you. Mrs Ratchett has been unwell and I'm here to see how she's faring."

"Another of your charitable causes," Mr Locke drily remarked.

"Indeed," Dr Locke replied. Addressing the others, she went on, "Forgive my rudeness but duty draws me elsewhere. Good evening to you all."

"One moment, please, darling," Mr Locke said as he took a gentle hold of her arm to stay her. "May I ask where you procured your delightful shawl from?"

"*Queshire's,* of course," Dr Locke replied with a smirk as she glanced at Mr Queshire. His expression remained stoic, however.

"When?" Mr Locke enquired. "Are you able to recall who sold it to you?"

"Yesterday," Dr Locke replied. "It was one of the assistants. I didn't take her name." She tilted her head. "Why?"

"It was my sister-in-law's," Mr Suggitt interjected in a sombre tone.

"The lady who was discovered upon Oxford Street," Mr Locke said.

Dr Locke looked between Mr Suggitt and her husband and enquired, "Truly?"

"Truly," Mr Locke replied.

"My wife crocheted it for her," Mr Suggitt said.

"She must therefore have it back," Dr Locke replied and, removing the garment, offered it to him. "With my sincerest condolences."

"Thank you," Mr Suggitt replied with a smile that failed to reach his eyes. Taking the shawl from her, he neatly folded it, and held it in his lap.

"Until tonight, darling," Dr Locke said to her husband. Allowing him to place a delicate kiss upon her cheek, she then approached the bar. Mrs Yates, upon seeing her, opened a door at the back and called for the landlord. Mr Locke therefore returned to his seat and, glancing back to the bar, saw his wife being accompanied from the room by a man he assumed to be Mr Ratchett.

He wasn't given long to ponder this, though, for the pub's main door was thrown open a second later by a girl of seventeen. She marched past the Bow Streeters, revealing naturally wavy, mouse-brown, shoulder-length hair, a fair complexion, and dark-brown eyes in the process. She wore an old, russet-coloured, ankle-length skirt, an off-white blouse, and a tattered, forest-green woollen shawl. Approaching the bar, she immediately slapped Mrs Yates across the face and yelled, "*Whore!*"

"Regina!" Mr Suggitt cried as he leapt to his feet and crossed the room.

Miss Regina Roberts spun around with wide eyes.

"What are you doing?" Mr Suggitt enquired from her.

"She's gone wild, that's what!" Mrs Yates screeched, holding her red face.

Regina turned sharply at that and, with a fierce scowl, attempted to climb over the bar, yelling, "You killed my mother!"

"None of that, now!" Mr Suggitt yelled as he wrapped his arms about her waist and dragged her from the bar.

"*Lemmie go!*" Regina screamed. Struggling against his grip as he lifted her off her feet, turned her around, and tried to drag her back toward the main door, she shouted, "You won't get my dad! I won't let you!"

"I don't *want* your dad!" Mrs Yates threw back.

Pushing down upon Mr Suggitt's arms, which were still tight around her waist, Regina shouted at Mrs Yates, "Then how come you came to live with us soon as he threw out Mum?! You wanted her gone from the start, you *witch*! You turned my dad against her!"

Managing to get Regina to the Bow Streeters' table, Mr Suggitt said, "Forgive me, but I must go home." He dragged her closer to the door, "Come on, Regina!" With one, carefully timed shunt, he successfully got her through it and said, "Don't give her the satisfaction. Your aunt and I will take care of you tonight."

The moment he released her, though, Regina stormed back into the pub and shouted at Mrs Yates, "I won't let this lie!"

"Come *on*, Regina!" Mr Suggitt insisted. This

time, his niece allowed him to lead her away, and the Bow Streeters heard a quiet, yet heated, discussion between the two about her behaviour in the few seconds before the door swung shut.

"An eventful evening," Mr Queshire remarked as he stood. "And a late one. Please forgive me but I, too, must be taking my leave. Good night to you all."

"Good night, Mr Queshire," Lady Owston replied, watching him leave. Draining her sherry glass, she placed her hand upon Miss Webster's arm and said, "Drink up, dear." Seeing Mr Locke preparing to depart, also, she enquired, "Shan't you wait for your wife?"

"Lynette is accustomed to visiting less-than-reputable establishments along the poorer thoroughfares," Mr Locke replied. "She feels it is her social duty to provide free care to those who could not otherwise afford a doctor's fee." He smiled. "She is also my wife and therefore capable of protecting herself." He picked up his cane, stood, and dipped his head. "Good night to you all." He turned upon his heel and left.

"I do believe it is time for us to leave, as well," Lady Owston remarked as she stood with much relief. Noticing someone she thought she recognised standing on the other side of the window, she pursed her lips and led Miss Webster and Mr Snyder out into the cold night air. "We should visit Mr Roberts again tomorrow morning," she continued whilst approaching the streetlamp. "To ask him why he lied about his mother-in-law living with him." She turned sharply toward the pub and, having her suspicions confirmed, enquired, "Miss Galway?"

"Hello," Miss Galway replied, wrapping her coat tight about herself as she approached. "Didn't know you was here."

"I see," Lady Owston said with a frown. "Is that why you were watching us through the window?"

Miss Galway's eyes bulged as she cried, "I

wasn't!"

"Come now," Lady Owston replied with irritation. "I saw you standing at the window overlooking our table."

Miss Galway pursed her lips and shifted her weight from one foot to the other. Realising it was pointless to continue denying the truth when she'd been caught out in a lie, she replied, "Fine, I was watching—but only because I wanna help the Bow Street Society."

"You've already been a tremendous help to us," Lady Owston replied in a gentler tone. "Go home, child. Aside from it being *far* too cold to be loitering outside of pubs, there is *still* a murderer walking around. In addition to the ne'er-do-wells and ruffians one may usually expect to find stalking the streets of London."

"I'll take you," Mr Snyder offered and gestured to his waiting cab.

"Nah, that's okay," Miss Galway replied. "Think I'm gonna go inside anyway; get something hot to eat."

"*Miss* Galway," Lady Owston scolded. "*Go* home." Pulling her own coat tight, she strode over to the cab and climbed inside. Miss Webster followed whilst Mr Snyder gestured toward the vehicle by way of making an additional offer to take Miss Galway home. Once again, she refused, however. Accepting her decision with reluctance, he returned to his cab and paid the lad he'd hired to watch it whilst he'd been inside. Once he'd climbed up into his seat, he looked back to the pub, but Miss Galway was already gone.

SEVENTEEN

"We came as soon as we heard," Lady Owston said in a trembling voice as she reached a grief-stricken Mrs Suggitt held tight by her husband's arms.

They were standing at the end of Moore Street, close to where some constables from the Metropolitan Police formed a human cordon. The officer's lamps cut through the early morning darkness, whilst the streetlamps at the opposite end of Moore Street illuminated a Black Maria and its driver. The vehicle spanned the cobbled road to prevent the curious entering from Queen Street. A small dot of light, emitted from the Maria's lantern, served as a beacon. A spell of heavy rainfall had recently subsided. Thus, the officers were clad in their thick, weighty coats. The dank air, caused by the rain's disturbance of the soot and dirt which covered the buildings, felt just as oppressive.

At Lady Owston's side were Misses Webster and Dexter; the three having been brought there by Mr Snyder who'd erred on the side of caution by remaining with his cab. Despite the early hour—four thirty, to be precise—all three women were wide awake yet subdued in their movements. Miss Dexter gripped her ankle-length, midnight-blue cloak as she looked down the street. Seeing the tenement building she'd visited with Mr Snyder earlier that day, she felt a shiver run through her. Although she'd not been present at the meeting at the *Turk's Head* public house, she'd been informed of what had occurred by Miss Webster during the cab ride over.

"When did it happen?" Lady Owston enquired from the Suggitts.

"A few hours ago," Mr Suggitt replied. His wife's shoulders shook as she buried her face in his coat.

"To *think* we only saw her this evening…" Lady Owston said, her voice cracking. "Perhaps we could've prevented this from happening."

"There was no suggestion she was in any danger," Miss Webster remarked in her usual monotone.

"Oh, *Agnes*, show some emotion for *once*!" Lady Owston scolded and pressed her handkerchief against her nose.

Miss Webster's mouth fell open, and she stared at her a moment. In a shaky voice, she replied, "Forgive me, Lady Owston, I—" Cutting herself short at the realisation she'd upset her employer and guardian, she then pursed her lips and fought to hold back the tears which threatened to fall.

"She's right," Mr Suggitt murmured. "None of us could've guessed my mother-in-law would be…"

Mrs Suggitt broke down into loud sobbing, prompting her husband to hold her closer to him and demand, "Where *is* that *blasted* inspector?"

"Was he the one to summon you here?" Lady Owston enquired after she'd dabbed at her nose and eyes.

"No," Mr Suggitt replied as he rubbed his wife's trembling back. "We received a telephone call at around two thirty this morning. Mr Trowel, a neighbour of Mr Roberts, called from the *Turk's Head*. Mr Trowel had been leaving for work when he'd noticed Abraham's door was ajar. Thinking he'd forgotten to lock it, Mr Trowel investigated to check all was well. When he—" His voice faltered. "When he pushed the door wider, he saw… *oh God,* I cannot speak it. It is too horrific!"

"She was mutilated," Inspector Woolfe interjected as he came up beside him. Looking to the Bow Streeters, he enquired, "Who told the meddlers?"

Mrs Suggitt howled into her husband's chest.

"Have a *heart*, Inspector!" Mr Suggitt hissed with a scowl. "My wife has just lost her mother to this fiend."

"And we'll catch him," Inspector Woolfe replied. "But until then there's nothing you can do, Mr Suggitt." He glared at the Bow Streeters. "or you. Go home—all of you."

"What a *foul*-tempered individual," Lady Owston remarked when he'd walked far enough away to be beyond earshot.

Miss Webster hummed in agreement as her own distress subsided.

"*Why* are they doing this?" Mrs Suggitt enquired through a sob. "What have any of us done to *them*?"

"I think I should take her home," Mr Suggitt informed the Bow Streeters.

"No, Clement," Mrs Suggitt said with a shake of her head. "We can't go home without Regina and Abraham."

"Where are they?" Miss Webster enquired.

"Inside," Mr Suggitt replied. "We brought them here after receiving Mr Trowel's telephone call."

"And they were with you both all night prior to that?" Miss Dexter enquired.

"Yes, after Regina's outburst at the pub, I took her to our home," Mr Suggitt replied. "Mr Roberts arrived at about half past midnight. He woke us from our beds. Mrs Yates had told him of Regina's behaviour, and he wanted to confront her about it and escort her home."

Mrs Suggitt's sobbing intensified but she'd turned her face toward them, her handkerchief clutched tightly against her lips.

"I took him into the parlour," Mr Suggitt continued as he stroked the back of his wife's head. "Where my wife joined us. We spoke to him together and convinced him to stay the night as Regina had already fallen asleep and it was too late to journey back home."

"Mr Roberts had seen Mrs Yates this evening, then?" Miss Webster enquired.

Mr Suggitt nodded and replied, "He told us he'd met her at the pub at closing—around eleven o'clock—and walked her home. Once there, my mother-in-law had told him everything Regina had said and done. He admitted he had been angered by his daughter's behaviour but also shocked. Mrs Yates tried to calm him, he said, but he had wanted to see Regina right away. Since they weren't sure if Regina would return home, and due to my mother-in-law being the focus of her rage, they decided it would be better if Mrs Yates waited at home. I don't think Abraham intended to stay with us but…" He took in a deep, shuddering breath. "…Abraham often sleeps outside the gates of the docks in the hopes of getting work first thing in the morning. We…" His voice faltered and then shook as he continued, "…We thought she'd be safe at home, as she had been so many times before."

Moved by the intensity of his emotion, Lady Owston dabbed at her eyes and enquired in a solemn voice, "Was she in the habit of leaving the door unlocked?"

"No," Mr Suggitt replied, sniffing hard. "They didn't have much but what they did have they were proud of. Mrs Yates and I rarely saw eye to eye, but she was family, nonetheless. How could *anyone*…?"

"That is what we intend to find out," Lady Owston soothed. "Could you tell me the address of the lodgings where the store's assistants reside?"

"Why?" Mr Suggitt enquired in return.

"We saw Miss Galway outside the *Turk's Head* when we left," Lady Owston replied. "She told us she would be going inside to buy a hot meal. She may have seen something therefore and I, for one, would like to speak with her before Inspector Woolfe puts the fear of God into her."

"Yes… of course, I…" Mr Suggitt said. Struggling to retrieve the information from his mind, at first, he then looked up and dictated the address to Miss Webster.

"Thank you, Mr Suggitt, Mrs Suggitt," Lady Owston said. "We shall be in touch. Goodbye."

The three Bow Streeters walked back to Mr Snyder's cab with heavy hearts and stomachs. Feeling nauseous at the thought of what had befallen Mrs Yates, Miss Dexter turned her mind to other matters and realised something. Stopping in her tracks, she glanced behind them. As she then hurried to catch the others up, she remarked, "I wonder where Mr Maxwell is."

"I truly have no idea, child, perhaps he is still tucked up in bed?" Lady Owston replied, climbing into the cab.

"He would have received Miss Trent's note as we did though, surely?" Miss Webster enquired as she joined her employer.

"The whereabouts of that journalist, as amicable as he may be, is *not* our immediate concern, ladies," Lady Owston said as Miss Dexter climbed in last and closed the doors over their knees. "After all, Mr Locke isn't here either."

Miss Dexter hadn't noticed Mr Locke's absence. Nevertheless, her thoughts returned to Mr Maxwell. Having received a note from him earlier, cancelling the invitation to dinner at his parents' home on account of his mother being ill, she assumed he must've stayed at his mother's bedside. Rather than be comforted by this assumption, though, she felt even more wretched. Should she not be at his side if his mother was seriously unwell? Perhaps not; she had yet to meet her so it would be inappropriate. Hearing Lady Owston give Mr Snyder the address, she felt the vehicle lurch forward and rattle as it made its way from the horrific scene. Yet, as she watched the darkened buildings pass by, and felt the chill of the

morning against her cheeks, she wondered what Mr
Maxwell was doing at that moment.

* * *

Dr Locke used her latch key to enter her home and saw the
lit kerosene lamp on the hall table left by their butler, Mr
Lyons. The arrangement had become a regular habit since
she'd started making night-time house calls to her patients.
This eve she'd been obliged to leave Mrs Ratchett's
bedside to assist with a particularly difficult birth at her
neighbour's house. She relieved herself of her coat and
hung it upon the stand by the door. Mr Lyons, having
duties to attend to come dawn, wasn't expected to keep
vigil until her return.

Therefore, she assumed she was the only one
awake as she placed a policeman's whistle beside the
lamp. She'd found it to be a most effective defensive
weapon for it summoned any constables who happened to
be within the vicinity. Her husband had procured it
through questionable means, though, so her possession of
it was kept a closely guarded secret between them.
Whenever she'd been obliged to use it, the arriving
constable had assumed a colleague had blown it. The
remaining items upon the hall table were a Chinese puzzle
box and finger trap.

Given her husband's resounding success as an
illusionist, and owner of the Paddington Palladium, they
enjoyed an upper middle-class status. As such, they were
counted amongst Booth's wealthy residents on Cleveland
Terrace. Nestled among Gloucester Terrace, Cleveland
Gardens, and Westbourne Terrace, Cleveland Terrace had
the then named Great Western Railway Station to its east.
To more recent minds, though, this same station is known
as Paddington.

The entire left side of the house's ground floor was occupied by Dr Locke's medical practise. At the front was her office, and at the rear was the waiting room for her wealthier patients. Meanwhile, a dining room was located at the front on the right side, with a guest parlour at the rear. Laid out across several floors, the remainder of the house served as the living quarters of the Lockes and their servants. Mr Greenham, their footman, and James, Mr Locke's personal valet, occupied rooms in the basement adjacent to the pantry and kitchen. Mr Lyons and his wife, who cooked for the Lockes, had a room in the attic. Belinda, Dr Locke's ladies' maid, and Veronica, the scullery maid, shared a room next door to the Lyons. Finally, Mr Lambert, the Lockes' groom and driver, resided above a small stable situated away from the residence.

Intending to put away her Gladstone bag, Dr Locke headed down the hallway toward her office. Before she reached it, though, Mr Lyons stepped out from the shadows and said, "Pardon me, ma'am."

Dr Locke spun around at once. Seeing the concern on his face, she felt a sudden weight upon her chest. In a soft voice, she enquired, "Where is he?"

"In his study; he retired to it shortly after returning at nine thirty."

"Has he eaten?"

"Yes; a cold supper I took to him at nine forty-five. I… saw his paraphernalia upon the sofa when I entered but, as per your instructions, didn't remark upon it."

"Very good."

"At four o'clock this morning, a messenger boy arrived with this for the master." Mr Lyons passed her an envelope with a 'B' stamped into its top-right corner.

Tearing it open and reading its contents, she then returned it to him and said, "Put it aside. He cannot assist the Bow Street Society tonight."

"Yes, ma'am."

"You may also secure the house and retire to bed."

"Yes, ma'am," Mr Lyons replied with a dip of his head. Whilst he went about securing the front door's many bolts and locks, Dr Locke climbed the stairs to the first floor and approached her husband's study. She knocked once and—as expected—had no response. Aware of her husband's habit to keep the door unlocked whenever he was inside, she turned the knob and entered.

Within, she found the lamp at half strength and the curtains drawn over the sole window. A fire, which had once been fierce, now smouldered in the hearth. The window was located on the back wall, overlooking the street, with the hearth on the right and the desk on the left. A collection of egg-cup-and-ball magic tricks was gathered upon the desk alongside sketches and handwritten notes for possible illusions. The lamp stood on the desk's corner adjacent to an opened, narrow, leather-bound box with green-velvet lining. If its indentations of a needle and vial were not telling enough, the sight of Mr Locke upon a sofa to the left of the door certainly was.

Lying on his back with his head closest to the door and his eyes closed, he had one shirt sleeve rolled up to his shoulder and a tourniquet tied tightly around his arm. Constructed from a canvas strap passing through two round bars, the tourniquet had a large screw positioned centrally upon it, perpendicular to some plates. The screw would be turned, clockwise, to pull upon the strap via the upper plate rising. The more the strap was pulled upon, the tighter the tourniquet became. Dr Locke recognised it at once as being the type preferred by surgeons. Mr Locke's arm hung over the sofa's edge with his hand resting upon the varnished floorboards. His other hand lay upon his stomach.

Noticing a vial lying on its side by her husband's hip, Dr Locke picked it up and read its label. As expected, the word *HEROIN* was printed upon it. A search of the sofa unearthed a needle wedged between her husband and the sofa's backrest. Both vial and needle were empty. Lowering her arms to her sides, she looked upon her husband's prone form and said through a sigh, "Oh, *Percy...*" He didn't respond, however. Thinking she would've been surprised if he had, she put the vial into her Gladstone bag and returned the needle to its box. Next, she held her compact's mirror close to her husband's lips. The steam which formed upon its glass told her he was still breathing. A careful lifting of one eyelid and then the other confirmed he was also under the drug's influence.

"I suppose I should be thankful you used the heroin *I'd* prescribed," she whispered. After all, she knew the vial had contained only a small amount of the drug. Nevertheless, experience had taught her not to accept things at face value. She therefore searched his frock coat and desk for additional vials he'd not told her about. When none were found, she stood in the middle of the room and pondered other possible hiding places. Most of his props were secured in an adjacent storeroom but, while it was likely some heroin was hidden there, her immediate concern was the study. She had known him to slip a vial or two onto a hidden shelf within the chimney breast so her next move was to put her arm up it. The shelf was found after a few seconds of feeling around but it was empty. She sighed, partly with relief and partly with concern; either her prescription was his only stash, or he'd found a new hiding place. As much as she hoped it was the former, her husband's past deceptions led her to suspect it was the latter. Rising to her feet and placing a soft kiss upon his forehead, she stroked his head as many questions posed themselves in her mind. Knowing none of them would be answered tonight, though, she picked up her bag, left the study, and locked its door. Her husband could easily pick it, of course, but she didn't want the servants to see him in that condition. "Good night," she whispered and retired to bed alone.

EIGHTEEN

Argyll Street, the thoroughfare opposite the *London Crystal Palace Bazaar*, was also the location of the lodgings for the *Queshire Department Store*'s assistants. Its proximity to the business was likely an attempt to eliminate poor punctuality. At the time, the impressive, burgundy façade of *Oxford Circus Station* on the northwest corner of Argyll Street, where it met Oxford Street, didn't exist. That would be realised a decade later by the Underground Electric Railways Company of London Limited (UERL). Therefore, when Lady Owston, Miss Webster, and Miss Dexter disembarked from Mr Snyder's cab at five fifteen, only a handful of people strolled down the street on their way to work.

"'Ere you go," Mr Snyder said as he leant down and handed Miss Dexter a miner's Davy lamp. Its tiny flame, housed within the lamp's narrow, cylindrical glass casing, illuminated as far as a foot in front of her. Beyond this, pitch blackness prevented any structures or obstacles from being discerned.

"Thank you, Sam," Miss Dexter said and held the lamp aloft.

"I'll be right 'ere if you need me," Mr Snyder said.

"We shall cry out if we need your assistance," Lady Owston informed him as she slipped her arm around Miss Webster's. "Let us press on, ladies."

Miss Dexter led the way along the narrow path and up the stairs to the lodgings' main door. There had been a frost during the night in this part of London which had left a thin layer of ice upon the surfaces. The ladies therefore took extra care in where they were placing their feet. Once they'd safely reached their destination, Lady Owston reached around Miss Dexter and knocked twice upon the door.

A few seconds later, the sash window to the door's right was lit up by a lamp. Its curtains were next pulled aside by a silhouetted figure who proceeded to unlock and lift the window. When they poked their head out, the Bow Streeters recognised a womanly form, but were unable to distinguish her facial features on account of the lamp's glare. Miss Dexter lifted her lamp, and the young woman at the window blinked and shielded her eyes with her hand. She demanded, "Who are you?! I'll shout for a constable!"

"That shan't be necessary; we're friends of Miss Galway's," Lady Owston replied. Placing her hand upon her chest, she introduced, "I'm Lady Owston and this," she indicated her companions, "is Miss Webster and Miss Dexter. We're from the Bow Street Society. The man sitting up on the hansom cab is Mr Samuel Snyder; he is also part of our group. Is Miss Galway at home?"

"Yeah; she's in a right state though," the woman replied.

"Oh *dear*," Lady Owston replied with a frown. "If you could let us inside, we will bring comfort to her."

The nameless woman remained silent and unmoving. After a moment, she withdrew from the window, slid it closed, and relocked it. The lamp was also extinguished.

"What do you suppose has upset her?" Miss Dexter whispered while they waited.

"We shall soon find out," Lady Owston replied as they heard footsteps approaching from the other side. This was followed by a bolt being slid back, a key being turned, and, finally, the door being opened to reveal their friend from the window.

"You'd best not be lying to me," the woman warned.

"May God strike us down if we are," Lady Owston replied, glancing over the woman's shoulder.

Looking behind her, also, the woman then eyed the trio before stepping aside and allowing them to enter.

"Thank you, Miss...?" Lady Owston probed.

"Smith," the woman replied and pointed to a room past the stairs. "I think she's in the kitchen."

"Excellent," Lady Owston replied. As Miss Smith stepped forward to take them there, though, Lady Owston lifted her hand and said, "there's no need to escort us. Please, you have already done a great deal."

Miss Smith grunted and shut the door. On the way to her own room, she muttered, "If you are lying Rose'll soon sort you out." The three Bow Streeters exchanged glances but Miss Smith slammed her door before they could respond.

"Perhaps Mr Snyder should have accompanied us after all?" Miss Dexter whispered.

"*Nonsense,*" Miss Webster rebutted. "We are no weaker for being women."

"We're not?" Miss Dexter enquired, feeling quite taken aback by not only the suggestion but Miss Webster's conviction when she'd said it. Miss Dexter thought back to all the times she'd blindly accepted she couldn't do something because of her sex. Reminding herself of all she'd achieved during the Dorsey case, though, and the other ladies' efforts during this one, she felt a warmth come over her. A smile also formed upon her lips as she realised Miss Webster was right; they *weren't* weaker for being women. "Yes, we're not," she agreed, moving in front of Lady Owston and Miss Webster to light the way.

Beyond the door indicated by Miss Smith was a modest kitchen warmed by an immense stove. Sitting at a table in the middle of the room was Miss Galway being comforted by a third young woman knelt at her feet. When the Bow Streeters had entered, both women jerked their heads upwards to see who it was. Yet, the moment she saw

Lady Owston, Miss Galway leapt to her feet, threw her arms around her, and cried, "Lady Owston! I'm sorry!"

Miss Galway's comforter stood also. She looked between Miss Webster and Miss Dexter and enquired, "What's going on? Who're you?"

"Miss Webster, Miss Dexter, and Lady Owston from the Bow Street Society," Miss Webster replied whilst Miss Dexter put the Davy lamp upon the table. "Miss Smith let us inside; we are friends of Miss Galway's."

Lady Owston pulled back from the embrace to see Miss Galway's face contorted by anguish. Searching her eyes for any hint of what might have distressed her, she enquired, "What*ever* is the matter, child? Surely you've not heard already?"

"Heard what?" Miss Galway enquired, confused.

Lady Owston pursed her lips together but waited until she'd guided Miss Galway back to her chair before she replied, "Mrs Sarah Yates, mother of Mrs Diana Suggitt and Mrs Maryanna Roberts, was murdered this night at home."

Miss Galway's breath hitched in her throat and her pink complexion paled as if someone had pulled a plug. Her wide eyes stared through Lady Owston whilst her hands and arms began to tremble uncontrollably. "No…" she whispered, shaking her head. "No, no…"

"Miss Galway?" Lady Owston urged as she placed a hand upon hers.

"*No*!" Miss Galway shouted, tugging her hand free as she did so. "*No*! It *can't* be right!" Leaping to her feet, she sought out the arms of her friend and demanded, "*Tell* them, Annie! It *can't* be right! It *can't*! It *can't*…" Miss Galway caused her friend to stumble as she collapsed into her arms, sobbing uncontrollably.

"Look what you've done," Annie scolded, glaring at the Bow Streeters as she held Miss Galway close.

"I don't understand…" Lady Owston confessed in

a soft voice. "Were Miss Galway and Mrs Yates close?"

"Nah," Annie replied. Rubbing Miss Galway's back, she said, "sshhh, Rosie. Calm down."

Lady Owston stared at the two and said, "Then I don't understand why—"

"She saw someone, okay?" Annie interrupted.

"I'm afraid you are going to have to give a far more detailed explanation than that," Lady Owston reproached.

Annie scowled at the Bow Streeters and, for several long moments, a tense hush descended upon the kitchen whilst she focused on soothing Miss Galway. Eventually, Miss Galway became passive enough to be led back to her chair. After easing her into it, kneeling beside her, and taking her hand, Annie whispered further assurances. Only when Miss Galway squeezed her hand in return and bowed her head did Annie continue. Addressing the others, she said, "Rose followed Mrs Yates and Mr Roberts from the *Turk's Head* pub tonight," she threw them a harsh scowl as she added in a malicious tone, "told me she was trying to help you lot out with some murder you're working on." She looked back to Miss Galway. "When Mrs Yates and Mr Roberts got to the end of their road though, Rose saw a bloke on the other side of Queen Street, lurking like he was up to no good."

"Did she see who it was?" Miss Dexter enquired, hoping to capture their likeness in a sketch.

Miss Galway shook her head.

"He stopped when Mrs Yates and Mr Roberts turned onto Moore Street, and then he followed them," Annie went on. "He was like a cat stalking a mouse, Rose said. The sight of it frightened her so; she scarpered back here without stopping once and woke me. Cried in my arms, she did—not as bad as this but bad enough. I'd only just got her calm when you turned up with your *news*." She spat out the last word with another glare cast Lady

Owston's way. "I'd told her the bloke wasn't anything to worry about, said he was probably coming home from seeing some woman and didn't want his wife finding out. Then *you* had to tell her *that*."

"In our defence, we had no conceivable notion Miss Galway had undertaken a task on behalf of the Bow Street Society," Lady Owston replied. "We engaged in conversation with her outside the *Turk's Head* public house, but *I* told her to come home. Miss Galway isn't a member of our group, although I know she wishes to be." Lady Owston sat at the table across from Miss Galway. "At what time did she see the man?"

"Around five past eleven, she told me," Annie replied. "Said she'd sat in the *Turk's Head* until closing time—eleven o'clock—when that Mr Roberts came to walk Mrs Yates home."

"And when did she awaken you?" Lady Owston enquired.

"Must've been almost half past midnight," Annie replied.

"We've got to tell Mr Queshire," Miss Galway told Annie through a sob.

"Not now, Rosie," Annie soothed. "I told you; he's probably asleep."

"You've attempted to speak with Mr Queshire already this evening?" Miss Webster enquired in her usual monotone despite her curiosity.

"Rose wanted to the moment she got back," Annie replied. "I told her he'd be asleep, but she pushed me, saying he could ask Mr Suggitt to warn Mrs Yates and Mr Roberts. We walked over to the store and spent about ten minutes knocking. Mr Queshire lives upstairs so I doubt he heard us. Rose didn't want to go but it was getting colder and I didn't fancy coming across the bloke that done in Mrs Roberts. I finally got her to come home with me about ten minutes later."

"At what time did you get back?" Lady Owston enquired.

Meanwhile, Miss Webster had begun to note the salient points.

"Must've been about... half past one?" Annie replied.

Lady Owston stood, and reaching across the table to place a gentle hand upon Miss Galway's shoulder, said, "Don't worry, Miss Galway. *We* shall tell Mr Queshire what has occurred. In fact," she straightened and looked to her fellow Bow Streeters who nodded their agreement. "We shall do so presently."

* * *

Lady Owston used the handle of her umbrella to knock upon the front door of the *Queshire Department Store* and waited. Its interior had been lit by the subdued glow of its gas lamps when she'd arrived. Thus, although she could neither see nor hear any sign of occupation, she was adamant Mr Queshire was up and about. Furthermore, with it being five forty-five in the morning, she knew there was only an hour or so left before the assistants were, undoubtedly, expected to arrive. When no immediate response came, she knocked several more times and called through the glass, "Mr Queshire?!"

A shadow was cast across the door, and Lady Owston glanced sideways at Miss Webster and Miss Dexter who were with her. The shadow increased in size as they heard someone approaching and, when the door was unlocked, the Bow Streeters stepped back. As Lady Owston had expected, it was Mr Queshire who stood in the doorway. He was attired in a freshly pressed, white shirt with sleeves rolled up to the elbow, and an apron tied about his waist. The apron covered his chest and legs, and he used its skirt to wipe some white, powder-like residue from his hands. He enquired, "Lady Owston? I wasn't expecting to find you on my doorstep at this hour. Has something happened?"

"Indeed, it has," Lady Owston replied. "Mrs Yates has been murdered."

Mr Queshire leaned his head forward and enquired, "*Pardon*?" He glanced at Miss Webster and Miss Dexter. "When? How?"

"We do not know," Miss Webster replied. "Have you spoken with Miss Galway at all this evening?"

"*No*," Mr Queshire replied with a curt shake of his head. "You are the first I've conversed with since leaving the public house last evening. Why?"

"She informed us she'd attempted to speak with you this evening but could gain no answer from her knocking," Miss Webster replied.

"I was no doubt sleeping so wouldn't have heard her," Mr Queshire said. "My bedroom is at the back of the building, you see."

"You have not been awake long, then?" Lady Owston enquired.

"A few minutes," Mr Queshire replied. When the ladies' gazes dropped to his attire, his did, too, and he explained, "I was adding some sodium hydroxide to a soap preparation I've been slowly simmering overnight."

"*Well*, ladies, we can gain no further ground this evening," Lady Owston said, turning toward her associates—only to spin around and cry, "Hessian sacks!"

"Pardon?" Mr Queshire enquired.

"You said you would check if the store had any," Lady Owston reminded him.

Mr Queshire stared at her and replied, "Yes… It doesn't."

"*Bother,*" Lady Owston said and released a soft sigh. "Never mind, let us return home, ladies, and have some much-needed rest. We may recommence our investigations in the morning. Good evening to you, Mr Queshire."

NINETEEN

The sounds of Mr Trowel's clamorous slurping filled the
Bow Street Society's kitchen as he ate a bowl of leek and
potato soup. Mr Snyder, who was sitting across from him
at the table, watched him devour the steaming liquid with a
warm smile and gladdened heart. The slurping ceased, and
Mr Trowel discarded the spoon into the bowl with a
clatter. He settled back in his chair with a satisfied smirk,
patted his belly, and said, "*Fine* soup, sir. *Fiiiiine* soup!"

"Want more?" Mr Snyder enquired, taking the
bowl.

Mr Trowel's smile broadened, and he replied,
"Give me a moment or two, lad, and I just might yet!" Mr
Eric Trowel was in his sixties. He bore every second of his
advanced years in the wrinkles on his face, the hunch of
his back, and the seizing of his knuckles. His fingers had
been curved like talons as he'd held the bowl. Yet, despite
the burden of his age, he spoke with a joviality wealthier,
younger men could only aspire to. He reminded Mr Snyder
very much of his late dad.

"By-and-by, thanks for comin' 'ere," Mr Snyder
said.

"Thanks for bringing me here!" Mr Trowel
exclaimed with a smile, referring to the cab ride there.
"But any way I can help Abraham and his family, I want to
do it. He's a good man, Mr Snyder, and he don't deserve
the trouble that's being dealt him."

It was obvious Mr Trowel and Mr Roberts enjoyed
a long-standing friendship. Therefore, on this basis, Mr
Snyder decided against fishing for more details on that
point. Instead, he enquired, "You woz the neighbour who
found Mrs Yates, wozn't you?"

"I was," Mr Trowel replied. Folding his arms and resting them upon the table, he tilted and shook his head as he added, "The devil himself came to call last night."

"We think Mrs Yates woz done in by the same bloke, or lass, who killed her daughter. From what you saw, do you think that's likely?"

Mr Trowel's gaze was intense as he replied in a grave tone, "There can be *no* doubt of that, sir. Her clothes was gone, just like poor Maryanna." He drew a horizontal circle in the air above his head. "Cut up here she was. Hair all gone and…" He rested his hands against his chest as he cupped the air. "*Gone.*" He folded his arms and put them back onto the table. "Dunno what happened to her clothes though. Inspector thought the one who done her in took them. I told him about her ring, too."

"Gone?" Mr Snyder enquired, recalling the glint of gold he'd thought he'd seen on her marriage finger the night before.

"*Gone*," Mr Trowel echoed. He looked to the empty bowl in Mr Snyder's hands, and the Bow Streeter stood to refill it from a large pot Miss Trent had prepared earlier.

As he ladled the soup into the bowl, Mr Snyder enquired, "What woz the rest of the room like?"

"Table was over, on her waist, like she'd pulled it down on herself." Mr Trowel replied, yanking the air toward him to mime the action. "Chair behind her was resting against the stove with her head underneath." Mr Trowel straightened as Mr Snyder set the bowl before him. Shovelling a spoonful into his mouth, that he held a moment to savour the taste, he continued, "I remember there was this… jar of lemonade on the table and two glasses, one in front of her and one on the other side."

"Woz the glasses empty?"

"No; hers was half-full, and the other didn't look like it had had any taken out of it," Mr Trowel replied, shovelling more soup into his mouth.

Mr Snyder rested his folded arms upon the table and enquired, "What woz you doin' up and about at that time of night anyway?" He momentarily bowed and tilted his head as he scratched his nose. "What time woz it again?"

"Quarter past two this morning," Mr Trowel replied.

"Yeah, that's right," Mr Snyder said, meeting his gaze once more. "What woz you doin' up at that hour?"

"I'm a knocker-up; first one's at half past three," Mr Trowel replied. "I don't know about the others until I see what the chalk on the doors or walls say when I get there. I've got to walk to my patch though, so I leave at half past two. If it wasn't for Mr Ratchett lending me the money for a cab this morning, I would've missed my first knock-up—and a bloke can't be doing that in a job like mine. He's gotta be relied upon, don't he?"

"You called the Suggitts from the *Turk's Head* pub at about half past two, yeah?"

"Yeah. I told Mr Ratchett to get a constable— which he did because I got one pulling me off my round when I was half done," Mr Trowel replied. Tilting the bowl toward him, he recommenced his clamorous slurping of the soup.

"Then what?" Mr Snyder enquired once he was finished.

"Took me off to the station, he did," Mr Trowel replied. "I thought he was one of them that don't like me doing what they think *they* can do for the same price. I told him where to go at first. Bobby or not, he wasn't gonna stop me earning what's rightfully mine." He prodded his chest with his thumb and shrugged a shoulder. "But then he told me why he was there, so I went with him. Wood, or whatever the beggar's name was—the inspector, you know?"

Mr Snyder nodded.

"*Him*," Mr Trowel continued. "He spoke to me and wrote down my statement and got me to sign it."

"Thanks, Mr Trowel," Mr Snyder said with a smile. "I'll get sumin' for you to take the rest of the soup 'ome in."

"That's *very* kind of you, sir. *Very* kind!" Mr Trowel exclaimed with a broad smile.

Mr Snyder stood and left the kitchen. Miss Trent, who'd been listening at the door, followed him to the foot of the stairs.

"From what he's told me," Mr Snyder began. "Mrs Yates woz almost definitely done in by Mrs Roberts' murderer. Woz lemonade, not coffee, but the top of her head woz cut off, so woz her breasts. Her clothes woz gone, too."

"She must've known who it was," Miss Trent said in a grave tone. "We'll have to wait for Dr Weeks' findings to be sure, though."

* * *

Yea, though I walk through the valley of the shadow of death, Inspector Woolfe inwardly recited as he strode down the narrow, dimly lit corridor. The doors he passed along the way were both ignored and forgotten about the moment he saw them. Upon reaching the corridor's far end, he read the brass plaque fixed to the left side of a set of double doors. Illuminated by the weak gaslight of a lamp above, it confirmed he'd reached his destination. He therefore entered the room beyond and, stopping just inside the door, glanced around for the man he'd come to see.

In the corner to the right of the doors was a desk strewn with plain paper sheets, unopened ink wells, pencils, match boxes, and a discarded pocket-watch. An

Empire typewriter sat in the centre of the desk. Old English style gold lettering spelt out its name on its curved-edge, black, flat cover. Although the design was first manufactured in Montreal in 1892, this model had accompanied its owner from Canada the following year. Inspector Woolfe had always admired its simplistic efficiency and had been warned about touching it in the past. Approaching the desk, he greeted the man huddled over the typewriter. "Dr Weeks."

A soft grunt sounded from the surgeon as he continued his typing.

Inspector Woolfe ran his gaze over his dishevelled appearance and realised he was still wearing the off-white shirt, old overcoat, frayed scarf, and fingerless gloves he'd seen him in only a few hours prior. The blood-stained leather apron was a new addition though. Akin to those worn by practitioners of meat cleaving, both it and Dr Weeks' tendency to refer to bodies as 'meat' had earnt him the nickname of 'The Butcher' among Metropolitan Police officers. By contrast, Inspector Woolfe had returned home for a stand-up wash, a shave, and a fresh set of clothes after visiting the crime scene that morning.

"Have you had any sleep yet?" Inspector Woolfe enquired.

"Nah," Dr Weeks replied and stretched his arms. Lighting a cigarette soon after, he tossed the packet onto the desk and resumed his typing. Meanwhile, Inspector Woolfe ran his gaze over the mess.

Case files were haphazardly stacked to the right of the typewriter. Atop the pile was a tin mug of steaming coffee—undoubtedly 'flavoured' with a shot or two of whiskey. A second tin mug nearby held several cigarette butts submerged in the putrefied coffee of the previous night. On the left of the typewriter was a copy of the *British Medical* Journal. It was open at an article by James Mackenzie, M.D., titled *TREATMENT OF ASEPTIC*

WOUNDS WITHOUT BANDAGES OR DRESSINGS. The corner of the page was folded over while tobacco fibres filled the Journal's central crease. Further old, well-thumbed copies of the Journal were strewn about the desk. They, like the rest of the room, were contaminated by the foul stenches of stale tobacco, lime, and carbolic. The most striking item on the desk, aside from the typewriter, was the thick copy of *Anatomy, Descriptive and Surgical*, third edition, from 1893. Originally written by Henry Gray with illustrations by Henry Vandyke Carter, this British edition was edited by Thomas Pickering Pick. Inspector Woolfe lifted its cover and the first few pages to peek at the colour plates of highly detailed, labelled illustrations depicting various parts of the human body.

Fixed to the wall to the left of the desk was an unpolished, mahogany box shelving unit. It was filled with more copies of the *British Medical Journal*, and the 1895 editions of the controversial *Lancet* publication. Resting against the journals' spines was a macabre postcard depicting a flayed, decomposing corpse lying on a high table. Five men in their twenties, wearing everyday clothing of shirts, trousers, waistcoats, and bowler hats, were standing behind the table looking, proudly, at the camera. A sixth man, sitting at the corpse's head with a scalpel in his bare hand, also had his head turned toward the camera. The unexpected words of *Happy New Year* were printed in large, spiral lettering in the postcard's bottom-right corner.

"My nephew," Dr Weeks said upon noticing Inspector Woolfe 'admiring' the postcard. "Third from the right." Picking up the mug of steaming coffee with one hand, he held out a file with the other. Inspector Woolfe took the file but waited for Dr Weeks to drink the hot beverage. The dead room's location in the basement served to prevent bodies from decomposing too quickly without the need for chemical-soaked bandages. It could also serve to bring on hypothermia in a man if he weren't too careful, though.

"Good morning, Dr Weeks," another medical man greeted upon entering the dead room. Switching his outdoors coat for a leather apron hanging on a stand behind the door, he then crossed to the far side of the room and uncovered a corpse lying on a slab. There were six slabs in total; each made of marble with a squared top supported by straight wooden legs. Although there was a lip around the slab's edge, it was no deeper than four or five inches. Three of the six slabs were occupied by body-shaped mounds covered by white sheets.

"What time did Mrs Yates die?" Inspector Woolfe enquired with a lifting of the file.

"S'all in there," Dr Weeks replied, gesturing to it. Inspector Woolfe watched him with expectant eyes. Releasing a deep sigh, Dr Weeks added, "Between half past midnight and when yer witness found her."

"And the lemonade?" Inspector Woolfe enquired.

Dr Weeks exhaled the smoke from his lungs. He'd not slept in over twenty-four hours and it showed; his eyelids involuntarily drooped while his movements were slower and more laboured. He wasn't too exhausted to be his usual charming self, however. "Riddled with damned arsenic…" he muttered as he stood and snatched the file back. Putting the cigarette in the corner of his mouth, he folded the file's front cover under the remaining pages and sat down at a long counter occupying the back wall.

Inspector Woolfe followed and ran his gaze over the complicated-looking pieces of scientific equipment. Upon the counter was an average-looking glass beaker with a stopper. The liquid inside was, Inspector Woolfe presumed, a sample of the lemonade. Inserted through the stopper was a straight, glass tube whose tip almost touched the beaker's base. Meanwhile, its top end resembled a poppy flower's seed pod. Also inserted through the stopper was a second glass tube whose tip ended about a centimetre after clearing the stopper's base. Above the stopper it curved to the right to resemble the letter 'P' before attaching to a small, glass chamber. The chamber, whose shape mimicked a bulb used in electrical lighting, was suspended horizontally above the stopper. A metal tube was attached to the centre of the chamber's rotund end. This, in turn, was attached to a long, horizontal, glass tube that passed through a second piece of tall apparatus and ended in a point. This second piece of apparatus had a brass base with a nozzle.

"*Don't* even *think* 'bout touchin' that," Dr Weeks warned as Inspector Woolfe leaned over the apparatus to take a closer look.

"I wasn't going to."

"Good," Dr Weeks replied, meeting his gaze. "'Cause that there's one of the most sensitive tests for arsenic there is, and I don't want ya messin' it up."

Inspector Woolfe habitually liked to hear how such tests worked. Yet, given Dr Weeks' mood was fouler than usual, he doubted he'd have the patience required to explain. He therefore stepped back and peered over Dr Weeks' shoulder at the bottles of nitric acid and zinc beside the apparatus. Noticing another piece of apparatus, he walked along the counter to take a closer look. It comprised of another average-looking, glass beaker, this time suspended over an open flame, with an open top. Sitting beside it were a bottle of hydrochloric acid and a batch of fine, copper mesh. Again, he assumed the liquid inside the beaker was a sample of the lemonade.

"Don't touch that either," Dr Weeks warned.

"Is this all just for the testing of arsenic?" Inspector Woolfe enquired as he returned to him.

"Yeah; Marsh Test," Dr Weeks replied, pointing at the first set of apparatus. "Reinsch Test," he added, nodding to the second.

Inspector Woolfe glanced over both sets of apparatus and gave a curt nod of his head whilst momentarily raising his brows. He said, "Impressive."

Dr Weeks eyed him as he turned the pages in his file. Whilst still not entirely convinced by the sincerity of Woolfe's compliment, he gave his findings, nonetheless. He said, "The jar of lemonade ya'll found on the table were laced with between three and five teaspoons of arsenic. Only thing in Mrs Yates' stomach— 'cept the usual acids—were lemonade. Ain't any arsenic in her tissues and were traces of lemonade and arsenic in her throat, in her mouth, and on her lips. Probably where she vomited so, if ya find her clothes, there'll be some on 'em, too." Dr Weeks stood and, taking the cigarette from his mouth, dropped it into the tobacco-saturated coffee mug on his desk.

"Our killer didn't intend to drink any of the lemonade he—or she—presumably brought with—" Inspector Woolfe cut himself short and plucked up the packet of cigarettes Dr Weeks had previously discarded onto the desk.

"If ya wanted one, ya should've asked!" Dr Weeks snapped, attempting to snatch them back.

"I saw a packet of *these,*" Inspector Woolfe replied, moving them out of his reach. "At the house of those meddlers, the Bow bloody Street Society."

Dr Weeks' hand shot back in an instant, and he stared at him with wide eyes.

Recognising the tell-tale signs of fear in the surgeon, Inspector Woolfe flattened his brow and narrowed his hard eyes. Through a clenched jaw, he enquired in a low, yet deceptively calm voice, "Have you been telling them things you shouldn't?"

Dr Weeks looked past Inspector Woolfe at his fellow doctor. Seeing he was engrossed in his work, though, Dr Weeks took a step back and, averting his gaze, replied, "Nah. Course not."

Inspector Woolfe closed the distance between them and leant forward to put their faces centimetres apart. In a low, hard voice he enquired, "Have you, or have you not, been telling the Bow Street Society things you shouldn't, *Dr* Weeks?"

The veins throbbed in Dr Weeks' neck as his heart raced. Feeling his leg muscles tighten, along with his shoulders, he glanced behind him before attempting to take several backward steps. At the same time, he reached behind him for the counter and replied in a tremoring voice, "I told ya... *nah*."

Yet, despite the distance Dr Weeks had put between them, Inspector Woolfe grasped the scruff of his shirt, pulled him off his feet, and plonked him down in front of him. Gripping Dr Weeks' shoulders, he leant forward, again, and enquired in a sardonic tone, "Do you want to try and sound a bit more convincing when you say that?"

Beads of sweat formed upon Dr Weeks' forehead, and he replied, "Those... damned cigarettes could've been anyone's."

"Yeah, they could've," Inspector Woolfe replied in a low voice. "But *you* are the doctor working on the Roberts murder case that *they* have been commissioned to investigate by the sister. And *you*," Inspector Woolfe gripped the ends of Dr Weeks' scarf, causing him to flinch, "are the only man I know who smokes *Turkish* cigarettes."

Dr Weeks' complexion turned pallid as he fixed his gaze upon Woolfe's with bulging eyes.

"If I find *any* evidence that you've been leaking confidential police reports to the Bow Street Society," Inspector Woolfe continued as he unknotted Dr Weeks' scarf. "I'll have your guts for garters—and that'll just be the beginning." He twisted the ends of the scarf to tighten it around Dr Weeks' neck in one fluid movement. "Understand?"

Dr Weeks' wheezed against the pressure on his throat as he replied, "Yeah…"

Inspector Woolfe released the scarf, sending Dr Weeks into a violent coughing fit, and said, "Good." He pulled Dr Weeks up by the shoulders and ran his hands over his coat's lapels. "Now," he gave a sudden tug of the material, causing Dr Weeks to grunt, and tapped his cheek. "Get some sleep."

Dr Weeks nodded through a few more coughs and kept his eyes fixed upon the policeman until he'd left the room. Feeling the pounding of his heart in his ears, and the throbbing of the veins in his neck, he stumbled back to his desk and retrieved a bottle of whiskey from its bottom drawer. Wiping the sweat from his forehead with his arm, he then collapsed into his chair and took a generous swig from the bottle.

TWENTY

"There are constables outside your front door," Lady Owston informed Mr Suggitt as she entered the kitchen via the basement's external stairs. Accompanying her were Misses Webster and Dexter, and Messieurs Maxwell and Snyder; the last having left his cab and horses at a nearby livery.

"Inspector Woolfe insisted upon it for our protection," Mr Suggitt replied. "Alas I fail to follow his logic; his suspicions firmly point at one of *us* being the devil who's slain our loved ones."

"Perhaps he hopes the murderer will attempt to slay a third?" Mr Maxwell suggested. Stark realisation struck him, however, and he hastily added, "*Oh God,* Mr Suggitt. I—I didn't mean that to sound—"

"*Who* are you?" Mr Suggitt interrupted.

Mr Maxwell tucked his notebook under his arm but, upon finding it was too cumbersome for him to offer his hand, tucked it under his other arm. When this, too, proved unsuccessful, he put it down on the table, wiped his hand upon his frock coat, and offered it to Mr Suggitt. He said, "Mr Joseph Maxwell of the *Gaslight Gazette*, sir." He felt Mr Suggitt's grip tighten. "A—And Bow Street Society member."

Mr Suggitt released his hand and enquired, "Why have we not met before?"

"I was only recently assigned to the case," Mr Maxwell replied.

Mr Suggitt enquired from Lady Owston, "Are such arrangements commonplace?"

"Miss Trent assigns whoever she deems appropriate for each case whenever she decides there is a need for them," Lady Owston replied.

"I see…" Mr Suggitt said with a sideways glance at Mr Maxwell. "Mr Roberts and my niece are aware of your visit this morning, He's in the dining room and she's in the parlour. Miss Trent informed me it was your preference to speak to them separately…?"

"Indeed," Lady Owston replied, removing her gloves. "Ladies are more inclined to speak their heart's secrets if their father isn't present to bear witness."

"I also intend to have Mr Roberts describe the clothes he last saw Mrs Yates wearing so I may sketch them," Miss Dexter interjected in a meek voice.

Mr Suggitt frowned and, casting a sideways glance at Mr Snyder, enquired, "But surely Mr Snyder would be better suited for such, or Regina? As they each approached her at the public house."

"Yes, but only Mr Roberts was at home with Mrs Yates prior to her death," Miss Dexter replied and downcast her eyes. "Aside from her murderer that is…" Momentarily closing her eyes to dismiss her imaginings, she met his gaze and added, "If Mrs Yates changed her clothes, and those were what the murderer took, then Mr Roberts may remember what they were."

"Unless he was the one who—" Mr Maxwell began.

"*Time* is of the *essence*," Lady Owston interrupted with a hard look to Mr Maxwell. "If we are to hear the answers, we require *prior* to the police discovering our presence."

"Y—Yes…" Mr Maxwell replied with flushed cheeks.

"Please *lead* the way," Lady Owston urged, addressing Mr Suggitt.

He felt sorely tempted to submit Mr Maxwell to Inspector Woolfe's mercy, however. It was only the painful recollection of his wife's precarious emotional state that stayed his hand. Climbing a steep, spiralled, stone staircase to the ground floor, he led them into the hallway and said, "I'd be appreciative if you would refrain from disturbing my wife; she is exhausted and hasn't eaten today. I fear your questions may ignite hysteria within her."

"We shall take *every* care not to do so," Lady Owston replied. "But we cannot promise we shan't. If the Roberts share information with us, which requires us to seek clarification from your wife, we are bound by duty to speak with her."

"I understand you are in an awkward situation," Mr Suggitt began. "Yet, while I admire and respect your group's dedication, I am fundamentally in agreement with Inspector Woolfe."

"As is your right," Lady Owston conceded. "However, since Miss Trent didn't receive written confirmation of your wife prematurely ending her commission with the Bow Street Society, we are obliged to do all in our power to unmask Mrs Maryanna Roberts' murderer."

"She would have ended it if her mother hadn't been…" Mr Suggitt said. Rubbing the bridge of his nose between his thumb and forefinger, he continued, "*Please* understand that I only wish to protect Diana as much as I can from this awful, *awful* business."

"The ultimate, and everlasting, protection you could give her though would be to permit us to discover who killed her sister and mother," Miss Webster stated.

"I know…" Mr Suggitt replied with a slouching of his shoulders. Indicating two doors, he said, "The dining room is second on the right, and the parlour is second on the left… If you *should* need me at all, pull twice on the bell rope in the corner of each room and my housekeeper shall fetch me." He half-turned. "I'm placing the welfare of my brother-in-law and niece in your hands against my better judgement. Please do not betray that trust."

"You have our words as Bow Street Society members that we won't," Mr Maxwell replied in a sombre tone.

"You may rely on us," Miss Dexter reassured.

"Thank you…" Mr Suggitt replied, lifting his shoulders and straightening his back. When he left them to enter a third room, his gait was also less encumbered.

"Mr Maxwell, *you* shall do me the privilege of joining Agnes and me in speaking to Miss Regina Roberts," Lady Owston said with a warm smile.

"Privilege…?" Mr Maxwell enquired as he rubbed his neck around the small bow of his cravat.

"Yes, *privilege*," Lady Owston repeated.

"Oh," Mr Maxwell replied, lowering his hand. Allowing a smile to form, then, he lifted his head, puffed out his chest, and added, "*Thank* you."

"Shouldn't Mr Maxwell assist us with Mr Roberts?" Miss Dexter enquired.

"*No!*" Mr Maxwell blurted out with a swift look from Lady Owston, to Miss Dexter, and back again. When Miss Dexter parted her lips to enquire after his reasons why, though, he stayed her voice by explaining, "He has met you and Mr Snyder before, Miss Dexter, and I'd only say, or do, the wrong thing." He extended his arm toward the parlour and, with a bow, addressed Lady Owston and Miss Webster. "Ladies first."

"As you wish, Mr Maxwell…" Miss Dexter replied in a subdued voice.

Mr Maxwell relaxed his arm and straightened at the sound. Watching Miss Dexter approach the door to the dining room, he felt his spirits wane and his joviality become overwhelmed by regret. Yet, although he parted his lips and took a couple of steps toward her, the opening of the parlour door kept him silent and obliged him to follow Lady Owston and Miss Webster.

"It's okay, lass," Mr Snyder soothed, placing a

gentle hand on Miss Dexter's lower back as he joined her at the dining room door.

"I know it is," she replied with a meagre smile. Taking a moment to gather herself, she then knocked.

"Yeah?!" Mr Abraham Roberts' voice called, prompting Mr Snyder to lead the way inside.

The first thing he and Miss Dexter were struck by was how dark the room was. Despite it being the middle of the day, heavy curtains had been drawn across the bay window on the far right, the gas lamps were lit, and a large fire was burning in the hearth. Mr Snyder presumed the curtains had been drawn to prevent the constables from spying on the residents, whilst Miss Dexter was grateful for the fire's warmth. In the middle of the room was a large, oak, extendable table with a polished top free of scratches and marks. An arrangement of wax flowers, housed within a bell-shaped, glass cover, formed the table's centrepiece. The room's remaining furniture consisted of a sideboard to one's left upon entering, and an oak, display cabinet opposite the door containing the Suggitts' best china.

Mr Roberts was sitting on the table's far side, facing the door. The puffy, dark circles beneath his bloodshot eyes made his gaunt features appear even more haggard. His tattered clothes were also in stark contrast to his opulent surroundings. He'd lifted his head when Mr Snyder had entered but then rose to his feet when Miss Dexter followed. He muttered, "Hello, miss."

"Please, sit, Mr Roberts," Miss Dexter replied as she took the chair opposite him. Mr Snyder waited until Mr Roberts had lowered himself into his seat before taking the vacant chair beside Miss Dexter's.

Mr Roberts rested his elbow and opposite hand upon the table. Bowing his head, he ran his free hand through his unkempt hair, occasionally gripping clumps of hair as he did so. He then lifted his head to meet Miss

Dexter's gaze and, gripping a large clump of hair at the back of his head, said, "Diana said you wanted me to tell you what her mum was wearing last night…"

Miss Dexter retrieved her sketchbook and pencil from her satchel but refrained from replying. In the past, she'd found people sometimes felt the need to fill silent gaps in conversation. In doing so, they often revealed information they might've otherwise been hesitant to share. Mr Roberts was no exception.

"…She also said you was all at the *Turk's Head* when Regina had a go at her grandmother," Mr Roberts continued. "You must've seen what she was wearing, then."

"I wasn't," Miss Dexter admitted. "Mr Snyder was, but you accompanied her home, Mr Roberts. If she'd changed her clothes once there, Mr Snyder wouldn't be able to describe them for me to sketch… *Did* she change her clothes?"

Mr Roberts dropped his hand and leant back in his chair. He replied, "Not while I was there." He dropped his gaze. "I should've stayed with her…" He leant forward once more and, resting both elbows upon the table, rubbed his face. A loud sigh escaped his lips as his shoulders slouched, his head bowed, and his hands ran repeatedly through his hair. Resting his head in the crook of his arms, he then gripped the hair upon his crown, and said in a muffled voice strained by emotion, "*Why* didn't I stay with her? I could've saved her… She could be alive today if I hadn't *left* her…"

"She woz at home," Mr Snyder said. "A place where she should've been safe. You wozn't to know."

Mr Roberts simultaneously released his hair, dropped his arms forward, and lifted his head. With a reddened face and eyes, he enquired, "But I knew where Regina was, didn't I? I didn't *have* to come here. I should've *stayed* with Sarah."

"Your wife was found on Oxford Street," Miss Dexter began. "Where anyone could see her or her murderer." She grimaced as Mr Roberts bowed his head and rested his forehead upon his arms. "I know it shall bring you little comfort, but…" Miss Dexter's voice became quiet as a lump formed in her throat at the sight of the distraught man. "…It wasn't possible for you to know, or even suspect, what would happen to Mrs Yates… Not even the Bow Street Society had an inclination. But you, and I," she glanced at her fellow Bow Streeter, "and Mr Snyder, may help Mrs Yates now by getting to the truth of her death. Between you both, I'm certain you can recall her clothes so I may sketch them, and *we* may locate them." She swallowed hard, "and, with the greatest of hope, her murderer."

Mr Roberts nodded against his arms. Sniffing hard, he lifted his head and shoulders from the table and dropped his arms to his sides. Keeping his head bowed, he replied, "She had on a grey shawl… Knitted. Lightish-grey, you know? With a… darker-grey, woollen dress underneath—or was it black?" He looked to Mr Snyder.

"I'll let Miss Dexter know what I remember once you've said yours," Mr Snyder replied.

Mr Roberts gave a slow nod and said, "Black boots, too."

"Any jewellery?" Miss Dexter enquired as she sketched and shaded the garments.

"Yeah…" Mr Roberts replied, rubbing his face with one hand. "A ring; gold, it was. Was her wedding ring, given her by her husband's mother. When times got hard, after Maryanna left, Sarah wanted to pawn it, but I told her no. She hated her husband but loved his mother."

"Why didn't you tell us Mrs Yates woz livin' with you when we asked?" Mr Snyder enquired.

Mr Roberts shook his head as he bowed it and replied, "I dunno…" Lifting his head sharply, he insisted, "nothing was going on between us." As he then bowed his head again, he muttered, "despite what Regina says."

"Was the ring plain?" Miss Dexter enquired.

"Yeah," Mr Roberts replied.

"Please, could you tell me if anything needs changing?" Miss Dexter enquired as she turned her sketchbook around and placed it in front of him. Mr Roberts lifted his head and, pulling the sketchbook closer, stared at the grey-and-black shaded drawing. "Yeah, that's them." He pushed the sketchbook toward her and fell silent. As he replayed the previous night's events in his mind, though, a sudden realisation hit him, and he enquired, "How'd you know I walked Sarah home?"

"Mr Suggitt told us," Mr Snyder replied.

Miss Dexter felt a shiver run through her as she recalled the conversation with Mr Suggitt outside the Roberts' tenement building that morning. Closing her sketchbook, she slipped it onto her lap, and rested her clasped hands upon it. She knew there would plenty of time for Mr Snyder to review the drawing once they returned to Bow Street.

Meanwhile, Mr Roberts rested his elbow upon the table and, leaning his head upon his hand, tugged repeatedly at the hair behind his ear. In doing so, he kept his face turned away from the Bow Streeters and his gaze fixed upon the closed curtains.

"Do you walk her home every night?" Mr Snyder enquired. "Did you walk her home the night Mrs Roberts woz done in?"

"Yeah, I do, but… not *that* night," Mr Roberts replied. "Sarah told me some bloke—some sailor she said—was in London for a couple of days and wanted to spend time with her. She told me she didn't need me walking her home because he would in the morning."

"What time did you walk her home last night?" Mr Snyder enquired.

"Eleven o'clock, closing time," Mr Roberts replied. "Got back home at quarter past. That's when she told me what had happened with Regina and where she'd gone." He dropped his arm to the table but kept his head turned away as he continued, "She told me to stay at home—" his voice faltered, "that Regina would be back come morning and I shouldn't worry." He clenched his hand into a fist. "I was angry though. I wanted to drag her back, to *make* her apologise."

"Did Mrs Yates bring any lemonade home with her?" Mr Snyder enquired.

"No," Mr Roberts replied, turning his head to face him. "And I already told Inspector Woolfe we don't keep any in the house."

"You left home, then, and got 'ere at abou'…?" Mr Snyder enquired.

"Gone midnight—half past, maybe?" Mr Roberts replied. "Clement and Diana told me to stay here, that it was too late to walk back and Regina was asleep besides."

"And woz she?" Mr Snyder enquired.

"Was she what?" Mr Roberts enquired in return.

"Asleep," Mr Snyder replied.

"Yeah," Mr Roberts replied. "I looked in on her…" He bowed his head and his voice became quiet as he went on, "…She was safe, cared for." He wiped his face and sniffed. "Sarah was alone…" He stared at the table as tears slid down his cheeks and his lips trembled. "I should've *been* there with her…" He said in a wobbly voice. "I should've—" He clasped his hand over his eyes as a sob erupted from his lips, and he broke down into uncontrollable weeping.

Feeling a tightening of her chest and a stinging of her eyes at the sight, Miss Dexter fought to suppress her emotions. Yet the more she saw and heard of the poor man's distress, the stronger her grief became until, finally, she stood and fled the room, muttering, "Excuse me." No

236

sooner had she stepped into the hallway and closed the door, did her tears erupt and her own, soft weeping commence.

"Miss Dexter?" Mr Maxwell enquired from across the hallway.

TWENTY-ONE

"Miss Roberts?" Lady Owston enquired as she entered the parlour. The fireplace stood opposite the door with—to Miss Webster's relief—a embroidered fireguard set before its hearth. Perpendicular to the fireplace were two plush sofas, each facing inwards toward the centre of the room. Miss Regina Roberts was lying sideways upon the sofa to the right with her bent elbow resting upon the sofa's arm. Her head was, in turn, resting upon the open palm of that hand whilst she browsed a copy of *The Bazaar, Exchange, and Mart, The Journal of the Household* lying in front of her. She hummed at the sound of her name but gave the new arrivals no further acknowledgement.

First published in 1868, the 'Exchange and Mart,' as it was commonly known, was one of many publications which catered to the pastime of fireside shopping. As the name suggests, fireside shoppers could browse their preferred publication and order their goods through the mail—often direct from the manufacturers. Although some publications and suppliers offered free samples of materials for dresses, linens, etc., with 'carriage paid,' formal orders were conventionally made on a cash only basis without discounts. Costing 2d per issue, the 'Exchange and Mart' included goods' advertisements and articles covering a range of topics, including sport, fashions, etiquette, the management of children, and items for the housekeeper's room. Naturally, Lady Owston had recognised the interior pages of the 'Exchange and Mart' the moment she'd laid eyes upon them. The fact it was in the Suggitt household surprised her, though. For, unless the *Queshire Department Store* had an advertisement in the publication, Miss Roberts—and, by association, Mr Suggitt—was supporting that establishment's competitors.

"Have you found something which greatly interests you?" Lady Owston enquired, pointing to the publication.

"I'm just looking," Miss Roberts replied, flipping over several of the pages until she'd reached one with a large picture. Since she'd thus far refused to even lift her head, let alone greet her visitors, Lady Owston decided to remind her of her matters. She therefore snatched the 'Exchange and Mart' out from under her nose, thereby obliging Miss Roberts to not only look up but also throw out her arm to retrieve it. Yet, Lady Owston was too swift for her, and all Miss Roberts succeeded in doing was throwing herself off balance. Catching herself by gripping the sofa's edge, she then scrambled to get back into a seated position as she demanded, "Give that back!"

"It isn't within my character to be rude, and certainly not in the presence of one who has lost as much as you," Lady Owston began. "However, on this occasion, I feel it is my duty to step outside the boundaries of etiquette to tell you to sit up straight, focus your attention, and listen."

"I don't have to listen to you," Miss Roberts retorted as she stood. Snatching the 'Exchange and Mart' from Lady Owston's hands, she dropped back onto the sofa and added, "you're not my mum."

"No; your mother is dead," Lady Owston retorted and sat beside her. "*Murdered*, and we—"

"I know she was murdered," Miss Roberts interrupted as she swiftly flipped through the pages of the 'Exchange and Mart.' "But the one who murdered her's dead, too, so it don't matter."

Lady Owston felt the weight of the young woman's words hit her as keenly as if she'd been slapped. Looking across to Miss Webster and Mr Maxwell, who'd sat on the sofa opposite, she then furrowed her brow and enquired from Miss Roberts, "Aren't you sad and afraid about your grandmother being murdered…?"

"No," Miss Roberts replied in a cool tone. "They done us all a favour."

"You do not wish to know who it was?" Miss Webster interjected.

"No," Miss Roberts replied.

"Even if it was your father?" Mr Maxwell enquired.

Miss Roberts lowered the 'Exchange and Mart' and, with a scowl, warned, "Take that back."

"He was the last person to see your grandmother alive," Miss Webster said.

"You don't know him, or me!" Miss Roberts shouted as she threw Miss Webster an equally dark look. "He wouldn't do that; he's not got it in him to kill someone."

"Why did you hate your grandmother so?" Lady Owston enquired.

"Thought that was as clear as the nose on your face," Miss Roberts retorted.

"I'm a little short-sighted," Lady Owston countered.

Although she retained her scowl, Miss Roberts glanced over Lady Owston with doubt in her eyes. Unsure as to whether she had been serious in her remark, she explained, "Because she got my mum out the house, so she could move in with my dad."

"How did she do that?" Lady Owston enquired.

Miss Roberts hesitated as she, again, glanced over Lady Owston's form. The tension in her face and shoulders visibly eased, though, as she replied in a calmer tone, "Told my dad lies about my mum. My mum didn't steal the housekeeping money, she wasn't drunk when it was taken, and she would've done anything for me when she hadn't had a drink. My dad didn't believe her when she told him she hadn't taken it but that was because Sarah had been filling his head with stones. It was her who told my dad to toss my mum out—and he did. Made her go to *that* life to make ends meet. He made her drinking worse by doing that, but Sarah couldn't stop even then. Whenever she got the chance, she was talking my mum down—to me, my dad, even to Aunt Diana. But Aunt Diana's on Mum's side, and mine. She just wanted us all to be back together; even asked my dad to have my mum back at home."

"Oh?" Lady Owston enquired.

Miss Roberts looked down at the 'Exchange and Mart' and, turning the page, studied the advertisement. She said, "I don't know if I should tell you."

"Would it be helpful if we told you we were friends of your aunt's?" Lady Owston enquired.

"It might…" Miss Roberts mumbled.

"In fact," Lady Owston continued with a warm smile. "We have been asked by her to investigate your mother's murder. I'm Lady Katheryne Owston and that is Miss Agnes Webster and Mr Joseph Maxwell; we are all members of the Bow Street Society."

Miss Roberts bit her lower lip as she looked to the others in turn. Addressing Lady Owston, she said, "Aunt Diana said you was coming today."

"Your aunt and uncle have been very kind to you, Regina," Lady Owston said. "They told us you and your father stayed here last night."

Miss Roberts nodded but returned her gaze to the 'Exchange and Mart.' Nibbling at her lower lip as she considered the possible good and bad consequences of opening-up, she then closed the publication and set it to one side. Shifting upon the sofa to face Lady Owston, she enquired, "If I tell you something, will you promise not to tell?"

"That very much depends upon what it is you have to say," Lady Owston replied. "But, if it's something connected to your mother's murder, it's your duty to tell us about it."

"What if I don't?" Miss Roberts enquired.

"Then, I'm afraid, it could mean the difference between us finding out who murdered your mother and not," Lady Owston replied, softly.

Miss Roberts frowned and, glancing at the door, said, "The night Mum died…" She bowed her head and picked at her fingernails. "Aunt Diana came to the house. She and Dad thought I was sleeping but I wasn't. I was behind the curtain though, so they didn't know. I listened…" She straightened and met Lady Owston's gaze. "Aunt Diana was telling Dad how sorry Mum was and how she was gonna get help. Aunt Diana and Uncle Clement was gonna take her in here so she could get away from the gin and stay off it. Dad told her he thought it was good news but said he didn't think it was a good idea for Mum and Sarah to live together. And, anyway, he said—" Miss Roberts pursed her lips and bowed her head.

"What did he say?" Lady Owston encouraged in a soft voice.

Miss Roberts closed her eyes and replied, "He told Aunt Diana he loved her, that it was her he'd loved all these years." Clenching her eyelids as she shook her head, she then lifted her head and continued in a hard tone, "She wasn't even surprised, or angry." She pursed her lips together, again, and bowed her head. In a quiet voice, she said, "She told him they'd talked about it before, and she still loved Uncle Clement. She told him it didn't change things though; she'd still help us as much as she could."

"What time did your aunt arrive and leave?" Miss Webster enquired as she recorded the revelation in her notebook.

242

"I went to bed at about half past nine because I've got to be knocked-up at four in the morning to go to the market," Miss Roberts replied. "Aunt Diana got there a bit after that. She was there a long time. I don't know what time she left but it was late because I was falling asleep by then."

"Did your father go out at all during the night?" Miss Webster enquired.

"No, after Aunt Diana left, he came to bed and we slept until we both got knocked up at four," Miss Roberts replied. "He walked to the docks to sleep at the gates and I walked to the market at Covent Garden to help sell the flowers."

"Where was your grandmother?" Mr Maxwell enquired.

Miss Roberts shrugged her shoulder and replied, "Dunno, probably working and out with some bloke. I didn't ask."

"Do you have any lemonade at home?" Miss Webster enquired.

"No," Miss Roberts replied. "My dad and me don't like it."

"Thank you," Lady Owston said with a warm smile. "You've been most helpful, and we *do* appreciate your speaking to us. I'm *quite* certain your aunt does, too. Mr Maxwell, would you be so kind as to inform Miss Dexter and Mr Snyder we are ready to proceed when they are?"

"Um, yes… of course," Mr Maxwell replied in a quiet voice as he felt the palms of his hands moisten. Standing, he turned, and felt his cheeks flush as he saw a fireplace where there ought to be a door. "Excuse me…" He mumbled, turning around and hurrying from the room. As he closed the door behind him, he released a sigh. The moment he looked to the dining room door, though, his heartrate quickened, and his stomach tightened. "Come on,

Maxwell, you can do this," he mumbled as he shuffled along the hallway toward the foot of the stairs. *It's not as if you've never spoken to her before,* he thought. *Or never upset her before.* He halted in his tracks as he felt his hair stand up on end. *What will I say?* He frowned and, wiping his forehead with his handkerchief, rounded the stairs. The sight of Miss Dexter softly weeping on the other side expelled his fear in an instant, though, and he strode toward her with an alarmed expression. He enquired, "Miss Dexter?"

She lifted her head and looked at him with wide eyes. Momentarily stunned into silence by his sudden arrival, she replied in a soft voice, "Mr Roberts required a moment."

Mr Maxwell's heart ached at the sight of her tear-stained cheeks and red eyes. Realising he was still holding his handkerchief, he offered it to her and enquired, "W-Would he like this?"

"No… But I would," Miss Dexter replied, taking it from him. "Thank you…"

"You're most welcome," Mr Maxwell said, feeling a warmth at the back of his neck.

Dabbing at the corners of her eyes, Miss Dexter enquired, "How is your moth—?"

"She's well, thank you," Mr Maxwell hastily interrupted. Offering a weak smile, he was keen to move the conversation away from the awkward subject of the cancelled dinner invitation. He therefore indicated the parlour and said, "Miss Roberts had some interesting things to say. After Lady Owston was forced to pull the 'Exchange and Mart' from under her nose. Apparently, Mr Roberts confessed his love to Mrs Suggitt on the night of Mrs Roberts' murder." Mr Maxwell toyed with his cravat. "Naturally, Mrs Suggitt rebuffed his affection."

"How *awful*," Miss Dexter replied with genuine regret.

244

"We only have Regina's word such a conversation took place, of course…" Mr Maxwell said in a feeble attempt to reassure her. Twisting his body to look back at the parlour door, he didn't notice Miss Dexter leaning forward to peer through the stairs' balusters at the same. Thus, when he turned back upon hearing her move closer a moment later, he inadvertently pressed his body against hers. They tensed in an instant but neither attempted to pull away either. Mr Maxwell's heart raced as he looked into Miss Dexter's smiling face.

"What are you thinking, Joseph?" She enquired.

"Um…" Mr Maxwell cleared his throat. "Well…" Clearing his throat a second time, he glanced around. Upon seeing they were still alone, he held her face in his hands and placed a tender kiss upon her lips. Miss Dexter's eyes widened at the touch but then closed as he kissed her again.

"Joseph…" She whispered through a soft exhale afterward.

Mr Maxwell released her and, attempting to step back, said, "F—Forgive me, Miss Dexter. I shouldn't have—"

"There's nothing to forgive," Miss Dexter replied as she took hold of his arm and eased him back to her. "We *are* engaged to be married."

You will cancel her dinner invitation and nullify your preposterous engagement, Oliver Maxwell's voice suddenly demanded within Joseph's mind, dashing his euphoria like a ship against the rocks. *This family will not be shamed by your vile, filthy habits*, the voice continued, propelling Mr Joseph Maxwell away from Miss Dexter. "P—Please…" He began, his stomach somersaulting.

"What is it?" Miss Dexter enquired.

As she attempted to move closer to him, though, he retreated around the stairs to put it between them.

Through the balusters, he said, "Please request Mrs Suggitt to join Mr Snyder and I in the dining room."

"But—" Miss Dexter began, cutting herself off when she saw him flee into the parlour. Utterly dumbfounded by what had just occurred, she stared at the closed door for several moments. When she realised he wasn't coming back, she looked at the handkerchief in her hands, and left the hallway in search of Mrs Suggitt.

TWENTY-TWO

Mrs Diana Suggitt felt chilled to the core despite the fire crackling in the hearth behind her. Sitting at the dining table, she gazed past Mr Maxwell's shoulder at an imagined horizon. Her hair was unkempt, her eyes were bloodshot, and her naturally pale complexion was insipid beneath a layer of tears. She repeatedly tapped her fingertips together as she rested the heels of her hands upon the table. Beside her sat Mr Abraham Roberts, whilst Mr Snyder was next to Mr Maxwell.

"Mrs Suggitt?" Mr Maxwell enquired.

Mrs Suggitt stilled her fingers and, looking at him without seeing him, replied in a hoarse voice, "Yes?"

"She's not up to this, can't you see that?" Mr Roberts interjected.

Mrs Suggitt brushed her hand against his and said, "No, I *must*; for Mother now as well as Maryanna." From Mr Maxwell, she enquired, "What is it you wish to know, Mr…?"

"Maxwell," he reminded.

"Oh yes, of course…" Mrs Suggitt replied, forcing a smile. "Mr Maxwell…" Her smile vanished, and she repeatedly tapped her fingertips together once more. "What is it you wish to know?"

Mr Roberts folded his arms and slouched back in his chair.

"You were at home all of last night, correct?" Mr Maxwell enquired.

"Yes… that is correct," Mrs Suggitt replied. "Alone at first… then Clement came home after speaking with the Bow Street Society at the *Turk's Head*. He brought Regina with him… and, much later, Abraham came."

"At what time did he arrive?" Mr Maxwell enquired.

"I've already *told* you that," Mr Roberts scolded. When Mr Maxwell didn't respond, though, he turned his head away and tightened his jaw.

"Half-past midnight, I believe," Mrs Suggitt replied and fixed her gaze upon her brother-in-law. "He was upset... Regina had argued with Mother—as your group witnessed, Mr Maxwell—and Clement had brought her here." She pressed a trembling hand to her forehead. "Forgive me, I—I've already said that." Lowering her hand, she clasped it with the other upon the table and rubbed her fingernails. "Abraham wanted to take Regina home so she could apologise to Mother. Clement and I convinced him it was too late to do so as Regina had already gone to bed. We invited him to stay the night also..." She momentarily held her bent fingers beneath her nose as she took in a deep, shuddering breath. "Abraham—" Her voice cracked, "...looked in on Regina and then retired to the second guest room. Clement and I retired to our own room."

"And no one left again until..." Mr Maxwell began, consulting his notebook.

"Mr Trowel called," Mr Roberts stated.

"Do you have any lemonade here, or did someone bring some back?" Mr Maxwell enquired.

Mrs Suggitt gave a curt shake of her head and replied, "I know—" She pressed her bent fingers to her lips to stifle a sob. Pulling back her trembling hand, she continued in a wobbly voice, "...how she was given the—" her voice cracked, again before she whispered, "*poison*." She blinked several times as she looked to the ceiling and took several slow, deep breaths. "None of us had any lemonade at all that night..." She looked back to Mr Maxwell, "either here or at the *Turk's Head*."

"The night of Mrs Roberts' death, you were at home all evening, too?" Mr Maxwell enquired, "With your husband?"

"Clement left soon after dinner, around… eight thirty, I believe," Mrs Suggitt replied and clasped her hands tightly upon the table. "He returned home a little after eleven thirty—as you already know. He told me of the conversation he'd had with your group about it last night. I…" She bowed her head. "Already knew the true nature of the business that had drawn him away from home that night. I didn't know on the night itself but afterward. He confessed it all to me and we later informed Inspector Woolfe of it also." She retrieved her handkerchief, dabbed at her red nose, and took several soft sniffs. "I don't condone my husband's actions, Mr Maxwell, but I understand why he felt he needed to do what he did."

"You lied for him when you were first asked about your whereabouts by the police. Has he also lied on your behalf though?" Mr Maxwell enquired.

"I… I don't understand," Mrs Suggitt replied, glancing at Mr Roberts.

"You went out as well on the night of your sister's murder, but not to find her as your husband had," Mr Maxwell said. "You went to see Mr Roberts."

Mrs Suggitt and Mr Roberts simultaneously looked at each other; she with parted lips, he with narrowed eyes.

"It's true, then?" Mr Snyder enquired.

Mrs Suggitt and Mr Roberts averted their gazes from one another. Whilst she then bowed her head and tugged at the corners of her handkerchief, he turned hard eyes to the Bow Streeters and replied, "Yeah, it's true. Who told you?"

"Your daughter," Mr Maxwell replied. "Who you thought was sleeping at the time."

"I wanted to convince Abraham to allow Maryanna to return home," Mrs Suggitt said in a soft voice. "Clement had agreed for her to live here awhile—to remove all temptation of the gin from her. I'd hoped… once he heard of our plans…" She looked to her brother-in-law who, again, averted his gaze. "Abraham would let her go home afterward."

"But he told you he loved you instead," Mr Maxwell said.

Mrs Suggitt turned wide eyes to him. Her lips quivered and fresh tears slipped down her cheeks. She parted and closed her lips as she looked between Mr Snyder and Mr Maxwell. Feeling a sudden hand upon her shoulder, she jerked her body away before seeing it was Mr Roberts. Her features crumpled at once, and she turned away from him whilst pressing the handkerchief tight against her lips to muffle the wheezing and sobbing which overwhelmed her.

Meanwhile, Mr Roberts ran his hand through his hair and stood. Pacing back and forth a while, he then returned to the table but continued to shift his weight from one foot to the other as he replied, "I *did* tell Diana I loved her—that I'd *always* loved her—but she told me she loved Clement." He folded his arms across his chest and nibbled at his thumbnail. "It was the answer she'd given me before, the one I'd been expecting. The stuff with Maryanna…" He shook his head and, sitting down, rested his elbows upon his knees. "…It made me feel bad. When Diana came that night…" He ran his gaze over her. "I thought it was another chance at happiness." His tone then hardened as he looked to the Bow Streeters and said, "I *loved* my wife; it was *her* I chose all them years ago, *not* Diana."

"But the drink made her into a monster," Mr Snyder remarked.

"Which could've made you think you'd chosen the

wrong sister," Mr Maxwell added.

"*No!*" Mr Roberts cried as he leapt to his feet. "I don't know *what* you're trying to say but I didn't murder my wife!"

Mrs Suggitt stood and, retreating to the window, put her back to the room as she continued to weep.

The sight immediately dispelled Mr Roberts' anger, and he dropped onto his chair with a sigh. "Look," he began, running his hand through his hair. "Neither me nor Diana done in Maryanna; you've got to look elsewhere for that."

"Would you like me to fetch your husband, Mrs Suggitt?" Mr Maxwell enquired in a gentle voice.

Mrs Suggitt shook her head.

"You don't have to do this, Diana," Mr Roberts urged.

"I do…" Mrs Suggitt replied, turning to face him once more. Although her lips, hands, and voice continued to tremble, and her tears continued to fall, she walked back to her chair and lowered herself onto it. "Please continue…"

"What time did you ge' to Mr Roberts' place?" Mr Snyder enquired.

"I believe it was… nine thirty," Mrs Suggitt replied. "I waited for half an hour after Clement had gone out before leaving. I knew Mother… worked until eleven o'clock—when the pub closes—so was confident I… could speak with Abraham without her influence. I was even more thankful to find Regina was already asleep when I arrived. Abraham and I talked about…" She bowed her head. "Well, you know what we talked about now." She clutched her handkerchief with both hands in her lap.

Meanwhile, Mr Roberts had put both elbows upon the table and was rubbing his mouth and chin with clenched hands. The redness around his eyes, and the way he stared up at the ceiling, betrayed the anguish that tore into his heart.

"I told him it wouldn't be awkward between us, despite his repeated confession of love," Mrs Suggitt said, prompting Mr Roberts to stand and pace once more. Rather than acknowledge his movement, though, she instead kept her eyes downcast and went on, "I reassured him I would continue to help him and Regina in whatever way I could. We left the question of Maryanna returning home unanswered for it was growing late and I needed to return home before Clement got back. I left at around ten thirty, arrived home at eleven o'clock and found Clement hadn't yet arrived." She took in a deep, shuddering breath. "I therefore hurried to change into my nightgown and slipped into bed. I must have lain awake for almost an hour before I heard the bedroom door opening. I turned my back to it and pretended I was asleep. I didn't want him to know I hadn't been at home all evening."

"And does he know now?" Mr Maxwell enquired.

"No…" Mrs Suggitt whispered through fresh tears and a shake of her head. With a trembling voice, she said, "I knew how it would look and… I didn't want him to think ill of Abraham. When Maryanna's… body was discovered… outside the bazaar, murdered, I thought the worst." She turned her head away. "I thought Abraham had murdered her so he could be with me. *That* is why I went to the Bow Street Society. I hoped you would discover the truth before the police did so I could, somehow, protect Regina from the *awful, awful* truth."

"*What* did you say?" Mr Roberts enquired from across the room. When she didn't reply, though, he strode over and enquired, "How could you think such a thing?"

Mrs Suggitt's shoulders shook as she covered her mouth and nose with the handkerchief.

"I would *never*—!" Mr Roberts yelled, causing her to flinch.

"I'm sorry, Abraham," Mrs Suggitt whispered.

"I *loved* my wife, Diana. If you *think* I could do *that* to her—cut her up and abandon her body for all to gawk at—you don't *bloody* know me at all!" Mr Roberts bellowed, pushing his chair over.

Mr Snyder and Mr Maxwell simultaneously leapt to their feet. The latter then hid behind the bulk of the former when Mr Roberts strode out the room. After the slamming of the door had caused Mr Maxwell and Mrs Suggitt to flinch, he pressed his hand over his ponding heart, whist she lost the last of her resolve and broke down into uncontrollable sobbing.

* * *

Miss Trent felt the caress of the cold wind across her face, smelt the sweet, dank scent of moss, and listened to the pitter-patter of rain against her umbrella. Attired in a black, silk, bustle dress and lace veil, she stood alone at an aged grave whose stone was blank; its memorial verse having been eroded by the elements long ago. She'd chosen it for its solitary spot in the cemetery's overgrown corner. Neglected and forgotten, it was clear no mourners would be paying their respects to the deceased. She felt a pang of guilt for not only taking advantage of this sad fact but also for not thinking to bring her own dedication of some kind.

"Inspector Woolfe suspects Dr Weeks is helping the Bow Street Society," Chief Inspector Jones' voice stated at her side.

"Did he say why?" Miss Trent enquired as she continued to gaze upon the grave.

"A discarded packet of Turkish cigarettes."

Miss Trent looked at him sharply. "That *careless* idiot!"

"You were all there when Inspector Woolfe noticed it in the Society's kitchen," Chief Inspector Jones pointed out. "Why didn't you remove it before he could do so?"

"Dr Weeks shouldn't have tossed it onto the table in the first place," Miss Trent retorted. Putting her hand upon her hip, she looked back to the grave and sighed. As Chief Inspector Jones then parted his lips, she added, "Don't say it, Richard."

"You don't know what I was going to say."

Miss Trent turned her head toward him and, tilting it, lofted her brow.

Chief Inspector Jones gave a weak smile and enquired, "Well, I did, didn't I?" Hooking his pipe onto his lower lip and igniting its tobacco with a match, he continued in a serious tone, "It's slender evidence to condemn a man on but Inspector Woolfe approached me personally, albeit off the record. That alone is enough to suggest he believes there's some truth in it." He took several puffs on his pipe. "I've told him to keep me abreast of any further developments in the matter."

"And Dr Weeks?"

"His reputation and position have yet to be publicly compromised but you should expect a withdrawal of his services from the Bow Street Society. Naturally, he hasn't stated such to me but, as long as Inspector Woolfe holds his suspicions, Dr Weeks cannot afford to be seen, or even rumoured to be, anywhere near you, the other Bow Street Society members, or its headquarters."

"They don't suspect your involvement with the Society, do they?" Miss Trent enquired as she, again, turned toward him.

Chief Inspector Jones shook his head and replied, "Nevertheless, as I'm certain you've already guessed, this must be our last meeting for a while."

254

"I had… But a part of me had also hoped I was wrong," Miss Trent replied in a sombre voice. As she looked back to the grave, its eroded surface suddenly held a darker significance.

"Goodbye, Miss Trent."

"Goodbye, Chief Inspector," she replied, listening to his feet traipsing through the wet grass as he walked away from her.

TWENTY-THREE

Miss Trent released the door, folded her arms, and lifted her chin upon seeing the visitor's face. In a cool tone, she said, "Oh. It's you. I suppose you'd better come in." She returned inside but only went as far as the foot of the stairs. Whilst the visitor also stepped inside and closed the door, Miss Trent held her arms tight against her chest and enquired, "What do you want?"

Rather than answer, though, the visitor stayed close to the door, scanned the hallway, and remarked, "You've done well for yourself, haven't you?"

"Don't, Polly. You've got no right to pass judgement on me. Say whatever it is you've come to say and leave."

Polly was in her late twenties with loose-curled, blonde hair tied into a ponytail beneath a brown bonnet. Her fair cheeks were tinged with pink from the cold, whilst her complexion lacked the usual smudges of soot from the trains which passed through the station accommodating the bar where she worked. She was attired in a modest, ankle-length, burgundy coloured dress and a black, woollen coat. She crossed the hallway to Miss Trent and said, "Dr Weeks sent me to tell you he can't do it anymore—helping the Bow Street Society, I mean.
Some inspector's on his back, and he don't want him finding out. I wouldn't have come here to stir up a hornet's nest, Becky. You know me more than that."

"Do I?" Miss Trent coolly retorted. "You told me you loved me and, days later, confessed you loved *him* more. For *weeks* I've not heard so much as a *whisper* from you."

"It's not like I *meant* to fall in love with him. He was a laugh and happy to give me a soft bed for the night. He then… just… grew on me, I suppose. Anyway, *you* could've come and seen *me*. Maybe said sorry for what you done?"

"I'm not getting into that again. You knew the rules," Miss Trent replied with a dismissive wave of her hand as she walked away from Polly. Turning upon her heel to face her once more, she continued, "You can tell Dr Weeks I received his message and shan't be contacting him again." She went to the door. "Thank you for telling me—" A sudden knock from the other side cut her off, however. Peering through the door's peephole, she saw Lady Owston, Miss Dexter, Miss Webster, and Mr Maxwell huddled together upon the porch. "You can't leave that way," Miss Trent said as she headed toward the kitchen. "You'll have to go out the back door."

"Why?" Polly enquired, hurrying after her.

"I don't want the other Bow Street Society members to know you were here," Miss Trent replied. Leading her through the kitchen, she unlocked the back door and held it open. When she looked back to Polly and saw the hurt in her eyes, though, she said in a soft voice, "Not because of our past, Polly." She held her arms. "But because they may accidentally inform Inspector Woolfe of your visit, and I don't want to see you in trouble."

The hurt dissolved from Polly's eyes, and a smile lit up her face. Placing a soft kiss upon Miss Trent's cheek, she whispered, "Thank you," before leaving through the open door and disappearing into the night.

* * *

"There are police constables absolutely *everywhere* at the Suggitt residence," Lady Owston informed Miss Trent whilst Miss Webster assisted her in removing her fur coat.

"There were a couple standing outside the front of the house," Miss Webster corrected and draped the coat over the stairs' handrail. Adding her own and Miss Dexter's to it, she then put Miss Dexter and Lady Owston's hats on top but kept her own on.

"Well, it certainly *felt* like they were everywhere," Lady Owston retorted, walking toward the kitchen. Mr Maxwell hurriedly moved ahead of her, though, and used his body to hold the door open for the ladies. Yet, although they thanked him as they passed, Miss Dexter avoided making eye contact and chose the chair furthest away from him at the table. Mr Maxwell, distracted by the lure of the hot stove, didn't notice this, however.

"I'm also expecting Mr Locke," Miss Trent said as she checked the time on the pocket watch she'd left at the head of the table. "I assume Mr Snyder will be along once he's settled the horses?"

"Yes," Mr Maxwell replied, heading straight for the stove to warm his hands.

"That will be Mr Locke," Miss Trent said as knocking sounded from the hallway. "Please, help yourselves to the tea." She indicted the array of tea things in the middle of the table and left.

Miss Webster poured some of the hot beverage for herself and Lady Owston. Meanwhile, Miss Dexter laid out her sketchbook on the table at the page with the depiction of Mrs Yates' missing clothing. Afterward, she accepted the teapot from Miss Webster and poured cups for herself and the others. When Miss Trent returned a few moments later, Mr Locke and Mr Snyder accompanied her, promptly taking their places at the table after making their formal greetings.

"I see you have once again neglected to remove your hat this evening," Mr Locke remarked to Miss Webster who dropped her cup with a clatter of china and a deluge of tea.

Leaping to her feet the moment she'd done it, she mopped up the dark liquid with her handkerchief and

258

whatever else she could find. In a hard tone, she replied, "I don't know what you mean, Mr Locke."

"Her *hat*!" Lady Owston cried as she, too, shot to her feet.

"Are you well, Milady?" Miss Webster enquired.

"Yes, yes, child!" Lady Owston replied with a dismissive wave of her hand. "I *just* recalled something I overheard at the *Writer's Club*. Two of the ladies were discussing how they'd never seen Mrs Gromwell without her bonnet."

"With all due respect, I fail to see the significance of such a conversation," Mr Locke remarked.

Miss Webster had stilled at her employer's words, though. Clutching her tea-sodden handkerchief, she fixed her intense gaze upon Lady Owston.

"I *know* why Mrs Gromwell doesn't remove her bonnet indoors," Lady Owston said.

"Please… don't," Miss Webster said in a quiet voice.

"I'm afraid I must," Lady Owston replied.

"I am *asking* you not to…" Miss Webster urged in a strained voice.

"What's going on?" Miss Trent enquired, looking between them.

"Agnes?" Lady Owston softly invited.

"I can't. You *know* I can't," Miss Webster replied, the strain on her voice worsening.

Lady Owston's eyes were filled with sadness as she felt her resolve waning. Placing a gentle hand upon Miss Webster's, she offered a weak smile and said, "I do, my child." She patted her hands. "Have no fear."

Miss Trent looked between them once more and demanded, "Could *someone* please tell me what's going on here? Whatever it is, Miss Webster, you'll have the Bow Street Society's full support."

"She keeps her hat on when indoors because she

bears scars from a fire," Mr Locke interjected.

All eyes turned to him at once.

"How did you...?" Miss Webster whispered, stunned.

"If I am recalling this accurately—please correct me if I am not—when we three entered the library at the Holdens' residence you, Lady Owston, at once crossed the room and hid the lit fire behind a guard. Afterward, you went to Miss Webster's side and hushed words were exchanged, presumably to ensure your secretary was not too overwhelmed by the fire's presence," Mr Locke said as he continuously scratched the back of his hand. "I did not remark upon it at the time as I considered it irrelevant. I was then reminded of it at the *Turk's Head* public house last night when I saw you flinch out the corner of my eye, Miss Webster. I had just struck a match. I therefore came to the, albeit assumed, conclusion you were afraid of fire. Most of such fears arise from the aftermath of past events, specifically, ones which were particularly painful." He paused. "While I do not wish to go into detail presently, I too have experienced such an event in my own life." He smiled. "Lady Owston's dramatic recollection of Mrs Gromwell's bonnet, and her stating she knew the reason for her not removing it, led me to suspect you wear your own hat constantly, Miss Webster, to hide scarring from the fire. A fact Lady Owston, as your employer and friend, would undoubtedly be aware of."

"You are a very observant man, Mr Locke," Lady Owston remarked with a heavy voice. Sitting down, she kept one hand on Miss Webster's and squeezed. "Agnes' parents were killed in the fire; she came to live with me soon after. She was only twelve at the time."

Miss Webster slowly lowered herself onto her own chair and slipped her hand into Lady Owston's. She said, "I remember waking up to my bedroom filled with smoke. My governess' room was adjacent to mine, so I rushed to her door and opened it. The flames burst out over top of me and singed my head. I screamed and reeled backward. My parents' room was on the other side of my governess'. Miss Potter had fallen asleep whilst reading and knocked her kerosene lamp from her bedside table. She always took a sleeping draught at bedtime, for I wasn't in the habit of waking up during the night, so she didn't awaken." Miss Webster's lips parted, and her eyes glazed over as she watched the events unfold in her mind's eye. "I was rescued by our butler. The fire had already taken hold by then... there was nothing to be done for my parents."

"My sincerest condolences," Mr Locke replied, a sentiment echoed by the others.

Drawn from her mind by their voices, she shifted her gaze to Mr Locke and explained, "Ever since that night, I've suffered with a crippling fear of fire; the smallest of flames may send my heart racing and the world spinning." She looked to Lady Owston who squeezed her hand between both of her own and gave a subtle nod of encouragement. Feeling bolstered by her guardian's support, she slipped her hand free and removed the pins holding her hat in place. When she pulled it away, a bare patch of flesh was revealed beneath. Its surface was roughened and maimed by heavy scarring that could have only been caused by severe burns.

"I'd always hoped my hair would return but it never did," Miss Webster continued. "I therefore took to wearing my hat and this." She turned the hat over to reveal a circle of real hair stitched together and attached to the underside of the hat's brim.

"You hide it quite well," Miss Dexter remarked in a saddened voice.

"But why wear false hair at all?" Mr Maxwell enquired.

"It lessens the chances of anyone glimpsing my scars should my hat slip at all," Miss Webster replied as she replaced her hat and secured it with pins.

"And it is called a *postiche*," Lady Owston interjected. "Made from actual human hair to blend with Agnes' own."

Mr Maxwell hummed in understanding.

"You were under no obligation to expose yourself in such a way, Miss Webster," Mr Locke said. "I admire your courage in doing so."

"Unfortunately, not *all* men are as liberally minded as you, Mr Locke," Lady Owston replied. "During the last century, wigs, specifically the tall, powdered type, were *most* fashionable. Yet, even as our century dawned, their popularity waned. Nowadays, they are not only out of favour but considered positively *shameful*. Men who wear them are accused of preposterous vanity whilst the women's crime is to be intentionally deceptive to attract the eye of a potential husband. Given the fact Agnes is still yet to be married at her age, the prejudice against her wearing a *postiche* would be monstrous."

"As sympathetic as we all are to your plight, Miss Webster, what significance does this have for the murders of Mrs Maryanna Roberts and Mrs Sarah Yates?" Miss Trent enquired.

"On account of the extreme disdain wigs, and the wearers of wigs, are held in by wider society, both the product and the wig-fitting service tend to be advertised in code," Lady Owston replied. "For example, women's wigs may be referred to as 'ladies' imperceptible hair coverings.' Furthermore, wig wearers strive to keep their secret at all costs. I've known ladies who have worn a wig, won a husband, and then proceeded to conceal the truth of their follicle deception for the entirety of their marriage. Only their hairdressers know they wear a wig as it is usually the hairdresser who fits it. It is therefore my strong suspicion, Miss Trent, the room at the top of the stairs in the *Queshire Department Store* contains such a wig-fitting service. It would certainly explain why Mr Queshire continues to deny it is anything but a storeroom. Yet, more than this, it would explain why Miss Galway was so afraid of us discovering its true use. Such a revelation would undoubtedly expose the customers concerned to unbridled ridicule and the store itself to a scandal it may not survive."

"Um, Lady Owston?" Mr Maxwell began as he twisted his cravat's small bow between his fingers. "If wigs are made from actual human hair, could it be possible for-for the scalps of Mrs Roberts and Mrs Yates to-to… to be made into one?"

Lady Owston simultaneously gasped and covered her mouth as she stared wide eyed at him in horror. "I… Agnes, my smelling salts." She held out her other hand and closed her eyes. Clenching her eyelids and lips together, she fought to dismiss the sickening imaginings filling her mind. Releasing a soft gag, followed by a sound of disgust as she tasted bile in her mouth, she then swallowed the latter and held the opened bottle of smelling salts beneath her nose. After taking several deep breaths, she felt her nausea subside enough for her to be able to open her eyes and speak again. Nevertheless, her hand trembled as she placed the bottle back into Miss Webster's hand and continued, "I… really couldn't say… Mr Maxwell." She took a large mouthful of tea. "The oldest method of wig making *I* am aware of is to make what is called a *weft,* a small, fringe-like thing which is sewn onto a foundation of net, silk, and other materials." She felt her nausea wane further as she focused on the cold facts of the industry. "More recently, however, a new method of wig making was developed in France; strands of hair are sewn directly onto flexible, flesh-coloured netting using a needle much akin to those used in embroidery. The netting allows the wig to have a more precise fit on the wearer's head. Netting could be secured to the underside of the…" She shuddered. "…but the… would have to be tanned into leather, I should think, a process which could take days *if* the wigmaker wanted to create a…" She released a soft grunt of disgust. "…high-quality finish." She took another mouthful of tea. "Besides," she fanned her face with her hand, "as I understand it, the hair used in wigs is foraged from overseas."

"Where is Dr Weeks? Surely, he could confirm if such a thing were possible?" Mr Locke enquired.

"Dr Weeks shan't be joining us, either tonight or at any other time," Miss Trent replied. "Inspector Woolfe has grown suspicious of the doctor assisting us in this case. Therefore, Dr Weeks has decided to cancel his membership of the Bow Street Society entirely."

"But how shall we know for certain about the wigs?" Lady Owston enquired with a desperate edge to her voice.

"By examining the wigs at the *Queshire Department Store* ourselves," Mr Locke replied with a smirk.

"How?" Mr Maxwell enquired. "If Mr Queshire refuses to acknowledge the wig-fitting service even exists, how are we to convince him to let us see the wigs?"

"By sending a lady in need of a wig, of course," Mr Locke replied with a twinkle in his eyes as he looked to Miss Webster.

"I couldn't possibly—" She began.

"But you must," Mr Locke interrupted. "Besides, the expectation would not be for you to approach Mr Queshire but for you to speak with the hairdresser who is, presumably confined to the room." He pulled Miss Dexter's sketchbook closer. "Meanwhile, Lady Owston and I shall distract Mr Queshire by enquiring after Mrs Yates' missing clothes and jewellery. It shall also provide me with an opportunity to see the layout of the store for myself in case my… nocturnal talents are required."

"*Mr* Locke!" Lady Owston scolded.

"That is, letting myself into a property without a key after dark," Mr Locke clarified.

"Oh… I see…" Lady Owston replied, feeling rather embarrassed.

"It all comes back to that store," Mr Snyder mused aloud.

Lady Owston hummed and replied, "There is certainly a strong suggestion our murderer is *one* of the people connected to the store. Mrs Roberts' shawl was sold there after being deposited in a basket which, theoretically, all our suspects had physical access to. Then there is the arsenic Miss Galway claimed she purchased on Mr Suggitt's behalf. Arsenic *he* claimed was to rid the store of rats; if *that* was also in the storeroom then, again, they *all* had access to it." She frowned. "No hessian sacks, however. I asked Mr Queshire about them again this morning when we told him of Miss Galway's attempt to rouse him."

"Mrs Yates also had access to arsenic as she purchased some on behalf of the *Turk's Head's* landlord. Although, as far as we could tell, she hadn't visited the *Queshire Department Store*," Miss Webster said. "Her being murdered does rather rule her out as a suspect, however."

"Unless she *did* murder Mrs Roberts and one of the others murdered her as revenge?" Mr Maxwell suggested.

"They were all together at the Suggitts' house all night though," Miss Dexter pointed out.

"They could be lying for each other; three out of the four have already done so," Mr Locke reminded her. "Of course, Miss Galway could have murdered Mrs Yates and created a fictitious stalker of Mr Roberts and Mrs Yates to give herself a reason to speak with Mr Queshire and thereby give herself an alibi."

"What would be her *motive* for murdering both women, though?" Lady Owston enquired.

"She is keen to become a member of the Bow Street Society and, by her own confession, disliked Mrs Roberts," Mr Maxwell replied.

"No; I do not believe such a preposterous reason," Lady Owston said. "Furthermore, Mr Locke, her ploy to provide herself with an alibi, as far as Mr Queshire was concerned, was unsuccessful for he didn't hear her knocking."

"True," Mr Locke conceded. "He is also a suspect though, is he not? Mrs Roberts caused a most undesirable scene in his store the day before she died and he, like all the others, had access to the storeroom wherein the donation basket was hidden—an initiative he personally manages—and the French Breakfast coffee was stored. I suggest we ask him to show us the batch of arsenic which was purchased from *Drummond's* when we speak with him tomorrow."

"You have read my thoughts," Lady Owston replied. "Regrettably, I must disagree with you with regards to Mr Queshire's position as a suspect. While I shall concede he *does* have access to the means of murder and, in Mrs Roberts' case, a possible motive, he does not have a motive for Mrs Yates' murder. I, for one, have also not seen any bottles of lemonade in his storeroom—though I shall also endeavour to enquire after it tomorrow."

"We cannot eliminate anyone as a suspect until we have completed our enquiries at the store," Mr Locke said.

A hum of agreement sounded from Miss Trent.

"Should I visit the docks tomorrow?" Mr Maxwell enquired. "Mr Roberts has told us he slept outside the gates after leaving home at the same time as Regina. Maybe someone saw him?"

"You could," Mr Snyder replied. "But it won't do you any good. Blokes who're not on the Quay-Gangers' lists, like Mr Roberts, don't get much attention as long as they do the work. Any man who's not lame can go to the gates and get work with no questions asked. Mr Roberts not being on the Gangers' lists means 'e's not known enough by them; means 'e could've sent a mate instead and got him to tell the Ganger his name. But even then, the Ganger's gotta remember it."

Mr Maxwell frowned and sat back against his chair.

"You can speak with Mr Ratchett at the *Turk's Head* instead," Miss Trent told him. "To see if he'll confirm Mrs Yates' story about the sailor and her explanation for the arsenic. He may have also seen Mr Roberts arriving to walk Mrs Yates home and, if she is telling the truth, Miss Galway leaving to follow them."

"Alone?" Mr Maxwell enquired with a hard swallow.

"No; Mr Snyder and Miss Dexter will go with you," Miss Trent replied and closed her notebook. "I think that concludes our meeting, everyone. Be sure to tell me of your findings and have a good evening."

* * *

Mr Joseph Maxwell hadn't lingered after the meeting, despite Miss Dexter inviting him into the parlour for a discreet word. He'd known what she'd wanted to discuss but couldn't bring himself to tell her the truth. He'd therefore mumbled a feeble excuse about not wanting to miss the last omnibus and left. He doubted she, or the others, accepted the reason for his departure, though, since the last omnibus wouldn't leave for several hours yet. When he'd unlocked the door to his room and stepped inside, then, he still felt the pangs of guilt for lying to them.

His room was in one of the many lodging houses

located within walking distance of Fleet Street. Cheap rent, a handful of furnishings, and minimal interference by the landlady meant he could come and go as he pleased and live in relative comfort. He was therefore surprised to see a lit lamp when he closed the door. Turning toward it, he then stepped back sharply at the sight of his father sitting in the armchair beside the cold hearth. Pressing his back against the door, he watched his father remove the cigar from his lips and exhale a thick cloud of smoke in his direction.

"Your landlady let me in, with a little monetary persuasion, of course," Oliver Maxwell said.

"I wasn't expecting you this evening, Father—" Joseph began.

"Where have you been? I've waited for you for hours."

"I—I was at work."

"No, you weren't. I went there first."

"My work with the Bow Street Society," Joseph replied.

Oliver stood and, tossing his used cigar into the grate, said, "Just as long as you weren't with your whore."

Joseph flinched at the last word. Parting his lips to reply, he discovered his vocal cords were paralysed by the intense nervousness he always felt in his father's presence. Unable to utter a single syllable, therefore, he closed his mouth and bent his knees as his father walked toward him.

"You're to come to dinner again tomorrow night," Oliver informed him. "Mr Lillithwaite and his daughter, Poppy, shall be in attendance. She's been unable to catch the eye of a suitor and her fading youth means she's increasingly becoming a burden to the family. I've reassured Mr Lillithwaite that his daughter will find a suitor in you provided he honours his promise of a generous dowry."

"But Father—" Joseph began, only to be cut off by

a hard, back-handed slap across his face. The force of which was enough to send him stumbling sideways, into the fireplace. Gripping the mantle shelf to break his fall, Joseph knelt upon the iron hearth and stared at the wall with wide, watering eyes. One side of his face stung like it was on fire. Hearing movement behind him, he flinched and ducked his head beneath the mantle shelf.

"You will *not* answer me back again, Joseph, and you will *certainly* not question my orders. Do I make myself clear?"

"Y—Y—Yes, F—Father," Mr Maxwell stuttered, fighting against the tremble which had overtaken his body.

Oliver gave a soft grunt of acceptance and, retrieving his hat, said, "I'll expect you to arrive promptly at eight." He walked away. "And wear some decent clothes; I do not want to be embarrassed." The sound of the door closing was like music to the terrified journalist who at once collapsed against the hearth in relief.

TWENTY-FOUR

Mr Locke held the door open for Lady Owston and Miss Webster to enter the *Queshire Department Store* ahead of him. Having leant on his walking cane whilst doing so, he now simultaneously swept it around to his front and pivoted upon his heel to follow them inside. As soon as he stepped onto the shop floor, the assistants behind the millinery and haberdashery departments' counters erupted into excited, yet hushed, conversations amongst themselves. Touching the brim of his top hat as he greeted each with a subtle nod and a warm smile, he soon caught the attention of the store's customers. Although older than the employees, they nonetheless returned Mr Locke's polite "Good morning" when he gave it on his way past.

"You have caused quite the stir, Mr Locke," Mr Queshire observed once Mr Locke had joined him at the perfumery department. Lady Owston and Miss Webster were also there; the former with an amused smile and the latter with a look of indifference as she glanced from Mr Locke to the millinery department.

"I can assure you it was not my intention," Mr Locke replied.

"Whether intentional or not, I would still like to thank you for it," Mr Queshire said. "I will undoubtedly witness an increase in customer numbers as soon as these ladies tell their friends the Great Locke shops here."

"As you know, my wife is already an avid supporter of your store; I am quite certain she shall be pleased my presence has assisted in its continued success," Mr Locke replied.

"Indeed," Mr Queshire agreed. Addressing the three of them, he enquired, "How may I be of assistance today?"

Miss Webster indicated the other departments with a hand bent back over her shoulder and replied, "I wish to purchase some leather gloves I saw the other day."

"And Mr Locke and I would like to steal just a *few* more minutes of your time—if it is convenient, that is?" Lady Owston enquired.

"But of course, I'm only too happy to help," Mr Queshire replied and opened the storeroom door. Whilst Lady Owston and Mr Locke entered ahead of him, Mr Queshire watched Miss Webster until she'd reached the millinery department. He then joined the others and closed the door.

"Pardon my saying, miss, but was that truly the Great Locke I saw?" the millinery department's assistant enquired from Miss Webster when she approached the counter.

"Yes, excuse me," Miss Webster replied, hurrying away to climb the stairs.

She was relieved to find the door to the hairdressing salon ajar and the loud cacophony of ladies' chatter drifting from within. Pressing her ear against the door marked *Staff Only*, she then turned its knob when she heard nothing coming from the other side. As she eased it open, though, she flinched at the squeak of its hinges. Glancing back to the salon, she was, again, relieved to see no one had emerged to confront her over her presence. She therefore slipped through the small gap she'd made and closed the door with a soft click. Noticing it had a bolt, she slid it into place and turned toward a short, windowless corridor.

At its far end was a second door that was also closed. Gas lamps with frosted glass shades and curved, brass brackets illuminated both ends of the corridor. Lined up in between was a set of four, identical chairs whose oval backs rested against the left-hand wall. Their armrests and seats were covered by plush, burgundy velvet and their rosewood frames were polished to a shine. Several oil paintings, depicting everyday objects in a variety of arrangements, hung on the wall opposite. Nowhere could she see a plaque or sign denoting the room's function, however. Relying upon assumption alone, she supposed the corridor was a waiting area, but for what?

She crept along the corridor but gasped when the door ahead of her opened and a man in his mid-to-late forties said, "Bonjour, may I help you at all?"

Miss Webster pressed her hand to her chest as her heart raced.

"Pardon moi, Mademoiselle, I didn't mean to frighten you," the man apologised with a distinct French accent. He had ashen-coloured hair tied into a ponytail, dark-brown eyes flecked with gold, and a fair complexion. Laughter lines could be seen in the corners of his mouth and eyes as he stepped into the light. He was attired in pressed, black trousers and frock coat, a crisp, white shirt with a high, starched collar, and a burgundy cravat. His waistcoat had black panels with gold, embroidered roses and brass buttons.

"You surprised me, that's all," Miss Webster replied with a weak smile.

"I'm Mr Vuitton, how may I help you?"

"A pleasure to meet you, Mr Vuitton. I'm Miss Agnes Webster; I'm here under the strong recommendation of my friend, Mrs Gromwell."

"Aaahh. Come in, s'il vous plaît?" Mr Vuitton invited as he stepped aside.

The room beyond was considerably smaller than the corridor; around six feet long by six feet wide. It was also windowless, with a single, wall-mounted gas lamp illuminating the space from the back-right corner. Standing against the wall opposite the door was an open, rosewood, ladies' bureaux with a chair, identical to those in the corridor, positioned in front of it. The bureaux's writing shelf was lowered but its drawers were closed and, presumably, locked. A free-standing mirror, identical to those she'd seen on the counter of the millinery department, stood on the left-hand corner of the bureaux's shelf. Above the bureaux was a set of three shelves lined with several walnut, faceless 'heads' on cross-shaped stands. Resting atop each was a splendid wig that had been painstakingly combed and arranged. Although the wigs were a variety of shapes and sizes, their colours were limited to natural tones. A Turkish-style rug, adorned with a burgundy, cream, and gold floral design, lay upon the polished, oak floorboards, whilst the walls were covered in burgundy, floral, textured wallpaper. Oak-framed bulletin boards, displaying advertisements for women's hair tonics, remedies, and "coverings," were mounted on three of the walls. An intricate, hand-drawn poster advertising the breadth of goods available at the *Queshire Department Store* dominated the fourth.

Mr Vuitton followed Miss Webster into the room and, indicating the chair in front of the bureaux, invited her to sit. As she did so, he retrieved a second chair from behind the door and set it down at a right-angle to hers. When he sat upon it, she could see his face reflected in the mirror.

"Mademoiselle, pardon my saying, but it seems to me you do not require a covering?"

"I'm grateful for your saying so, sir. But, alas, I have hidden my shame well." Miss Webster removed the pins from her hat, placed them into a pile upon the bureaux's shelf, and lifted her hat to reveal the scarring beneath.

Mr Vuitton rose to his feet and, peering down at her head, furrowed his brow. He enquired, "What is the cause of the scarring?"

"I was involved in a fire at my home as a child. I opened a door, and the flames burnt my scalp."

"May I touch it, mademoiselle?"

"You may," Miss Webster replied despite the nerves it bore in her. No one other than Lady Owston and her maid had ever laid a finger upon it. She therefore flinched at his initial touch and watched his reflection in the mirror with bated breath. Rather than crimple his face in disgust or make a sardonic remark as she'd feared, though, he studied her head as intently as a doctor would. His fingers were also light and unobtrusive against her flesh as they traced the lines of her scarring.

"Do you use hot crimping irons, hot pins, or any other means to make your hair wavy?" Mr Vuitton enquired.

"No," Miss Webster replied.

"And you have applied A.G. Edwards & Co.'s *Harlene* remedy for baldness and *Koko for the Hair* to no avail?" Mr Vuitton enquired.

"Nothing has worked; I'm deathly afraid of the rest falling out, too," Miss Webster replied, surprised by how much she'd revealed. Not even Lady Owston was aware of that fear.

"And you have used lemon juice rubbed into the scalp?" Mr Vuitton enquired. "Washed your hair, and rubbed it hard, every night with a teaspoonful of salt and one scruple of quinine added to a pint of brandy you have mixed well?"

"Yes, both. Happily, my hair is still intact. It is only the patch of baldness that refuses to disappear."

"Oui, mademoiselle," Mr Vuitton agreed and retook his seat. "It is sometimes the practise of madames… that is, how do you say? Married women… Err, pardon, non. Practice of older women to wear lace mantillas; I do not think such an accessoire would suit you, however. I can show you some *postiches* which match your colouring, but the position of your baldness makes it difficult to cover without increasing the size of your head. And a bigger head is *most* unbecoming, oui?"

"Oui," Miss Webster replied with a weak smile.

Mr Vuitton picked up her hat and, standing, examined it beneath the light of the gas lamp. He enquired, "And you have tried to hide your baldness by brushing your remaining hair over?"

"Yes, but my hair isn't thick enough to hide it entirely," Miss Webster replied, her hope waning with each moment he spent examining the hat. When she'd agreed to investigate the mysterious room at the top of the stairs, she'd fully expected to find a charlatan. After discovering the opposite, though, she'd grown keen to hear his opinion on her situation, and had forgotten her reason for coming as a result. "Is there *nothing* you can do?"

"Mais oui, mademoiselle," he replied with a broad smile and returned her hat. "Stay here, s'il vous plaît, and I shall return."

Miss Webster felt elated by the news as she watched him leave. It was little wonder Mrs Gromwell had come to see him if she suffered from a similar affliction— *Mrs Gromwell*! Miss Webster leapt to her feet as the memory of Lady Owston's revelation at the Bow Street Society meeting exploded into her mind. Scolding herself for becoming caught up in her own situation, she scanned the shelves for any mousy-brown or blond wigs.

Finding none, she reached beneath the bureaux's shelf and opened the cupboard. Inside were piles of small, square boxes. She glanced over her shoulder and, taking out each box in turn, opened its lid to peer at the colour of the wig inside. Moving onto the next when the first didn't match her criteria, she then repeated this process until she found a mousy-brown wig. No sooner had she taken it from the box though did she hear footsteps approaching in the corridor. Slipping the wig into her coat's inside pocket, she returned the empty box to the cupboard, closed its door, and straightened just as Mr Vuitton entered.

"I have this *postiche* and this *postiche*," he announced, presenting her with two hairpieces: one a chocolate-brown in colour, the other a dark, chestnut.

Miss Webster forced a smile onto her stoic features and, turning toward the mirror, allowed him to place each *postiche* upon her bald patch in turn. Reminded of the fact she may have a dead woman's scalp concealed on her person, she swiftly said, "The first, I think."

"Excellent choice, mademoiselle. I'll wrap it for you."

"Thank you," Miss Webster replied before holding her breath as he reached into the cupboard. When he took out the empty box, she'd put there moments before, she studied his face but saw no hint of suspicion or confusion. Keen to distract him nonetheless, she enquired, "For how long have Mr Queshire and Mr Suggitt been offering this service?"

"Monsieur Queshire, trois years," Mr Vuitton replied, wrapping her *postiche* in tissue paper and putting it into the box. "Monsieur Suggitt does not know it is done; he was angry when Monsieur Queshire and I told him about it, so Monsieur Queshire said for me to go on but not to tell Monsieur Suggitt."

"Do you make the coverings?"

"Non, Monsieur Queshire buys from mon amie, Monsieur LeGarde, in Paris. He is a wig maker of the first class," Mr Vuitton replied as he tied a red ribbon around the box. "I, err, how do you say? Mend the wigs if they are broken after going on the ship."

"Have you had any new wigs delivered lately?"

"Non, we will get some at the end of this week," Mr Vuitton replied, holding out the box to her.

"Thank you, monsieur. How much do I owe you?" Miss Webster enquired. Once he'd named the amount, she gave him the necessary monies, thanked him, again, and left. As she strode down the corridor, she was thoroughly pleased with both her purchase and what she'd discovered.

TWENTY-FIVE

Mr Locke dropped his gloves into his top hat and placed his top hat upon the table. Lying his cane on the window ledge beside him, he brushed his fingers against the sash window's lock to determine its design. The metallic, swing arm was indicative of a dual locking mechanism. He knew the bottom of the window's frame would have a deep, brass recess screwed into it. A rounded hook on a pivot, mounted to the underside of the window's mobile component, would 'catch' the recess' outer edge as the window was slid closed. The compression of the swing arm would then secure the hook within the recess. Not only would it prevent someone from sliding the window up from the outside, it could potentially dissuade someone from attempting to enter at all. From experience, Mr Locke knew the sound of breaking glass could be loud enough to rouse whoever was inside. He knew a method of entry that didn't require such extreme measures, but refrained from employing it in this case. Instead, he took a seat at the table beside Lady Owston, with Mr Queshire sitting opposite.

"How is Miss Galway?" Lady Owston enquired. "I couldn't see her in the store."

"She didn't feel quite ready to return yet," Mr Queshire replied. "Her recollection of someone pursuing Mrs Yates, mere hours before she was murdered, has had a profound affect upon her. She's terrified the murderer may have seen her watching. The sooner your group identifies him the better."

"When did she tell you this, if she has not returned?" Mr Locke enquired.

"This morning; I meant she hadn't returned to her duties," Mr Queshire replied. "Naturally, I sent her back to the lodgings when I saw how much the matter still upset her."

"Alone?" Mr Locke enquired with a lofted brow.

"Yes; why ever would I not?" Mr Queshire enquired in return. "It isn't an unreasonable distance to walk in the daytime."

"Perhaps, if you were not 'terrified' the man who murdered two women would seek you out. Although, I am certain you considered such a thing," Mr Locke replied in a sardonic tone.

Mr Queshire's gaze hardened as he looked upon the Bow Streeter.

"I presume she did not arrive for work yesterday?" Mr Locke enquired.

"She did not," Mr Queshire replied.

"Naturally; otherwise she would have informed you of her fear then," Mr Locke said, maintaining his sardonic tone.

Mr Queshire narrowed his eyes and tightened his jaw.

"I am nonetheless intrigued by your waiting until this morning to speak with her, however. Given that Lady Owston notified you of Miss Galway's attempt to rouse you from your sleep on the very morning of Mrs Yates' murder," Mr Locke continued in a more sombre tone. "Personally, curiosity alone would have compelled me to leave my store at once to speak with the assistant concerned. You did not inform Mr Queshire of the reason behind Miss Galway's attempt to rouse him at such an early hour, did you, Lady Owston?"

"No, I don't believe I did… And you didn't ask me either, Mr Queshire," Lady Owston replied.

"I was still trying to digest the news of Mrs Yates' murder," Mr Queshire said. "And I was told yesterday morning, by Miss Annie Simkins—another of the store's assistants—that Miss Galway was unwell. Due to Mr

Suggitt being, predictably, unable to return to work, I was obliged to take on his duties in addition to my own. Put quite simply, Mr Locke, I could spare no time to visit Miss Galway, or even speak with her on the telephone, until this morning when she arrived for work."

"She purchased arsenic on Mr Suggitt's behalf, did she not?" Mr Locke enquired.

"She did," Mr Queshire replied with a scowl. "As Mr Suggitt has *already* confirmed."

"May I see it?" Mr Locke enquired.

"*No*," Mr Queshire replied. Shifting his gaze to Lady Owston, he continued, "It was only a few grams and I've already exhausted them. I used two slices of buttered bread, to sprinkle the arsenic on, which I placed in the basement as bait for the mice."

"I thought it was an infestation of rats you had?" Mr Locke challenged.

"*Rats, mice*, they are the same to me," Mr Queshire rebuked with a glare. "Their specific biology is irrelevant when they are chewing through expensive silks."

"*Mr* Queshire, have any further items been donated to your stock?" Lady Owston interjected to calm his growing irritability.

"I've not personally taken receipt of any garments but there were some new ones in the basket," Mr Queshire replied. Casting a sideways glance at Mr Locke, he added, "You may check it if you wish."

"I do," Mr Locke replied with a smirk. Standing, he made no noise as he moved around the table and lifted the basket's lid. Although he had his back to Mr Queshire's, he looked at him out the corner of his eye but saw no attempt to scrutinise his search.

"Have you sampled your soap yet, Lady Owston?" Mr Queshire enquired.

"No, I'm afraid I haven't," Lady Owston replied.

Completing his search, Mr Locke closed the basket's lid and faced the others empty-handed. He enquired, "There are no clothes elsewhere, Mr Queshire? You mentioned a basement; perhaps we should check if any clothes were put there by mistake?"

"Absolutely not," Mr Queshire replied as his shoulders visibly tensed. "I've cooperated considerably more than I ought to, and been exceptionally patient with you and your associates, Mr Locke." He thrust back his chair and stood, avoiding a collision with Mr Locke due to the Bow Streeter's quick reflexes. Stepping around his chair and pushing it back under the table, he cast a glare between them and said, "There are *no* donated garments aside from those in the basket. The fact I take in any at all has the potential to ruin me, which is why I was reluctant to tell Lady Owston of it in the first place. She, unlike you, at least had the decency to be fair with me. If you wish to accuse me of something, Mr Locke, then I would suggest you do so now. Yet, know you are at risk of having a court case brought against you for slander."

"My good fellow," Mr Locke replied with a smirk as he moved toward the window, thereby putting the table between him and the irate store owner. "I can assure you I have enough money to tie you and your store up in legal bureaucracy, appeals, and hearings for years to come. Since you have resorted to reselling subpar goods as new, thereby defrauding your trusting customers, I rather suspect your financial affairs are not so buoyant. I therefore suggest you refrain from threatening gentlemen with court proceedings unless a distant, rich relative suddenly dies and you inherit a substantial sum of money." His smile faded as he turned to face him and, with a grave expression, continued, "Besides, my request to see your basement came from a desire to fulfil a commission given to the Bow Street Society by Mrs Diana Suggitt, not from a vindictive quest to ruin you." He neared the table and lowered his voice. "Do not misunderstand me, however. Should you feel obliged to commence court proceedings against me, I would have no qualms in not only ruining you financially but also legally and morally. A man does not threaten such extreme measures unless he feels threatened himself. My question is inevitably this, therefore; *why* do you feel threatened?"

Mr Queshire rested the knuckles of his clenched fists upon the table and, leaning over them, replied, "You are quite correct, Mr Locke; I *do* feel threatened but not because I'm hiding the stolen garments of two murdered women." He glanced over his shoulder at the basket behind him. "As you've seen, the basket doesn't contain any—and neither does the basement, which you'll have to take my word for. Your persistent challenges to the answers I've freely given, though, have served to make me suspect you think I had some part in these crimes. I did not. Yet when a man is shown the shadow of a hangman's noose, and he does not deserve to have his neck placed within it, he is apt to be defensive." He removed his hands from the table and straightened. "I have told you the truth, despite your trying of my patience, Mr Locke, but now I must ask we end our conversation here. I'm still understaffed on account of Mr Suggitt's continued absence so I would appreciate the opportunity to return to the management of my store."

"Of course," Lady Owston replied, prompting Mr Locke to loft a brow.

"Thank you," Mr Queshire mumbled as the tension eased in both his face and voice.

"But first tell me; why do you think we are looking for Mrs Yates' clothes?" Lady Owston enquired.

The corner of Mr Queshire's mouth twitched. "An assumption on my part," he replied in a cool tone. "I presumed the same man who murdered Mrs Roberts murdered her mother, ergo Mrs Yates' clothes would have been missing like her daughter's."

"Do you have any lemonade in the storeroom, or perhaps upstairs?" Lady Owston enquired.

"No, I don't like it; even with sugar I find it too bitter for my palette," Mr Queshire replied.

"*Thank* you, Mr Queshire," Lady Owston said with a broad smile as she stood and headed for the door. "I know how *valuable* your time is. I really *do* appreciate your sparing some of it for us."

"You're always welcome to it, Lady Owston," Mr Queshire replied with his usual charming smile and followed her as she left. Meanwhile, Mr Locke returned to the window to collect his cane and remind himself of its locking mechanism. For reasons unknown, the identification he'd made had already slipped his mind. He therefore ran his hand over the lock before looking over the room's floorboards. Seeing no indication of a trapdoor to the basement, he concluded the entrance must be elsewhere. Currently at a loss as to where it could be, he plucked his hat and gloves from the table and left the room to join the others at the perfumery department's counter.

"You *will* send my condolences to Mr and Mrs Suggitt and their family?" Mr Queshire enquired from Lady Owston. "I've not seen them since it happened."

"But of *course*," Lady Owston replied. Catching sight of Miss Webster by the millinery department, she waved to get her attention. "There's Agnes."

"Excellent, thank you. Good day, Milady," Mr Queshire said.

"Good *day* to you, too," Lady Owston replied. Watching him as he returned to the storeroom, she then hurried across the shop floor to greet Miss Webster.

Meanwhile, Mr Locke, having had an idea, glanced at the perfumery department's assistant to ensure she was distracted by a customer before slipping past and approaching the storeroom door. With his back against it, to keep the shop floor in view, he turned the knob and eased the door open a crack to peer inside. He saw Mr Queshire sliding down the sash window and securing its lock. When Mr Queshire then turned toward the door, though, Mr Locke was obliged to close it with a click and retreat to the counter in the middle of the room. *Why had Mr Queshire decided to open and close the window after we'd left?* He pondered. Hearing the thud of the storeroom door, he looked up and saw Mr Queshire crossing the room toward the stairs.

Noticing Lady Owston and Miss Webster deep in conversation at the millinery department, Mr Locke considered instructing them to return to Miss Trent at Bow Street whilst he searched the *Queshire Department Store* for the missing clothes. A cursory glance at his surroundings obliged him to abandon the idea, however. As the reception he'd received had proven; there were too many ladies here who'd recognised him. Such attention would make slipping into restricted rooms unnoticed impossible. He therefore left his current spot to re-join his fellow Bow Streeters.

"I didn't have time to inspect it properly, but I have it concealed in my coat," Miss Webster informed Lady Owston in a hushed voice.

An unusual point at which to enter a conversation, Mr Locke mused. The fact Miss Webster had felt the need to conceal whatever it was she had, led him to decide against enquiring after its nature. He therefore resigned himself to the role of spectator whilst browsing the hairpins for a gift for his wife. All were ornate and intricately decorated. Yet, it was the glint of gold nestled among them that caught his attention. Leaning over the counter to take a closer look, he realised it was a ring. *There had been mention of a ring*, he thought. The fog in his mind refused to lift, however. Nevertheless, he glanced over at the assistant and, seeing she was speaking with a customer, grabbed the ring with a cluster of hairpins and dropped them into his palm. Turning so his back was to the counter, he picked up the ring and slipped it over his thumb before dropping the hairpins back into the tray. Since he'd yet to put his hat on, he placed it on the counter and pulled on his leather gloves to conceal the ring. He then turned to his fellow Bow Streeters and said, "If you ladies would be so kind as to take my hat and wait in my carriage outside? I shall be but a moment."

"Where are you going?" Miss Webster enquired.

"To investigate a most curious incident," Mr Locke replied.

When he left the store with them and strode down the street, though, Lady Owston remarked to Miss Webster, "peculiar behaviour, indeed."

Meanwhile, Mr Locke sought out the service alleyway running adjacent to the buildings' rear. Once found, he counted the gates until he reached the one belonging to the *Queshire Department Store*. As the storeroom window overlooked the rear yard and, consequentially, the gate, he refrained from scaling the wall. Instead he jumped, gripped the wall's flat top, and used his upper body strength to pull himself high enough to peer over. There was no one in the storeroom and nothing seemed out of place in the yard. *What was Mr Queshire doing at the window, then?* He pondered. Pulling himself higher, he saw a set of slanted, wooden doors beneath the window. Presuming them to be the elusive entrance to the basement, he pulled himself up and over the wall before lowering himself down on the other side. Keen to not be discovered he placed his feet onto the yard's cold, stone floor, bent his knees and back, and crept over to the doors.

They were secured with a cast-iron chain and heart-shaped padlock. The latter was engulfed by rust to the point Mr Locke doubted its key could release it, let alone one of his picks. Clearly it had been some years since this entrance had been used. His thoughts returned to the basement's internal entrance; even if he could locate it, the state of the external doors meant his entry point would also have to be his exit point. Such a strategy would be dangerous as, if he were caught by either Mr Queshire or his employees, he'd have no choice but to remain in the basement. The thought of wearing the Metropolitan Police's own brand of jewellery wasn't an attractive one. He therefore conceded to the unpleasant reality that an attempt to penetrate the basement posed a risk greater than his chance of success.

He looked up at the storeroom window and, after seeing the room remained vacant, left the yard in the same manner he'd entered. Once in the service alleyway, he brushed the dust from his frock coat and strolled back to his fellow Bow Streeters on Oxford Street.

TWENTY-SIX

From her vantage point of the pew beneath the window, Miss Dexter thought the absence of customers gave the *Turk's Head* public house's dilapidated interior an eerie atmosphere. If she hadn't known of her fellow Bow Streeters' visit the other evening, the cobwebs, dust, and stained wallpaper would've convinced her no one had set foot in the place for years. Weak gaslight in dirty sconces assisted the light from the fireplace in casting dancing shadows across the floor. This, coupled with the rumble of thunder in the distance and the pitter-patter of rain against the window, made her glad for the company of Mr Maxwell, Miss Webster, and the pub's landlord, Mr Ratchett.

Mr Maxwell was sitting beside her on the pew whilst Miss Webster had taken the stool opposite to ensure her back was to the open fire. The moment Miss Dexter had seen the flames within the hearth upon entering, she'd encouraged Mr Maxwell to join her on the pew with a gentle nudge of his arm. She'd doubted Miss Webster would air her preference for the stool, and neither she nor Mr Maxwell were going to reveal Miss Webster's phobia to Mr Ratchett, so Miss Dexter had manoeuvred them all to ensure the stool would be left vacant.

Mr Ratchett was in his late fifties with broad biceps, rounded shoulders, and a hunched back. He'd moved his stool away from the table before lowering himself onto it with stiff-moving knees and a soft grunt. His chestnut-brown, unkempt hair had grey flecks at its edges, which mirrored the colour of his closely cut sideburns. A cream shirt clung to his muscular arms, whilst an old, crumpled apron hung from his waist to rest upon dark-brown trousers.

"Thank you for speaking to us at what must be a

difficult time," Miss Dexter said.

"Anything to help out the Roberts," Mr Ratchett replied in a voice dragged from the depths of his chest. "Still can't believe what 'appened; wife's beside herself."

"Mrs Yates took care of your wife the night Mrs Roberts died, didn't she?" Mr Maxwell enquired with pencil poised.

"Yeah," Mr Ratchett replied. "Jenny's got sickness of the lungs."

"Wasn't Dr Locke with her?" Miss Webster enquired, recalling the visit the other evening.

"Nah; I've not got much trust in women doctors, but we can't afford a regular one," Mr Ratchett replied. "All Dr Locke could do for Jenny was give her some tonic and tell her to rest up. Mrs Yates took over most of Jenny's care."

"But Mrs Yates finished work early that night?" Mr Maxwell enquired as he made his notes.

"Robbie McDonald came and collected her," Mr Ratchett replied. "Them two went back a long way. We all did; I was a Merchant Seaman with Robbie until I met Jenny. He's always held a candle for Sarah."

"Mrs Yates told our associate, Mr Snyder, that Mr McDonald sailed from London the day after Mrs Roberts' murder," Miss Webster began, referring to her previous notes. When Mr Ratchett nodded, she enquired, "Did Mr McDonald know Mrs Roberts at all?"

"Not that I know of, but I'll tell you who she *did* know—and who came looking for her the night she died, too. Sarah's other son-in-law, Mr Suggitt," Mr Ratchett replied. "Came in about a quarter past nine. I told him Mrs Roberts was barred and she'd not come in besides. He got all het-up but then left. I told Sarah about it when she came down about fifteen or so minutes later. I let her leave early because she and Robbie wanted to make the most of their time. He's gonna be heartbroken when he gets back to port and finds out she's gone."

"Do you have any idea when that may be?" Miss Webster enquired.

"I'm afraid I don't; months, a year even?" Mr Ratchett replied. "Depends if he decides to change ships when he gets to the other end."

"Arsenic," Mr Maxwell stated as he tapped his notebook with his pencil before leaning upon it with his bent arm. "Mrs Yates bought you some for the mice from *Eastleigh's* chemists, didn't she?"

"She did," Mr Ratchett replied.

Mr Maxwell hummed and absently chewed the end of his pencil. Grimacing at the bitter taste of wood a moment later, he straightened his back and wiped the spittle from the pencil onto his trouser leg.

"May we see it, please?" Miss Webster enquired with mild disgust at Mr Maxwell's actions.

Mr Ratchett grimaced as he forced his reluctant joints into motion and stood. Waddling over to the bar, he retrieved a brown-paper packet from the shelf beneath the counter and, returning to the others, tossed it onto the table. It was sealed and clearly marked with the *Eastleigh's* stamp. Dropping back onto his stool, he said, "The police wanted to look at it, too. I've not had a chance to use it yet, what with Jenny's illness and then Mrs Yates' murder."

"What did the police say when you showed it to them?" Miss Dexter enquired.

"Not much, just thanked me for showing it to them," Mr Ratchett replied. "They came the day before Sarah was murdered, probably trying to say she killed her daughter. I showed it to them to make a point."

"You don't believe Mrs Yates was responsible for Mrs Roberts' death, then?" Mr Maxwell enquired. "They weren't on speaking terms, after all."

"Sarah loved her children—*all* of them," Mr Ratchett replied in a hard tone. "She talked harshly about Maryanna but that was her way of protecting herself. That girl hurt all of them with her drinking; there was no need for it, either. Was just like her dad."

Mr Maxwell frowned as he was reminded of his own father. He therefore resumed his notetaking to push the thoughts from his mind.

"The night Mrs Yates died, did Mr Roberts walk her home at closing?" Miss Dexter enquired.

"He did; got here at eleven o'clock and left with her," Mr Ratchett replied.

"Did you see anyone watching them or, perhaps, following them when they left?" Miss Webster enquired.

"Now that you mention it, there was someone, a young woman who sat by the door," Mr Ratchett replied. "Soon as Abraham came in, that young woman watched him. I'd caught her watching Sarah, too. Then, when they left, she got up and walked out after them."

"Can you remember what she looked like?" Miss Dexter enquired as she retrieved her sketchbook from her satchel.

"I think so," Mr Ratchett replied. "She was small, like the size of a twelve-year-old or something. She was older than that though; I could tell by looking in her face." He closed his eyes. "Wiry, blond hair she had, in a bun at the back." He gestured to the base of his skull. "Wore a skirt and a blouse; can't remember what colours."

"Was there anything unusual about her face? A large nose, maybe? Distinctly coloured eyes?" Miss Dexter enquired as she sketched out the description.

Mr Ratchett clenched his eyelids as he concentrated but, after a few moments, lifted and dropped his hands with a weary sigh and shook his head. Opening his eyes, he replied, "Sorry, I can't remember. It was closing time and I was tired. I just wanted to get them out and check on Jenny."

Miss Dexter frowned; it wasn't the most detailed of descriptions and her sketch was faceless besides. She therefore decided against showing it to him and closed her sketchbook.

Whilst she completed her notes, though, Miss Webster said, "I believe we met the young woman shortly after leaving here the other evening."

Miss Dexter put her sketchbook back into her satchel and inwardly scolded herself for not making the connection between Mr Ratchett's description and Miss Galway. Yet, on reflection, she realised it would've been impossible for her to have done so since she'd never met Miss Galway. Offering Mr Ratchett a soft smile, she said, "Thank you, again, for your help."

* * *

Mr Roberts turned the ring over in his fingers as he scrutinised it with a furrowed brow. Sitting on a sofa in the Suggitts' parlour, he was leaning forward with his elbows resting upon his knees. Sharing the sofa opposite were Lady Owston, Miss Webster, Mr Maxwell, and Miss Dexter, whilst Mr Locke stood beside the fireplace. Several moments passed, during which the Bow Streeters studied Mr Roberts' face. It soon became apparent that, the longer he examined the ring, the more his features tightened, and the redder his eyes became. In a hushed voice, he said, "It's Sarah's… The initials engraved on the inside are her husband's." He lifted bloodshot eyes to Mr Locke. "Where did you find it?"

"In a tray of hairpins at the *Queshire Department Store*," Mr Locke replied.

Mr Roberts sat up and, looking between Mr Locke and the others, enquired, "What was it doing there?"

"Mrs Yates didn't take it there?" Miss Webster enquired, her monotone causing the question to sound more confrontational than she'd intended.

"Nah," Mr Roberts snapped, glaring at her. "She never went near the place."

"Perhaps your daughter, then?" Mr Maxwell suggested. "Or Mr and Mrs Suggitt?"

"When're they supposed to have done that?" Mr Roberts demanded with hardened eyes. "She was *wearing* the ring the last I saw her."

"Well…" Lady Owston cautiously began. "There is the possibility one of them murdered your mother-in-law because they suspected she murdered your wife."

"You're *mad*," Mr Roberts replied.

"It isn't madness to consider all possibilities," Lady Owston retorted. "Besides, we still include *you* among our suspects, Mr Roberts."

"I *didn't* murder my wife—*or* my mother-in-law!" Mr Roberts yelled with a fierce glare.

"Whomever the guilty party is, they deposited the ring at the store," Mr Locke interjected. "Regardless of whether it was done to divert suspicion away from themselves, it is clear the only possible time the murderer could have dropped the ring into the tray would have been the morning after Mrs Yates' death, due to her being murdered so early in the day."

"Sarah didn't kill Maryanna; she hated the drink, but she loved her daughter," Mr Roberts replied through a clenched jaw. "Anyway, Diana, Clement, Regina, and me couldn't have killed Sarah because we was all here when she died. We told you that."

"Indeed, you did," Mr Locke replied. "But more than one of you has admitted to lying to protect another. Why would any of you not do so again?"

"I'll show you why," Mr Roberts replied, getting to his feet and opening the window. Addressing the constable standing outside, he said, "Get Inspector Woolfe here; tell him I want to talk to him."

The constable looked past Mr Roberts and, seeing the Bow Streeters, hurried away to fulfil the request.

"I want you to hear this from him," Mr Roberts told them once he'd closed the window.

TWENTY-SEVEN

The night was drawing in when Lady Owston, Misses Webster and Dexter, and Messieurs Locke, Maxwell and Snyder stood around the central counter in the *Queshire Department Store*. Sitting side-by-side before them were Mrs Ruth Holden, Mrs Diana Suggitt, Miss Regina Roberts, and Mr Abraham Roberts. Mr Bartholomew Holden gripped the top of his wife's chair as he stood between it and Mrs Suggitt's. Mr Clement Suggitt stood behind his wife, holding her hand against her shoulder. Mr Edmund Queshire stood beside Mr Roberts' chair, whilst Mr Roberts' held his daughter's hand in her lap. Meanwhile, Dr Percy Weeks was bent over the counter of the haberdashery department with his folded arms resting upon the glass and a cigarette perched in the corner of his mouth. Standing beside him was Inspector Caleb Woolfe, whilst two uniformed constables loitered on the street beside an imposing Black Maria.

"Four days ago, the Bow Street Society was commissioned to investigate the murder of Mrs Maryanna Roberts, and now we are ready to reveal who we believe took her life," Lady Owston said as she lifted a thick file for all to see.

Mrs Suggitt stifled a gasp with her handkerchief and tightened her grip upon her husband's hand. He had stood erect at the news and placed his free hand upon his wife's other shoulder. At the same time, Miss Roberts had pursed her lips and put her other hand upon her father's, Mr Roberts had momentarily averted his gaze, Mr Holden had sidestepped to hold his wife's chair with both hands, and Mrs Holden had rolled her eyes and tutted.

"Here we go," Inspector Woolfe remarked as he put a cigarette between his lips and lit it with a match. "I told you what would happen if you carried on meddling."

Exhaling the smoke toward the group, thereby causing Mrs Holden and Mrs Suggitt to wave it away, he added, "Perverting the course of justice by conspiracy; that's what this is."

"I thought you wanted to know the truth, too," Miss Roberts challenged.

Inspector Woolfe flashed a yellow-toothed smile and replied, "I do, but we're not going to hear it from them. They're bloody meddling civilians; they don't know anything about how a case *should* be investigated. There are proper rules to follow, strict methods when recording evidence, and ways suspects should be questioned."

"I still think we should hear what they've got to say," Miss Roberts countered.

"Can we *please* get on with this?" Mrs Holden urged. "We have a dinner engagement at eight."

"Two of my family have been murdered and you're worried about dinner?" Mr Roberts enquired with a scowl.

Mrs Holden lifted her chin and replied, "I wouldn't expect someone like *you* to understand."

"You *what*?!" Mr Roberts cried, leaping to his feet.

"*Oh*!" Mrs Holden cried, wide-eyed, as she sat bolt upright and reached for her husband. "*Bartholomew*!"

Mr Suggitt stood between Mrs Holden and Mr Roberts, though, and warned the latter, "*Stop* it. You getting into trouble won't help anyone."

"*Sit down*," Inspector Woolfe warned in a loud voice. His hard eyes followed Mr Roberts to his chair before shifting back to Mrs Holden upon hearing her mutter something under her breath. "Do you want to share that with the rest of us, Madam?"

Mrs Holden turned her head toward him with parted lips when she realised she'd been overheard. Lifting her chin once more, she turned her head away and replied, "No. Thank you."

"Good," Inspector Woolfe said. Shifting his attention back to Lady Owston, he went on, "Let's hear it, then; your theory, before I'm obliged to arrest everyone for brawling."

"Thank you, Inspector," Lady Owston replied and opened the file. "Mrs Maryanna Roberts and Mrs Sarah Yates were poisoned with drinks laced with arsenic— French Breakfast Coffee for Mrs Roberts and lemonade for Mrs Yates. The scalps and breasts of each victim were removed and taken by their murderer. Their clothes were also stolen and, in Mrs Yates' case, so too was her gold wedding ring. From descriptions Mr Suggitt and Mr Roberts gave, our artist Miss Dexter sketched the victims' missing clothes."

Miss Dexter held up her sketches and both Mrs Suggitt and Mr Roberts averted their gazes. At the same time, Mr Holden looked at the sketch depicting Mrs Roberts' missing clothes with sorrowful eyes, whilst his wife stifled a yawn, and Mr Queshire maintained a stoic expression and folded his arms.

"Mrs Roberts' body was discovered in the doorway of the *London Crystal Palace Bazaar's* Oxford Street entrance," Lady Owston continued. "Her body having been taken there in a hessian sack by her murderer."

Inspector Woolfe narrowed his eyes and glared at Dr Weeks who was scratching the back of his neck with his head down.

"Are you listening, Inspector?" Lady Owston enquired.

Inspector Woolfe grunted.

"Was that a yes or a no?" Lady Owston enquired as politely as she could.

"Yeah, I'm listening," Inspector Woolfe replied.

"*Excellent*," Lady Owston said with a fleeting smile. "On account of where Mrs Roberts' body was found, we had to consider the possibility her murderer was a stranger. At that point in time, this was a more probable scenario than the alternative. Yet, when we later learned *how* she was killed, the likelihood of this scenario disappeared, and we instead concluded she was murdered by someone she knew.

"We came to this conclusion for three reasons: a) She was poisoned, a weapon most frequently utilised in closed quarters, b) The poison was put in coffee, a beverage she would *certainly* not have chosen if gin was available, and c) she wouldn't have accepted or drank the coffee if it had been offered by a stranger. On the surface, reason b may appear to support the stranger theory as it seems to demonstrate a lack of intimate knowledge about Mrs Roberts. Yet, given her public preference for gin, a stranger would've been more inclined to offer an arsenic-laced bottle of that drink than coffee.

"Reasons a) and c) may also be applied to Mrs Yates' murder. She, unlike her daughter, *was* given her preferred choice of beverage by her murderer—lemonade. This fact *does* demonstrate a more intimate knowledge of Mrs Yates so again, we suspected she, like her daughter, was murdered by someone she knew. The simple fact Mrs Yates was murdered *in* her *own* home strengthened our opinion. Her requirement that her son-in-law escort her home after work demonstrates an awareness of possible danger at night. It would've therefore been against her instincts to invite a stranger into her home when she was alone. As a result, we entirely dismissed the possibility of our murderer being an unknown entity. This dramatically decreased our circle of suspects for both murders. Due to the similarities between the two crimes, in terms of chosen weapon, corpse mutilation, and items stolen, we also quickly concluded we were seeking the same person, or persons, for *both* deaths. Mr Locke?"

"Thank you, Lady Owston," Mr Locke said as he accepted the file from her. Turning the page and taking a few moments to refresh his memory, he continued, "Mrs Roberts' body was identified by Metropolitan Police Constable Fraser for two reasons. The first: she was a prostitute known to frequent the area. The second: she was the sister-in-law of the *Queshire Department Store's* assistant manager, Mr Clement Suggitt. It was he who was notified of Mrs Roberts' murder by Constable Fraser. Afterward, Mr Suggitt broke the news to his wife and Mrs Roberts' sister Diana, via telephone and told her not to travel to Oxford Street. She, in a state of great distress, at once went to Bow Street and commissioned the Society to investigate her sister's murder. The reason she cited for the commission was a lack of confidence in the Metropolitan Police's willingness to identify the murderer of a 'fallen woman,' such as Mrs Roberts."

"That's—" Inspector Woolfe began through a growl.

"A simple statement of facts and no attempt to sully anyone's reputation," Mr Locke interrupted.

"It still doesn't make it true," Inspector Woolfe remarked and crushed out his cigarette.

"The Bow Street Society's experience with the Dorsey case compelled us to refrain from blindly accepting our client's innocence. It also highlighted the need to consider *everyone* as a suspect until evidence against their guilt could be uncovered; Mrs Suggitt was no exception to this." Mr Locke looked to her as he returned the file to Lady Owston. "She commissioned our services, but she was not above our suspicions."

"I, my secretary Miss Agnes Webster, and Miss Georgina Dexter, were assigned to investigate the case by the Bow Street Society's clerk, Miss Trent," Lady Owston began as she turned to the relevant page. "We travelled to Oxford Street with Mrs Suggitt in the Bow Street Society's hansom cab, driven by Mr Samuel Snyder who, unbeknownst to our client, had also been assigned to the case. Mrs Suggitt informed Miss Webster, Miss Dexter, and me of an incident which had occurred at the *Queshire Department Store* the previous day, one which had an altercation between Mrs Roberts and another customer at its centre."

"I presume you are referring to *me*?" Mrs Holden interjected.

"Indeed, she is," Mr Locke replied as he absently scratched a sore patch on the back of his hand. Briefly retrieving the file from Lady Owston and referring to the next passage, he continued, "We were told by Mr Queshire and his shop assistant, Miss Rose Galway, that Mrs Roberts propositioned your husband." Mr Locke shifted his gaze to the man in question but continued to address Mrs Holden as he said, "You naturally took offence to such behaviour and threatened to leave the store. Mr Queshire therefore intervened and removed Mrs Roberts despite her violent physical, and verbal, abuse toward him. When the request was made for your identities, Miss Galway granted it. By contrast, Mr Queshire, for reasons of propriety and reputation, had intended *not* to do so."

"As is only proper," Mrs Holden remarked.

"Under normal circumstances, I would be inclined to agree with you," Mr Locke replied with a smile. "However, we were investigating a murder. Thus, we were obliged to question *anyone* who could, potentially, be involved. You and your husband were suspects because of your altercation with Mrs Roberts. If Miss Galway had *not* let slip your names, we may be still trying to track you down even now."

"When Miss Webster and I spoke to you at your home, Mrs Holden, you made it *abundantly* clear you not only had a low opinion of Mrs Roberts, but you thought she was of the 'criminal class.'" Lady Owston said. "Furthermore, you stated her murder wasn't unfortunate."

"It wasn't," Mrs Holden replied in a cool tone.

"How could you *say* such a thing?" Mrs Suggitt enquired in disbelief. "Do you have *any* idea what was done to her?"

"She was a *foul* creature who squandered her God-given life in the gin houses," Mrs Holden replied.

"That doesn't mean her murder was a *good* thing!" Mrs Suggitt cried.

"I now see why your sister was as *foul* as she was; uncontrollable emotion is evidently a family trait," Mrs Holden sneered.

"The only foul creature here is *you*!" Mrs Suggitt cried as she attempted to slap Mrs Holden. She was pulled back to her chair by her husband's arm, though. Distraught and ashamed by her own emotions, she turned and buried her face in his waistcoat with shaking shoulders and unbridled weeping.

"As I told you at the time," Mrs Holden began as she peered down her nose at Lady Owston. "Neither my husband nor I would slay another human being; it is against God's Commandments."

"You also told us you'd visited the *Theatre Royal* on Drury Lane until nine thirty on the night of Mrs Roberts' murder," Lady Owston replied. "Furthermore, that you returned home at ten o'clock and, while your husband read in the library, you retired to bed."

"A story which your husband confirmed during my conversation with him at the *Royal Coachman* public house on Hill Street," Mr Locke interjected.

"And *why* would he *not*?" Mrs Holden scoffed.

"Indeed," Mr Locke replied and shifted his gaze to Mr Holden. Seeing the trepidation in his eyes and face, he considered sparing him the humiliation a full disclosure of the facts would bring. Yet, after reflecting upon Mrs Holden's uncouth behaviour, he decided a full disclosure could prove fortuitous to Mr Holden in the long term. He therefore continued, "You did not remain in the library, Mr Holden. Instead, you left your home and sought out Mrs Roberts. She, by your own admission, was just one of the women who regularly satisfied your carnal needs in exchange for monetary payment. Needs which your wife could not, for propriety's sake, fulfil." To Mrs Holden, he said, "You have my sympathies."

Mrs Holden chewed her tongue in indignation.

Mr Locke continued, "Yet you did not simply have 'services rendered,' Mr Holden; you told her she would not receive any further coin from you should she behave in a similar manner to the way she had acted earlier in the day. In your own words, you wanted to remind her 'of her place.' You also paid her only half the amount you usually would—*after* she had 'verbally' rendered her service to you—partly because she was inebriated at the time and partly because of her earlier behaviour. Am I recalling this correctly, Mr Holden, or would you like to make some amendments?"

"*Disgusting,*" Mrs Holden sneered.

"Be *quiet,* woman," Mr Holden countered. "*I* am your *husband*; I shall find my pleasure wherever *I* see fit."

"Maryanna was *sick*, she needed *help*," Mrs Suggitt interjected in a shaky voice. "Not for men like *you* to take advantage of her."

"I did *nothing* of the kind," Mr Holden replied. "I paid her for the pleasure she gave me." His features softened and his voice became laced with regret as he continued, "I enjoyed a warmth from her I couldn't ever hope to receive from my wife. Ruth and I married for convenience; it is a lonely and soul-destroying existence to be in a loveless marriage. I'm not ashamed to admit that, when I heard of Maryanna's death, I was sad beyond measure."

Fresh tears slipped down Mrs Suggitt's face as she continued to glare at Mr Holden.

"I *swear* to you, on my *word* of honour as a gentleman," Mr Holden insisted.

Mrs Suggitt looked up to her husband who gave her shoulder a gentle squeeze. Dabbing at her eyes with her handkerchief, she replied, "I still can't condone your behaviour, Mr Holden, but… I am comforted by the knowledge her part in your life was a positive one."

"Thank you," Mr Holden whispered.

"It was your reaction to her death which convinced me you were not responsible for it, Mr Holden," Mr Locke said.

"And it was your vehement disgust and dislike of her, Mrs Holden, which had Miss Webster and I convinced *you'd* had no part in the poor woman's murder, either," Lady Owston interjected.

"Yet these were mere assumptions," Mr Locke continued. "The evidence of your innocence would come when we scrutinised the practicalities of either of you committing the act. Dr Weeks, we have a vague idea of when Mrs Roberts was murdered but could you clarify it for us, please?"

Dr Weeks straightened and looked to Inspector Woolfe. When the policeman gave no objection, he replied, "It were between midnight and four in the mornin'. She were then found by Constable Fraser at six."

"As I suspected. Thank you, Doctor," Mr Locke said with a smile. "Mr Holden, even at midnight, your meeting with Mrs Roberts, at approximately ten forty-five, was over an hour before the earliest time at which she could have died. Furthermore, you only remained with her for a few minutes. You then returned home and climbed into bed at eleven forty-five where, as both you and your wife stated, Mrs Holden was asleep. On the surface, therefore, it would appear neither of you had any practical opportunity to murder Mrs Roberts. And yet," he held up his finger, "you each had *motive* in the form of the earlier altercation. You had each been humiliated by it, if for different reasons. Could it be one, or perhaps both, of you murdered her because of this? You could have lied for each other and your servants, who dressed you the following morning, could have unwittingly provided you with an alibi. Why would an alibi be required? Because the murderer, having stolen her clothes, left Mrs Robert's shawl at the *Queshire Department Store.* You each could have risen early enough to return to Oxford Street, abandon the shawl at the store, and return home in good time to be 'awakened' by your servants.

"This scenario did not play out, however, for two reasons. As a regular customer of the department store, you, Mrs Holden, would have been aware of Mr Queshire's routine reluctance to discuss his customers with those who had no right to the information. You would assume, therefore, your name would not be uttered in connection with the altercation with Mrs Roberts. Why, then, would you go to the trouble of disposing of Mrs Roberts' shawl at the very establishment where the altercation took place? The answer is you would not. You had absolutely no reason to suspect anyone would visit you to ask after your altercation with Mrs Roberts. You could have therefore simply retained the shawl without fear of consequence. The presence of the shawl on one of the store's dummies the very morning *after* Mrs Roberts' murder, though, tells us this was *not* the case. Which leads me onto the second reason. It is my belief, Mr Holden, that despite you being unable to recall it when I asked you what Mrs Roberts was wearing the last you saw her, she *was* in fact in possession of her shawl at that time."

"It does look familiar, yes," Mr Holden admitted as he scrutinised Miss Dexter's sketch for a second time.

"Mr Queshire adorned the dummy with the shawl on the *night* of Mrs Roberts' murder when he was alone in the store," Mr Locke continued. "Due to the fact she *was* wearing it during your meeting with her, and Mr Queshire did *not* mention he had received a late-night visit from you or your wife, it is our conclusion neither of you had any practical opportunity to dispose of the shawl before our visit. As a result, regardless of any semblance of motive or practical opportunity to commit the deed, you are both innocent of Mrs Roberts' murder. Since there was no tangible connection between either of you and Mrs Yates, we also believe neither of you were responsible for her death."

"May we leave, then?" Mrs Holden enquired.

"Yeah," Inspector Woolfe replied. "Go home."

"*Thank* you," Mrs Holden said. Allowing her husband to take her arm and help her to stand, she then pulled her arm free and stomped out of the store.

"I *am* sorry about Maryanna's death," Mr Holden said in a soft voice as he addressed both the Suggitts and Roberts.

"Thank you," Mr Suggitt replied.

A little of Mr Holden's sadness was eased by this and, after biding goodbye to the others, he followed his wife into the night.

TWENTY-EIGHT

"I appreciate you not revealing the existence of the second-hand basket to Mrs Holden," Mr Queshire said to Mr Locke once the harpy and her spouse were beyond earshot.

"She had not placed the shawl *within* it, so it was unnecessary for her to be made aware *of* it," Mr Locke replied.

"But someone here did," Mr Maxwell interjected. "The storeroom, where the basket is kept, is never locked so, theoretically, any of you could've put the shawl there."

"Earlier, I stated Mrs Suggitt was not above our suspicions," Mr Locke began. "Once we had eliminated the Holdens as possible suspects, we turned our scrutiny to all those who were close to both victims, Mrs Suggitt included. Yet, before we explain our conclusions regarding our client's level of guilt, we must first explain those relating to her husband."

"As Mrs Roberts' brother-in-law, it should have fallen to *you* to intervene when her behaviour around the Holdens became unpalatable," Lady Owston began. "Instead, it was Mr Queshire who felt obliged to confront her and, subsequently, remove her from his store."

Mr Suggitt averted his gaze and swallowed to ease the tightening of his throat.

"According to Mr Queshire, you would distance yourself from Mrs Roberts whenever she visited the store, an allegation you have never denied," Lady Owston went on. "Your wife, on the other hand, would converse freely with her sister where all the customers could see. Thus, your behaviour couldn't have been born from a decision to disown your wife's family. During our conversation at the *Turk's Head* public house, you admitted you'd never made a secret of your dislike for Mrs Roberts. We must therefore assume you distanced yourself from her for the same reason. Regardless, however, Mr Queshire had felt unable to request your assistance *because* of your reaction to Mrs Roberts' past visits to the store.

"Yet, your feelings toward your sister-in-law ran deeper than a simple dislike of her; you yourself told us you thought she was making the lives of her husband, her daughter, and even your wife a misery."

"She was," Mr Suggitt replied as he took his wife's hand.

Lady Owston hummed and, after a fleeting smile, continued, "But it was your *wife's* pain specifically, caused by her being constantly disappointed by her sister, which compelled you to offer Mrs Roberts two hundred pounds to leave London. An offer, though generous, she refused. She also threatened to tell your wife of it, and it was this reason which, you believed, had brought her to the store."

"Yes, it's true," Mr Suggitt replied in a low voice.

"You've already admitted to us this was the reason you decided to look for her on the night she died," Lady Owston continued as she turned to another part of the file. "In addition to her usual haunts, you visited the *Turk's Head* public house where its landlord, Mr Ratchett, informed you she'd not been in all evening. You were reportedly agitated by this news but left regardless. It wasn't *you* who first informed us of your search, however. Mrs Sarah Yates, Mrs Roberts' mother, had been informed of your visit, by Mr Ratchett, shortly after you'd left. *She* told us of it. Furthermore, Mrs Roberts had been *barred* from that establishment on account of her having caused trouble there in the past. One must therefore wonder *why* you would even check the pub at all. Mrs Yates and her daughter hadn't been on speaking terms prior to Mrs Roberts' death so, surely, it would've been unlikely she'd have gone there. *Perhaps* you wanted everyone to *see* you *without* Mrs Roberts so you could *prove* you hadn't seen her all evening when her body was eventually discovered?"

"Don't be ridiculous," Mr Suggitt rebuked. "I was at home in bed by a quarter to midnight; ask Diana."

"She's already lied for you once," Inspector Woolfe remarked.

Mr Suggitt looked from Inspector Woolfe, to Lady Owston, and back again. When neither aired an objection to the accusation being laid at his door, he cried, "I didn't murder my sister-in-law!"

"Why not?" Mr Locke challenged. "You had the motive; you wished to ensure she held her tongue over your proposition. You had the opportunity: your wife, who has already lied for you by telling the inspector you were at home together all evening, could have lied about the time you came to bed. You had the means: there is a tin of the French Breakfast coffee, used to administer the arsenic to Mrs Roberts, both in the storeroom here and, in your own words, at your residence. Furthermore, you requested Miss Galway purchase some arsenic from *Drummond's Pharmaceutical Chemists* on your behalf. Though Mr Queshire confirmed it was indeed for a rat infestation in the basement here, you could have easily stolen the arsenic and given it to your sister-in-law. Then there is the shawl; as assistant manager, you could have placed it in the second-hand clothes basket without anyone's suspicions becoming aroused."

"Your guilt does *appear* certain, Mr Suggitt," Lady Owston said in a sombre tone. "And yet the certainty wanes when one scrutinises whether you had the *capability* of not only murdering Mrs Roberts, but also her mother and, in addition to their murders, mutilating their bodies. Yes, you initially lied about your whereabouts on the night Mrs Roberts died. Yes, you failed to tell the police about the argument between Mrs Roberts and the

Holdens, and, yes, you told Miss Dexter you didn't want the Bow Street Society to investigate anymore. However—"

"He did what?" Mrs Suggitt interrupted in a hushed voice. Looking up at her husband, she enquired, "Clement, is this true? Did you tell them to stop investigating?"

"I did it for you, my darling," Mr Suggitt replied as he sat down on Mrs Holden's vacant chair and took his wife's hands in his. Holding them close to his chest, he looked into her eyes with an intense sadness in his own. "I could see how much pain you were in and I couldn't bear it. I thought… if we just let the *police* do their duty, it would be resolved sooner, and this nightmare would be *over*."

"*Oh,* my *darling*," Mrs Suggitt whispered and threw her arms about him.

"I'm so sorry, Diana. I never meant to hurt you," Mr Suggitt said as he held her close and wept into her shoulder.

"Hush," Mrs Suggitt soothed, stroking the back of his head with a trembling hand. "It is done, my darling."

"However, as we have all just witnessed, you are sincere in your love and devotion to your wife, Mr Suggitt," Lady Owston said. "The murder of her sister, though enabling you to be rid of her once and for all, would have devastated your wife as it has now. The same consequence has been born from the death of your mother-in-law. Thus, while you *are* capable of lies and deception—uttered to protect your wife—you are *not* capable of murdering the two most important women in your wife's life. The love and devotion you feel for Mrs Suggitt simply wouldn't allow you to commit the deed. Mr Maxwell?"

"Thank you," Mr Maxwell replied as he accepted the file from Lady Owston. Turning to the relevant page, he puffed out his chest and continued, "And so, ladies and gentlemen, we go back to Mrs Suggitt." He smoothed his frock coat with one hand, cleared his throat, coughed, and cleared his throat again. "Inspector Woolfe, was there any hessian sacks at the Suggitts' home?"

"No," Inspector Woolfe replied in a flat tone.

"Thank you," Mr Maxwell said with a smile. When Inspector Woolfe's glare was intensified by this, though, Mr Maxwell's smile vanished, and he felt his face warm. Wiping his palms upon his frock coat's skirt and shifting his weight from one foot to the other, he continued, "Um…" He turned away from Inspector Woolfe and referred to the file. "Ah, here we are." He glanced at the Suggitts. "Mrs Suggitt lied about being at home the night her sister died."

"I *beg* your pardon?" Mr Suggitt enquired as he lifted his head to regard Mr Maxwell.

"She lied… about being at home… the night her sister died," Mr Maxwell replied.

"Is this true?" Mr Suggitt enquired from his wife.

"I was going to tell you…" Mrs Suggitt whispered.

"While you were out looking for her sister, she was visiting Mr Roberts," Mr Maxwell said.

Mr Suggitt furrowed his brow and looked down the row to his brother-in-law. Mr Roberts' hard eyes were fixed upon Mr Maxwell, however.

"When she got there, at around nine thirty, she thought Miss Regina Roberts was asleep behind the curtain; so did Mr Roberts," Mr Maxwell continued as his natural colouring returned. "Mrs Suggitt already knew her mother wouldn't be there because she was working at the *Turk's Head* public house until eleven o'clock like she did every night. Mrs Suggitt told Mr Roberts she wanted her sister to live with her so she wouldn't be tempted by the gin anymore. Rather than celebrate this good news though,

Mr Roberts, again, confessed his love to Mrs Suggitt. Miss Roberts, who was *awake*, had overheard all of this."

"You did *what*?" Mr Suggitt hissed, addressing Mr Roberts, as he rose to his feet.

"I didn't return his affection, darling!" Mrs Suggitt cried, standing to block her husband. "I reminded him, as I had so many times before, that I love *you*!"

Mr Suggitt's hands clenched at his sides as he demanded, "Is that correct, Abraham?"

"It is," Mr Roberts replied in a grave voice as he stood also. "I loved Maryanna, Clement, but the drinking… I was losing her to it. When Diana came to see me… I thought it was another chance at happiness, but I *respected* what she told me. *Nothing* happened between us."

"They're telling you the truth, Uncle," Miss Roberts reassured as she too stood. Moving around Mrs Suggitt, she placed a gentle hand upon Mr Suggitt's arm and begged, "*please*, Uncle Clement. Aunt Diana did tell Dad she loved you. She also said she'd still help us before she left, and Dad came to bed."

"*Listen* to her," Mrs Suggitt whispered, her trembling hands gripping the lapels of her husband's coat as tears poured down her face. "I *love* you, Clement."

Hearing the intense emotion in his wife's voice, Mr Suggitt finally shifted his gaze to her and, all at once, his anger evaporated. Putting his arms around her and pulling her into an embrace, he said, "I love you, too, my darling." He kissed the top of her head and added in a hushed voice, "I believe you."

"When Mr Snyder and I spoke to Mrs Suggitt, after Miss Roberts had told Lady Owston of the overheard conversation, she said she'd left Mr Roberts' residence at ten thirty. She, um…" Mr Maxwell said and flicked back a couple of pages in the file. Realising he'd gone too far, he turned another page and ran his finger down the typed lines. Finding what he was looking for, he continued, "When she returned home, at approximately eleven o'clock, Mr Suggitt hadn't returned. She retired to bed and, after lying awake for almost an hour, heard the bedroom door open, and she pretended to be sleeping." Mr Maxwell rested his hand on his cravat. "Mrs Suggitt had the same access to the French Breakfast coffee and arsenic as her husband, as well as the second-hand clothes basket *if* he had told her of its existence. Mr Suggitt has already confirmed in his own account though that she was indeed asleep in bed at a quarter to midnight on the night her sister died. She therefore had *no* opportunity to commit the murder before her husband came home.

"She, like Mr Suggitt, *did* lie to us on several occasions. Firstly, to protect Miss Regina Roberts: she hired the Bow Street Society because she suspected Mr Roberts of murdering her sister. She wanted *us* to discover the truth before the police did so she could protect Miss Roberts from it. Secondly, she lied on her husband's behalf about their being at home all evening. Thirdly, she lied to her husband about visiting Mr Roberts because she wanted to protect her brother-in-law. Lying and murdering are two *very* different things though, and she had no motive for killing either victim. Thus, like with her husband, we have concluded she, too, is innocent of these crimes for these reasons. Mr Snyder?"

"Mr Roberts," Mr Snyder began as he accepted the file from Mr Maxwell. "You tellin' Mrs Suggitt you loved her is a reason for you wantin' your wife dead. You got French Breakfast coffee at your house with no dust on the tin; everythin' else on that shelf woz covered in it so someone must've used the coffee. Miss Dexter asked 'bout the sacks and you told her you didn't have any, which we thought woz true as we couldn't see any either. There's loads of sacks at the docks though so you could've got one from there." Mr Snyder sniffed and wiped the underside of his nose with his thumb. "Your daughter's just said you went to bed after Mrs Suggitt left. We know, from Miss Roberts, you woz both knocked up at four o'clock in the morning; you to go sleep outside the dock gates, and she to go to Covent Garden. That doesn't give you any time to do in your wife between the two times Dr Weeks said. We think you never got near the arsenic Mrs Yates had bought either because Mr Ratchett still had it when we asked him. We can't check with the Quay-Gangers at the docks, about you bein' there or not, as you're not a Royal but we don't think you ever had a sack at home either. So, even though you lied about Mrs Yates livin' with you and Mrs Yates not talkin' to your daughter, you didn't do in your wife. Mostly because the reason doesn't make sense: you'd do in Mr Suggitt before you done in Mrs Roberts if you wanted to be with Mrs Suggitt because Mrs Roberts wozn't livin' at home. You'd tossed her out on her ear when you found out she'd been tea-leafin' the housekeepin' monies."

"He was the last person to see Mrs Yates alive though," Inspector Woolfe pointed out. "He walked her home, remember?"

"When was Mrs Yates murdered, please, Dr Weeks?" Mr Locke enquired.

Again, Dr Weeks looked to Inspector Woolfe who gave a soft grunt of approval.

"It were between half past midnight and quarter past two in the mornin' when whatshisface found 'er," Dr Weeks replied.

"Mr Trowel," Inspector Woolfe interjected.

"Yeah, 'im," Dr Weeks replied with a nod.

"The Suggitts said Mr Roberts got to their house at half past midnight, and he stayed the night," Mr Snyder began. "That means Mr Roberts didn't have any time to do in his mother-in-law either." Mr Snyder rested his large hand on the file's open page. "But getting' back to his wife, there woz two hours when her body was put somewhere."

"Given the fact she was placed in a sack, a difficult feat at the best of times, with some ease," Lady Owston said. "One must presume the process of—" She referred to the file, "*rigor mortis* had yet to take place. Therefore, one must be inclined toward the earlier time of midnight for when Mrs Roberts was murdered. Between the later hours of four o'clock and six o'clock, when the body was discovered, the sack, with body, would have had to have been stored somewhere safe."

Mr Snyder nodded and resumed, "Mr Roberts wouldn't of been able to take it back home because Miss Roberts or Mrs Yates could've come back. We've got no one sayin' 'e went to the *Queshire Department Store* to drop off the shawl either. We don't think Mr Roberts done in either victim, then, Inspector."

Inspector Woolfe glared at Mr Snyder but knew he was making sense, which angered him further. Woolfe also knew the greater number of meddlers compared to police meant a confrontation would do him little good. Angered at being cornered for a second time during this investigation, but conceding he needed to know the truth, he released a soft sigh that sounded more like a growl and enquired, "If I agree with you—*if* I do—that Mr Roberts wasn't the one who murdered his wife, am I right in next assuming you think his daughter was responsible? Because she's the only one you haven't ruled out yet."

"No, I'm afraid not, Inspector," Miss Dexter replied with a meek smile. "Thank you, Sam." She accepted the file from Mr Snyder and, placing it on the countertop, quietly cleared her throat. "Once one assumes Mr Roberts is telling the truth about where he was the night Mrs Roberts died, one must further accept Miss Roberts' account. She couldn't have possibly murdered her mother, Inspector. Even if we were to consider the chance of her father and aunt lying to protect her, Miss Roberts had no reason to murder her mother; she loved her and wanted her back home."

"Pardon my interruption," Mr Queshire began as he dropped his hands to his sides and moved toward Miss Dexter. "But isn't there a possibility you're *all* neglecting to consider?" He looked between them all. "It's a ghastly thought but, given the tragic circumstances, I feel it's my duty to draw attention to it."

"And what's that, sir?" Inspector Woolfe enquired.

"He is referring to the possibility they *all* murdered Mrs Yates because *she* murdered Mrs Roberts," Miss Webster said.

"It has to be considered," Mr Queshire muttered as he sheepishly looked to his feet.

"It's a preposterous idea," Mr Suggitt remarked.

"He's right, though," Inspector Woolfe interjected. "It's a possibility."

"Mrs Yates openly admitted to her feud with her daughter when Mr Snyder conversed with her," Miss Webster resumed. "She also told Mr Snyder that Mrs Roberts had been barred from the pub, and confirmed Mr Roberts' story that he had been forced to ask his wife to leave the family home because he'd discovered she'd stolen the housekeeping money to purchase gin." Miss Webster referred to her previous notes. "Mrs Yates didn't deny living with her granddaughter and son-in-law, citing the reason she was doing Mrs Roberts' job—taking care of the family—for her. According to Mr Ratchett, Mrs Yates was taking care of the unwell Mrs Ratchett when Mr Suggitt had come seeking Mrs Roberts.

"At half past ten, on the same night, a sailor by the name of Mr Robbie MacDonald came to the pub to escort Mrs Yates away so they could spend some time together. An arrangement confirmed by Mr Roberts—who hadn't needed to escort his mother-in-law home that night because of it—and Mr Ratchett. The landlord and Mr MacDonald were old friends, so he would've at once recognised him when he'd arrived. According to Mrs Yates and Mr Ratchett, Mr MacDonald left London on the morning Mrs Roberts' body was found. Though it *is* possible the sailor *could* have murdered Mrs Roberts and then left it is *highly* unlikely. As for Mrs Yates, we couldn't eliminate her as a suspect as she could have slipped away from the sailor's company and murdered her daughter. With Mr MacDonald out at sea, there was no immediate way we at the Bow Street Society, with our limited resources, could confirm her story. When Mrs Yates was also murdered, we had to scrutinise this theory even more."

"Our murderer was arrogant; he, or she, brought his own lemonade to Mrs Yates' residence for, according to Mr Trowel's account, there was a jar of it on the table and two glasses," Mr Locke began. "Mrs Yates *did* know her murderer for reasons we outlined earlier. While Mr Roberts, Miss Roberts, and the Suggitts *had* been eliminated as suspects for Mrs Roberts' murder it does appear, at least in theory, one, or all of them, could have murdered Mrs Yates as revenge for her murdering her daughter. Mr Roberts, Miss Roberts, and Mr Suggitt had *all* visited the *Turk's Head* public house, where Mrs Yates had been drinking lemonade, the night of her murder, after all. Though unlikely, *one* of them *could* have stolen said lemonade to lace it with arsenic. Their subsequent answers to our enquiring after that beverage, in which they denied having ever possessed it, could have been simple lies."

"At this point, we must return to Mrs Roberts' shawl, deposited in the second-hand clothing basket in the storeroom here, however," Lady Owston began. "Also, Mrs Yates' ring, identified by Mr Roberts, which was found, by Mr Locke, in a tray on the haberdashery department's countertop only today. Mrs Yates *could* have brought the shawl here and given it to the one of the assistants as a donation, though no account of that ever having taken place has emerged. Furthermore, the Suggitts, Mr Roberts, or Miss Roberts *could* have deposited the ring into the tray *after* murdering Mrs Yates—and encouraged the others to lie to provide an alibi—except for one, important detail. Inspector?"

"None of them have been allowed to leave the Suggitt place since we brought them back from Moore Street this morning," Inspector Woolfe said.

TWENTY-NINE

The corner of Mr Queshire's mouth twitched, and he replied, "I see…" A fleeting, yet contrived, smile graced his lips as he folded his arms and strolled away from the group toward the front door. Stopping as a glance outside reminded him of the constables' presence, he faced the others and continued, "But, if they are all vindicated, you must inevitably return to your original supposition that a stranger had killed both victims?"

"You are presuming we have exhausted our list of suspects," Mr Locke replied and approached Mr Queshire. "Time and time again during the course of our investigation, we were brought back to here, the *Queshire Department Store.*"

"The altercation between Mrs Roberts and the Holdens, Mrs Roberts' shawl being displayed on a dummy the morning after her murder, the French Breakfast coffee in the storeroom, the arsenic purchased by a store assistant, Miss Galway, and then Mrs Yates' ring in the tray," Mr Maxwell interjected.

"From the moment I saw a customer entering the room marked *Staff Only* at the top of the stairs, I have been plagued by the question of 'why.'" Lady Owston began as she went to Mr Locke's side. "*Why* was she going into that room? *Why* was Miss Galway so *deathly* afraid when I remarked upon it? *Why* did she repeatedly refuse to divulge the room's true use? And *why* were you, Mr Queshire, so keen to make me believe it was nothing more than a storeroom?"

"I can't believe you're still fixated on *that*," Mr Queshire sneered.

"Finally," Lady Owston said. "The answer came to me when Mr Locke remarked upon Miss Webster's choice to always wear her hat indoors."

"What's that got to do with anything?" Inspector Woolfe enquired.

"Patience, inspector," Lady Owston replied. "Agnes?"

Miss Webster removed the pins from her hat and placed them in a pile upon the counter. Lifting her hat to reveal the patch of bald, scarred flesh beneath, she informed Inspector Woolfe, "I lost my hair as a child, during a fire at my home."

Inspector Woolfe's hardened facial features softened as he looked upon the disfigurement.

"The experience left me with an intense fear of fire," Miss Webster continued. "When Mr Locke, Lady Owston, and I visited the Holdens' residence, we were invited to wait in their library. A fire was burning in the hearth and Lady Owston, knowing of my fear, shielded the fire from my view using a guard. Later, at the *Turk's Head* public house, Mr Locke noticed me flinch when he lit a match. Therefore, at our next Bow Street Society meeting, he commented upon my never removing my hat when indoors. This prompted Lady Owston to recall a fellow member of the *Writers' Club,* Mrs Gromwell, who never removed her bonnet when indoors either. While at the club, Lady Owston had overheard some other members discussing the matter, but the significance of their conversation wasn't fully appreciated until Mr Locke's remark."

"I had seen Mrs Gromwell leaving the room at the top of the stairs earlier in the day," Lady Owston began, her gazed fixed upon Mr Queshire. "When I attempted to speak to her about her presence there, she, like Miss Galway, became extremely frightened. She spoke to me of shame and how she had lied to everyone. I was still in the dark until Mr Locke said what he did, and I made the comparison between Miss Webster and Mrs Gromwell. I realised each wore either a wig or a hairpiece, though Miss

318

Webster's is attached to her hat. As you know, Mr Queshire, ladies who wear wigs are seen as deceptive by wider society. Yet they still have a requirement to be deemed beautiful by potential suitors. The wig-fitting service, which operates out of that room." She pointed upward. "Meets the demands of these ladies while still keeping their shame a closely guarded secret."

"I thought we'd agreed *not* to have such a service, Edmund?" Mr Suggitt challenged.

"*You'd* decided not to have such a service on the basis of so-called 'propriety,'" Mr Queshire retorted. "But you forget this is *my* store and it shall provide whatever service *I* deem suitable."

"While Mr Locke and I were speaking with you in the storeroom today, Mr Queshire, Miss Webster snuck upstairs to see what she could find," Lady Owston revealed.

"You had no right to do that," Mr Queshire reprimanded.

"Too right, they didn't," Inspector Woolfe interjected as the tension returned to his face. "Anything could've happened."

"I met a lovely Frenchman called Mr Vuitton," Miss Webster replied with a smile. She reattached her hat to her remaining hair with the pins and walked behind the haberdashery department's counter. "He confirmed you had no knowledge of the service, Mr Suggitt, and even spoke to me of various treatments I could try to encourage the regrowth of my hair. While he was out of the room for a time, I searched the bureaux and found this," she reached beneath the counter and took out a small, brown-paper packet. Moving back around the counter, she offered the packet to Dr Weeks and enquired, "Could you examine this, please?"

Inspector Woolfe moved closer to Dr Weeks and enquired, "What is it?"

"We believe it to be a wig made from a tanned human scalp," Miss Webster coolly replied.

Mrs Suggitt clapped her hand over her mouth to stifle a gasp whilst Mr Suggitt looked from the packet, to Mr Queshire, and back again with wide eyes.

"Maryanna's scalp was…" Mr Roberts muttered, his voice trailing off as he stared at the packet.

"Indeed," Lady Owston replied.

Dr Weeks took the packet, opening it upon the millinery department's counter, and examined it with a magnifying glass. Turning it over and holding it up to the light a moment later, he said, "Can't say for sure if it's human or animal, but it's flesh of some kind." He tossed it back onto the paper. "I can run some tests but I ain't gonna be able to say for sure one way or another."

"Thank you," Miss Webster replied as she wrapped the wig.

"It is *certainly* not the usual layer one would fine underneath the netting in a wig, even in the more modern ones," Lady Owston began. "Furthermore, one would expect to see small bumps where the individual strands had been threaded into the material. There are none on this example, however."

"What're you saying, then?" Inspector Woolfe enquired. "Mr Vuitton murdered Mrs Roberts for her scalp?"

"Nah, but it *was* someone connected to this store," Mr Snyder replied and joined his fellow Bow Streeters in looking to one person.

"*No!*" Mrs Suggitt gasped, clinging to her husband when she saw who they were looking at. At the same time, Mr Roberts had leapt to his feet to lunge for them but was held back by Inspector Woolfe.

"You murdered my wife!" Mr Roberts yelled at them as he struggled to free himself from Inspector Woolfe's vice-like grip.

"Stay back!" Inspector Woolfe ordered, lifting Mr Roberts off his feet and plonking him down beside his chair.

Mr Queshire's face was stoic and his eyes cold as he enquired, "And *why* would *I* murder Mrs Roberts and Mrs Yates? Neither of them visited the wig-fitting room."

"Because Mrs Roberts humiliated you in your store, and Mrs Yates humiliated Mr Suggitt in front of her customers," Mr Locke replied. "You admitted you had allowed your emotion to overwhelm you when you had removed Mrs Roberts following her altercation with the Holdens; a natural reaction given the fact she had physically and verbally abused you in front of your customers. She made you appear weak in an environment where you were not only respected but admired. Then, at the public house, when Mrs Yates scolded her son-in-law for his angry reaction to our questions, you made a remark, 'such unnecessary behaviour,' I believe it was. We had presumed, at the time, you were referring to Mr Suggitt's behaviour, but you were not. You were referring to Mrs Yates'. She had belittled him into submitting to her, thereby making him appear weak and feeble-willed."

"Looking back on Miss Galway's behaviour whenever you were in the room, or she was talking about you," Lady Owston began. "I see now she was deathly afraid of you, too. Furthermore, when I confronted you over the selling of second-hand goods, your persona morphed into something very ugly indeed. I had never felt threatened in a man's presence until then."

"And then there was your other comment," Miss Webster began. "In which you spoke of keeping Mrs Roberts safe if she had returned to the store, even after it had closed. We thought you were speaking hypothetically. You were, in fact, admitting she *had* returned to the store *after* it had closed. She was likely looking for her sister. Seeing an opportunity to enact your revenge upon her, you invited her in, probably to the storeroom, and prepared her a cup of French Breakfast coffee."

"You used the arsenic which Miss Galway had purchased, and which you could not produce when we asked to see it today, to lace the coffee," Mr Locke said. "Mrs Roberts drank it and died within minutes. You then proceeded to beat her body, remove her clothes, scalp her, take her breasts, and wrestle her remains into the sack." He swallowed the bile that had escaped from his stomach at the thought of such horrors. "Given you live above the store, a fact you have freely admitted, you would know when the servicemen would usually start their rounds. Therefore, you waited until you were certain no one would be around before carrying Mrs Roberts' body to the doorway of the *London Crystal Palace Bazaar*. It was an establishment you were already aware of on account of its second entrance being located opposite Argyll Street, which is, of course, where the lodgings for your assistants may be found. The shawl you mended and placed upon the dummy, as you described, in time for the store opening the next day. I must admit it was rather fortuitous my wife purchased it, otherwise we may not have been able to make the connection."

"Edmund, is this true?" Mr Suggitt hissed.

Mr Queshire clenched his jaw and lifted his chin whilst keeping his hard gaze fixed upon Lady Owston.

"Miss Galway, keen to impress us to become a Bow Street Society member, followed Mrs Yates and Mr Roberts home," Lady Owston began. "When they neared their destination, however, Miss Galway noticed a man lurking on the other side of the street. She couldn't see his face but was so frightened by his behaviour, she ran home and awoke her fellow lodger, Miss Annie Simkins, to tell her what had happened. By the time Miss Webster, Miss Dexter, and I arrived to question her about what she'd seen at the pub after we'd left, Miss Galway was in *such* a state of distress. She explained how she and Annie had come here to try and rouse you from your sleep but could gain no answer. To belay her fears, we came here that night, too. You were fully dressed when you came to the door." Her voice and expression became dejected as she continued, "You said you had been adding sodium hydroxide to the soap mixture you'd had simmering all night. Though, it was *you* Miss Galway had seen, *you* who had murdered Mrs Yates, and it was *you* who was... disposing of her flesh and... scalp."

Mr Queshire's hands clenched into fists beneath his elbows.

"After leaving us at the *Turk's Head* public house," Mr Locke began. "You returned here and laced a jar of lemonade with arsenic; presumably, you had seen her drinking it while she spoke to Mr Snyder. Taking it and two glasses, you went back to the pub but waited outside until Mrs Yates left with Mr Roberts. You could not loiter outside their home as you did not know where they lived. After following them back, you expected Mr Roberts to leave again once he had been informed of the incident with Miss Roberts you yourself had witnessed that evening. Several minutes later, Mr Roberts did indeed leave, and you waited a little longer before going inside. You may have enquired of a passing neighbour which room was the Roberts'—that detail we can only assume— but eventually you found it and you knocked. Mrs Yates answered and your suspicion she would be alone was confirmed. She probably recognised you from earlier in the evening and you no doubt gained entry by lying about a message from Mr Suggitt. Once inside, you poured the lemonade for you both and killed her. Afterward, you did the same to her body as you did Mrs Roberts' except for transporting it elsewhere. You took her clothes and ring and, upon returning here for a second time, dropped the ring into the tray."

Mr Queshire closed the distance between himself and Lady Owston and said in a low voice, "I do hope you enjoyed the soap I gave you, Milady." A smile crept across his lips. "For it was Mrs Roberts' *flesh* you were rubbing between your vile legs."

"Ugh!" Lady Owston cried as she covered her mouth.

Mr Locke at once took a gentle grip of her arm and guided her back to enable him to place himself between her and Mr Queshire.

"I could deny it, of course," Mr Queshire continued in the same, cool tone. "Claim Miss Galway was the one who had murdered both women to garner the attention of the Bow Street Society but to give the credit of *my* work to a *woman* does *not* sit well with me."

"Oh my God…" Mrs Suggitt whispered before gagging into her handkerchief. In response, Mr Suggitt held her tight against him. Meanwhile, Mr Roberts glared at Mr Queshire from around Inspector Woolfe's bulk, whilst Miss Roberts held her arms tight about herself and stared at the floor with an ashen complexion.

"I overheard Miss Galway telling Annie Simkins of the man she'd seen following Mrs Yates when the two tried to rouse me," Mr Queshire resumed. "I was covered in blood at the time so, naturally, I couldn't come to the door."

Miss Roberts stood and moved into her father's waiting arms.

"I listened at the window and it was then I knew Miss Galway had to be my next source of material," Mr Queshire said.

Miss Dexter huddled close to Mr Snyder, and the cabman put his arm around her.

"When Miss Galway came to work this morning, she told me what had happened," Mr Queshire continued. "It was evident she hadn't seen me for she wouldn't have confessed it to me if she had. Still, I had resolved to be rid of her—she was a liability anyway, as you saw when she blurted out the Holdens' name, Lady Owston. I convinced her to remain in the basement until this evening when I would notify the police a man was following her. I told her it was too dangerous to return to the lodgings, or to leave the store, for the man had probably followed her home and then here. She was so gullible she believed every word I said and trusted me entirely."

"I saw you at the window earlier, I thought you had put something on the outside ledge, but you were, in reality, making sure we had not left and gone straight to the external entrance to the basement," Mr Locke said. "You had, undoubtedly, read the *Gaslight Gazette's* account of my nocturnal exploits during the Dorsey case and feared I could break the lock on the external basement doors."

"I am not concerned about being exposed, Mr Locke; I would do it all again," Mr Queshire replied. "I merely wanted the opportunity to remind Lady Owston of *her* true place by putting Miss Galway's body on her doorstep. I knew Inspector Woolfe distrusted the Bow Street Society, and I hoped he would arrest and hang her."

"But *why*?!" Miss Roberts cried.

"You do not like women very much, do you?" Mr Locke challenged Mr Queshire. "Your interrogation of my wife over her chosen profession was testament to that."

"Mrs Yates reminded me of my mother," Mr Queshire stated matter-of-factly. "My mother had presumed to tell me what to do, had presumed she could control my life as she'd controlled my father's. Women are parasites to be stepped upon, Mr Locke. Yet we allow them to gain more and more control every day—*women* journalists, *women* doctors, *women* artists, and writers. They shall never be satisfied until they have dominated us all." He smirked. "But do not misunderstand me; I didn't kill Mrs Roberts and Mrs Yates to right a political injustice, far from it. You're correct in your assumptions about how I murdered Mrs Roberts and Mrs Yates and why. Yet I also wanted *revenge* for every wrong done to me by women. Those who visit my store are greedy, lecherous vermin who think it is their birth right to bark orders at me and scold me when things do not go their way." His smile grew. "I wanted them all to have a taste of their own foulness once they'd realised they'd been bathing in the flesh, and wearing the scalps and clothes, of their dead peers. The wig *is* Mrs Roberts' scalp; you will find Mrs Yates' here, too." He neared Mr Locke to look over his shoulder at Lady Owston. "Do you remember the soap batch I said was gently simmering when you came to me about Miss Galway's visit?"

"Yes…?" Lady Owston whispered as the colour drained from her face.

"It was Mrs Yates' flesh I was using, naturally," Mr Queshire replied.

"Oh my God…" Lady Owston whispered. She lifted her hand to her mouth as a terrible idea occurred to her. In a subdued voice, she enquired, "Mr Queshire… where is Miss Galway?"

"In the basement, of course," Mr Queshire replied with great relish. "I killed her over an hour ago."

EPILOGUE

Inspector Woolfe had sworn the Suggitts, Roberts, and the Bow Street Society members to secrecy until Mr Queshire's formal plea hearing. Once the guilty plea had been entered, Mr Maxwell's article was published in the next evening edition of the *Gaslight Gazette*. It read:

DEPARTMENT STORE FROM HELL EXPOSED

The owner of the *Queshire Department Store*, Mr Edmund Queshire, today pleaded guilty to two counts of murder at the Central Criminal Court, the Old Bailey. The sentence of death was passed by the black-cap-wearing judge, the Right Honourable Sweet, and shall be carried out in a matter of days. Newgate Jail has already announced Mr Queshire's execution will be held away from the macabre curiosity of the public eye.

Mr Queshire was arrested for the murders of Mrs Maryanna Roberts and Mrs Sarah Yates following an investigation by the Bow Street Society, the group having been commissioned by a relative of both victims, Mrs Diana Suggitt. Upon being identified as the person responsible, Mr Queshire readily confessed to his crimes with relish and even showed the Bow Street Society members, and Metropolitan Police Inspector Caleb Woolfe, the horrors which lay in the store's basement. To those of a sensitive disposition, your correspondent recommends you cease your reading now.

The body of a third victim, Miss Rose Galway, who was a sales assistant at the department store, was found hanging, naked, from the basement's beams. She had been mutilated in the same fashion as Mrs Roberts and Mrs Yates and, like they, had been poisoned. She with a cup of French Breakfast coffee laced with arsenic. The missing clothes of all three women were shown to the group by Mr Queshire, he having deposited them within a basket located in the basement's corner.

In Mr Queshire's rooms upstairs, Inspector Woolfe and the Bow Street Society members discovered a large pot on the stove. It contained a heavy mixture, pale in colour, which the store owner identified as being the remains of Mrs Yates' missing flesh. It had been reduced in mass through the process of boiling and mixed with sodium hydroxide to create a soap preparation. Mr Queshire confirmed he had sold batches of such soap, containing the flesh of Mrs Roberts, within his store. Any ladies who have recently purchased soap from the *Queshire Department Store* are therefore requested to deposit it, sealed or otherwise, at their nearest police station. An additional request regarding ladies' head coverings, purchased from the same establishment, has also been made by Inspector Woolfe.

The sound of knocking disrupted Miss Trent's reading of the article. The discomfort she'd felt upon being reminded of the macabre details subsided as she left her office and opened the front door. A man wearing a flat cap was stood on the porch carrying a leather bag.

"Is this the place for the Bow Street Society?" He enquired.

"It is. I'm Miss Rebecca Trent, clerk of the Bow Street Society, Mr…?"

"Daniel Holland, locksmith, come to fix a new lock to your front door. Mr Locke asked me to come by."

Miss Trent lofted a brow and enquired in a sardonic tone, "*Did* he?" She placed her hand upon her hip. "This is the first *I've* known about the arrangement. Could you wait here while I telephone him, please?"

"Whatever you say, Miss Trent," Mr Holland replied with a lift of his cap.

Closing the door and sliding one of its many bolts into place, she returned to her office and picked up the telephone receiver. Instructing the operator where to place her call, she then waited whilst it was connected before hearing Mr Locke's voice utter a greeting in her ear.

"I have Mr Holland standing on the Bow Street Society's porch," Miss Trent informed him.

"Who?" Mr Locke enquired. "Ah, yes, Mr Holland. Was he scheduled for today?"

"I wouldn't know; *I* wasn't the one who organised his visit."

"My sincerest apologies. I had every intention of informing you of my plans when I made the arrangement, but clearly my memory failed me on this occasion."

Miss Trent heard a faint rustling of papers.

"I have supplied him with a lock of my own design to fit to the front door," Mr Locke continued. "It shan't prevent someone of *my* skill from entering the premises uninvited, but your average housebreaker would find it an incredible challenge. As agreed, I have put forth the capital for the lock's installation and provided Mr Holland with instructions as to the procurement of the monies. If you so wish, I may be able to attend Bow Street in… an hour but, personally, I do not think my presence shall be necessary, do you?"

"I think it would be wise for you to confirm he is indeed the locksmith you arranged, Mr Locke, considering the safety of every Bow Street Society member, and myself, would be under threat if he isn't. I'll expect to see you in half an hour." She then replaced the receiver, thereby ending the call.

* * *

The rhythmic trotting of the hansom cab's horses went unheard, and the cool breeze went unfelt by Mr Joseph Maxwell as his senses became muffled by a daydream. In his mind's eye, he watched the events of the previous night's dinner at his parents' house. He recalled the pleasant company of Miss Poppy Lillithwaite; his father's choice for his bride-to-be, the delicious meal, and the words of praise his father had given his exemplary behaviour. It had all gone better than he could've hoped and, tonight, he'd had the satisfaction of seeing his article on the front page of the *Gaslight Gazette*. Yet, despite these two wonderful occurrences, there was a strange feeling of numbness dulling his elation.

"Oi! Time to ge' out!" the cab driver bellowed from above.

Mr Maxwell was jolted from his daydream and, seeing they'd arrived at his lodging house, scrambled from the cab. "Apologies," he mumbled as he paid the amount agreed upon prior to his departure from Fleet Street.

The cab driver looked to the coin and gave a soft grunt. As he then geed his horses and drove away, Mr

Maxwell crossed the pavement to his lodging house only to catch sight of something familiar in the corner of his eye. He looked down the street and thought he recognised both the driver and vehicle of a second hansom cab parked a few metres away. Approaching it with caution at first, he then quickened his pace when his suspicions were confirmed. He greeted, "Good evening, Mr Snyder."

"Evenin', Mr Maxwell," Mr Snyder replied with a smile and a touch of his hat.

"Has Miss Trent sent word of another case she wants me to investigate?"

"Nah," Mr Snyder replied.

"Then… what are you doing here?"

"There's more important things in life than murders and crime," Mr Snyder replied with a lift of his head to indicate Mr Maxwell's lodging house. "Best to go on in, lad."

"Am I in trouble?" Mr Maxwell enquired, placing his hand upon his throat.

"Best to go on in," Mr Snyder repeated with a smile.

Mr Maxwell looked over his shoulder at his lodging house and back at Mr Snyder. Rubbing his throat, he swallowed the lump that was forming and walked back along the pavement at a slower pace than before. When he reached the lodging house's front door, he stopped and looked back down the street at Mr Snyder. The cab man was still smiling, which unnerved Mr Maxwell further, but it was clear he wasn't going to reveal anything more. Mr Maxwell therefore entered the building and climbed the two flights of stairs to his floor when he saw no one in the hallway. As he stepped onto his landing, he saw another familiar figure standing outside his door. "Georgina?"

Miss Dexter turned at the sound of his voice and smiled. "Joseph," she said as she crossed the landing to meet him. "Where have you been?"

"I was at work; what are you doing here?"

Miss Dexter's smile vanished as she halted at his abrupt response. "I had to speak with you," she replied in a quiet voice. Bowing her head and clasping her hands together against her skirts, she continued, "You were so startled at the Suggitts' house after our kiss. I'm... not like Mrs Roberts, Joseph." She momentarily met his gaze. "*Please,* do not think ill of me."

"I don't," Mr Maxwell said, closing the gap between them. "You could *never* be like Mrs Roberts."

"Then why did you flee?" Miss Dexter enquired as she lifted sad eyes to him.

How he wanted to kiss her, to hold her. Then, as it had done so in the Suggitts' hallway, the voice of his father echoed in his mind. It said, *why couldn't you have been more like your brothers? Both successful, and both married well... Dowry, Joseph. That's what you need, a decent dowry... nullify your preposterous engagement... This family will not be shamed by your vile, filthy habits.* The memory of his father's slap also caused his face to ache, and he realised why he'd felt so numb. The dinner with Miss Lillithwaite at his parents' house, the plans for them both which his father had made abundantly clear, the fury with which his father had received the news of his engagement to Miss Dexter; it all led to one horrifyingly inevitable outcome. An outcome echoed by his father's voice in his mind: *nullify your preposterous engagement.*

"Joseph?" Miss Dexter enquired, concerned.

"Georgina, I..." Mr Maxwell began. Unable to look at her, though, he downcast his eyes and said in a hushed voice, "I must break our engagement."

"No," Miss Dexter gasped. "You can't be sincere in your words."

"I am..." Mr Maxwell mumbled. "This is how it must be."

"I don't understand," Miss Dexter replied in a

shaky voice. "I thought you wanted us to be wed? You gave me your word all you had promised would come to pass. You put your hand over your heart, and you *promised* me."

Feeling sick to his stomach, and still unable to look at her, Mr Maxwell hurried to his door and said, "*Please,* Georgina, don't make this any harder than it already is. It's ended, my love. I'm sorry."

"Sorry? Is that *all* you can say?" Miss Dexter enquired through a sob.

Yet, Mr Maxwell kept his back to her and his hand upon the doorknob. He felt disgusted with himself for treating her this way, but he couldn't weaken, he *mustn't* weaken. *You will not answer me back again, Joseph, and you will certainly not question my orders*, his father's voice echoed in his mind. Unlocking the door, he replied, "Y-Yes, it-it is, I'm sorry." As he turned the knob and pushed the door open, though, her voice stayed him.

"Do not come to me again, Joseph," she said in a shaky voice. "Never did I think you would ever lie to me… or that you could be so *cruel*!"

Hearing the rustle of her skirts when she hitched them up, Mr Maxwell turned and saw a glimpse of her red, tear-stained face as she rushed past and down the stairs. Intense regret and sorrow struck Mr Maxwell like a lightning bolt at the sight. Thus, without thinking, he ran to the bannisters and shouted, "Georgina!" Yet she was already gone.

* * *

"Saying thank you isn't sufficient to describe what I'm feeling, Miss Trent," Mrs Suggitt said as she sat beside her husband in the Bow Street Society's kitchen. "But I shall regardless, not only on my behalf but also my sister's and mother's: thank you."

"We only did what you asked us to," Miss Trent replied. "But your thanks are still gratefully received."

"Here is a cheque for your group's fee," Mr Suggitt said as he retrieved a folded piece of paper from the inside pocket of his coat. "I trust the amount is satisfactory?"

Taking it from him, Miss Trent checked the amount and replied, "Yes, very satisfactory. Thank you." Slipping it into a pocket concealed within her skirts, she then took a sip of tea and enquired, "What are your plans, now that there is to be no trial?"

The Suggitts exchanged wary glances but it was Mr Suggitt who replied, "Mr Queshire has bequeathed the store to me."

"You're not accepting it, surely?" Miss Trent enquired.

Mr Suggitt averted his gaze to his wife, shifted his weight and cleared his throat. With a sheepish glance to Miss Trent, he replied, "We plan to, yes."

"But your sister was murdered there, so too was Miss Galway," Miss Trent reminded them.

"Which is even more of a reason to ensure some good comes from this horror," Mr Suggitt countered with more conviction. "Naturally, the store's name will have to change but, already, footfall has increased. The people of London wish to visit the place where such ghastly deeds were carried out."

"Abraham has agreed to help Clement with the refurbishment of the store's interior," Mrs Suggitt said.

"*Minus* the salon, storeroom, and wig-making service, of course," Mr Suggitt interjected.

"And Regina is to become a sales assistant, while *I* take on the role of manageress to ensure the safety of the store's female employees," Mrs Suggitt added.

Miss Trent released a sigh and replied, "I can't say I follow your logic, but I can understand the reasons behind your decision." She offered a contrived smile. "And I wish you luck in your new endeavour."

"Thank you, Miss Trent. This is something Clement and I simply must do," Mrs Suggitt replied.

"Forgive my intrusion but my husband said I could find you here," a woman's voice said from the kitchen door, prompting the three of them to simultaneously look toward its owner. From their vantage point, they could also see the open front door in the distance. Standing beside it was Mr Locke who was supervising Mr Holland's installation of the new lock.

"Good afternoon, Dr Locke," Miss Trent greeted as she and Mr Suggitt stood. "You've already met Mr Suggitt, I believe?"

"Yes, good afternoon," Dr Locke replied.

"This is his wife Mrs Diana Suggitt," Miss Trent introduced. Once the ladies had exchanged pleasantries, she enquired, "How may I help you?"

"I have been led to believe the Bow Street Society is in need of a member with medical expertise. Is that correct?" Dr Locke enquired in return.

"It is," Miss Trent replied, wondering how she'd come by such information. The sound of Mr Locke's voice drifting from the hallway, however, furnished her with an excellent guess. She therefore resolved to remind him of the importance of discretion once the Suggitts had left. "Will you excuse us a moment, please?" Miss Trent enquired from them as she joined Dr Locke in the doorway. Once she'd garnered their assent, she stepped out into the hallway with Dr Locke and closed the door. In a low voice, she enquired, "May I ask why you wish to know?"

"I had thought that obvious, Miss Trent," Dr Locke replied. "I would like to apply for the position."

Enjoyed the book? Please show your support by writing a review.

DISCOVER MORE AT...
www.bowstreetsociety.com

GASLIGHT GAZETTE

News about the Bow Street Society

Price: 1*d.*

SUBSCRIBE
to the
GASLIGHT GAZETTE
for...

- **NEWS** about **BOW STREET SOCIETY** releases

- **NEVER-BEFORE-SEEN** deleted scenes and unused drafts from past books and short stories.

- **FIRST LOOK AT NEW STORIES** Subscribers are first to read new casebook short stories

- **SNEAK PEEKS** of future releases...and **MORE!**

A FREE monthly publication delivered directly to your electronic mail box.

SUBSCRIBE *now:*
www.bowstreetsociety.com/news.html

Notes from the author

Spoiler alert*

I first came across the Whitechapel Murders case (aka Jack the Ripper) when I was around fifteen years old. I read a book—I don't recall if I'd borrowed it from the school's library or a public one—which was supposedly based upon a newly discovered diary of Sergeant George Godley. Godley was a Metropolitan Police officer who worked with Inspector Aberline on the case. I think it may have been *Jack the Ripper: The Final Solution* by Steven Knight. Regardless, it stayed with me long after I'd finished it. Even now, I can still envision a drunken Inspector Aberline being roused by Godley.

In the years since reading the book, I've discovered it has received mixed reviews from both Ripperologists and general readers. This hasn't stopped me, like most with an interest in true crime, from having a fascination with the Whitechapel Murders. I've watched several films & documentaries and read several books on the subject. At the time of the murders themselves, everyone had a theory, including Sherlock Holmes creator Sir Arthur Conan Doyle. He suggested it could've been *Jill* the Ripper, as midwives could walk the streets, covered in blood, and no one would've remarked upon it.

Obviously 'Jack' wasn't the murderer's actual name—at least as far as we know. Jack was simply a name attached to an otherwise unidentified man, in the same way John Doe is attributed to unidentified male corpses today. The reason why it became attached to the Whitechapel Murderer was largely because a letter—allegedly from the murderer—sent to the Central News Agency of London, was signed 'Jack the Ripper'. In November of 2016, I was lucky enough to look upon the actual 'Dear Boss' letter, as it's since become known, while attending a Victorian Crime evening at the National Archives in Kew, London. When one considers how much paper is simply thrown away these days, it's truly amazing the letter has survived the hundred-plus years since its creation.

In 2011, I read *Sweeney Todd – The Demon Barber of Fleet Street* by Thomas Peckett Prest, a prolific writer of Penny Dreadfuls in the nineteenth century. The very first time I learnt of Sweeney Todd was while watching an episode of *Coronation Street*. One of the characters, while eating a pie, referred to the story. I remember asking my mother who Sweeney Todd was and she told me. Like the Whitechapel Murders, the story of Sweeney Todd has always intrigued me. I wanted to read the original story all the movies and books were based upon so I ended up buying, and reading, the above title.

The foundation of the idea behind the murders in *The Case of The Lonesome Lushington*, and the man responsible, is an attempt to combine the Jack the Ripper and Sweeney Todd crimes. This is why Edmund Queshire's first victim, Mrs Maryanna Roberts, is a prostitute fallen on hard times. It's also the reason why Queshire mutilates his victims' bodies, why he turns their flesh into soap and their hair into wigs, and why he tries to sell these items in his department store. According to Peckett Prest's story, Todd had the flesh of his victims baked into pies by Mrs Lovett who sold them in her shop, hence the reason behind the reference in the *Coronation Street* episode.

A Jack the Ripper victim partly inspired the domestic circumstances of Maryanna Roberts—Annie Chapman. While conducting research into the lives of the Ripper victims, for an unrelated project, I came across a photograph of Annie with her husband, John. She, like Maryanna, had been the victim of circumstance and alcoholism. The photograph of Annie, smartly attired in an impressive dress with neatly styled hair, and John standing beside her with his hand on her shoulder, reminded me Annie Chapman, like all the Ripper's victims, were real people. They'd had a life unrelated to the Ripper and people who cared for them. As far as I'm aware there hasn't yet been a television series or film focusing on the victims' lives alone. Personally, I think it's long overdue.

Maryanna Roberts, her family, and the second victim, Mrs Sarah Yates, are all members of the working social class. This was intentional on my part, along with the decision to involve the Society's cabman, Sam Snyder, in the investigation. Those familiar with the first book, *The Case of The Curious Client,* will know he didn't conduct any of the interviews like he does in *The Case of The Lonesome Lushington.* I wanted to show the reader this other side of London society without resorting to the clichés often associated with the Victorian Era, e.g. all poor people were criminals. I also didn't want to fall into the trap, as a writer, of only focusing on crimes among the middle or upper classes.

There is a strong theme of shopping and consumerism running through the book. While thinking of the title for the first book, I knew there were certain themes which ran through it. One of these themes was curiosity—both being curious oneself and being curious to others—which is why the book was given the title it was. When it came to *The Case of The Lonesome Lushington,* I wanted to take the concept of themes further. I therefore decided to have a predominant theme running throughout the book which helped highlight a particular aspect of Victorian society. In this instance, the themes became consumerism, Oxford Street, and the varieties of establishment one could expect to encounter, e.g. chemists, department stores, etc. I intend to continue in this vein with all future Bow Street Society books. Not only to create a sense of place, but also to give each book its own distinct identity.

Inspector Caleb Woolfe, the investigating officer for the Metropolitan Police, is far from happy about the Society's involvement in the case. His resistance to their efforts is more than simply his personal opinion, however. In *Sir Howard Vincent's Police Code 1889*, a constable is instructed to "on no account move it or anything surrounding it; or allow any other person to do so" (p.117) when first called upon to investigate the corpse of a victim of foul play. The much later *"Police-Duty" Catechism and Reports*, by H. Childs of 1903 gives further clarification to these orders:

> *Ques.* In the case of a death by violent means, what steps should be taken?
> *Ans.* Remain by the body until properly relieved; send messenger for inspector and divisional surgeon; not allow the body to be moved, or room or place or anything about it to be interfered with; exclude the public, [and] give no information to public except by permission of superior officer.

Obviously, the above was published after the year in which *The Case of The Lonesome Lushington* is set (1896). Nonetheless, "exclude the public" would've been covered by Vincent Howard Code's instruction of not allowing "any other person" to move a body. In short, Inspector Caleb Woolfe is merely doing his job.

As a result, the Society isn't revered by the police or given privileged access to evidence like other literary detectives, such as Sherlock Holmes and Hercule Poirot (the creation of Agatha Christie). It would've certainly made it easier for me, as the writer, to follow the tradition of the amateur detective who's unconditionally trusted by the police. Yet, at the same time, it wouldn't be realistic. Realism and accuracy are two things I strive for while researching, planning, and writing the Bow Street Society books and short stories. By putting the obstacles in the Society's way, in the form of the police's resistance etc, I also hope to show how resourceful and ingenious the Society members can be. They have to draw upon every skill and piece of knowledge they possess to solve the case. I think the Society's investigation in *The Case of The Lonesome Lushington* is a perfect example of exactly how the group goes about this.

~T.G. Campbell
August 2017

MORE BOW STREET SOCIETY

The Case of The Curious Client
(Bow Street Society Mystery, #1)

WINNER OF FRESH LIFESTYLE MAGAZINE
BOOK AWARD APRIL 2017

In *The Case of The Curious Client,* the Bow Street Society is hired by Mr Thaddeus Dorsey to locate a missing friend he knows only as 'Palmer' after he fails to keep a late night appointment with him. With their client's own credibility cast into doubt mere minutes after they meet him though, the Society is forced to consider whether they've been sent on a wild goose chase. That is until events take a dark turn and the Society has to race against time not only to solve the case, but to also save the very life of their client…

On sale now in eBook and paperback from Amazon. Also available for free download via Kindle Unlimited.

The Case of The Spectral Shot
(Bow Street Society Mystery, 3)

When Miss Trent is paid a late night visit by a masked stranger the Bow Street Society is plunged into its most bizarre case to date. New faces join returning members as they encounter unsolved murders, the contentious world of spiritualism, and mounting hostility from the Metropolitan Police. Can the Society exorcise the ghosts of the past to uncover the truth, or will it, too, be lured into an early grave...?

On sale now in eBook and paperback from Amazon.
Also available for free download via Kindle Unlimited.

The Case of The Toxic Tonic
(Bow Street Society Mystery, #4)

When the Bow Street Society is called upon to assist the *Women's International Maybrick Association,* it's assumed the commission will be a short-lived one. Yet, a visit to the *Walmsley Hotel* in London's prestigious west end only serves to deepen the Society's involvement. In an establishment that offers exquisite surroundings, comfortable suites, and death, the Bow Street Society must work alongside Scotland Yard to expose a cold-blooded murderer. Meanwhile, two inspectors secretly work to solve the mystery of not only Miss Rebecca Trent's past but the creation of the Society itself...

On sale now in eBook and paperback from Amazon.
Also available for free download via Kindle Unlimited.

SOURCES OF REFERENCE

A great deal of time was spent researching the historical setting of *The Case of The Lonesome Lushington.* This research covered not only the physical setting of London in 1896 but also communication technology (such as typewriters and telephones), medicine, the Metropolitan Police, Pharmaceutical chemists, and ladies' fashions to name but a few. Thus, a great deal of information about the period has been gathered, to inform me of the historical boundaries of my characters' professions and lives, which hasn't been directly referenced in this book. Where a fact, or source, has been used as to inform the basis of in-book descriptions of interiors, street names, items, and geographical locations *et cetera* I've strived to cite said source here. Each citation includes the source's origin, the source's author, and which part of *The Case of The Lonesome Lushington* the source is connected to. All rights connected to the following sources remain with their respective authors and/or publishers.

BOOKS

1897 Sears Roebuck & Co. Catalogue: Introduction by Nick Lyons (Skyhorse Publishing, 2007)
The following citations are from the above book:

"Millinery Department" section, specifically entries No. 23484 (*The Murray Hill Ladies' Leghora Flat Straw Hat*) & No. 23494 (*The Olympia*) p.320
The Murray Hill Ladies' Leghora flat straw hat and The Olympia in the millinery department at the Queshire Department Store.

"Millinery Department" section, pp.319-321
Materials adorning the decorated hats, and their varying heights, sold in the millinery department at the Queshire Department Store.

"Corset Department" section, specifically entry No. 23639, p.324
Nursing Corset in the hosiery department of the Queshire Department Store.

"Rubber Hair Pins" section, p.334
Rubber hair pins sold in the Queshire Department Store.

"library and Office Furniture" section, specifically entry No. 9250 "A $25.00 Book Case for $16.75," p.593
Mr Holden's bookcases.

"library and Office Furniture" section, specifically entry No. 9266 "A $16.00 Desk for $10.75," p.593
Mr Holden's desk

*****

Stevens, Serita Deborah with Klarner, Anne <u>The Howdunnit Series: Deadly Doses: A Writer's Guide to Poisons</u>, (Writer's Digest Books, Cincinnati and Ohio, 1990)
The following citations were taken from the above book:

"Two: The Classic Poisons: Arsenic, Cyanide, and Strychnine," p.11
Dr Weeks' findings, specifically Maryanna's Roberts' stomach being inflamed and arsenic being present in her throat.

"Appendix D: Poisons by the Time in Which They React," p.274

Dr Weeks' statement that arsenic can start working in as a little as one minute.

*****

Stratmann, Linda <u>The Secret Poisoner: A Century of Murder</u> (Yale University Press, New Haven and London, 2016)
The following citations were taken from the above book:

"CHAPTER FIVE: The Suspicions of Mr Marsh," pp.66-67, specifically the suggestion that Marsh had applied heat to produce the odour of Garlic to detect the presence of arsenic.

Dr Weeks' statement that arsenic smells like garlic when heated and that he got this smell after he had executed the Marsh Test.

"CHAPTER FIVE: The Suspicions of Mr Marsh," p.70, specifically the explanation of how, in 1837, Swedish chemist, Jöns Jacob Berzelius, modified the Marsh Test apparatus to weigh any resulting arsenic.

Dr Weeks' statement regarding his having weighed the arsenic to determine there were about three teaspoons' worth.

"CHAPTER FIVE: The Suspicions of Mr Marsh," p.74, specifically the explanation that arsenic was so widely used in the nineteenth century that it could be in the material used to make a chemist's apparatus.

Dr Weeks' explanation of the widespread use of arsenic and how it's in the apparatus the Marsh Test relies upon.

"CHAPTER FIVE: The Suspicions of Mr Marsh," pp.72-73, specifically the explanation of Orfila suggesting ways of ensuring sulphuric acid and zinc were free of impurities, the explanation of how Professor Orfila and physician and chemist, Jean-Pierre Couerbe, discovered arsenic in the bones and flesh of corpses, they'd not considered to have been poisoned with arsenic, and the explanation of 'normal arsenic' and Orfila's announcement of how 'normal arsenic' could be easily identified compared to ingested arsenic due to 'normal arsenic' not being water soluble. *Dr Weeks' explanation that sulphuric acid and zinc could have arsenic in them, too, if one doesn't make sure they're free of impurities first, Dr Weeks' description of the story of Professor Orfila and Physician and chemist, Jean-Pierre Couerbe, and Dr Weeks' explanation of 'normal arsenic' and how it's not soluble in boiling water where a poisoner's arsenic is.*

"CHAPTER FOURTEEN: Expert Witnesses," p.197, specifically the description of a discovery by veteran chemistry professor at the Royal Institution, William Brande, that the arsenic found by a Reinsch Test used by Professor Taylor to prove a woman by the name of Miss Bankes had been murdered by a Dr Smethurst, had been introduced by the copper gauze used in the Reinsch Test. *Dr Weeks' statement that one must ensure the copper one uses is pure otherwise it can mess up the test.*

"CHAPTER SIXTEEN: MATRIMONIAL CAUSES," p.217, specifically the explanation of the Pharmacy and Sales of Poisons Act coming into force in 1869 and how, because of it, the following applied: no one could sell, compound or dispense poisons unless they were a pharmaceutical chemist, no one could buy a poison

unless they were known to the chemist or were introduced by someone known to the chemist, and all sales had to be recorded in a book, together with the buyer's name and address.

Dr Weeks' explanation of the same Act and of the above criteria it imposed. Also, Dr Weeks' statement that buyers must give their name and address, and the descriptions of the poison books at Drummond's Pharmaceutical Chemist's and Eastleigh's

Illustration "10 James Marsh's apparatus for the separation of arsenic"
The Marsh Test apparatus in Dr Week's mortuary.

*****

Baren, Maurice Victorian Shopping (Michael O'Mara Books Limited, London, 1998)
The following citations were taken from the above book:

"The Chemist's Shop" chapter, pp.81-89
PURE DRUGS ONLY sign in the window of Drummond's Pharmaceutical Chemists, that shop's exterior, and the products featured in the advertisements pinned to that shop's interior wall.

"Fireside Shopping" chapter, pp.105-108
Fireside shopping and how orders worked, the publication, contents and cost of the Exchange, and Mart, The Journal of the Household.

*****

Chapter Three: Details of Death's subsection Examining a Body at the Scene. Crime Investigation: The Ultimate Guide to Forensic Science, (Parragon, Bath, 2007) p.47, specifically the Rigor Mortis section.
Dr Weeks' explanation of the rigor mortis process.

Gordon, Peter & Doughan, David DICTIONARY OF BRITISH WOMEN'S ORGANISATIONS 1825-1960 (Foreword by Sheila Rowbotham) (Taylor & Francis Group) **(London and New York, 2013)**
Lady Owston's Writers' Club.

* * *

INFORMATION SHEETS

Museum of the Royal Pharmaceutical Society Information Sheets
The following citations are from the above source. The sheets were downloaded as free PDFs from the Royal Pharmaceutical Society's Museum information sheets webpage:
http://www.rpharms.com/learning-resources/information-sheets.asp

"INFORMATION SHEET 15: DISPLAY GLASSWARE"
Glass bottles containing varying amounts of coloured water in the window display of Drummond's Pharmaceutical Chemists, the names and descriptions of the onion, swan neck and pear carboys, and the name and description of the Specie Jar (including its label).

"INFORMATION SHEET 12: DISPENSARY BOTTLES"

The origins of the "carboy" name, their original contents and purpose, the nineteenth century use of carboys, the alternative name of "Shop Round," the potential reasons behind the use of specific colours for the liquids in window display bottles, the cylindrical jars on counter containing lozenges, and the various bottles on the shelves behind the counter at Drummond's Pharmaceutical Chemists.

"INFORMATION SHEET 11: BALANCES, WEIGHTS AND MEASURES"

The scales on the counter at Drummond's Pharmaceutical Chemists and of the specific use of Troy weights for prescribing and dispensing of medicines despite the Avoirdupois weights and measures being favoured in the Medicinal Act of 1858.

* * *

MAPS

Booth, Charles Booth's Maps of London Poverty East and West 1889 (reproduced by Old House Books) *purchased from* **Shire Books http://www.shirebooks.co.uk/old_house_books/**
Where the Head of the Mob Squad, Inspector John Conway, had been born in the East End of London (Stepney), the locating of the Holdens' residence on Hill Street in Mayfair (number 200, Hill Street is a fictional address), the locating of the Suggitts' residence on Reeves Mews, and the location of Reeves Mews and its surrounding areas. Also, the direct quoting of the names of Booth's social class classifications in reference to the households on Reeves Mews and its surrounding areas, Moore Street, Edgware Road, Nutford Place, and the lane

*to the rear of Molyneux Street and south of John Street.
Also the locating of Mr Roberts' residence on Moore
Street, and the locations of Moore Street, Queen Street,
Edgware Road, Nutford Place, and the lane. Also, the
locating of the fictitious Turk's Head Public House on the
corner of Edgware Road and Queen Street and of its
clientele consisting of the residents of Moore Street and
the lane.*

* * *

MUSEUMS

The Museum of London
Timeline on wall of the Museum of London.
*Thames Embankment having electrical streetlamps since
1878.*

The Old Operating Theatre & Herb Garret Museum
Online Surgical Instrument Collection, specifically a
Surgical Tourniquet, c. 1870. (2002:028H)
http://www.thegarret.org.uk/collectionsurgical.htm#19
90002
The Surgical Tourniquet Locke uses.
.

* * *

VIDEOS

Magneto Era (1876-1900) by PHONECOinc
Published on 23rd August 2013 on www.youtube.com
*Basic description of the telephone in the Bow Street
Society's Headquarters.*

* * *

WALKS

The Alleyways and Shadows Old City Ghost Walk with Richard Jones
Attended: Saturday 16th July 2016
http://www.london-walking-tours.co.uk/
Spiked window attachments as burglar deterrents.

* * *

WEBSITES

Lee Jackson's *The Victorian Dictionary*
http://www.victorianlondon.org/index-2012.htm
The following sources are all taken from The Victorian Dictionary website

Jackson, Lee Chronology 1801-1901
The location of the first public lavatory for ladies in 1884 (Regent Circus).

Cassell & Company Limited, The Queen's London. A Pictorial and Descriptive Record of the Streets, Buildings, Parks and Scenery of the Great Metropolis in the Fifty-Ninth year of the reign of Her Majesty Queen Victoria, 1896

Photograph of the Victoria Embankment, from Charing Cross Station and accompanying description used as historical reference sources for basis of the in-book descriptions, history and location of the Victoria Embankment, the Victoria Embankment's Promenade, Albert Embankment, and the third Thames Embankment division running Millbank to Battersea Bridge.

Photograph of Regent Circus and Oxford Street, looking east and accompanying description used as historical reference sources for the basis of the in-book description and locations of Oxford Street and Regent Circus. The description accompanying this photograph was also used as an historical reference source, in conjunction with Dickens, Jr., Charles "Police Force" entry Dickens' Dictionary of London, 1879, *for the basis of Inspector Woolfe belonging to the E Division of the Metropolitan Police.*

Photographs of the Water-Lily House, Kew Gardens and The Palm House, Kew Gardens and their accompanying descriptions used as historical reference sources for basis of the in-book descriptions and history of each location.

The Pocket Atlas and Guide to London, 1899
The location of the London Crystal Palace Bazaar.

Dickens, Jr., Charles "London Crystal Palace" entry Dickens' Dictionary of London, 1879
The location of the London Crystal Palace Bazaar and direct source of the quote "cheaper kind of fancy goods" in Chapter Two.

"BAZAARS AND ARCADES" Routledge's Popular Guide to London, [c.1873]
The location of the London Crystal Palace Bazaar.

Black's Guide to London and Its Environs, (8th ed.), 1882
Name, construction, and Architect of the London Crystal Palace Bazaar.

Dickens, Jr., Charles "Police Force" entry Dickens' Dictionary of London, 1879
Used as an historical reference source, in conjunction with the description accompanying the photograph of Regent Circus and Oxford Street, looking East from Cassell and Company Limited, The Queen's London. A Pictorial and Descriptive Record of the Streets, Buildings, Parks and Scenery of the Great Metropolis in the Fifty-Ninth year of the reign of Her Majesty Queen Victoria, 1896, *for the basis of Inspector Woolfe belonging to the E Division of the Metropolitan Police.*

Punch: "DIRECTIONS TO LADIES FOR SHOPPING," Jul-Dec. 1844
Ladies waiting in private carriages for store employees to come to them.

"How to Make Tea and Coffee" entry Cassells Household Guide, New and Revised Edition (4 Vol.) c.1880s [no date]
The coffee in the Queshire Department Store's storeroom having been prepared twice weekly, left to cool, heated on the stove when required, and drunk mid-morning and lunchtime. Also concurrent reference to this being the habit of the English middle classes at the time.

"Income and Management" Chapter, Cassells Household Guide, New and Revised Edition (4 Vol.) c.1880s [no date]
Miss Webster's statement regarding Lady Owston's household taking in deliveries of sacks of potatoes every month.

Bell's Life in London and Sporting Chronicle, 27 January 1883
Maryanna Robert's Convict Supervision Office photograph, specifically Locke's identification of the photograph's origin, Maryanna's fingers being spread across her chest, and her shoulders being held by the hands of unseen men.

Phillips, Watts, Chapter III Rag Fair. The Wild Tribes of London, 1855
Lady Owston's description of the Rag Fair's location, its methods of business, and its clientele.

"OMNIBUSES" – Reynolds' Shilling Map of London, 1895
Oxford Street being included as a stop on many of the omnibus routes.

Wynter, Andrew, Chapter 12 – A Chapter on Shop-Windows. Our Social Bees; or, Pictures of Town and Country Life, and other papers, 1865
Lovely hues being formed in the coloured liquids filling the window display bottles at Drummond's Pharmaceutical Chemists on account of the gaslight shining through from the shop's interior. Also the use of polished mahogany.

Sims, George R., How the Poor Live – Chapter 12, 1883
Dock Labourers sleeping at the dock gates in the hopes of being picked for work the next morning, Royals, Quay-Gangers, and Dock Labourers waiting around for late ships.

Krout, Mary H. A Looker-On in London. Chapter 9: Women's Clubs (1896), 1899
Lady Owston's Writers' Club, the bulletin board, and the club's Presidents and Vice Presidents.

Greenwood, James, Toilers in London, by One of the Crowd [James Greenwood], Umbrellas to Mend, [1883]
The job of a Knocker-Up, specifically the times written in chalk on walls and doors by customers, constables taking jobs, and the requirement to allow oneself enough time to get to one's patch before the first customer needs waking up.

Staffe, Baroness How to take care of the hair: The Lady's Dressing Room, trans. Lady Colin Campbell, 1893 - Part II (cont.)
Hair used in wig making foraged from overseas, use of hot pins and hot crimping irons to make hair wavy, lace mantillas being worn by old ladies, advice to not increase size of head by applying false hair, and recipes for preventing hair loss.

A.G. Edwards & Co.'s "Harlene" World-Renowned Hair Producer and Restorer advertisement, 1891
Mr Vuitton's reference to this product.

Koko for the Hair advertisement, 1891
Mr Vuitton's reference to this product.

*****

The Victoria & Albert Museum
http://www.vam.ac.uk/
The following two citations come from the above website:

Article: History of Fashion 1840-1900
http://www.vam.ac.uk/content/articles/h/history-of-fashion-1840-1900/
Miss Webster's attire, specifically her "leg-of-mutton" sleeves and the angle she wears her hat (according to this source hats were generally worn squarely on the top of the

head. Also, Mr Edmund Queshire's appearance,
specifically his clean-shaven face and his three-piece suit.
Also, frock coats having become more associated with the
older, or more conservative, gentleman.

Online Collection: Pair of Wedding Shoes
http://collections.vam.ac.uk/item/O146173/pair-of-
wedding-unknown/
Lady's Owston Court (or 'Louis') shoes.

*****

***The Tudor Links* Article: 1896 Winter Blouses**
http://www.tudorlinks.com/treasury/articles/1896winte
rblouse.html
References to blouses as a 'waist' or 'waists.'

***Elizabeth Montague Letters'* Article: Bluestocking**
Circle
http://www.elizabethmontaguletters.co.uk/the-project
Elizabeth Montague and the origins of the Bluestocking
Circle's name.

***A Victorian.com's* Article: Servants and the Servant**
Question: The butler
http://www.avictorian.com/servants_butler.html
The Holdens' butler's attire.

NYP Corporation - National Burlap Manufacturer's
***Nursery Supply Blog* Entry: The History and Uses of**
Burlap Posted on Tuesday, May 3rd, 2011 at 4:51 pm
http://nyp-corp.com/blog/the-history-and-uses-of-
burlap/
Dr Weeks' statement that hessian fibres were found in
Maryanna's hair and that her body was transported in a
hessian sack.

Vale and Downland Museum – Local History Series
Downloadable PDF: <u>Sacks for Hire by Reg Wilkinson</u>,
downloaded from *the Wantage Museum's* website.
http://wantage-museum.com/wp-
content/uploads/2013/04/Sacks-for-Hire.pdf
*Hessian sacks being used for the transportation of bushels
by farmers, Sack Hire Companies and their depots, and
sacks' links with coal.*

Tlucretius.net's Article: <u>Victorian Slang</u>
http://www.tlucretius.net/Sophie/Castle/victorian_slang
.html
*The use of the slang term "Lushington" to denote a
drunken person.*

Sunset Times website
http://www.sunsettimes.co.uk/
The first signs of dusk at four thirty in the afternoon.

UCL Bloomsbury Project's website's article: <u>London
School of Medicine for Women</u>
http://www.ucl.ac.uk/bloomsbury-
project/institutions/london_school_medicine_women.ht
m
*The existence and legality of the London School of
Medicine for Women.*

Historic England's website article: <u>Oxford Circus
Underground Station entrance on north-west corner of
Argyll Street and Oxford Street</u>
https://historicengland.org.uk/listing/the-list/list-
entry/1401022
*Construction of the Oxford Circus Underground Station
and by whom*

British Medical Journal website, specifically item **Br Med J 1896;1:267** from the online archive: **TREATMENT OF ASEPTIC WOUNDS WITHOUT BANDAGES OR DRESSINGS** by James Mackenzie, M.D
http://www.bmj.com/content/1/1831/267
Reference to the name of this article, and its author, in Chapter Fifteen

Creative Review website's article: **Under the Skin: the evolution of Gray's Anatomy**
https://www.creativereview.co.uk/under-the-skin-the-evolution-of-grays-anatomy/
Background, name, and interior of the thirteenth edition of Anatomy, Descriptive and Surgical from 1893.

BBC News website's article: **How The Lancet made medical history** by Martin Hutchinson, BBC News Online staff
http://news.bbc.co.uk/1/hi/health/3168608.stm
The Lancet was controversial in 1896.

Printed in Great Britain
by Amazon

41779232R00209